One Dead Tory

When John Bullock, the brash Tory leader of Beechley borough council, arrives at the Town Hall to find calls for his resignation and dissent among his followers, he is not unduly worried. A man with parliamentary ambitions, he relishes confrontation and taking centre stage. This is more than can be said for the local police, who took a few knocks at the recent poll tax riots: how could they predict that before the week was out they would have far worse than a few unruly anarchists on their hands?

The day's massive demonstration against John Bullock's proposed spending cuts soon turns nasty, even though the leader, surprisingly, has failed to turn up for the council meeting after an important lunch engagement. Busy with the rioters, Beechley police feel they have far more important things to worry about than a telephone call from an anxious Mrs Bullock to report her husband missing . . .

Then Detective Sergeant Judy Best comes across John Bullock's dead body up on the North Downs, and a full-scale murder investigation begins. Recently promoted to the CID, Judy needs to prove her mettle to her grumpy and unpredictable boss, Detective Superintendent Manningbird. However, the team's enquiries turn up not only murder but blackmail, illicit sex and large-scale corruption. Then Judy finds herself up against a secret society which extends from the highest echelons of the local council, to the richest of Beechley's businessmen and into the police force itself . . .

By the same author:

UPPERDOWN
EMPIRE BORN
DEAD FIT

One Dead Tory

Stephen Cook

MACMILLAN
LONDON

First published 1993 by Macmillan London Limited

a division of Pan Macmillan Publishers Limited
Cavaye Place London SW10 9PG
and Basingstoke

Associated companies throughout the world

ISBN 0–333–60205–6

9 8 7 6 5 4 3 2 1

A CIP catalogue record for this book is available from
the British Library

Phototypeset by Intype, London
Printed by Mackays of Chatham Plc, Chatham, Kent

Chapter One

John Bullock strode towards the town hall of the London Borough of Beechley, buttoning up his double-breasted blue blazer and staring hard at the two men who hovered at the foot of the white stone steps. One of them wore a dirty denim jacket and held a large piece of paper across his chest saying NO MORE CUTS in uneven felt-tipped capitals. The other, with a fuzzy pony-tail and a silver earring, had a carefully made placard on a pole which said 'Bullock must go'; he waved it around jerkily, like a severed head on a pike.

'Morning, Mr Bullock,' shouted the man with the earring and placard, his voice a mixture of aggression and *bonhomie*. 'I hope you and your Tory group are going to see a bit of sense and change your minds today.'

Bullock paused for a moment and studied his adversary calmly, as if deciding whether to use the double-barrelled shotgun or the high-velocity small-bore rifle. He was a large, meaty man, and his cool grey eyes gave nothing away.

'And I hope,' he said evenly, 'that you and your sort are going to lose a day's pay over all this day of action nonsense. You're breaking your contracts of employment.'

The man with the earring was Steve Ditchley, leading light of the Beechley Joint Shop Stewards' Committee. He followed Bullock angrily up the steps, jabbing a nicotine-stained forefinger at the politician's broad, impassive back. A young constable with a spotty face watched edgily from ten yards away, shifting his weight from one large black shoe to the other.

'This action's been properly balloted, Mr Bullock,' shouted Ditchley, the *bonhomie* evaporated from his voice. 'The whole borough's grinding to a halt. You'll change your tune when you see the demo this afternoon. We'll have you, Bullock, you'll see.'

The only reply he got was the rhythmic flapping of the large swing doors as Bullock disappeared into the town hall, a flat-faced modernist building with stone friezes depicting scenes of civic harmony which

1

had been hard to find in Beechley in recent times. Even this prosperous slice of south London, its centre of gravity in the tidy, owner-occupied suburbs working their way towards the North Downs, had suffered a serious riot over the poll tax three months earlier. A crowd of two thousand had besieged a council meeting, hit the chief executive over the head with a placard, and put six policemen in hospital.

'Tory scumbag,' muttered Ditchley, retreating slowly to the foot of the steps and propping up his placard against the wall. 'Like talking to sodding Mussolini.'

Ditchley restored his grooming with a pull on his pony tail, rolled himself a thin cigarette, and resumed asking people approaching the town hall not to cross the picket line. Most of them gave him a wide berth and hurried past, eyes fixed silently on the ground, whereupon Ditchley informed them with chatty menace that they were scabs and would suffer accordingly. Maybe not today, maybe not tomorrow, but one day – definitely . . .

Inside the town hall, Bullock replied to the over-smiling welcome from the neatly permed woman on the enquiry desk with a curt nod and a wave of his black attaché case, and continued up the broad main staircase to the committee room where the Conservatives were gathering to plan their strategy for the afternoon's council meeting. For the first time in his three-year leadership, John Bullock was under pressure from his own side. Secret plans to keep the poll tax below £300 in the following year by making a ten per cent cut in all the council's spending had been leaked to the *Beechley Examiner* the previous week. Now there were whispers that some of the Tory councillors thought the cuts too drastic and were getting cold feet, especially with another dose of street action on the way. A rebellion, a split, was on the cards.

'Morning, ladies and gentlemen,' said Bullock jauntily, heading for the end of the long table, taking the only chair with arms, and opening his attaché case with a brace of loud, authoritative clicks. It was a few minutes after 11 o'clock, and most of the other Conservatives were already present, standing in groups with heads together in earnest conversation. They halted in mid-sentence to return the leader's greeting in a ragged, obedient chorus and hurry to their seats.

'Right, then, let's get on with it,' said Bullock, settling himself with his papers and glancing round the wood-panelled room, his jaw jutting slightly as if in warning that he wasn't going to stand any nonsense. He was a successful surveyor and estate agent, forty-six years old, with pleasant, regular features and hair that was still blond and wavy. But what many noticed first about him was his open-pored, shiny nose, which he wiped frequently with a wine-coloured handkerchief from his breast pocket. There was also something impassive and inexpressive about him as he looked out on the world, counting and assessing.

'I think I should start by telling you that I had a meeting yesterday with Mr Rutter, who still wishes to be referred to as the chief executive rather than the managing director,' said Bullock, a vindictive tone hovering in his flat voice.

A nervous ripple ran around the group. It was not the first time that Bullock's determination to restructure the council along business lines had been resisted by the bureaucracy. The latest notion was that rate-payers – or chargepayers, as they had become under the poll tax – should be referred to at all times as customers, and Rutter was dragging his feet on that as well.

'And what was Mr Rutter's view of the current situation?' asked Simon Pilkington, deputy leader of the group, stroking his red-dotted blue silk tie. He was a smooth young management consultant who, like Bullock, had Parliamentary ambitions. A copy of last week's *Examiner* – TORIES IN NEW CUTS SHOCKER splashed over the front page – was on the blotter in front of him, and an equivocal gleam was in his eye.

'His view,' said Bullock, fixing a dead grey stare on Pilkington, 'was that there was a general election in the offing, and that we ought to bear in mind that there could be a significant change in the national context before too long. Or words to that effect.'

'And what was your response to that, John?' murmured Pilkington, studying his fingernails as if he already knew the answer. The tone was patronizing, and Bullock shifted his bulky body and head backwards so that his returning stare was directed down his shiny nose.

'My response, Simon, was that if he was trying to tell me that a half-baked bunch of pillocks and windbags was going to dislodge a party with ten years of achievement under its belt and its finger on the pulse of the country, then he ought to have his head examined. In fact, I offered to arrange for him to see a specialist – privately, of course.'

He looked challengingly round the group, which consisted of businessmen with heavy faces, a colourful assortment of middle-aged women wearing unsuitable jewellery, and a scattering of serious young men with value-for-money eyes. Bullock could always be relied upon to trample down any doubts about Conservative policy which had been sown in their mind by the travails of the new poll tax, and they rewarded his latest pugnacious sally with little nods and chuckles.

'Bravo, John,' said Elspeth Gorringe, a scrawny woman with thin henna-coloured hair, flashing her gold teeth at him.

'As for his view that we should in some way soft-pedal our agenda,

3

I reminded him in no uncertain fashion that we increased our majority at the local elections last month on a platform of further economies and efficiencies, and that we aren't going to allow threats of violence from the great unwashed to prevent us from pushing the programme through. And I hope we're not going to have to spend too much time on these rumours about what you might politely call a failure of nerve on our own side.'

His eyes returned pointedly to Pilkington, who was glancing around nervously, fingering his tie with one hand and the newspaper with the other. He cleared his throat and intervened quickly, before Bullock could score more direct hits.

'One question I, er, through the chair, think we have to address before we go much further, is the small matter of how a preliminary working paper of our financial steering group could find its way into the press like this? And, indeed, what do we say about it? There'll be a lot of pressure about that at full council this afternoon.'

Smiles evaporated, silence fell, and eyes swivelled to Bullock. The suggestion had got around that he had leaked the document himself in order to get the row over and done with before real budget planning got under way in the autumn, and to put pressure on the fainthearts in the group.

'There's a leak inquiry under way, Simon, as you already know,' said Bullock, lowering his tone to introduce a hint of menace. 'And I only hope the culprit doesn't turn out to be present in this room now – or to be one of the senior officers of the council, for that matter. As for what we say about it, you won't be surprised to know that my view is we should stick to our guns, both at the meeting and at any press conference afterwards.'

'Bullock battles for Beechley!' chirped Elspeth Gorringe, her wild-eyed smile freezing as everyone ignored her.

'The only problem with what you say, John,' said Pilkington swiftly, 'is that if we do indeed push through ten per cent cuts across the board, then there's a serious danger that the riot we had this year about the poll tax will be followed next year by another one about service cuts. Quite irrespective of what happens this afternoon.'

'Am I hearing you right, Simon?' said Bullock, leaning suddenly forward, quizzical and sarcastic, his nose shining fiercely now, like a weapon polished for combat. 'Because that strikes me as rather a pink point of view. The lower the poll tax, the less chance of protest by the ordinary people of the borough, surely.'

Two spots of colour had appeared on Pilkington's creamy cheeks. He had been to public school and Oxford, and didn't feel he should be worsted by a man like Bullock, who had left Beechley Grammar School at seventeen years of age, and gone to no university at all.

'Yes, John, of course,' said Pilkington, his voice tetchy. 'But I think I ought to point out once again that this idea of pegging the poll tax at three hundred pounds has never been formally adopted by the ruling group. In fact, it was rather plucked out of the air by yourself at the local elections. During your victory speech from the steps of the town hall, if I remember rightly.'

Bullock looked slowly round the room, an expression of incredulity on his face, as if the deputy leader were proposing incest or collective hara-kiri. His eyes met those of each councillor in turn, challenging them silently to signal loyalty or dare to join the upstart. One by one they submitted to the dominant male.

'Thank you, Simon,' said Bullock, his victory complete. 'I was under the impression that you'd got what you wanted over this document when you successfully inserted the cancellation of the Market Walk leasing scheme. Now it seems you want to reopen the debate, reverse the new economies we're planning, and throw our election-winning poll tax strategy overboard. Well, I'm quite happy to do that, Simon. That's how democracy works. Providing, of course, there's a seconder.'

Most of the councillors conceived a sudden fascination with the pattern in the grain of the mahogany-veneer table. Fifteen seconds went past, a few throats were cleared, a few fingers drummed gently on blotters, and Pilkington's chin sank slowly towards his chest. The spots of anger and humiliation on his cheeks were now a deep scarlet.

'No? Well, there's your answer, I'm afraid, Simon,' resumed Bullock, taking the wine-coloured handkerchief from his breast pocket and giving his nose a thorough wipe. 'So if you don't mind, we'll move on to the proposal to deduct a day's pay from all council staff taking part in today's strike. I notice they describe it as a day of action, which I can only assume is some kind of joke – rather unusual on their part.'

Bullock suddenly glanced at his watch and looked round the group.

'And by the way, I'd be glad if we could move through the agenda reasonably quickly, if you don't mind – I've got a lunch to get to.'

'What, you're not coming over to the George?' asked a fat woman called Cynthia Piles. The slap-up meal before every council meeting – once a gift of the ratepayers to their elected representatives, but paid for individually since the Bullock era began – was the only bit she was really interested in.

''Fraid not, Cynthia,' said Bullock, giving her a look which hovered between distaste and lasciviousness.

'Down with municipal socialism!' said Elspeth Gorringe, giving the air a puny punch.

'God,' muttered Pilkington. 'It's like something out of *Animal Farm*.'

Chapter Two

By two o'clock the High Street had been closed to traffic, with the town hall barricaded off and surrounded by policemen. Chief Superintendent Blackman, a tall, tubby man who headed the local division of the Metropolitan Police, was determined that the violent scenes of the poll tax riot would not be repeated. He stood on the town hall steps, holding a small leather-covered cane behind his back, as the protest march, waving banners and emitting thin shouts, came into view.

'Here come the bleeding lefties,' muttered the tall, thin Superintendent standing next to Blackman, thumbs hooked behind his breast-pocket buttons. 'God knows why they bother any more – you'd think they'd have got the message by now.'

'Part of history, you mean? Yeah, but the trouble is, you can't write 'em off,' said Blackman, an edge of anxiety in his voice. 'Just, er, check there are no gaps in the barriers, will you, Jack? And let's have a few more troops round the front here.'

The Superintendent, who had bumped up the front-line numbers once already and was worried about leaving the rear unprotected, raised his eyes irritably to heaven and moved away, talking into his radio. As he did so, the chanting began.

'Bullock, Bullock, Bullock!' called a voice from the front of the demonstration, distorted and amplified tinnily by a megaphone.

'Out, out, out!' came the roaring but ragged response, reverberating around the plate glass and tall façades of the High Street. The head of the march was a hundred yards away now, level with the half-empty town centre redevelopment pushed through by Bullock, but its tail was still coming round the corner from the assembly point in Churchill Park, half a mile away. Some of the police lined up at the foot of the steps were shifting uneasily, fastening the chin straps on their helmets or pulling on black leather gloves. Twenty or thirty more officers were moving round from the side streets, plugging gaps in the cordon.

'Who do we want?' came the tinny voice through the megaphone. It belonged to Steve Ditchley, who had left picket duty at noon, sunk a few quick pints in the Highwayman, and was now marching confidently at the head of his army.

'Bullock!'

'And when do we want him?'

'Now!'

The Chief Superintendent gave a tut of nervous irritation and turned to the chief executive, who had come out of the building to survey the scene and was standing at the head of the steps, shifting edgily and twitching his shoulders.

'You'd think they could manage something a bit more original for a special occasion like this, wouldn't you, Mr Rutter?' said the Chief. 'I've heard this kindergarten stuff a thousand times before.'

Barry Rutter, a lean, pinstriped man with glasses, smiled jumpily, his fingers suddenly flying to his domed forehead and fluttering down the two-inch scar dating from the poll tax riot. The wooden edge of the placard had split the flesh neatly to the bone, and three months later the stitch marks were still visible around the thin, violet-coloured groove. The first wave of the crowd, placards twitching and jerking in time to the chant, was surging towards them.

'The slogans do seem to concentrate rather on changing one vowel in the leader's name and making it plural,' said Rutter, the strain in his voice undermining the attempt at jocularity. 'Hardly original, I quite agree.'

The Chief Superintendent's attention had switched back to the street, where Steve Ditchley, wearing a green and blue nylon bomber jacket, had reached a traffic island across the road from the cordon and was climbing unsteadily on to an aluminium stepladder. A couple of press photographers moved stealthily forward as he wavered on his perch, like some bright but ragged specimen in an aviary. He waved his megaphone wildly and a sudden hush descended on the protestors.

'OK, comrades!' he yelled raucously. 'Testing, testing, one, two, three – can you hear me down there at W.H. Smith? Before I hand you over to Mavis Tench of Nalgo, I'd just like to congratulate everyone on a magnificent turnout this afternoon. Bloody magnificent, comrades! Bullock and his fellow Tory councillors are going to get the message loud and clear – bollocks to Bullock! No more cuts in Beechley!'

There was a roar of approval.

'Thank you, Steve,' yelled Mavis Tench, in a shrill, wheezing voice. 'Thank you, comrades. As you know, the theme of this day of action is jobs and services. The Tories have made it clear through their henchmen in the mass media that they want to axe hundreds of jobs and hand the few remaining services over to their cronies in the private sector. Well, I've got news for you, Mr Bullock: it ain't gonna happen!'

There was an answering roar from the crowd, which now filled the entire High Street and was milling around in the June sunshine. The banners of trade union branches, their Victorian scenes of toil and solidarity depicted on vast scarlet backgrounds, splashed the view like poppies in a field of wheat.

'Comrades, we all know that councils round the country are facing huge cuts because of the disgraceful cash limits imposed by this heartless Tory government. That's bad enough. But what we're facing in Beechley is ten times worse, comrades! They could actually spend ten per cent more next year in Beechley without going through the Government's capping limits. But Bullock and his henchmen are proposing to cut ten per cent across the board. There'll be charges for meals on wheels! Day nurseries closed! Libraries cut! It's blind ideology, comrades! Naked social vandalism!'

Barry Rutter stood and listened for a few minutes longer, occasionally studying the front of his suit and brushing it nervously with the back of his fingers. Then he looked up at the Chief Superintendent with a ghost of a smile, his green eyes inscrutable behind thick lenses.

'Well,' he said. 'It looks fairly harmless, thank God – can't see poor old Mavis starting a riot. Class Warfare not much in evidence, in spite of the rumours.'

'I think the unions warned them to stay well clear,' said Blackman, removing his flat hat and running his fingers over a few oily-looking strands of grey hair. 'I don't think they want their demo spoiled by the smellies, any more than we do.'

'So we can get the meeting under way, can we?'

'I think so, sir.'

Blackman gave him an unpractised salute, and Rutter glided back into the shadows of the entrance lobby.

Most of the councillors had got into the town hall through the car park under the rear extension, a piece of concrete brutalism grafted on the rear of the building in the 1960s. They were standing about in the pale oak-panelled council chamber producing little bursts of nervous laughter as they exchanged anecdotes about dodging the demonstrators. Rutter walked over to the Mayor, a wisp of a Liberal Democrat sitting at the podium, checking his watch and sweating freely in his robes and chains. Above his head loomed the borough's green and white coat of arms, a trio of beeches on a hill with the motto *in urbe agoribusque virtus*.

'John Bullock's not here yet,' said the Mayor irritably. 'I'm going to start without him if he doesn't show up in five minutes.'

'Well, I, er, saw him leaving the town hall on his way out to lunch,' said Rutter, blinking like a mole in daylight and fingering his scar again. 'It's not the sort of meeting he'd want to miss, is it? I'll get my secretary to phone around, try to locate him.'

Rutter disappeared through the door behind the podium. The Mayor glanced crossly around the chamber and up at the public gallery, which was nearly full and guarded by several police officers. At the table in front of the podium the council's chief officials, all of them balding, bespectacled men in grey suits, were smiling and examining the smart new plastic name plates which Rutter had just had made for them.

After a final look at his watch the Mayor picked up the large oak gavel, banged it on the podium, and declared the meeting was about to start. In the public gallery behind the councillors there was a mild rumpus as two overweight teenage girls draped a green and yellow banner over the balcony reading 'Books not Cuts', and were promptly hustled out by a couple of constables to cries of 'Shame!'

'Let that be a warning to people that we intend to conduct this meeting without demonstrations or interruptions,' said the Mayor, his voice thin and tense. 'Anyone who wants to wave their arms around and shout slogans can leave the building and join the rabble on the streets.'

'Tory stooge!' yelled a bearded man in a black leather jacket, jumping to his feet at the back of the gallery. 'Why don't you . . .'

The rest of his message was lost in a gargle as a blue-clad arm went round his throat and he, too, disappeared. The Mayor banged mightily with his gavel again and declared the meeting open, despite the absence of John Bullock.

'I can only assume he was delayed at lunch . . .'

There were jeers and elbows prodded into neighbours' ribs on the Labour benches, which were gearing themselves up for a knockabout afternoon. Bullock was notorious for his interest in food.

'. . . or, indeed, something to do with his business interests . . .'

'Shame!' shouted Ashok Patel, a tubby and nervous London Regional Transport manager who had recently become leader of the Labour group. The previous incumbent, a trade union official, had made the mistake of giving his support to the town centre redevelopment project just as the property slump was turning it into a white elephant.

'. . . so I trust that's all right with you, Mr Pilkington?'

Pilkington rose to his feet, looking unusually subdued. Even the lunch at the George had failed to restore his spirits after the humiliations of the morning.

'I think so, Mr Mayor. I've no doubt the leader will arrive shortly, and I expect we're going to spend the initial part of the meeting listening to the party opposite wasting time with their usual clichés and synthetic outrage.'

Patel was on his feet like a jack-in-the-box, pointing a stubby finger at his opponent.

'I'd just like to remind the gentleman,' he snapped, 'that the outrage is certainly not synthetic and that much of it comes from people who made the unfortunate mistake of voting for his party. Perhaps that's why the leader has decided to hide himself away in a cupboard today – he's in a blue funk.'

There was an explosion of shouting and fist-waving on the Tory side, punctuated by thuds from the Mayor's gavel. Politics in Beechley had become more uninhibited in recent years, and it had been known for councillors to jostle each other and exchange threats in the corridors. Feelings were running especially high today, and fortunately Elspeth Gorringe's shrieks about jumped-up Pakis were drowned in the general hubbub.

Eventually the Mayor enforced an uneasy calm and debate began on Labour's emergency motion of no confidence, tabled in response to the *Examiner* leak. But bursts of shouting and jeering still reached the ears of the councillors from the demonstration at the front of the building, and when Patel was five minutes into his harangue there was a sudden explosion of noise and the sound of running feet from just outside the chamber.

Patel paused and whispered anxiously to the Labour councillors around him, who looked like spectators at a dog fight who had suddenly realized they might get bitten themselves. The Mayor had his gavel raised and his mouth open again, unsure what to say, when the high double doors of the chamber burst open and two blue-uniformed council security men fell through them backwards. They were followed by a group of twenty unkempt young people, a small avalanche of beards, pony-tails, shaven heads, Rasta locks, tattoos, earrings, gold teeth, nose studs, baggy trousers, sleeveless T-shirts and black boots laced high above the ankle.

The councillors suddenly fell as silent as a well-behaved class of schoolchildren. Barry Rutter grasped his head in his hands, as if to protect it from renewed assault. Only the Mayor stood up, trembling like a terrier confronting a bulldog.

'Who are you people?' he shouted, eyes popping. 'How dare you?'

The ragged intruders grouped together, like Vikings at a beachhead;

11

one of them, a beefy youth with long blond hair, put his foot on the back of a security man, who was lying motionless with his legs drawn up like a foetus. Then they glanced at each other, nodded, and launched into a chant, jabbing their dirty fingers at the Mayor in a clear case of mistaken identity.

'Hello, Mr Bullock,
We know you're upper class
So you can take your spending cuts
And stick them up your arse!'

The crescendo of the final phrase was spat out staccato, and the angry group began to repeat the chant, advancing slowly towards the podium where the Mayor stood quaking and speechless in his outsize robes. Barry Rutter, imitated by some of the chief officers, was beginning to lower himself under the table, and the councillors were shuffling sideways along the benches, away from the barbarian invaders, trying to keep fear out of their faces.

But before the intruders could reach their quarry, there was a thundering of even heavier feet from outside the chamber, and a helmetless platoon of police officers burst through the doors, panting and tripping over each other. They leapt on the chanting gaggle with clumsy rugby tackles and neck locks, and within seconds the blue carpet in the aisle was covered with bodies rolling and fighting like dogs in the dust. The spectators in the public gallery were on their feet and cheering, as if they were Romans at the circus.

'Class Warfare!' gasped Barry Rutter, climbing grey-faced to his feet and turning to the Mayor. 'Blackman assured me it couldn't happen. They must have got in the back way.'

'Outrageous,' stammered the Mayor, still pop-eyed. 'Where were the police?'

'All out the front, listening like sheep to Mavis Tench. Ah, there's the Chief Superintendent himself.'

Roger Blackman had appeared at the main doors and was moving through the battlefield where his men were quickly taking control and frog-marching their prisoners from the chamber, bent double in arm-locks. As he passed one khaki-clad form, writhing on the ground, he gave it a nasty little jab in the kidneys with his toe-cap.

'Er, sorry about this, chief executive,' said Blackman, meeting Rutter in front of the podium. At their feet a young blond policeman, his face scarlet and his teeth bared, was kneeling and twisting the wrist of a youth with his head shaved except for a four-inch orange pigtail. The youth's face was pressed deeply into the carpet, which muffled his squeals of pain.

'So where did they spring from?' demanded Rutter angrily, fingers running down his scar again. 'They only operate in Camden and Lambeth, according to you. The unions had banned them. And then they come storming in the back door.'

The Chief Superintendent raised his palms in surrender, and sagged heavily against the bench behind him.

'Can't count on anything these days, I'm afraid, sir. New demands being made on the police all the time, society's fragmenting, and the police have to pick up the pieces. To be honest, I didn't think anyone would know you could get in at the back, through the car park.'

Rutter let out his exasperation in a long burst of breath, like a balloon going down. Near by, the orange-pigtailed youth was being pulled to his feet, the side of his face swelling into a brown and purple bruise. Elspeth Gorringe popped up in the first row of benches, waving a thin gold-ringed fist at him and telling him in a salivary screech that he was a piece of scum.

'There'll be thousands of pounds' worth of damage by the time this is over,' muttered Rutter, watching a spiky-haired girl lying on her back kicking at two officers, her boots scoring deep grooves in the wooden panelling on the walls.

'Yeah, property's all you care about, mister chief executive,' gasped the orange-haired youth, submitting to the handcuffs. 'What about people, eh? They don't fucking matter, do they?'

The blond officer grabbed his pigtail and twisted it savagely, propelling him towards the doors. The youth bent and twisted to avoid the pain, but his bruised and contorted face appeared upside down beneath his arm and he fixed Rutter with a wild glare.

'What about all the homeless, then?' he yelled. 'What about the kids on the streets, begging like animals? Eh? What's your council doing about it all, then? Fuck all, that's what!'

Rutter and Blackman stared at him as he disappeared through the door, glanced in silent embarrassment at each other, and quickly turned away to watch other intruders being dragged away like motley sacks of grain. The sounds of battle gradually subsided, to be replaced by excited chatter from the councillors as they returned to their places and readjusted their papers. Elspeth Gorringe had sagged in a corner, breathing stertorously, her eyes closed and her lips in a happy smile. Blackman cleared his throat.

13

'Just about takes care of them, then. Your Mr Bullock turned up yet, by the way?'

'What?' said Rutter, who was dusting imaginary particles off his suit. 'Er, no, I don't believe he has. Can't think what's happened to him. Not like him to miss a meeting, especially if there's a scrap going on.'

'Hmm,' said Blackman, pushing his flat hat on to his head and twisting it into position. 'let's hope they haven't ambushed the poor bugger on the way over here – that would be all we need.'

Chapter Three

Thursday, 3.30 p.m.

Dorothy Bullock was entertaining two women friends to tea when the phone rang in the hall. She paused in her animated description of the unreliability of modern Italian washing machines, tutted with irritation and excused herself. Her guests resumed a silent appraisal of the furniture and fittings, sipping tea and leaving heavy traces of lipstick on the delicate white cups.

'I do like these curtains, Dotty,' said Annabel Silver, with a trace of sarcasm, as her hostess returned. 'Are they Dralon?'

Dorothy was walking slowly back into the sitting-room with her forehead creased in a frown. She was an unassuming woman in her mid-forties with disappointed hazel eyes, brown hair, and a large mouthful of even teeth.

'Don't be rude, Annabel,' she said absently. 'They were here when we came and we haven't had time to get this room redecorated yet. Anyway, there's nothing wrong with Dralon.'

'Sorry, Dot, only teasing,' said Annabel, a ripe-looking brunette in a flowery tent dress who had been to girls' public school with Dorothy years before. 'What's up? You look sick as a parrot, as my so-called husband would say.'

Dorothy made a flapping gesture with one hand.

'Oh, nothing,' she said. 'It's just that they've lost John.'

'*Lost* him?' said Betty Damson, a stringy blonde perched on the edge of the sofa, overdressed in a candy-striped shirt and high-heeled white shoes. 'What do you mean, lost him? It's not as if he's a handbag or a bunch of keys, is it?'

'Or a dog,' said Annabel, more mischief in her dark eyes. 'You'll have to start keeping him on a lead, Dotty. Keep him from straying.'

'Oh, shut up, Annabel,' snapped Dorothy, breaking suddenly out of her reverie and throwing herself into a chair, where she bounced slightly on the pneumatic cushions. 'That was the town hall on the phone. Apparently he hasn't turned up for the council meeting.'

15

'Doesn't sound like John,' remarked Betty sharply. 'I thought he lived for his politics these days.'

Betty was the wife of Nigel Damson, John Bullock's partner in the firm of Bullock and Damson. John had asked Dorothy to befriend her in order to sweeten the business connection, but relations between the two women had remained awkward and cool.

'Is he at work instead?' asked Annabel, suddenly serious and supportive.

'Oh, he won't be at work,' said Betty, draining her teacup decisively. She felt her husband was taking an unfair share of steering the firm through the collapse of the property market while John Bullock was off playing councillors and getting himself selected as a Parliamentary candidate.

'No, he's not at work,' said Dorothy, giving Betty a resentful glance. 'They've checked. I hope he hasn't had an accident or anything. And there's this horrible demonstration going on down there, about the cuts – they might be having another riot, for all I know.'

Annabel put down her teacup with a rattle of spoon in saucer, got up, and put a matronly arm round Dorothy's slumped shoulders.

'Don't worry,' she cajoled. 'He'll turn up. Knowing him, he's been delayed over some lunch or other – was he out to lunch today?'

'He's always out to lunch,' muttered Betty in the background, bitterly.

'Yes, I think he did say something about a business lunch,' said Dorothy, brightening a little and looking up at Annabel, eager for more comforting words.

'There you are, then,' said Annabel, jolly and encouraging. 'Or he's gone up to town for an urgent business meeting. John can look after himself, you know that.'

Dorothy gave Annabel a brilliant smile. The large spread of even teeth was still an impressive sight, although a few of them were tinged with grey now.

'Come on, then,' said Annabel gaily, as if suggesting a game of hockey on the lawn. 'Let's have this tour of the new house, then. I suppose there's nothing you can do about the ghastly name? I mean, Jumpers – it's like something out of a porn movie.'

Betty rose stiffly from the sofa and followed the other two, her mouth a tight line of pale pink. She had long coveted this house for herself and her husband Nigel, and she particularly liked the name; but the Bullocks had beaten them to it and snapped the place up cheaply when the previous owner's computer company had suddenly gone bust.

Dorothy took them dutifully round the five bedrooms and three bathrooms, hardly needed now that their teenage son and daughter were away at boarding schools. The other two women uttered little cries and murmurs of appreciation, although from time to time their eyes hardened, focusing on the greasy, child-high stains on the wallpaper on the stairway, or the brown marks on a wash-basin, or the greying pair of Y-fronts hanging half-out of the linen basket. The tour ended in the kitchen, fitted throughout with oak cabinets larded with fretwork.

'Oooh, it's lovely,' moaned Betty painfully.

'D'you think so?' asked Dorothy, head on one side, one wing of brown hair touching her shoulder. 'I'm wondering whether to have it re-done.'

'This kind of thing *is* a bit old hat these days,' said Annabel, running her finger idly along the granite-look worktop. 'I'd like to get one of those free-standing butcher's block tables, you know – on wheels?'

Annabel pulled her big sun-glasses out of her hair and on to her nose as they passed into the garden, wandered around the smooth lawns and primped flower-beds, and surveyed the knee-high grass in the empty acre of paddock. The house, built in brick with multiple gables and a steep, sweeping roof in mellow red tiles, was tucked into the top of Hunter's Combe, a fold of the downs on the southern edge of the borough of Beechley. All around stood hangers of magnificent beeches which had come almost intact through the great gale three years before.

'Well, I'd better be off,' said Betty, curtly, when they reached the gravel drive. The other two made no effort to prevent her going, and waved her off down the hill in her white Fiat Uno. Then they exchanged glances of complicit relief, went inside again and settled to a more intimate conversation, starting with the latest developments in the affair Annabel was having with a professional tennis coach.

'Shall I tell you what he wanted to do the other night?' she said, lowering her voice and leaning closer to a fascinated Dorothy. 'Dirty bugger – I didn't let him, I can tell you.'

When Annabel, too, left at half-past four, there was still no word of John. Dorothy rang the Tory group secretary at the town hall, heard a brief account of the invasion of the council chamber by Class Warfare, and was told he had still not turned up.

'Oh, God, I hope those awful people haven't set on him and beaten him up somewhere,' moaned Dorothy.

'Oh, no, don't worry, the police have got tabs on them,' said the secretary. 'But I think all the councillors were a bit shocked after the invasion – they finished the meeting very quickly and just went home. I'll give you a ring the moment your husband shows up.'

Dorothy moved into the sitting-room and began clearing away the tea things. She had been strikingly slim and beautiful when she and John Bullock had married twenty years before, but now the body beneath the blue skirt and white blouse was beginning to thicken. There was a bulging green vein on the back of one calf, and the set of her back and shoulders hinted at a certain restlessness, as if life had not yet given her enough.

She busied herself in the kitchen, deciding what to cook for dinner, as if it was a normal afternoon. But all the time she was listening for an engine coming up the winding lane, dreading that it might be a police car bringing an officer to tell her that John had been run over and killed. By the time she had prepared the vegetables, wiped every surface and put every object in the kitchen into its appointed spot, it was six o'clock and she could suppress the foreboding no longer. She walked into the hall to dial the local hospitals.

She was about to lift the telephone when it rang. The bell sounded as loud as a fire alarm in the hushed house, and she jumped back with a little cry. Then her heartbeat settled back and she lifted the receiver to hear the voice of Nigel Damson at the other end.

'Dotty?' His voice was an upper-class drawl, adopted and honed because he thought it a business advantage, and she pictured the lean, dark head and the five o'clock shadow. 'Just wanted to let you know, John's car's still in the office car park. So he must be still around in Beechley somewhere.'

'Oh, thanks, Nigel.' Dorothy struggled to keep her voice even, but it sounded shrill. 'You haven't seen him today, have you?'

'Only this morning, when he came in and made a few phone calls before going over to the town hall.'

'But he left his car at the office?'

'Yes – he's got a space at the town hall, as you know, but he usually walks there and back for the exercise.'

'How was he this morning? Did he seem all right to you?'

'Bit wound up, I suppose, but he had a difficult day ahead. He's not been in touch, then? The town hall rang me mid-afternoon to see if he was here.'

'Not a word from him. I'm beginning to get a bit worried.'

'He'll show up, Dotty,' said Nigel jovially. 'Probably when you least expect it – proverbial bad penny. Don't get yourself in a state. And give us a call if we can help.'

18

Dorothy put the phone down slowly, wondering how well it would suit Nigel if John did disappear. The merger between John Bullock and Company and Damson and Vizard had really been a takeover by John's firm, and there had been something unforgiving in Nigel's smile ever since. She shook her head to clear it of suspicious thoughts and dialled the hospitals with an unsteady finger.

The news that none of them had admitted him produced a sense of relief that was quickly swept aside by larger fears. She wandered into the sitting-room and watched the shadows of the tall beeches advance towards her across the lawn. Had he been suddenly called up to town over some secret business crisis? She knew vaguely that the town centre redevelopment had been running into trouble because no one wanted to lease the shops. Had he been called to one of the schools because of an accident to one of the children? That was ridiculous, though – the school would have rung her, here at the house.

So was it something more personal, some mid-life crisis that had been developing like a cancer under that blank exterior of his? Had despair or a secret scandal made him decide to end it all, throw himself in a river or under a train? Would he be found in the morning, parked up some hidden track with a hosepipe round to the exhaust? John would never commit suicide, surely. Perhaps he had emptied his bank account and taken a plane to Rio. Maybe Penelope Moggeridge, the secretary with the thin legs, had gone with him.

As the evening dragged by, her speculations lurched round in fruitless circles. She left the dinner uncooked, made herself a cheese sandwich, and ate only three bites of it. The phone stayed silent, the house was quiet, and she began thinking how isolated she was here, how any maniac prowling the bush-fringed downs could descend upon her, like a fox on a cooped chicken. She rang Annabel, but her husband Rex told her irritably that Annabel was out at her exercise class. She stood at the sitting-room window and watched the last pale streaks of light fading into a deep blue sky, and an owl hooted somewhere in the trees: since they'd moved in both she and John had thought they'd seen someone prowling near the trees, in the evenings. She set off rapidly round the house, pulling curtains across all the windows, locking the doors, and snapping on all the lights. Then she poured herself a large whisky from an ostentatious crystal decanter with a thistle-shaped stopper, and called the police.

Beechley police station, a grey box of 1960s concrete on the edge of the town centre, was slowly coming back to normal. The canteen was clearing of the weary officers from other divisions who'd been drafted in for the demo and stayed on to process their arrests. Steel-grilled vans lurched out of the rear yard, heavy with their built-in bullet-proof laminate and big policemen slumped on the seats, yawning or re-reading the morning's crumpled tabloids. Among the thirty people arrested, half a dozen Class War stalwarts were facing a night in the cells, including the ginger-headed boy with a pigtail. People were still reporting assaults and damage to property and the front office was full of officers struggling to take statements from men and women made incoherent by pain, anger or drink. A call from an anxious wife about a missing husband was the last thing they wanted.

'He's probably gone out for a few drinks with his mates, madam,' said the harassed WPC on the communications desk, pushing a damp lock of hair out of her face. 'That's the usual explanation. Why don't you give it till the morning and call back if he hasn't showed up?'

'I don't think you quite understand,' said Dorothy, her voice becoming shrill and faltering under the effects of the neat whisky. 'He's not the sort of man to go on silly, disgusting pub crawls. He's the leader of the borough council.'

Eventually she was put through to Chief Superintendent Blackman, who was still up in his office holding a post-mortem with half a dozen Superintendents and Inspectors and drafting a report to Area head-quarters and the Commander in charge of public order at Scotland Yard.

'I hope to God she's going to tell me the silly sod's turned up,' Blackman told his cohorts wearily, hand over receiver, as he waited for the connection. 'A council leader gone AWOL will be as much use as a hole in the head.'

'Let's hope the guy hasn't got a hole in the head himself,' muttered the Inspector in charge of the front office, who had just brought up a bizarre statement from an Asian shopkeeper with poor English who'd come in to report seeing a youth crossing a piece of waste ground with a body in a wheelbarrow. The shopkeeper had apparently challenged the youth, who'd said his mate had got a bang on the head in a pub fight and he was taking him to hospital.

Blackman put on a formal tone and greeted Dorothy with a couple of polite pleasantries. They had met inside the barricaded town hall during the poll tax demonstration, when Dorothy had delivered her husband to the back door in a rain of half-bricks and the police had rushed her inside for safety. As Blackman talked to her now, his eyes closed in martyrdom and his head fell forward on to his spare hand, as if it was suddenly too heavy to balance on his well-fleshed neck.

'Have you tried all the friends and colleagues who might know where he is? You have. Clubs, drinking haunts? Oh, did she? I'm sorry. And no unpleasant phone calls or threats? Hang on, let me write this down: silver Mercedes estate, JB 492? OK, we'll check if it's still there. And I'll have the accident and incident reports double-checked. Yes, round every police force in the country, if you wish. Not like him, mmm? People do behave out of character from time to time, Mrs Bullock – I'm sure he'll turn up by morning. If not, we'll think about a search and putting it out to the media. Yes, the moment we hear anything. Don't worry, and try to get some sleep.'

Blackman replaced the receiver and looked round his white-shirted colleagues, his face gloomy and interrogative. His large fingers began to drum softly on the polished wooden desk.

'Playing away,' murmured the Superintendent eventually, shrugging his shoulders. 'Has to be. Got carried away, forgotten what time it is.'

'I thought that would be the favourite,' said Blackman, staring at him disdainfully. 'But it doesn't exactly explain the no-show at the council meeting, does it?'

'I don't know about that,' said the Superintendent, already huffy at signs that the afternoon's lapses were going to be laid at his door. 'Some people can't resist a quick jump after lunch.'

'Well,' said Blackman. 'I happen to have met his wife, and I don't think that's very likely.'

'There's still this body in a barrow job,' said the front office Inspector, brandishing the statement from the Asian shopkeeper. 'We can't afford to just ignore a report like that. Or it might be a kidnap.'

'Mmm,' said Blackman with impassive sarcasm. 'So why has nobody heard from the kidnappers yet?'

'Might be worth a word with Special Branch up at the Yard,' said a thin Chief Inspector with narrow eyes. 'I know this one's on the right side, but you never know what some of these politicos get up to.'

Blackman pushed himself slowly to his feet, swallowing a gurgle of wind and shaking his head with a mildly incredulous smile. 'It's getting late, gentlemen,' he said. 'And if I don't get home I'll be taking another phone call from another angry woman. Just get that message round, will you, Bill? Description, details, all cars, all stations. Back to the fray in the morning.'

Friday

The working day at the town hall began with a mass meeting of staff in the council chamber, hastily convened by Barry Rutter and punctuated by bangs, shouts and the tinkling of broken glass from men re-glazing the windows smashed by Class Warfare. Everyone except the tightly permed receptionist looked at each other and shook their heads when Rutter asked who'd seen John Bullock after the group meeting. The receptionist, fingering the big plastic beads looped round her neck, related in a wavering voice how a large man with a crew cut and dark glasses had come in saying he had a car outside to take the leader to lunch; but she had failed to get a reply from Bullock's office and the man had waited impatiently for a few minutes and left. A teenage clerical officer said he thought he'd seen Bullock walking across the car park at the back, but he wasn't sure. Rutter walked gloomily back to his office, wondering if he should ring the police. He decided to wait.

The only advance in the police inquiry had come in the early hours of the morning when a patrol car finally called at Bullock's office to check his Mercedes, sighted there by Nigel Damson at 6 o'clock the previous evening. The small car park at the side of the office was empty, and there was nothing and nobody to indicate where the car might have gone. It was added to the stolen and suspect list on the Police National Computer, and the news was given to a distraught Dorothy when she phoned the police mid-morning. A WPC and a sergeant were despatched to get a statement from her, and for a while the police worried they might be dealing with a kidnapping, best handled under a news blackout. But in the late afternoon Scotland Yard's press bureau issued a picture of Bullock with his car number and a statement that they were 'concerned over his whereabouts'. The local evening TV bulletins ran the photograph with a run-down of Bullock's recent political exploits.

Rumours, theories and off-colour jokes rattled round the police station. Bullock had got out of his depth in an operation running hard currency into Eastern Europe; a pile of clothes had been found on Brighton beach, and Bullock was doing a John Stonehouse, faking his own death; organized criminals had muscled in on the town centre redevelopment and were displeased about the lack of progress. In the CID office, Detective Inspector Colin Borden wondered aloud whether they were dealing with another victim of the maniac who'd done two unsolved, motiveless murders near the crest of the North Downs.

'We don't even know if there's been a crime yet, let alone a murder,' said his colleague Judy Best, glancing up irritably from a wad of statements on the previous day's vandalism. 'And as I remember it, the other two victims were a slightly built woman and a frail old man who lived by themselves in isolated houses. From what I saw of him when he toured the station that time, it wouldn't be quite so easy to strangle John Bullock.'

'OK, Judy,' said Borden, raising his hands and eyebrows. 'Don't take it too literally, I was just chatting.'

'Sorry, Colin,' said Judy, reaching for her half-eaten cheese roll. 'It's just that my particular problem right now is, how the hell do you prove that it was this yob rather than that yob who lobbed a brick through Iqbal Hussein's window? The descriptions are all rubbish – they'd fit about half the teenagers in the division.'

'The answer is, you don't bother,' said Borden with a played-out sigh, getting up and walking to the window with his hands shoved in his pockets. 'You know that as well as I do. We'll end up just doing the ones where we've got a ready-made arrest, or the little buggers were caught by the cameras, or there was personal injury. The rest are just insurance jobs. Paperwork. Crap. Don't take it so seriously.'

'And what about this body in the barrow?'

'Doesn't ring true. Someone's telling porkies – or drinking too much.'

'You're an old cynic, in spite of all this born-again stuff,' said Judy, pushing the statements back into a folder and brushing crumbs from the front of her white blouse. She had been in the CID for under two years, and had just been promoted to sergeant, prompting complaints of tokenism from some of her longer-serving male colleagues. She smiled warmly at Borden, one of the few who'd helped and supported her, a little dimple appearing in one cheek.

'Just a realist,' corrected Borden, returning the smile with interest. 'And when it comes to this John Bullock affair, I've got a feeling that it's going to be a lot more nasty and complicated than everyone wants to think.'

Chapter Four

Saturday, early morning

Up on the downs, four miles south of Beechley town centre, the day dawned with a cloudless sky. An orange sun climbed slowly out of the grey smudge of the eastern horizon, its low light sparkling through the dewdrops on the grass and the newly spun spiders' webs in the bushes. Small birds in the ragged clumps of yew and hawthorn chattered and squawked irritably, while away beyond the M25 a pheasant repeated its clueless call, half-way between a cluck and a squeak. The blue of the sky lightened, the night chill began to fade from the air, and at half-past six a few joggers and dog walkers began to arrive on the edge of the escarpment from the shadow-laden slopes and valleys below.

There were wiry men with wispy beards and tight bicyclists' shorts clinging to their pulsing thigh muscles, pink-faced girls with breasts lolloping under outsize T-shirts, and overweight businessmen with desperate eyes and rasping breath. They toiled up the rutted tracks, past copses fouled by rotting mattresses and the carcasses of washing machines, wiping sweat from faces perspiring in the early morning sun. A few cars were now grinding up Tupwood Lane, parking in the National Trust car park on the top of Halliloo Hill, and disgorging brisk-looking women with inquisitive terriers or men in tweed jackets with amiable Labradors. The owners set off over the open down, shouting or flourishing sticks at the dogs, which crashed and bounded around the undergrowth near the car park or stood together with ramrod tails, sniffing and trembling.

Judy Best sat in her black track suit on the bench at the summit of Halliloo Hill, looking out over the weald of Kent and Sussex, an undulating patchwork of colours ranging from turquoise-green to the shadowy purple of ripe plums. It was a picture punctuated by church spires and brick-built Victorian institutions on hillsides – schools or asylums. Trails of mist around the valley bottoms were rising and evaporating in the growing warmth, while an early train rattled out of

24

the tunnel towards the coast and the first plane of the morning rose silently in the distance above Gatwick.

She had grown up near the downs, twenty miles further west, and the view reminded her of childhood picnics on the slopes of Box Hill and teenage walks holding hands with anxious, spotty boys. Her move to Beechley from the inner city, where she'd rarely felt safe on the streets in or out of uniform, had prompted her to take up running again, and the half-way pause on Halliloo Hill was part of her regular route. This morning seemed the clearest and most peaceful of the year so far, and she spread her arms along the back of the bench, closing her eyes and tipping her head back so her pale-blonde, bobbed hair touched her track suit collar. She breathed deeply, contemplating the temptation to walk home rather than run. It would stymie her target of twenty miles a week, but it would prolong the outing in the delicious morning air. What the body would lose, the soul would gain.

She opened her eyes again drowsily as she heard the footfalls of another runner thumping laboriously towards her up the slope. It was a beanpole of a man in a white T-shirt and black nylon shorts, elbows pumping like bony pistons, big hands flopping loosely. Judy watched him and prepared to smile or say good morning, but he passed with studiously downcast eyes, as if the ground in front of him was particularly interesting today. Everyone who came up here seemed to hanker for a solitude they would never get anywhere so close to the overspilling metropolis, and averted looks and perfunctory grunts were the general habit. This man's feelings about those around him were expressed in the message YOU FAT BASTARD, printed in black on the back of his retreating shirt. Judy was caught between amusement and indignation, wondering if it amounted to the offence of using threatening words and behaviour.

She glanced at her watch and saw it was nearly half-past eight. The country below her was coming to life now, with the trickle of traffic on the M25 nearly a mile away swelling into a steady stream heading for the hypermarkets, the DIY superstores, the mother-in-law's place, the Channel ports. Just below the lip of the chalk escarpment, a farmer whistled and shouted as he held the gate open for a herd of Friesians fanning out into a field of pasture. One of the cows suddenly bellowed and broke into a lumbering run, kicking and bucking like a filly. A group of boys in shirts and shorts flashed with fluorescent orange and lime green were riding bicycles through the farmyard, heading for Slump Quarry, the huge disused chalk pit tucked into a fold of the downs, just below Halliloo Hill. Over to her left was the lip of the quarry, steep and dangerous, defended by a barbed wire fence and green danger notices put up by the National Trust.

Judy idly watched the boys as they rode past the crumbling arches of the old lime kilns and into the pit which had once provided the acid, powdery mortar for the building booms of Victorian London. The undulating floor of the quarry, spattered with bushes and clumps of small trees, was ideal terrain for juvenile risk-taking and had been worn into a skein of paths by the sort of fat-tyred machines the boys were riding. She continued to watch as they wheeled and skidded a hundred and fifty feet below her, their shrill calls and curses cutting cleanly through the fresh morning air.

Most of them were chasing each other round the tight corners, taking bumps so fast they sailed through the air like miniature stuntmen, but a boy in a tangerine T-shirt broke off from the pack and headed away from Judy, pedalling faster and faster towards the grey-white face of the pit. His momentum took him ten or fifteen feet up the loose, steepening chalk, and he stood up on the pedals, leaning to one side and then the other as he pushed and strained for more height. Then suddenly gravity and the gradient defeated him, he stalled and hung motionless for a second, and then neatly whipped the bike round to hurtle, whooping, back to the bottom. As he went through the trick a second and third time, legs stuck out stiffly on the descent to show how easy he found it, Judy wondered how safe the quarry was, and whether the boys' parents and the owner of the land knew what they were up to.

She decided it was not her problem and was about to stretch her limbs and set off home when she threw a final look down into the quarry and noticed that the boy in tangerine was no longer on his bike. He was crouched next to a large purple-flowered bush, as if clutching an elbow or leg, his machine thrown down in a heap behind him. Judy screwed her eyes up against the growing brightness and looked harder, convinced at first that he had confirmed her worries by falling off and injuring himself. But suddenly he sprang to his feet and ran down towards his friends, yelling and waving his arms like an ungainly insect. She couldn't hear what he was shouting, but the rest of the boys turned, rode towards him and skidded to a halt in a ragged circle. As their heads followed his pointing arm, they threw themselves off their bikes in a jumble of handlebars and spinning wheels, and sprinted towards the bush, slipping and slithering on the loose and rising ground. The boy in tangerine, instead of showing the way or following, sat down suddenly, as if his legs had dissolved, and let his head slowly sag on to his hands.

26

By now Judy was walking rapidly towards the rim of the quarry, breathing harder as her pulse speeded up and her neck and chest tightened painfully. But when she saw the boys clustered on their knees around the clump of bushes, peering and pointing like trackers round the most recent footprint, the adrenalin overwhelmed her and she broke into a headlong run along the path which skirted the lip of the quarry. 'I don't believe it!' she heard herself panting. 'I don't believe it!'

At first the ground was smooth and the gradient gentle, and she could take her eyes off the path and look to her left, over the strands of barbed wire, at the huddle of bright shirts in the bottom of the quarry. Then the way downwards broke off from the ridge path and took her suddenly into clusters of stiff little hawthorn bushes whose branches snagged at her and sprayed drops of cold dew in her face. The ground was hard, with a slippery wet skin, falling away steeply in ruts and steps, and she tried desperately to cut her speed, milling her arms and wondering whether to risk cutting her hands by grabbing at the hawthorns. Then one of her feet went into a long, greasy slide, and she was bumping and sliding on her hip and shoulder to a painful, gasping halt.

She lay there for half a minute, waiting to see if any of the pain persisted, staring at the sky and trying to gain some composure. Then she sat up, deciding that whatever it was down there wouldn't go away in the ten minutes it would take her to reach it at a safe pace. It might just be an escaped animal, an abandoned pet, something someone had dumped which the boys thought was valuable. The quarry was screened from her now by the undergrowth, and when she got to her feet, wiping her muddy hands on her track suit and testing out a ricked ankle, she trotted slowly downhill, wondering if her careful plans for a leisurely weekend would have to be abandoned.

The look on John Bullock's face was as cool and unimpressed as ever, as if death was just another item on the agenda which he would wrap up with a few businesslike phrases and put to the vote with the sang-froid of a man with a large majority. He was lying on his back in a huge wild buddleia bush, cradled by the thick purple stems and half-hidden among the trailing mauve-coloured pokers and long furred leaves. A cloud of marbled white butterflies was fluttering over him, to and from the flowers, and it looked almost as if he had selected the spot and settled down for a peaceful nap. Standing over him, cold and pale with shock, Judy hoped for a wild moment that the eyelids would suddenly blink, that a shine would return to the glaucous irises, that he

27

would hold out his hand and ask her calmly to help him up.

But it was clear from the first glance that John Bullock was never going to rise to his feet again. His skin was a waxy yellow colour, a couple of bluebottles were dabbling in the lozenge of greenish mucus descending from one nostril, and his feet and legs were wrenched into impossible angles, like broken sticks. His grey flannels and blue blazer were torn and covered with chalk dust, and the knot of his tie was pulled sideways, as if somebody had grabbed it and tried to strangle him. One hand was resting on his chest, palm turned outward, as if he'd realized at the last moment, before the untroubled composure of his handsome mouth could change, that no amount of votes would save him from a murderous attack.

Suddenly revolted by the open eyes, Judy reached over to try to close them, but quickly thought better of touching anything. The kids had already trodden the ground around the bush into a scuffed welter of footprints which would badly upset the scenes of crime team. She stepped back and used both hands to pull her hair from her face, stretching her eyelids and feeling her arms trembling slightly. Corpses were nothing new to her, but the death of a political leader was a fresh departure: very un-British, especially in a hitherto tranquil place like Beechley. She had one dead Tory on her hands.

'Please, miss, is he really dead?'

It was the boy in the tangerine shirt who had wandered up behind her. He was about ten, with straw-coloured hair, standing in the full sunlight shading his eyes and squirming his bony knees together, as if his bladder was full.

'Yes, I'm afraid he is,' said Judy, stepping out of the shadow which still surrounded the resting place of John Bullock. The boy nodded seriously, unsurprised.

'My friends went to phone the police,' he said. 'At the farm.'

'Good for them,' said Judy. 'I'm a policewoman too. I happened to be sitting at the top there and I saw you find him.'

'Has he been murdered?'

'Could be.'

'Will you find out who did it?'

'Hope so.'

The boy's thin features suddenly puckered in rejection of the ugly evidence of mortality that been thrust before his eyes.

'There was all that, that stuff,' he whimpered. 'You know, coming out of his nose.'

Judy put an arm round his thin shoulders and steered him over to the hillock where he'd left his bike, and they sat down together to wait for help to arrive. She asked him about school and his favourite TV programmes while he gave monosyllabic answers and scrawled violent patterns in the dust with a twig. Presently they heard the whooping and mewing of the sirens, and a blue light flashed through the poplars on the road along the valley, which marked the boundary between the Metropolitan Police district and Kent. One of Beechley's area cars was the first to bounce dustily along the track into the quarry, the bare arm of the officer in the passenger seat resting along the top of the door. An ambulance was lumbering in two hundred yards behind.

'Hello, Judy,' said the officer, surprised, as he climbed out of the Rover and tucked his white shirt in round his spreading stomach. 'What you doing here? We got a shout there was a body in the bushes.'

'There is,' said Judy grimly. 'And I just happened to be passing. This is the young man who found him, so we'll have to get his details in a minute. I'll just hand him over to the ambulance crew for a bit and take you to the spot.'

Judy knew both the uniformed men from vague introductions in the canteen, and they remembered her because she had a rare but memorable smile and was the only woman Detective Sergeant on the district. She took them over to the butterfly bush, where they whistled under their breath and wiped their brows with their forearms as they stood looking at the body.

'Well,' said the driver eventually, clearing his throat. 'It's definitely that whatsisname, political one we were meant to look out for. Saw his mug shot on the telly last night.'

'That's right,' said Judy. 'John Bullock, Conservative bigshot and leader of the council. They'll be rattling their cages in Downing Street over this one. Powerful man.'

The bush was out of the early morning shadow now, and the sunlight was playing in Bullock's dusty hair and glancing off a tooth which was just visible through the pale, placidly set lips. The paunchy officer, his shirt escaping from his trousers again, was squinting up the face of the quarry, shading his eyes. The top thirty feet was a near-vertical cliff of glittering white chalk, while the remaining hundred feet or so was a steep grey scree ending in a debris of brick-size limestone blocks dotted with scrub and bushes.

'Well, he's fallen from power now, all right,' he muttered. 'About a hundred and fifty feet, by the look of it. You can see some of the marks where he slid down the loose bits.'

'Did he fall or was he pushed?' said the driver. 'Nice little job for you and your mates, Judy. I'll just go and break the good news, get the hordes on the move.'

'While you're at it,' said Judy, 'can you get them to give Inspector Borden a ring at home? I think he ought to know about this one.'

'Borden, eh? Reckon this is one for the vicar?'

'Come on,' said Judy reproachfully. 'Just because he's got religion doesn't stop him being a good detective.'

The boys who had raised the alarm had ridden back to the quarry and joined their friend in the tangerine shirt at the ambulance, where the PC with the wayward shirt was taking their names and addresses. Meanwhile the farmer, a stout brown man in his fifties with his trousers held up with a piece of orange twine, had walked down to the quarry in a bow-legged gait and was leaning casually against a post. Judy went over to talk to him while she waited for the police surgeon and the scenes of crime team.

'You a copper?' the farmer asked her, smiling enigmatically. 'Plain clothes?'

Judy nodded.

'Who is it this time, then?' His manner was casual, almost amused.

'No formal ID yet, sir,' said Judy.

'Not that council leader, is it?'

'We can't confirm identities until next of kin have been informed. Anyway, what d'you mean, this time? This a regular occurrence, or something?'

'Oh, there's been a few in here over the years,' said the farmer, narrowing his eyes and looking away down the valley as if he was assessing the coming harvest. 'Chopped-up wives, buried gangsters, couple of teenagers fell off the top. You get lots of dead 'uns in quarries. Murder, is it?'

'Could be,' said Judy. 'You notice anything over the last couple of days? Any unusual activity, any noise or lights at night, that sort of thing?'

The farmer turned down the corners of his mouth and shook his head, looking away again.

'Nah. To be honest with you, there are so many ruddy odds and sods traipsing around the place I don't take much notice. Long as I can keep the buggers out of my fields, I don't care what they get up to. You get all sorts of daft goings-on, mind. Weird types from up town wandering around on drugs. People lighting fires and having barbecues at midnight. Idiots trying to climb up the quarry face.'

30

'Anything like that the last couple of days?'

'You're a keen one, aren't you?' said the farmer, looking straight at her for the first time, his eyes blue and sly. 'Didn't have girl detectives in my day. Like it, do you? All those young chaps?'

Judy controlled her irritation, told him someone would be round to take a statement from him, and walked over to the swelling group of police vehicles. The routines of murder were well under way: the surgeon had confirmed it was a suspicious death, the coroner had been informed, attempts were being made to track down the pathologist, and the head of the Area Major Inquiry Team had been alerted. Chief Superintendent Blackman had apparently volunteered to forgo a morning on the golf course and drive up to Jumpers himself to break the news to Dorothy Bullock.

The farmer was right, thought Judy, walking off by herself for a moment, scuffing her battered trainers in the loose gravel. Quarries seemed to attract furtive and disreputable behaviour, like public lavatories and underground walkways. People felt such places were already soiled and abused, and that a contribution from them would go unnoticed, undiscovered. They could flirt with the danger of sudden drops and crumbling cliffs, or sniff around to see what secrets and skeletons might be uncovered from the past. And the excavation of the earth was a powerful reminder of burial and disposal, as if the ground had been loosened on purpose to receive the latest residues of human vice. The lip of the quarry nearest to the Halliloo Hill car park was clearly a favourite dumping ground: dark lines of detritus trailed down the quarry face, like mascara-filled tears on a pale, lumpy face.

Judy heard the gentle tooting of a car horn behind her, and turned to see an ageing green estate car pulling up, with the features of Colin Borden just visible behind the reflections on the grimy windscreen. He got out and walked over to her, wearing his lined and weary smile.

'Dragged you out of the garden, did they?' asked Judy, nodding at his grass-stained jeans and blue T-shirt.

'You know me,' he said. 'I'm happier at work. Didn't know you spend your weekends looking for bodies, though.'

'Sheer luck, if that's the right word. But it's the man we want, I'm afraid.'

Judy led the way under the police tape towards the buddleia, where a large cream-coloured tent was being erected by a group of men in green overalls who were having difficulty getting rid of the butterflies. She was irritably aware that Borden was watching her closely, with a concerned expression, as if to gauge how shaken she was. She felt the familiar double-bind tightening around her: if you were upset by the violence and brutality in police work, you were just a plonk, you weren't up to the job; if you weren't upset, then there was something wrong with your emotions, you weren't a proper woman. She stopped angrily and confronted him, hands clenched inside her track suit pockets.

'Look, Colin,' she said tersely. 'I was here first and I want to work on this case. I don't want to find myself turfed off the team because of some macho bullshit, OK?'

'OK, OK,' he said. He hunched his shoulders and his tone was defensive, as if such thoughts were miles from his mind; but he was still studying her round, small-featured face with some secret interest.

'So I'll be on the inquiry, definite, working with you?'

'It'll probably be run by a Superintendent from AMIT. But there'll probably be dozens working on it, so I don't see why not.'

'Yes, Colin, but the selection and the day to day stuff will be mainly down to you, everyone knows you're the best investigator in the district.'

'Flattery will get you everywhere,' he smiled. 'But I suspect it's not going to be simple and it's not going to be easy. There'll be political complications, and all sorts of pressure for a quick result.'

'I know,' said Judy, relaxing into a smile. 'But don't worry, we've got God on our side if you're on the team.'

'That's right,' murmured Colin, turning away and walking towards the tent. 'That's right. So I'd better take a butcher's at the mortal remains.'

Chapter Five

Saturday, 10.30 a.m.

By late morning the sun was shining brilliantly out of a clear blue sky and a wide slice of the downs had been taken over by dozens of police officers and their vehicles, gradually squeezing everyone else out. A vanload of officers had parked on Halliloo Hill and taped off a half-mile strip of land around the quarry, preparing it for a finger-tip search in the afternoon. But dogs kept invading the area, prancing and barking when they were chased or shouted at, and runners and walkers indignantly questioned harassed PCs about why they were being excluded from their usual stamping ground.

'Are you *aware* that this is National Trust land?' asked a woman in stout shoes, blinking resentfully at a panting officer who had finally managed to see off a persistent Alsatian with a slavering red mouth.

'Yeah, but it's murder, see?' gasped the PC, wiping his sweaty face. 'That good enough for you?'

'No, I'm afraid it's not. Do you always talk to members of the public in that insolent way?'

'Only when it's necessary, madam. Move along, please, and don't forget your pooch. Looks like it's got diarrhoea.'

'Well, really!'

Down in the quarry a mobile control centre with a black and white dome in the roof dominated the cluster of police vehicles parked at conflicting angles fifty yards from the box-shaped tent which covered the body. Superintendent Bryan Manningbird had arrived from the Area Major Inquiry Team to take charge of the investigation and was talking to Colin Borden and Judy Best while everyone waited for the pathologist. The coroner's officer had arrived and was hunched in a corner, struggling awkwardly with sheaves of paper. Manningbird, widely known as Fat Man, had a great bag of a body with tiny warts in the grey folds of skin beneath his eyes. He remembered Judy from her time as a WPC in London's docklands, when a young investment analyst she knew had been murdered in a gym and she'd been caught up in the inquiry.

33

'You seem to be making a habit of this,' said Manningbird, his bright little eyes running over her sceptically.

'Habit of what, sir?' asked Judy, smiling innocently, displaying her tidy rows of even teeth.

'First at the scene, that sort of thing. Bit of a coincidence. I don't suppose this one's a personal friend as well?'

''Fraid not,' said Judy, brightly. 'And this time I'm in the CID. Gives me a head start working on the case – doesn't it, Colin?'

Borden nodded, and Manningbird grunted noncommittally. A PC came in balancing a tray and handed them plastic cups brimming with grey-brown coffee. Manningbird was gingerly sipping at his when a car outside backfired like a pistol shot, making him start and spill the hot liquid down his dirty blue suit. He cursed thickly and they all peered through the window to see Professor Martin Binder, a neat man with watery eyes and a shock of white hair, climbing out of his rusting Morris Minor estate car. He was wearing a leather-elbowed tweed jacket and a knitted green tie, and was carrying a battered leather case. Borden nudged Judy.

'Told you he'd be wearing that 'orrible tie,' he said. 'It's been in more breakfasts than you've had hot dinners.'

'And not only breakfasts, knowing his job,' said Judy jauntily. Manningbird gave her a reproachful look and she immediately regretted her attempt at schoolboy machismo. It was the kind of thing she'd often condemned in arguments with colleagues about canteen culture.

They took Binder down the path of lumpy chalk to the tent where half a dozen men in green overalls were busily coming and going like bees around a hive. He stepped briskly into the overalls handed to him, crushed a green cap over his shock of white hair, pulled out a notebook and pencil, and snapped on some rubber gloves. Then he gave them a mirthless grin, took a deep breath like a diver going underwater, and ducked beneath the canvas. As he disappeared into the gloom, a scenes of crime man came up to Manningbird and offered him a clutch of plastic bags containing several small objects.

'Contents of jacket pockets, sir, and a few things that were lying about,' he announced. 'Couldn't get into the trouser pockets without disturbing it too much. No wallet so far.'

'Thanks. Right, gents ... and, er, lady ... let's go and have a look at these while the Professor's wrestling with the rigor mortis.'

When they climbed back up the steps into the control centre, a perspiring uniform sergeant in shirtsleeves turned round from the radio console and spoke excitedly to Manningbird.

'Sir, they've found the car, up at the top!'

Manningbird fixed the sergeant with his little, mole-like eyes, waiting for more.

'In the car park at the top of the hill, sir. The driver of one of the carriers checked out the index number. Er, JB 492. Silver Merc estate.'

'When did you say this car was reported missing?' asked Manningbird, turning to Judy and Colin.

'Early hours of yesterday,' said Borden.

'So it's been on the stolen and suspect register for more than thirty hours, everyone on this patch's meant to be looking for it, and someone's only just had the bright idea of checking the car park of a well-known local beauty spot.'

Manningbird stared vindictively at the sergeant, who looked back helplessly, pink-faced, mouth half open.

'That's right,' said Borden, impassively.

'Bleedin' plods,' snorted Manningbird. 'Get the scenes of crime mob up there, and make sure they put a half-mile cordon round the car as well, will you? And tell them I'll be up there when I've talked to the Prof. Now, let's have a look at the debris.'

One bag contained the wine-coloured silk handkerchief from Bullock's breast pocket, darkened in patches by the oils collected in its frequent journeys across the owner's shiny nose; another some small change, which had fallen on the ground beneath the bush, and a gold blazer button from the bottom of the chalk slope; and a third one contained a slim diary, covered in black leather, from his inside jacket pocket. The diary had London Boroughs Association embossed in gold on the front.

'Like the bloke said, no wallet,' murmured Manningbird, riffling through the diary. 'Now, where are we, right, May, June, here we go: 14th June. It says 11 a.m. group, whatever that is, 1 p.m. DK, Black Swan, 3 p.m. council meeting.'

Judy and Colin crowded silently round to study the week's cryptic entries, neatly written in pencil or thin black felt-tip. Judy noticed that today's space was marked Exeat, James; Bullock should have been driving right now up the tree-lined avenue of some public school, shaking hands with a gangling teenager in a blazer, taking him off in the silver Mercedes for lunch at a posh roadhouse. But instead of all that, he was going to be carried off to the mortuary in a huge plastic sheet, hands and feet tied into bags like a tramp trying to keep out the cold, and cut up like a dead animal. She forced herself to concentrate on the diary as Manningbird's pork-sausagey fingers turned the pages one by one.

At the front there were pages of information about local government, with small mug shots of fat-faced office holders with moustaches and brilliantined hair grinning self-importantly, and a few pages for personal information where the spaces had been left blank; at the back the half-dozen pages left empty for notes had several jottings and a few phone numbers with a first name or an initial next to them. Manningbird grunted, snapped the diary shut and dropped it back into the plastic bag.

'Right,' he said. 'Last seen just before lunch on Thursday, right? Shouldn't be too difficult to locate DK and see if he showed up at the Black Swan. Who was the last person to see him, as far as we know at the moment?'

'Someone at the town hall, I think,' said Judy. 'The meeting in the morning was the Conservative councillors' group, working out policy before the council meeting proper.'

'Mmm. I can see a big trawl of the town hall coming up. Sooner the better.'

There was a rap at the door and Borden opened it to find Professor Binder standing there, protecting his pale, sad eyes from the sun with a hand held up at his forehead, like a salute gone wrong.

'Come on in, Prof.,' said Borden. 'Can I get you a nasty cup of coffee from the mobile canteen?'

'Er, I think not,' said Binder, climbing the two wobbly steps and sitting down on a bench, his leather case at his feet. There was a slight aroma of last night's whisky on his breath, and he pulled his fingers wearily down his cheeks, exposing the intimate watery pinkness inside his lower eyelids.

'Sorry we can't offer you anything stronger,' said Borden; his voice was sincere but a slight raising of the eyebrows betrayed the dig. Binder flapped his hand casually, as if fending off an annoying insect.

'What d'you make of it, then?' asked Manningbird, leaning against the side of the van, his shirt buttons parting slightly to reveal the blubber-white skin of his paunch.

'I often wish I had a thousand pounds for every time I've said this sentence,' said Binder. 'But death appears to have been caused by a massive blow or blows to the head.'

'Sustained during a fall or a jump from the cliff top?' asked Borden. Binder turned down the corners of his mouth, shook his head, and addressed them like a group of students, catching the eye first of one, then another; he had a clear, light voice, with precise consonants and upper-class vowels.

'Unlikely, I'd say. My tentative opinion is he died before he went over the edge of the quarry. My reason for saying that is that the kind of cuts and abrasions consistent with a fall – you may have noticed the grazes on the hands and on one cheek – look as if they were sustained after death. No bruising and bleeding and redness, as when you or I fall over on the pavement, but dry, yellowish scratches instead. I suspect those leg fractures happened post mortem as well.'

'So what about these fatal head injuries?' asked Borden. 'There didn't seem to be much blood.'

'That's quite often the case in fatal head injuries. In fact, the absence of blood makes me particularly interested in the large red mark just beneath the right ear. Now that is definitely a bruise – a massive bruise – so the blow must have happened while the body was still alive and the blood was still moving round the body. There's been at least one blow to the back of the skull as well, hard enough to depress the skull but again not hard enough to cause significant bleeding. I suspect we'll find that one or the other, or the combination of the two, caused the death.'

'Type of weapon?'

'Couldn't say for certain. Something large, with a rounded face, without any sharp edges which would cut the skin. A big round stone, an unusually large paperweight, perhaps, something of that kind. I'll probably be able to say more on that after the post-mortem.'

'And how long d'you think he's been dead?'

Binder squinted at the low plastic ceiling and pulled ruminatively at a few strands of his bushy white hair. His manner and dress, even his motor car, reminded Judy of how men looked in films made in the forties and fifties, before she was born; he was stuck in a post-war time warp of baggy grey flannels and semi-military mannerisms.

'Fair old time. He's cold and floppy, and rigor mortis usually relaxes like that about thirty-six hours after death. There's some decomposition already, which is why the poor chap is beginning to leak a bit. So I'd say he was probably lying out here in the sun all yesterday. Very tentatively, I'd say somewhere between noon and midnight on Thursday.'

'Could you give us a more precise time?'

Binder shook his head, leaning down to pick up his case and put his little sketch book into it.

''Fraid we can never be as precise as you chaps would like. The temperature of the body's the most helpful thing if it's still cooling down, but this one's been dead long enough to reach the ambient temperature, so even that won't be much help—'

'So when d'you want to do the carving?' broke in Manningbird briskly.

'First thing this afternoon?'

'That's fine. We'll see you at the mortuary at, what, three o'clock?'

Judy stepped outside with the Professor and waved him off. The Morris Minor coughed and lurched its way out of the quarry, past the officer logging all movements and the gatepost where the farmer still lounged, an expression of amused tolerance on his nut-brown features as he watched the comings and goings.

Manningbird and Borden followed her out of the control centre, on their way to look at the Mercedes and the lip of the quarry. The Superintendent's wheezy breath and great sack of a body made Judy decide against suggesting that they should go on foot, climbing around the edge of the quarry. She offered instead to drive him up there in his unmarked police Cavalier while Borden followed in his green estate car with the peeling paintwork. As they drove towards the farmer, he waved them down, and Judy wound the window open impatiently.

'You going to be much longer?' he asked, jeeringly, leaning on the car window sill and riveting Judy with his hard little eyes. ''Cos this is upsetting my cows, see?'

He was so close she could smell the sourness of his breath and the dungy animal-smell of his clothes. She suppressed a wince and looked away from him, to the right, where the Friesians were grazing placidly in fetlock-high grass dotted with buttercups.

'They look perfectly happy to me, sir,' she said, turning back to the farmer and winding up the window slowly. 'But no, we won't be long now.'

She accelerated away before there was any reply, and she and Manningbird exchanged the long-suffering, impassive glance of police officers confronted with the never-ending obtuseness of the British public. The conversation moved quickly back to the docklands case.

'What's happened to Ron Slicer?' asked Judy evenly, staring out of the window as they turned on to the main road and headed along the valley under the green lip of the downs. Inspector Ron Slicer had bullied her and tried to implicate her boyfriend in the killing, and one of Judy's reasons for joining the CID had been to try to do the job better than the likes of him.

'Ron?' said Manningbird, twisting the thin brown line of his lips. 'He's out at Heathrow, looking for stolen suitcases.'

'Change of scene for the lad, eh?'

'Could say. He was a bit wild on that case of yours. Complaints didn't help.'

Judy grinned and shook her head, remembering the sleek, badger-like head, the neat moustache and incisor teeth, the inexhaustible well of anger and stroppiness, the constant jumping to prejudiced conclusions. She glanced over at Manningbird and saw his face contorting with a sudden confusion.

'That, er,' he said in a strangulated voice. He stopped the sentence, cleared his throat, and started again. 'You, er, still knocking around with that, er . . . '

'That black guy, you mean? Clinton?'

'Er, yeah.'

''Fraid not.' Judy stared out at the ripening grain fields curving smoothly towards the tree-lined escarpment as the car slowed and turned up towards Halliloo Hill. 'It was him or the police force, in the end. He couldn't understand why I wanted to stay in after what happened to him – and to me, for that matter.'

'So why *did* you stay, then?'

Judy avoided his eye, which was suddenly concerned and avuncular, and looked out at the approaching clusters of dark-green yew trees. The road steepened as it plunged under the shade of the canopy of foliage, and the car's automatic box jerked the engine into a lower gear. She searched for a summary of her long hesitations. It seemed the right thing? She wasn't going to let the bastards get her down? She was ambitious? She enjoyed meeting people and helping them, like a Miss World contestant?

'You know what it's like,' she said eventually. 'Didn't want to lose the pension.'

Manningbird grinned as the car reached the road's summit and they caught a glimpse of the hazy greyness of London in front of them. They coasted downhill for half a mile, then turned right up the narrow Tupwood Lane which would take them to the car park on Halliloo Hill. The lane was blotched with sunlight falling through the beech copses, where car tyres had pressed black ruts into the mulch of last autumn's leaves.

'Bit of a lovers' lane up here,' said Judy. 'Someone might have seen something Thursday night.'

'We'll put it out at the press conference. And we'll put boards out asking people to come forward.'

'They won't be keen – the hills are probably alive every night with the sounds of people getting their leg over someone else's wife.'

'You're definitely developing a police officer's mind, Judy,' said Manningbird. 'I'll give you that much.'

A hundred yards from the car park a uniformed constable recognized the police index number and waved them through. Behind them, Borden had to stop to show his warrant card. By the time he'd parked, Judy and Manningbird were already watching more men in green overalls fussing round the silver Mercedes parked in the furthest corner of the car park, half hidden by clumps of bracken. The car's doors and tailgate were all wide open, as if there'd been an explosion inside it.

'Was it locked when you found it?' Manningbird asked one of the men in overalls.

'No, sir. Wide open, keys in the ignition. Amazing nobody's nicked it.'

'Today's car thief requires a challenge, perhaps. Anything obvious? Any decent prints?'

The man shook his head, hands on hips. There were drops of sweat standing on his receding blond hairline, and several of them suddenly rolled forward and dripped off the end of his nose. He wiped his face with a green-covered arm.

'Not really,' he said. 'There's his briefcase, also not nicked, a few personal effects – pair of spectacles, box of tissues, maps, usual stuff. We'll bag it all and get it back to the lab so we can dust it properly, eliminate the victim's prints, an' all that. Few footprints round about, but the surface doesn't help. Too dry, especially with all this loose stuff they've spread around to fill up the holes.'

He kicked irritably at one of the split flints in a patch of loose orange-brown sand.

'Signs of struggle, bloodstains, objects being dragged?' asked Manningbird.

'You can have a look round the back of the vehicle, sir. Surface looks as if it might have been flattened, but some dog was round here earlier, sniffing at the car and kicking up the dirt.'

Judy moved closer and leaned forward to look at seats upholstered in grey leather and a dashboard crowded with little dials and gauges. The rich smell of the leather reached her nostrils, a sudden whiff of wealth and luxury, of posh hotels and expensive shops. She read the spines of the tapes stacked in a recess below the player: *Great Arias from Puccini, The Best of Sinatra, Tschaikovsky's Greatest Hits.* She thought of Bullock's big, shiny-nosed face on last night's TV, now lying in a bush with insects crawling on its open eyes: she'd have put him down for brass bands and *South Pacific,* but this fitted better – popular classics and easy listening, a musical massage for the man who has everything. Which tape had accompanied him on his final drive?

' "I Did It My Way"?' said Borden, who had appeared at her elbow.

'Nah. "Nutcracker Suite",' replied Judy, her voice as expressionless as his.

'You're sick,' said Colin, sucking in air and wincing. 'You know that?'

'Course I'm sick – I joined the Met Police. Let's join Fat Man and see where he took the final tumble.'

They walked slowly across the down to the spot where Manningbird was standing in a group of officers, looking intently at the ground. On the near side of the barbed-wire fence, the grass was dusty and yellowing under a sun which had long since sucked up the overnight dew. But on the far side there were little clumps of vegetation between the fence and the cliff, and it was clear that something large had passed through them, crushing the spindly hedge parsley and breaking off the delicate flowers of knapweed and scabious. Another green man was using tweezers and a little stiff brush to remove any bits of fabric and fluff on the barbs of the two strands of wire.

'Plenty of room below that bottom strand,' Manningbird was saying. 'So under he goes, and then over the edge. Would be the bleedin' place where everyone comes up to peer over the edge, wouldn't it? Fat chance of any decent marks.'

Far below they could see the police vehicles, parked higgledy-piggledy, some of their roofs marked with huge numbers for identification by helicopter. Officers and civilians – legless from this perspective, like stumpy figures in distorting mirrors – sauntered around the little cream-coloured tent, snatches of their conversation floating up on occasional stirrings of breeze.

'Ready for the meat wagon?' shouted one officer cheerfully.

Judy didn't catch the reply, but thought she heard the word 'ripe'. She walked away on her own, suddenly nauseated by police work and the way it robbed people of normal reactions to death and suffering. Many of these officers had seen bodies decomposing in cupboards, lying in car parks with hatchets in their skulls and floating, bloated and putrescent, in ponds or rivers. A phrase from an A-level session on Greek tragedy surfaced in her mind, and it occurred to her she hadn't seen much pity and terror in people's reactions to the morning's discovery. The boy in the tangerine shirt, his little face puckered and his chest heaving like some captured bird, was the only exception.

41

Judy stopped and looked back, round the curve of the quarry's rim, to the spot where the others were standing, hands in pockets. Her eye traced the line between them and the bottom of the pit, where all the police paraphernalia added to the litter of the crumbling kilns, the broken-down sheds, the clumps of bushes and briars. There were places on the steep grey-white scree, towards the bottom of the quarry face, where the surface seemed to be newly skimmed, as if by a heavy object; and for a sudden second, the bright morning faded and she saw John Bullock, flanelled legs and blazered arms flailing loosely, plunging and bouncing downwards under a dark sky, like an unwanted doll tipped into some gigantic dustbin.

Chapter Six

'I'll wait in the car,' said Borden carefully, looking straight ahead through the windscreen as he pulled on the handbrake.

'Don't be daft,' said Judy. 'Come in and have a coffee. It won't take me long to change.'

Borden hadn't invited Judy in when they'd stopped for him to change at his home twenty minutes earlier, but it wasn't the best of times to start introducing wife and children. Now he smiled nervously and followed Judy up the tiled path of the red-brick Victorian villa, past a bed of unpruned rose bushes and three overflowing dustbins. Her flat was on the first floor, and he kept his eyes on the thin brown stair carpet as she led the way upwards through the drabness and musty odours of the house's common parts.

Judy's front room was filled with sunlight falling on an Indian cotton rug striped in ochre and vermilion. She made mugs of coffee and disappeared into the bathroom, leaving him to pace the floor and study the pictures: a Japanese print of a big wave about to engulf a small boat, and a framed photograph on the bookcase of a twelve-year-old Judy, muffled and moody, on a windswept English beach with desperately grinning parents. He stole a look along the corridor into the still-curtained bedroom, where a pink duvet trailed off the foot of a low bed and a white nightdress lay tangled on the floor. Then the sound of the shower stopped, and he hurried back to the front window, humming 'All My Hope on God is Founded' in between sips of black coffee. The green crest of the downs was just visible in the distance, above the crenellated ridge tiles of the houses opposite.

'Ready?' asked Judy, coming back into the room in an aroma of shampoo, track suit replaced by a blue skirt and white, high-necked blouse. She was brushing out her wet hair, which looked darker than its usual white-blonde and hung closer to her neck and face, making them thinner and more vulnerable.

43

'Let's go, then,' said Colin jovially, putting down his coffee mug. 'But listen, you sure you're feeling up to it?'

She flashed him a warning look, collecting her bag and stuffing the hairbrush into it without replying. He apologized and followed her out, pulling the door closed behind him, noting the flimsiness of the single lock, but saying nothing. Ten minutes later the unmarked Cavalier they had picked up from the police station was winding through the rising curves of Hunter's Combe Lane towards Jumpers, family home of the late John Bullock.

'Not what you'd call a council estate,' murmured Colin, taking a hand off the wheel and gesturing vaguely at the high garden walls, the five-bedroom façades in mock-Georgian or Tudor, the clumps of rhododendron and azalea which still carried a few fading blooms of orange or mauve.

'Just look at these names,' said Judy. 'Beechlands, Paddocks, Merlins, Rosemullion. It's not much better than Mon Repos or Dunroamin, really, is it? You'd think these toffs would have a bit more imagination.'

'What d'you want – Xanadu?' said Colin. 'From what I hear the best name for this bloke's place would be Dungazumpin.'

'That's pure prejudice, Colin. And why's it so quiet, that's what I want to know? You'd think no one actually lived here.'

'It's a dormitory, isn't it? This lot'll all be out making their millions. And if the wives are at home by themselves, they'll all be cowering behind their big dogs and burglar alarms.'

'Now then, Colin, don't get bitter. You're a servant of *all* the people, remember.'

The gravel in the driveway of Jumpers was so deep that getting to the front door was like struggling across a sandy beach. As Judy recovered from turning her ankle a second time, she noticed a well-dressed woman through the big window of the front room, going round polishing the ornaments.

'Look at that,' she stage-whispered over her shoulder to Borden, who had found a line of paving stones through the gravel and was making quicker progress. 'Even the cleaning women wear strings of pearls round here.'

Judy was expecting a pretentious set of chimes when she pressed the button at the side of the varnished oak door, but instead there came a sober, straightforward ringing sound. The woman she had seen through the window was there in seconds, a yellow-brown duster hanging loosely in her hand: she had brown hair, and her hazel eyes were

44

slightly bloodshot and had a lost, bewildered expression.

'Mrs Bullock home?' asked Judy.

'I'm Mrs Bullock,' muttered Dorothy, as if she didn't quite believe it.

'I'm so sorry,' said Judy. 'I thought . . .'

She abandoned the explanation and did the introductions, the sun scorching the back of her neck and beads of sweat breaking out on her forehead and upper lip. Dorothy blinked a lot and seemed slow in understanding, and Judy wondered if she'd been sedated; but eventually she nodded and led them into the cool, parquet-floored refuge of the hallway. A woman with luxuriant dark hair and a lot of lipstick appeared at the kitchen door and leaned on the jamb, folding her chubby brown arms and staring at them with an expression which told them she wasn't impressed.

'Mrs Silver,' said Dorothy, gesturing weakly with one hand. 'She's looking after me. School friend. Police again, Annabel.'

Annabel nodded, saying nothing, and turned back into the kitchen. Dorothy took them into the sitting room with the big window looking over the lawn, which appeared almost white in the flood of sunlight. They all sank into the pale yellow armchairs and sofas, and Judy's eyes went straight to the silver-framed wedding photograph on the huge TV cabinet of polished wood. There it was again in a fresher, leaner version – John Bullock's big-jawed, impassive face, the calm eyes, the shiny nose and glossy hair. She found it hard to believe that Dorothy's tightly pinched mouth could really contain the palisade of brilliant teeth revealed in her wedding smile.

'I haven't got all that long,' said Dorothy, looking vaguely round the room. 'Annabel and I have got to go and collect the children from school.'

'Yes, of course,' said Borden soothingly, leaning forward and clasping his hands between his knees, which were raised and splayed awkwardly by the depth of the chair. 'Just a couple of things at this stage, Mrs Bullock – your husband's movements on Thursday, and whether you've got any idea how this might have happened?'

Dorothy shrugged her shoulders slowly and opened her hands, which seemed too small and delicate for a body beginning to spread into middle age. She looked round the room again, as if her eyes were going to light on something which might give her the answers.

'Well, it was a fairly important day for him, I suppose,' she said, slowly. 'He said he was going to the office, then to the Conservative group meeting, then to this council meeting in the afternoon.'

'Did he say when he expected to be home?'

'No, but he usually rings me towards the end of the day to say when he'll be getting away.'

'And no call on Thursday?'

Dorothy shook her head.

'Did he say anything about lunch?' asked Borden. 'Who he was meeting?'

'Well, nothing specific or anything.'

'Do you know who DK is?'

'DK?' She paused for a moment, wincing in the effort to push aside her distress and think. 'Don't think so. Why?'

'It's in his diary – lunch, Black Swan, DK.'

Dorothy shook her head. Colin was about to speak again when the door opened and Annabel Silver walked in with a tea tray – a china cup for Dorothy, Judy noticed, and lumpy earthenware mugs for the two of them. She looked over at Borden, but his attention seemed to have shifted to Annabel's lush cleavage as she bent to set down the tray. Judy watched her give him a discreet little smile as she straightened up and left the room.

'Do you know if your husband had any enemies, Mrs Bullock?' Judy asked quickly, before Colin could re-focus. 'Had he received any threats?'

Dorothy shook her head and blinked, as if Judy had addressed her in Serbo-Croat; she evidently expected all the questions from the male officer.

'Was he worried about anything? Or were you?'

Dorothy paused for a moment, then suddenly began talking freely, as if a tap had been flicked on. She didn't know that much about John's affairs, because he wasn't much of a talker, tended to keep things to himself. But things hadn't been all that easy for him recently, one way or another. Politics had been difficult, so had work. Because of the poll tax, and the riot, and now this new row over the cuts, he'd been spending more and more time at the town hall. At the same time business was difficult because of the recession, and she knew that his partner was increasingly fed up at being left with most of the burden. But perhaps the worst thing, she said, had been some of the Conservative group turning against him, threatening a public split or an attempt to get rid of him as leader. That had worried him, all right. He'd come home one night the previous week and let rip about Simon Pilkington.

'He's the deputy leader?'

'Yes. He thinks John's too radical, you know, too Thatcherite, trying

46

to change too much too quickly. John was spitting blood about him, said he was going to have to knock heads together.'

'Were those his actual words?'

'Words to that effect. This was all in the build-up to Thursday's meeting.'

'So would you call them enemies, or is that too strong?'

Dorothy gave a bitter little laugh and stared at the dark blue carpet, linking her fingers. Judy got her first real glimpse of the teeth.

'You know what it's like in politics,' said Dorothy. 'Your worst enemies are always on your own side.'

'Sounds a bit like the police force,' murmured Colin, staring innocently out of the window to avoid a warning glance from Judy.

'But I suppose it all began with the seat,' said Dorothy, looking up, suddenly brighter as the new thought occurred to her. Judy and Colin exchanged glances, puzzled.

'What seat?' asked Judy cautiously. Dorothy was clearly a bit overwrought, and a neurotic ramble about furniture was the last thing they needed.

'You don't know?' asked Dorothy, looking from one to the other, eyebrows raised. 'You can't have been reading your newspapers, then. The Parliamentary seat. Beechley South-East.'

'Ah, yes, sorry,' said Judy, relieved. 'What happened?'

'Well, you know Sir Magnus Oakley is retiring at the next election?'

'Politics aren't my strong point. But go on.'

'John was after the nomination, and everyone thought he'd get it quite easily. Then Pilkington went in for it too. It was outrageous, a direct challenge to John, just to spite him. He was livid. You just don't do that sort of thing.'

'So what happened?'

'Well, Pilkington was excluded quite early on, which rankled rather. Or so I've been told. He could hardly have been surprised, though – he just didn't have enough experience. And John went on to get the nomination.'

'So how well did those two work as leader and deputy after that?'

Dorothy shrugged her shoulders weakly.

'It was awful. And as I say, it was coming to a bit of a head.'

Judy looked at Colin, unsure where to go next. He had discarded his flippant look of a few minutes earlier and was paying attention, eyes wrinkled in concentration. He gave Judy a tiny nod and turned a thumb towards his own chest.

'And what were you saying about strains with his partner, Mrs

Bullock?' he asked gently. 'The Mr Damson in Damson and Bullock, presumably?'

'That's right – Nigel Damson. And it's Bullock and Damson, actually. I'm not sure Nigel and John ever saw eye to eye, really. They didn't really choose each other as partners, you see, it was sort of forced on them by the merger. But John always tried, I do know that much. That's why we had them round to dinner, and he encouraged me to be friendly with Betty.'

'Mrs Damson?'

'That's right,' sighed Dorothy. 'It wasn't easy, I can tell you. She's so touchy. And so, well, jealous.'

'Of what?'

Dorothy related how Betty had always coveted Jumpers and suspected John of hearing that it was about to come on the market, concealing the news from her, and snapping it up in a private deal. In fact, it wasn't like that at all, Dorothy said. Nigel had also known it was coming up but had deliberately omitted to tell Betty because he knew they wouldn't be able to afford it. And now there was a big atmosphere.

'Big enough for anyone to do, er, this?' asked Colin.

'The murder, you mean? Nigel? Or Betty?'

'Or Simon Pilkington.'

Dorothy was sitting up straight, eyes wide, as if the thought had only just struck her. Judy noticed the red tendril of an inflamed vein running from the tear duct to the iris of one eye. Dorothy swallowed heavily.

'Listen,' she said carefully. 'Are you sure somebody killed him? Mightn't he just have fallen over the edge? After all, it's pretty dangerous up there.'

'What would he be doing walking up there when he had such a busy day?' asked Colin, watching her closely.

'He might not have gone up there till later, when it was getting dark. His car was down in town until the evening.'

'That's right – according to Mr Damson. But in that case, where would he have been all afternoon, missing the council meeting?'

'I don't know, maybe something came up, or he was depressed . . .'

'Depressed? Are you suggesting he might have taken his own life, Mrs Bullock? You said he was worried.'

'No . . . I don't know,' said Dorothy, her voice and hands beginning to tremble.

'Did he leave a note, or anything like that?'

'No, no – I haven't found anything.'

48

Dorothy closed her eyes and lowered her head, shaking it slowly, as if she wanted to abandon the battle to think and talk. When she picked up a cushion, holding it tightly to her waist and rocking slightly, Judy and Colin quickly picked up their mugs of tea and looked away. Judy stared at the oil painting of a ruined castle on a cliff which hung above the fireplace, and Colin took an interest in a rack stuffed untidily with women's magazines. For a while the silence was only disturbed by the sound of their gulping, its tempo at odds with the ticking of the brass carriage clock on the mantelpiece.

'Just one more thing,' said Judy quietly, putting her mug back on the brightly coloured tray. 'How were things between you and your husband – were you getting on all right?'

Dorothy opened her eyes, looked at Judy reproachfully, then closed them again. This time tears the size of the pearls around her neck squeezed out between the lids and slid slowly down her face to the corners of her tightly clamped mouth. A harsh voice interrupted from the side of the room, where Annabel had silently opened the door and started listening.

'I think that's enough for now, don't you?' she said. 'The last thing she needs is your insulting questions. And it's time we set off to get those poor children.'

Colin and Judy rose to their feet, apologizing and straightening their clothes. Judy offered Dorothy a leaflet about the local victim support group, which Annabel grabbed from her hand. They would need to search the house, said Colin, and possibly take away some of the dead man's things. Dorothy, wet-faced, nodded; they would be back by the evening. The two detectives let themselves out and drove off in silence.

'Better get down to the post-mortem,' said Colin eventually, looking at his watch.

'Yes,' said Judy. 'What d'you make of it, then?'

'Strikes me he had more enemies than friends.'

'Too right. But I suppose he didn't get where he is today, et cetera. What struck me was, she's not telling us everything. Seemed quite keen on the idea of accident or suicide.'

Colin glanced across at her, interested, and had to swerve suddenly to avoid a green Jaguar which appeared on a narrow corner.

'Sorry. Think they own the road, these millionaires. It might just be natural reluctance to believe your dear departed husband got mixed up in violence or skulduggery.'

'It might. But I got a feeling it was more than that.'

'Oh, no,' said Colin heavily, sagging against the driver's door as if she had pushed him. 'Not the dreaded female intuition. I wondered how long it would be before that one dropped in to say hello.'

'Not intuition, actually, Colin,' said Judy, coolly. 'Observation. You're not a male chauvinist, are you, by any chance?'

'Me, never. You mean, her not wanting to say anything about how they'd been getting on? I thought that was understandable, too, actually. You've got to remember she's in shock.'

'True. But the way she reacted more or less told us that things weren't going too well between them, and I'd like to know a bit more about it.'

He looked across with one of his smiles, boyish in spite of the leathery wrinkles, and Judy reminded herself that he was married and had got religion.

'You want to get your snout right down to the bottom of the laundry basket, don't you?' he said.

'That's right,' said Judy flatly. 'No truth without understains.'

'Typical woman,' he said, the grin yielding to a grimmer expression. 'Rolling about in the dirt.'

Chapter Seven

Saturday, 3 p.m.

'Good job he wasn't out there another couple of days, eh?' said the coroner's officer, a little man with droopy eyes and a toothbrush moustache. 'This weather, we'd have had another jolly green giant on our hands. Like that pensioner they found in a high-rise the other week, eh? Talk about a niff.'

He opened the door and grinned cheerfully as Manningbird and his team trooped past him into the warren of rooms behind the mortuary. As well as Colin Borden and Judy Best, there were half a dozen other police staff: a scenes of crime man, an exhibits officer, a photographer, a scientist from the forensic laboratory and the area press officer. None of them responded to the officer's grin except the press officer, a bald man with bad skin who came to more post-mortems than was strictly necessary and was suspected of being a ghoul.

Professor Binder was already there, wearing green rubber boots, a gown and a plastic apron, and for five minutes there was general shuffling and rustling as everyone put on the same kit. Manningbird used the time, as he wrestled with a tight pair of boots, to tell Judy and Colin that the briefcase from Bullock's car had turned out to contain a recently recorded cassette tape among the wads of council papers.

'Didn't have time to hear it myself,' grunted Manningbird. 'But Jim Duncan's had a listen and apparently our man was up to no good.'

'You ready, gentlemen?' interrupted Binder, checking them over like an officer about to lead a patrol into enemy territory. They nodded, breathed in, and stepped one after the other over the knee-high wall between the changing rooms and the mortuary itself.

The fully clothed body of John Bullock, hands and feet still bagged up, was lying on a stainless steel table under the bright fluorescent lights, guarded by two aproned mortuary attendants, a redhead and a dark, slim man, who looked to be still in their teens. They were leaning against a pillar, cracking jokes and chatting about the pubs where they planned to spend their Saturday night. Judy forced herself to walk up

51

to the table and look down at the corpse, expecting once again the sense that the living person was only a thread or a breath away, that the body might at any moment blink, swing its legs down to the floor and declare it was feeling a bit peckish. But this time, in this harsh and antiseptic place, it was different. The body seemed dirtier and deader than it had in the quarry, its eyes more stony and opaque. It was more like a thing and less like a person, and instead of feeling shocked at the absence of movement and vitality, she felt astonished that this object lying before her could ever have breathed or spoken, could ever have been filled with the tumult of feelings and appetites which lift people from the earth and push them through the world. She quickly began to feel calmer, no longer secretly worried that the body would suddenly contort and scream when the knife sliced it open from throat to groin.

Already Binder was removing the bags from the hands and feet, and the camera began clicking and whirring as he guided the photographer round the body, asking for shots from this angle and that, pointing out the grazes on the hands and face, the little tears and patches of dirt on the trousers, the missing button from the blazer. Then the others stood back and watched while Binder started using strips of tape to lift fibres and dirt from the hands, and when he had finished doing that he used sharp little spatulas carefully under all the fingernails, dropping the little curls of dirt in tiny containers. Then he took swabs from every orifice of the face, cut a lock from the dusty hair, and used some tweezers to pluck hairs from the eyebrows. Judy nudged Colin with her elbow.

'Beauty treatment, sir?' she stage whispered. 'Eyebrows? Waxing? Manicure?'

The two of them were standing silently about six feet from the body, next to a trolley laden with scalpels, a rubber mallet, a chisel and a stainless steel saw. He had been watching soberly and glancing solicitously at Judy from time to time, but now he frowned at her, half amused and half disgusted.

'You're as bad as the coroner's officer,' he said.

'You know the score, Colin,' she said. 'You've got to make the jokes to protect yourself – so come on, loosen up.'

Binder was now peering closely at the great purple-black mark on the side of the neck, testing it gently with his latex-covered fingers. Then he straightened, squinted up into the fluorescent lights, and felt his way round the scalp with a gentle kneading movement, as if he was washing its hair. A scattering of chalky dust floated down to the steel surface beneath the head.

'Right, gentlemen,' he said, looking round them all in his professorial manner. 'I'm not sure we've learnt anything new so far, although with any luck some of the tapings and so on will eventually tell us something about where he was and what happened to him before he found his way into the quarry. So I think we'll have the clothes off. And I think I'd better shave the scalp so we can have a proper look at these injuries.'

It took Binder and the assistants ten minutes, heaving and pulling and occasionally cutting the cloth with scissors, to remove the blazer and trousers, the black slip-on shoes, the grey socks, the white cotton shirt. The shirt was stained and soiled, but the underpants were a clean grey-white; the thought crossed Judy's mind that Bullock's wife, who no doubt put his clothes out for him every day as if he were still a schoolboy, had perhaps known on Thursday morning that strangers were going to see her husband in his underwear. The clothes were bagged up and labelled by the exhibits officer, and Judy stared at the naked body as Binder bent over and carefully took a clipping of the dark pubic hair. Then he started shaving the head, using his large stainless scalpel, the size of a table knife, like a cutthroat razor.

The body was strangely ordinary and unimpressive, a great inert mound of pale flesh, with the torso turning a greenish colour in the area of the liver. She had expected the local political strongman to have a powerful, hairy torso, but the chest looked soft and girlish, with big nipples and a few wispy blond hairs. His thighs looked thin and puny, his knees and feet unnaturally large, and it was clear from the twisted angles in his legs that both of them were broken, one above and one below the knee. The fall into the quarry had also damaged the elbows, shoulders and hips, but there was something colourless and anaemic about the injuries. They seemed to blend undramatically into the yellow waxiness of the dead flesh, like scratches on thick parchment. Binder finished shaving the scalp, leaving the head like a lump of pale dough with a bizarre fringe tumbling around the forehead; then he noticed Judy's interest and moved down to join her.

'Just as I thought,' he said, rotating the two ends of one leg in opposite directions and producing a slight grinding noise. 'These injuries would have caused massive bruising and discoloration if they'd happened before death. As it is, I'm confident they happened afterwards. The fact that there were fractures suggests the fall would most likely have been during rigor mortis, between about six and thirty-six hours after death. Otherwise the body would probably have been floppy enough to avoid breakages of that kind.'

The woman mortuary assistant, her red hair matched by pale, freckled

53

skin, made a joke about stuffing pillows as she gathered up the pile of hair from the steel table. Binder asked her to help him, and there was more grunting and squeaking of rubber gloves as they turned the body over. Most of the back was a deep, red, meaty colour, like liver, where the blood had settled and congealed under the skin; but the buttocks and shoulders were flat and pale, as if something had been pressing against them. Binder bent over the marks eagerly, testing and prodding.

'Aha. Now the lividity here is most interesting. If he'd been killed where he was found, I dare say the white marks would have been in long vertical stripes, where his weight rested on the stems and branches of the bush. As it is, it looks as if the weight was resting on the buttocks and shoulders for a sufficient period after death for the lividity to become fixed like this.'

Manningbird put his hands on his knees and peered at the whitish patches, his face greyer and his breath more laboured than usual.

'How long, exactly?' he asked. Binder glanced at him, his sad eyes full of reproach.

'Come now, Superintendent, you've done enough of these cases to know that exactitude is a rare luxury when it comes to timing. Approximately is the word I'd prefer. And I'd say he spent at least six hours after death in some sort of sitting position. And possibly quite a lot longer, because the lividity is very fixed and definite.'

'You mean, sitting in a chair?'

'Probably not, because the paleness doesn't stretch very far down into the thighs, which take a good deal of the weight on a chair. Possibly on a hard surface such as the floor, with the knees up, putting most of the weight on the point of the buttocks, and leaning against something with the shoulders.'

'Car boot, perhaps?'

'Less likely – he'd probably be on his side there, unless it was an estate car, of course. Corner of a room, large box – something like that, perhaps.'

Manningbird straightened up, grunting with the effort, and looked at Colin and Judy, who had gathered round to look at the marks.

'So,' said Colin. 'If he was killed at lunchtime, he was kept somewhere until the evening, and possibly well into the night, before he was dumped at Slump Quarry.'

'And even if he wasn't killed until later, it wouldn't have been as late as, say, midnight,' said Judy. 'Nobody would be likely to dump a body after daylight, and it gets light at about four a.m. at the moment.

54

So something like eight in the evening looks like about the latest time for the death.'

'Mmm,' said Binder, sceptically focusing his watery eyes on her as he moved round to the head again. 'Don't get too carried away, Sergeant. It's more of an art than a science, you know.'

The shaving of the scalp had revealed that the big purple mark under one ear was not the only injury: there was a dent in the back of the skull, about four inches across, where the flesh had gone purple, and Binder was gently running a finger over it, back and forth, like a man tickling a cat.

'Whatever hit him definitely had a rounded profile,' he murmured. 'Left the skin intact, but dented the bone and fractured it. But it probably wouldn't have been fatal on its own – it's the other chappy round the side I've got my eye on, and that probably didn't damage the bone at all. Oh well, better have a look inside.'

The body was turned on its back again, and the head propped up on a wooden block with a half-moon cut in it to accept the back of the neck. Then Binder picked up his bright, heavy scalpel and cut a neat line across the scalp from the top of one ear to the other. The blade went cleanly through to the skull, producing no blood, and Binder began working it forward close to the bone, peeling away the rubbery grey flesh of the scalp, pulling it towards the forehead, turning it inside out and pulling it forward over the face, like some hideous blubbery mask with the fringe of hair still poking from beneath it. Then, more delicately, he began to work the other way, towards the injury and the base of the skull. Straight away he encountered swollen, puffy flesh, little dark lumps of congealed blood and the fractured section of the skull, which looked like the top of a boiled egg after someone had bashed it with a spoon. He looked up and nodded at the photographer, who stepped forward and started taking more pictures.

'So far, so good,' he said, grinning at the three detectives standing in a close group. They had all pulled their masks up, and the parts of their faces which were still visible seemed to reflect the greenish shine of their plastic aprons. The warmth of a dozen people in the confined space of the mortuary was making the atmosphere steadily thicker, and the opening of the body had added a new smell to the background odour of disinfectant: the heavy, sweetish, butcher's shop smell of decaying flesh and blood. The three said nothing, and Binder turned round, took a light helmet with a plastic visor from the male attendant, and disappeared underneath it, picking up a small electric tool with a stainless circular blade three inches across.

The others stepped involuntarily back as the saw tore and buzzed through the bone, throwing out a gritty, yellowish dust. As Binder steered it through the shape of a large diamond, with a little notch to allow it to be replaced precisely afterwards, a few thick drops of gore oozed out on to the stainless steel table. Binder lifted off a section of the skull the size of a two-pint mixing bowl, handed it to the assistant and began deftly peeling off the covering of the brain, which came away like a skin of tough white latex. Underneath, shining and mysterious, lay the brain itself, with its delicate whorls of grey and the palest pink; but the lower part of the right side of it was disfigured and swollen with a stain of dark red and purple, climbing upwards from the site of the great bruise under the ear. Binder snatched off his helmet and lowered his nose towards it, like a hound on a scent.

'Ah yes!' he exclaimed. 'Just what I suspected. A massive sub-arachnoid haemorrhage. The blow by the ear must have ruptured the vertebral artery, causing extensive bleeding up into the brain which would have meant immediate unconsciousness and a pretty rapid death, by the look of it. Sort of thing you get occasionally with the rabbit punch.'

'Sub what, professor?' muttered Colin, peering forward into the opened skull, his eyes screwed up squeamishly.

'The arachnoid is one of the membranes covering the brain, between the dura mater and the pia mater,' said Binder, standing back while more photographs were taken. 'The dura mater is the one I just peeled off, rather like a rubber johnny, don't you think? Anyway, blood pumping under the arachnoid from a ruptured artery puts massive pressure on the brain, with the kind of result you see before you. Now, if you'll excuse me, I think I'll just get the brain right out so we can have a closer look. There's just a chance the haemorrhage was natural, so we'll have to check for berry aneurisms.'

None of the police staff had the stomach for a full explanation of this one, and Judy turned away as Binder began probing down the side of the open skull with his scalpel, like someone loosening a pudding before turning it out of the bowl. She walked down to the end of the mortuary, breathing steadily and deeply to tame the stirrings of nausea in her stomach. When she turned round and walked back, the brain was sitting on the side of a sink, like a head on the shelf of a charnel house, and Binder was peering into the empty skull.

'Haemorrhage in the bottom of the cranial cavity,' he said, squinting up at her sideways. 'Care for a look? No? I quite understand, my dear, quite understand.'

The next time Judy's patrolling took her past the table, Binder was cutting down the front of the body, peeling back an inch-thick covering of yellow fat. Then he picked up a heavier knife, cut through the ribs, and lifted out a plate-size section from the front of the ribcage.

'Why are you bothering with the rest, now you've worked out what killed him?' asked Judy, trying to keep her attention off the powerful smell of putrefaction rising from the opened torso. She was beginning to feel angry, as if some unrelenting ritual mutilation was being carried out.

'Because, my dear,' said Binder, glancing at her severely, as if she were some first-year student, 'I don't want my learned friend for the defence standing up in court and saying: "Tell me, Professor, are you aware that the deceased had a heart condition? No? And so can you be sure that he did not die of a heart attack when he saw the weapon raised in front of him?" I have to be able to say that natural disease did not contribute to the death. I also need to have a closer look at the site of the blow, and the contents of the stomach may tell us something.'

He began working with his scalpel up into the neck, and a few seconds later pulled out the tongue and oesophagus, cut them away from the top of the stomach and carried them over to the draining board like a length of mangled reddish rope. Judy resumed her patrolling of the mortuary, studying the mechanism of the handles on the fridges, the design of the taps on the sinks, anything to keep her mind from dwelling on the beastly nature of the human body. But each time she turned there was another reminder: the intestines, grey and shiny, pulled out and piled on the thighs, the liver and lungs lying by the sink like dog meat in a butcher's shop, the red-headed mortuary attendant – still smiling and chatting – using a steel jug to ladle soupy black blood from the gaping cavity. The crown of creation was just a pile of meat and offal.

Colin started patrolling with her, asking her about her holiday plans and telling her how he and his family would be going to Majorca again. They were deep into the relative merits of villas and hotels, swimming pools and beaches, when Manningbird called them over to the sink. Binder had finished putting a series of deep slices through the liver and was dabbling in the sloppy grey bag of the stomach, which emitted the acidic stink of vomit.

'The Prof. says the stomach's virtually empty,' Manningbird told them. 'Which could mean he was killed before lunch, or that he was killed so long after lunch that the meal had been digested.'

'Will the blood and urine samples be any help on alcohol and so on?' asked Judy, trying to think of intelligent questions to keep her emotions down.

'Not much good for alcohol after about twelve hours, I'm afraid,' said Binder, who had slit open the atria and ventricles of the mauve-coloured heart and was making delicate cuts across the back of it to inspect the condition of the coronary arteries. 'But other drugs, including cannabis, can leave traces for up to a fortnight.'

'Tory boss in dope shock,' said Judy; the mood was lifting now the end was in sight.

'Stranger things have happened,' said Binder, poking with the point of his scalpel at the whitish deposit in one of the slit-open arteries. 'Look at that – this chap was a candidate for a heart attack in a few years. Too many expense-account lunches, I dare say.'

'D'you mean those two tiny blood vessels are what keep us alive?' asked Judy, steeling herself to lean closer to the draining board, which was swimming with the multicoloured and malodorous organs.

''Fraid so,' murmured the Professor, popping a bite-sized piece of heart muscle into a jar of preservative. 'Serious design fault, in my opinion.'

'You'll have to get on to your boss about that, Colin,' said Manning-bird, a little sparkle in his mole-like eyes. 'Get him to put out a new model.'

'Hate to think what your ticker looks like, Bryan,' said Colin, placidly. 'Ready for a transplant, I should think.'

'Yes,' said Binder, blinking his watery eyes at Colin. 'Let me know when the Almighty's got *Homo sapiens* mark two on the drawing board – I've a number of important recommendations to make.'

On the table, the forensic scientist had finished taking fingerprints and the attendants had begun to reconstruct the body, working rapidly in their eagerness to start their Saturday night out. They put the cut-out section of skull back in place, pulled the scalp back over it, and sewed the two edges together with what looked like a sailmaker's needle. One of them replaced the plate-sized section of ribs while the other dropped the intestines and dissected organs into a plastic bag and stuffed them in the cavity of the body, like the giblets of a supermarket chicken. Then they began the needlework on the chest, and in a few minutes the only sign the body had been opened and pillaged was the large three-foot seam down the torso and the shaven rear part of the head.

Binder finished making his notes and leaned his back on the draining board to run through a summary of his findings with them: a massive haemorrhage caused by the blow under the ear, probably struck from in front of the victim with a heavy, round-headed implement. As he talked, Judy found herself contemplating the corpse again, but this time with a new feeling of calm and relief. It was no longer like catching a glimpse of a side of beef in the back of a butcher's van, all gory, with flakes of yellow fat and strips of white bone. One of the attendants was covering it with a gown now, pulling it over the arms, completing an image of finality and rest. As they all filed down the mortuary to the changing rooms, Judy felt a strange urge to stop and say goodbye, to touch the face or hand: she had never met John Bullock, and suspected she wouldn't have liked him, but she had got to know his corpse quite well and now there was a strange twinge of loss in the knowledge she would never see it again. But she didn't stop, for fear the gesture would be noted by her colleagues and used in evidence against her.

They paddled their boots in a little pool of disinfectant, threw their gowns and aprons in a bin, and sat on the little dividing wall to swing their stockinged feet back from the hall of the dead to the land of the living. But there was silence among them as they changed, each taken up by their own thoughts about the fragility of the curtain which separated the two places. Judy was just pulling on her shoes when the door from the corridor opened and the droopy-eyed coroner's officer put his head round it.

'Can't do you steak and kidney pie,' he grinned at them. 'But there's a nice cup of tea and a biscuit if you fancy it.'

Chapter Eight

Colin Borden drove them back from the mortuary to Beechley police station, with Manningbird wedged tightly in the front passenger seat, and Judy slumped against the door in the back. She felt tired and nauseated by the post-mortem, her nostrils still full of the smell of decomposition. The route took them past the new Beechley Multiplex, where they got caught in Saturday evening traffic – John Bullock had pushed through the planning permission for the cinema, despite warnings from officials that the roads couldn't cope. Eventually Manningbird broke the silence.

'Never really get used to it, do you?' he said, wriggling sluggishly. 'I mean, they try and keep it neat and tidy, but it's like a bleeding abattoir by the end, isn't it? Piles of bits everywhere.'

'How many you done, Bryan?' asked Colin, drumming his fingers on the steering-wheel and watching a couple of laughing teenage girls in jeans, their hair catching the slanted evening sun.

'God knows. Forty? Fifty? Too bloody many.'

'The weird bit is the brain,' said Judy, her voice slightly slurred by the thick saliva that had gathered in her mouth through the long, hot afternoon. 'I can just about handle all the wet red stuff, it's just like another RTA. But the gleaming grey bits – they tell you it's the most powerful computer in the universe, but when it's all neatly sliced like that it just reminds me of some ice-cream dessert you see on TV.'

'Makes you wonder a bit about the old soul, eh, Colin?' said Manningbird, twisting his larded grey neck to wink at Judy. 'Prof. didn't quite seem able to find it anywhere.'

'That's hardly surprising,' said Colin impassively, still looking out of the window. 'Given that it left the body some time ago.'

'Yeah – not long after birth, the more I hear about Mr Bullock. I gather this tape confirms your worst suspicions of what they get up to in politics.'

They reached the stained grey slab of the police station, and the heavy security gate slid back to let them into the rear car park. Inside the station, they headed straight for the canteen, past the noticeboard with its news about pension schemes, football teams and old bangers for sale. Manningbird bought tea for them all, and Colin earned himself disgusted stares by asking the tired black woman behind the counter to make him a fish finger sandwich.

In the incident room at the far end of the first floor, half a dozen CID men with their jackets off were gathered round a TV with a bad picture. The news was on, showing lines of officers in blue overalls, on their hands and knees in the sunshine on Halliloo Hill. There was a clip of Manningbird, bulgy-bodied and small-eyed, appealing for information about 'this barbaric killing of a most distin-guished citizen'.

'Anything from the search yet, Jim?' asked Manningbird, approaching a blond man with a lean face and biceps straining against well-ironed white shirtsleeves.

''Fraid not, sir,' replied Detective Sergeant Jim Duncan in his slurred Scots accent. 'Unless you're interested in dog turds, old coins and discarded condom packets.'

'Right then, let's have a listen to that tape from his briefcase, then.'

'It's all set up in one of the interview rooms.'

A dozen of them trooped down the corridor and crowded into the bare white room, most of them leaning shoulder to shoulder against the wall. Manningbird jammed himself into the little chair with metal arms while Judy sat down opposite him, sipping the sweet canteen tea. Duncan poked and punched at the buttons on the twin-track tape machine as if he were getting in some sparring practice.

'OK, pin your ears back,' he said eventually, delivering a final jab to the start button and leaning back with folded arms. A series of echoing bangs and thuds issued from the machine as someone on the tape struggled to set up the recorder and get it working properly. Then suddenly they heard a hard Cockney voice, half jocular, half aggressive.

' . . . you, John?'

'Yes, it's me.' The second voice – flat, cautious, noncommittal – was obviously nearer the microphone, and clearer.

'You wanted some proof, right?'

'That's right.'

'Right, well, I've got a tape recording of you and the lady concerned, and I'm going to switch it on and stick the phone next to it. OK?'

'Er, OK.' There was an undertow of anxiety beneath the middle-class tones of the second speaker. He cleared his throat with a gentle rasping noise, as if preparing himself for a verdict.

There was more clattering and thumping, as if the telephone at the far end of the recording was being put down on a table and shifted about. Then another sort of conversation began, as fuzzy and distant as a bad satellite connection.

'. . . keeping all right, have you, Bill?' It was a woman's voice, throaty, matter-of-fact, attempting to preserve a sophisticated sheen on a down-market accent.

'Yes, not so bad.' It sounded like the second voice again, but very indistinct. The ribald male excitement stirring in the interview room was beginning to make Judy feel uncomfortable, and she kept her eyes fixed in her half-empty mug.

'And what are we going to do today, Bill? Have you been a bad boy again? Or d'you want to be a baby?'

There was a synchronized, muted 'Woo-er!' from around the interview room, its atmosphere rapidly heating and thickening in the press of bodies. Judy glanced up briefly at the semicircle of badly suppressed grins, the nervous shifting of shoulders: the woman on the tape had clearly touched something in all of them. For a moment her eyes met those of Manningbird, which were hard and unamused.

The next few phrases were lost between the fuzzing of the tape and the noise and shushing in the interview room, and then the woman was heard telling her client to get his clothes off because she was going to punish him severely. The theatrical pleadings and whimperings which followed were curtailed by a click, and the first voice returned, rougher and more triumphant than before.

'. . . you there, John?'

'Er, I'm here.' The second voice was on a higher pitch now, eaten at the edges by fear and defiance.

'That enough proof for you, John? Or should I say Bill?'

'It could be anyone on that tape. You couldn't prove it was me, or anyone else, for that matter.'

'Don't piss about, John, I've got photos of you going in and out of the flat. Looking very furtive, if I may say so. Would you like to have a look at them? Or perhaps I should take them straight to your wife?'

For a moment there was silence both on the tape and in the interview room. The detectives either looked at the floor or exchanged uneasy glances, pondering the victim's dilemma. 'Bang to rights,' muttered one of them, as the voice on the tape resumed.

62

'So let's talk business, shall we, John?' it said, calmer but more vindictive as it moved from the battle to the terms of surrender. 'The figure's five thousand, like I told you yesterday, all right?'

'This is blackmail,' came the reply, defiance and pomposity gaining the upper hand for the moment.

'Too fucking right it's blackmail, you soft-headed git. Very quick on the uptake, John – you go to university, or what?'

'You won't get away with it. You're a common criminal.'

'Shut your gob, John, and listen. You know the car park on Halliloo Hill? On the North Downs – your neck of the woods.'

'Yes, I know it.'

'Be there one o'clock today, with the money. Park down at the end, on the right, by the big tree. There'll be more instructions for you there – got that?'

'I can't get the money that fast.' The second voice was sullen, but thoughtful.

'Don't make me laugh, John. You've already had a day to sort it with the bank manager. That's petty cash, circles you move in. One o'clock, right?'

'I'll have to think about this.'

'Do that, John. And don't do anything silly like getting in the old bill.'

'Since you're committing a crime, that's exactly what I ought to do.'

'Yes, John. But if I'm not back in town by four, my mate here is going to deliver all this stuff to the newspapers, isn't he? With a copy to your lady wife, of course. Wouldn't go down too well, now, would it?'

'You dirty fucker.'

'No, you're the dirty fucker, John, and I've got it on tape. Five grand. One o'clock.'

The dialogue was ended abruptly by the loud whirring sound of the dialling tone, followed by a few seconds of stertorous breathing and the click of the tape recorder being switched off. Jim Duncan reached out a muscular arm to switch off the machine, and everyone looked at Manningbird, crouched in his tight chair like a toad.

The heat was becoming unbearable, and the sweaty closeness of her male colleagues intensified Judy's sense of oppression at the perversity of men and their sexual behaviour. She wanted to get home, to sluice the reek of John Bullock's decaying innards from her mouth, to clear her mind of toms and their pathetic, lust-ridden clients. Manningbird suddenly wiped a grey paw over his moist face, levered himself up and waddled out into the coolness of the corridor. The others trooped after him, back to the incident room.

63

'We can take it this is Bullock's voice, all right?' Manningbird asked Duncan, over his shoulder.

'Yeah. The Chief Super knows him, so he had a quick listen earlier on. Confirmed it.'

'Mm. How did he react?'

'Looked a bit shocked, to be honest. Said he was sorry for Bullock's wife – and that he's had the chairman of the Conservative Party on the phone.'

'Saying what?' Manningbird scowled, gnawing at his grey lower lip.

'Anything he could do to help, that sort of thing.'

'Meaning, get your bloody finger out and arrest someone.'

Manningbird stood with his back to the window, leaning against the sill, the evening sun gleaming behind him on Beechley's little clutch of tall office buildings. His face was in shadow while his sparse grey hair was lit up from behind like a straggly halo. The others perched on tables or pulled up plastic chairs. Colin sat beside Judy, giving her another of the solicitous glances which irritated her.

'Rather confirms your thoughts on the marital relationship,' he muttered. She nodded grimly as Manningbird began talking.

'Well, I think the gent who made this phone call could help us with our inquiries,' he said. 'And he could start by telling us how he made a recording like that – the one of the tart and the client.'

'Tart must've been in on it,' said Jim Duncan.

'Must be a note of her number somewhere among Bullock's things,' said Colin. 'Get to her, should be able to get to him.'

'And with any luck that'll be it,' said Duncan. 'Bullock goes to meet blackmailer, they have a barney, the guy bangs him on the head and tips him over the edge.'

'Only trouble with that,' cut in Judy, 'is that Bullock's partner says his car was still parked down in town at the end of the afternoon.'

There was a pause while Duncan and several others looked at Judy warily, as if she was a strange child who had pushed her way into the playroom and was trying to spoil their fun.

'But maybe Damson's misleading us all,' said Colin, leaning back in his chair with his hands in his pockets. 'From what Mrs Bullock was telling us this afternoon the relationship between Bullock and his partner wasn't all that good.'

Judy turned in her chair to face him. 'You mean Damson was in on the blackmail?' she said sceptically. 'Surely not.'

'Perfectly possible.' Colin's smile was almost playful. 'And then there was his other lunch date – the one in his diary.'

'What about it? We already know he didn't go to that.'

'Do we? We know he didn't go to it in the car which called for him, that's all.'

'Look, Colin, what are you driving at?' Judy could feel herself reddening: this was suddenly a private altercation, with everyone else as ringside spectators.

'I'm driving at the fact we know very little so far. Bullock might have met the blackmailer, or gone to the lunch, in a taxi.'

'And the blackmailer would borrow his keys and take his car up there later? Why would he bother? He'd just be more likely to get caught.'

'There you are, you see – all we've got is questions.' Colin looked smugly round at his colleagues, while they grinned back, taking pleasure in the baiting.

'What d'you mean, all we've got is questions?' Judy flared. 'We all know that, Colin, for Christ's sake.'

Manningbird suddenly held up a hand as if he were stopping a stream of traffic.

'All right, you two, all right. Let's not have any pointless arguments. There's still of lot of routine stuff to do on this. And I want it done carefully because there's a lot of people watching us, as Jim was pointing out earlier.'

'What about the Prime Minister?' said Duncan sarcastically. 'I'm surprised she hasn't been down to shake the widow's hand in front of the cameras.'

'Give her time, Jim,' said Manningbird. 'But in the mean time, I want a proper transcript of that tape done tonight, before you all bugger off to the boozer. And in the morning we'll have another look at his diary and search his stuff. Starting at eight, all right?'

Judy looked at her watch and saw it was nearly eight o'clock already. The brush with Colin had increased her need to get home and switch off, but her antennae told her as she shuffled towards the door that she'd have to spend the next hour or two down at the Cat and Mouse, buying her round with the others and making it clear she wasn't throwing her teddy in the corner just because someone had challenged her.

It took her the duration of the first drink to give Jim Duncan and the others the detail of how she'd stumbled on the body. She found herself dramatizing it, doing a clumsy piss-take of the farmer's accent; but she sensed resentment and jealousy in the interest around her, and the familiar implication that none of all this was suitable for a woman. All the while she was irritably aware of Colin Borden, perched on a tatty stool just out of earshot, chatting to the chain-smoking barman. When she saw him draining his glass, she stepped away from the group and sat on the stool beside him.

'You off, Colin?'

''Fraid so. Early start and all that.'

'Were you having a go in there, or what?' Judy took a swig of her lager and grimaced: the second never tasted as good as the first. Colin looked at her carefully for a moment.

'No. But I thought it was too early to start assuming anything very much.'

'Fair enough. It's just that it came over like a bit of an assault. Favourite police pastime – taking the piss out of a Doris. The others loved it.'

Colin smiled ruefully, gripping his forehead between finger and thumb, and she found her train of thought pausing while she studied the homely lines around his eyes. They formed a perfect fan-shape, running back from the corner.

'Yeah, sorry, Jude, I realized a bit too late that's how it was coming over. You going to hold it against me?'

'Could you rephrase that? No, Colin, it's just that I was hoping you'd treat me as a colleague, not as a woman. But one moment you're being bloody Sir Galahad, and the next you're doing me over. It's as if I've got to be attacked if I refuse to be protected.'

'Nowhere's a woman's world, though, is it?' His eyes were offended, defensive. 'It's not just the police force.'

'But in the police it's worse. You staying for another?'

He shook his head, smiling ruefully.

'Wife and family to take into consideration?'

'That's right. I'm late enough already. You want a lift home?'

'No thanks. See you tomorrow.'

She looked at his retreating back until she caught sight of Jim Duncan watching her do it. His eyes were narrow and alert, and she looked away irritably. Duncan had regarded himself as top detective sergeant until her promotion, and he wasn't going to want her taking a leading role in this case. The barman asked her from behind his haze of smoke how life was treating her, and she swapped platitudes with him while she finished her drink.

The evening was still warm as she set off home. She passed several pubs where crowds were standing outside in T-shirts, laughing extravagantly and slopping their drinks on the pavement. It was just the sort of night where a wrong move or word by a police officer could set off a running lager-fuelled punch-up, and she felt grateful she wasn't in uniform and on duty, fighting off drunks and scooping up bodies. She gave a wide berth to the shouting queue and the smell of hot grease outside a fish and chip shop.

Then she was out of the town centre, walking through streets of terraced Victorian houses where the televisions glowed blue through gaps in the curtains and canned laughter gusted through widely opened windows. They'd have seen the bit on the news about John Bullock, their local council leader; they'd probably been shocked, said it was a terrible thing, even if they hadn't voted for him. What would they say if they knew that a married man from the party of family values was visiting a prostitute?

As she turned a corner she was suddenly facing south, and the lumpy black crest of the downs formed a new horizon beneath the remnants of turquoise and crimson in the darkening sky. Dorothy Bullock would be up there, in the big house tucked into the fold in the hills, comforting her children with the help of her friend, the big brunette: everyone hoped that wealth could cushion you from the cruelties and tragedies queueing up to destroy human happiness, but it couldn't. Judy told herself it was tiredness, combined with lager on an empty stomach, making her hand tremble as she slid her key into the lock.

Ten minutes later, chewing a sandwich and staring out at the dark line of the downs again from her unlit front window, she had recovered her knowledge that grieving for others wasn't her job. And in any case, would it be grief, pure and simple, that John Bullock's widow was feeling now? Or was there a sense of relief as well? Had she known what her husband was up to, and was that knowledge the thing that she'd been concealing this afternoon? And now there'd be insurance policies, money from the business, a future even more secure. When Judy finally fell asleep with the radio still on she dreamed that Dorothy Bullock, smiling and wearing shiny green waders, was standing with a rod at the edge of a flooded quarry, pulling out huge silver fish with no eyes.

Chapter Nine

Saturday, 9 p.m.

'All right, Mavis – what's your alibi?'

Steve Ditchley was on his third pint now, which meant the jokey phase. It had been preceded by sober analysis of the post-Bullock political situation in Beechley, and would be followed by heartfelt ranting about basic trade union principles and the iniquity of the Tory government.

Mavis Tench fixed him with her shrewd little eyes as she waddled up to the bar of the Pig and Whistle in her pale green Crimplene slacks and tent-sized brown cardigan. She was the *grande dame* of the labour movement in the borough, and she wasn't going to be drawn into cheap banter with a newcomer like Ditchley. He was a socialist of the 1980s, confused and frustrated, whereas Mavis could remember times when there really were such things as Labour governments. When she reached her third drink she would probably recount dewy-eyed tales of 1945, when Britain's war heroes sent Churchill down the road and voted for progress and reform.

'Pint, please, Stan,' said Mavis calmly, manoeuvring her backside on to a bar stool, where it drooped over the edges like a bag of sand. Only when the straight glass was standing in front of her and she had paid the barman did she return her attention to Ditchley.

'Evening, Steve: did you say something?'

Ditchley roared with exaggerated laughter and fiddled with his earring, but his eyes remained cold. His little group of retainers, most of them shop stewards like himself, laughed as well. Mavis was queen of the clerical staff – another reason for mutual suspicion – and looked round at them all, unimpressed. Ditchley stopped laughing and stabilized himself with a pull on his pint and a wipe of his mouth. He was wearing his best waistcoat tonight, with front panels in a dark paisley pattern and a purple silk back, and it gave him a sleek and sinister air.

'Say something, Mavis?' he said, rolling his eyes and adopting a

68

policemanly tone. 'I most certainly did. I was merely enquiring, in the politest possible manner, of course, about your whereabouts on the night of the demise of our esteemed council leader.'

He looked round, enjoying the grins of the men with lagers in front of them and fags in their fingers. Mavis took a long drink, drawing back her upper lip so her teeth were visible like brown stumps through the side of the glass.

'I'm afraid I don't consider it a laughing matter,' she said, putting down her glass and panting gently. 'He might have been anathema to us politically' – she pronounced it *anafema* – 'but he was still a human being, with a wife and family. Ask not for whom the bell tolls, Steve. Ask not.'

'What's bells got to do with it, Mave?' asked Ditchley, winking at his mates and prompting a little rash of sycophantic jokes about large Bell's and the bells of hell going ting-a-ling for John Bullock.

'Forget it, lads,' said Mavis, raising her eyes to heaven. 'Bit above your heads. My alibi, as it happens, is that I was round the corner at the labour rooms conducting a review of the day of action. What's yours, Steve?'

'Mine?' Ditchley spread his hands and raised his eyebrows, all innocence. 'I was there with you, Mavis – you remember that.'

'I do, Steve, I do. Until opening time, at any rate. Coppers had you in yet?'

A sudden silence fell on the group, and Ditchley's eyes narrowed behind the smokescreen from his roll-up. Mavis knew the remark would hit a sore spot, and now she looked innocently around the bar, as if to check out the Saturday night clientele. The Pig and Whistle, an unmodernized Victorian pub full of engraved glass and beaten-up wooden panelling, stood at the corner of a narrow street a quarter-mile from the town hall. It was the unofficial watering-hole of trade unionists, Labour Party people, and the more hairy types from Beechley Polytechnic. Now it was filling rapidly with bodies, beer fumes and shouted conversations, and the blue-grey cigarette smoke spiralled and swam in the last rays of the evening sun filtering through the red and yellow lozenges in the front windows. Ditchley was in his element, and he wasn't going to let this gibe from Mavis stop him from playing it for laughs. He held his hand up in the air and snapped his fingers.

'Aha, I get it,' he said with exaggerated sarcasm. ''Cos the old bill banged me up and infringed my civil rights after the people's demo against the poll tax, they decide to look me up now, right? Their suspicions are aroused 'cos I'm not bawling my eyes out over Bullock, so they come round on Sunday morning and boot down the door of my flat. It doesn't take them long to find my collection of severed human heads in the fridge, and right at the front is the ugly mug of poor old Bullock – something like that, eh, Mave? Bang to rights?'

'I shouldn't joke about it if I was you, my son,' said Mavis, almost jocular. 'Any bother to do with the town hall and your name will pop out of the computer. That's how they operate these days. They'll be knocking on your door any moment now, you mark my words.'

'And what will I tell 'em, Mave? You seem to have it all worked out, so you tell me.'

'I dunno, Steve – what *are* you going to tell 'em?'

It was the latest of several clashes between Mavis Tench and Ditchley since the poll tax riot, which had sharpened their political disagreements. The demonstration which ended in running battles and blood on the town hall steps had been organized by the Anti-Poll Tax Federation, and Mavis, under pressure from the Labour group on the council, had succeeded in pushing through an official boycott by the trade unions. But Ditchley and his friends had lobbied unofficially for a big turn-out of union members, and he had been photographed by the *Beechley Examiner* at the front of the march, teeth bared, pony-tail flying and a length of two-by-two in his hands. The Tories had had a field day calling him 'the real face of Labour', and for a while the police suspected him of being the one who split Barry Rutter's forehead open.

'Now, come on, Mavis, let's not be silly about this,' said Ditchley, eyes glinting slyly through a sudden show of reasonableness. 'If the old bill does show up, what I tell 'em is what I know: I have a bit of a set-to with the old bastard when he walks through our picket lines, which is nothing out of the ordinary, and that's the last I see of him until some homicidal maniac steps in and shoves him over the edge of Slump Quarry. Simple as that. But there is one thing I do feel a bit bad about, Mavis, and I think you ought to know about it.'

'What's that, then, Steve?' said Mavis, eyeing him cautiously.

'His wife. I fancy her something rotten.'

Mavis winced and turned away as Ditchley smiled maliciously round his semicircle of sniggering admirers and drained the half-pint remaining in his glass. In politics Mavis was thick-skinned and astute, but she lived with her sister, a thin and mild-mannered shop assistant, and had never learnt to cope with the crude cock-waving of male group behaviour. The joke, which Ditchley repeated whenever he got the chance, was that she was married to Nalgo at an early age but was still waiting for the marriage to be consummated.

'Very fit-looking woman, got all the proper bits,' Ditchley continued, matter-of-fact, as if explaining the controls on a motor car. 'You remember her the night of the people's demo, don't you, lads? Drove up to the town hall to drop the old man off and ended up being rushed inside by the old bill. Couldn't guarantee her safety, and all that. In fact I do hear tell it was her gave first aid to the poor old chief exec. when someone cracked his bonce for him. Used to be a nurse. Wouldn't mind checking out her bedside manner myself, know what I mean?'

'You've got a sick mind, Steve,' muttered Mavis, giving him a sideways look full of distaste and proffering her empty glass to the barman.

'Yeah, but it doesn't mean I'm a bleedin' murderer, does it?' said Ditchley sulkily, on the brink now of the glassy, impassioned stage of the night's indulgences. 'You really want to know who killed him, you should be talking to old Todger here – go on, Todge, tell her.'

Todger had been sitting quietly at the edge of the group wearing a black leather jacket over a white T-shirt and a black baseball cap turned around so that its peak pointed down the back of his neck. His face, dented and pitted like an old kettle, looked as if it had been kicked and punched regularly since birth; his nose was broken, several teeth were broken, and most of the blood vessels in his cheeks were burst like tiny flowers. He worked as a labourer in the gardening department – shortly to be privatized – and liked people to think he was well connected in the underworld of south London.

'Yeah, well,' said Todger thickly, tapping the ash off his fag with a calloused finger and looking mysteriously at the floor. He would tell enquirers with a sinister stare that the four letters tattooed on the knuckles of his right hand stood for 'all coppers are bastards.' The police knew what it meant without asking, which was why they had administered some of the damage sustained by Todger over the years.

'Come on, someone,' said Ditchley unpleasantly, taking the first sip from a new pint. 'Reach behind him and wind him up, will you?'

Todger looked up with a glint in his pale eyes which turned from murderous to abject as he remembered that Ditchley was top dog in the present surroundings.

'Yeah, well,' he said. 'Bullock was messing around with some heavy duty characters. That's about the size of it. Can't say more than that, really.'

'Criminals?' asked Mavis sharply. 'Is that what you mean?'

'You might call 'em criminals,' said Todger, taking a huge final drag and grinding out his stub on the wooden floor. 'I might even call 'em criminals. But they call themselves businessmen. Businessmen who don't fanny around, if you get my meaning.'

Todger was emitting clouds of smoke from his mouth and nostrils, like some battered dragon. Mavis gave the explosive, high-pitched wheeze which was her version of a laugh.

'Come on, Todger,' she said. 'You've been reading too much Mickey Spillane. Nobody likes Tory council bosses, but don't get carried away.'

'You'd be surprised, Mavis, you'd be surprised,' cut in Ditchley, shaking his head as if sadly disappointed with the standards of today's political leaders. 'What d'you think this town centre business is all about? Market Walk, or whatever they call it?'

'Come off it – Kingswood and his lot? They might be the lowest form of life, but they don't go around breaking legs and concreting you into flyovers. Besides, they'd no reason to get rid of Bullock – he was in cahoots with them. Gave 'em everything they wanted.'

'Yeah, but the project's stalled, innit?' said Ditchley. 'They built the bleedin' thing, and now nobody wants it.'

'Not Bullock's fault if the market's gone down, is it?' said Mavis. 'He's given them all they need – cheap land, planning permission – the lot.'

'I can see you're not up to date, Mave,' said Ditchley, exchanging smirks with Todger. 'I'm disappointed in you – I thought you kept your ear to the ground.'

Mavis studied them for a moment, like a headmistress carpeting a brace of smart-arse twelve-year-olds. 'Come on, then,' she said severely. 'Out with it.'

'It's in the document, ain't it?' said Ditchley, smug in the power of superior knowledge. 'The one that leaked. The *Examiner* didn't mention it 'cos they don't know their arse from their elbow – just went on about social services. You seen the cuts document, Mave?'

'No,' said Mavis, wriggling defensively on her stool. 'No one has, except the Tories and a few officials. Bloody *Examiner* won't hand it over to Ashok.'

'No, they wouldn't, would they?' said Ditchley. 'But I seen a copy yesterday, from my special sources. Council's not going to lease the offices after all – tucked away in the small print.'

'What? That was part of the deal. Gave Kingswood a guaranteed tenant.'

Ditchley shook his head, his pony-tail flapping on the dark silk of his waistcoat. He raised a knowing finger to the side of his nose.

'Only an option, wasn't it? First refusal, sort of thing. And now they are refusing – part of the cuts. Keep the bloody poll tax down.'

'Totally out of order,' said Todger, shaking his head and turning down the moist nicotine-clogged corners of his mouth. 'Those boys don't like it one bit.'

'They are not happy,' said Ditchley, separating the words with careful emphasis. 'They're already lumbered with a load of shops they can't let – that's your Tory-engineered recession for you. But the shops was the jam, and now they're having the bread and butter taken away too, thanks to Mr John bleeding Bullock. You beginning to see a pattern here, Mave?'

'They don't like it one bit,' repeated Todger, pulling the brim of his baseball cap round to the side of his battered head, as if to signal the seriousness of the situation. Mavis grinned at them pityingly.

'Nice idea, lads,' she said. 'But it's completely over the top. The cuts document isn't going to happen, necessarily, and anyway these blokes play a longer game than that. The Tories'll give 'em what they want in the end, everyone knows that. They're all in each other's pockets. Kingswood's not stupid enough to kill the goose that lays the golden egg. This is just another hiccup, like all the others on that development. Look, here's Ashok – you tried this one on him?'

She reached out to grab the sleeve of Ashok Patel, the leader of the Labour group, as he tried to sidle past them unnoticed. He hauled an interested smile on to his face as he turned towards them, but his brown eyes betrayed his dismay at the prospect of conversation with Steve Ditchley and friends as their fifth pint approached. He was wearing a white shirt and red tie, and had been playing the part of responsible opposition leader in early evening TV interviews: dreadful crime, no stone unturned, tributes to tough but honourable opponent. All of that would be class treachery in Ditchley's book.

Patel listened politely to Mavis's summary of the Ditchley–Todger scenario, his stubby fingers buttoning and unbuttoning the jacket: his trade union comrades watched him beadily, hunched over their pints like gnomes. As Mavis finished, Patel seemed to conclude that he should treat the situation as informal, left the jacket unbuttoned and slid his hands into his trouser pockets.

'Well, as you know, I've been concerned for some time about the nature of the relationship between the Tories and the town centre consortium,' he said uneasily. 'Perhaps you can let me have a full copy of this cuts document, Steve, and we can pursue it further.'

Ditchley closed his eyes, shook his head, and smiled smugly, as if taunting a child with a sweet.

'Uh-uh,' he said, 'no can do, Ashok. Special sources.'

Mavis accused Ditchley of being childish, while Patel muttered something about getting it out in the open on Monday, and attempted to sidle away. Mavis grasped his arm again, asking him if he could imagine the cancelled lease as a motive for murder. His eyes swivelled nervously, one hand jumping out of his pocket to button his jacket, despite the oven-like heat in the pub. There were a few drops of perspiration sitting on the top lip of his handsome, well-fleshed face.

'Come on, Ashok, we're not going to quote you,' said Ditchley, jeeringly.

'No, no, of course not,' said Patel, grinning uncomfortably. 'I just wouldn't like to prejudice the police inquiry in any way. The situation's very delicate at the moment. But obviously they'll have to follow up every possible line of inquiry.'

'You're sitting on the fence again, Ashok,' said Ditchley, in a low and menacing sing-song. 'Tell us what you really think, for a change.'

Patel was stung; his face darkened, and he eyed Ditchley and his coterie with distaste. The annual elections for the joint shop stewards' committee would be coming up in the autumn, and he had already taken discreet steps to boost the prospects of several candidates who had hopes of defeating Ditchley for the chairmanship.

'What I really think, eh, Steve?' said Patel, warmly, taking a drink from the half-pint of stout Mavis had bought for him. 'Well, if you must know, I'd favour the cock-up theory here, not the conspiracy. Some nutter, some bizarre accident. They still haven't explained this body in a barrow thing that was reported in the *Standard* last night . . .'

Ditchley snorted with derision. Todger exposed his shattered teeth in a knowing smile of dissent, and pulled the brim of his cap to the back of his neck again, as if putting a gearstick back into neutral.

' . . . all right, you can laugh, but stranger things have happened. There were several assaults on Thursday by your mates from Class Warfare . . .'

'Hold it right there,' shouted Ditchley, thrusting a forefinger so close to Patel's nose that he swayed instinctively backwards and spilled the drink of a student with a glass stud in her nose, who gave him a vicious stare. 'You know bloody well we told Class bloody Warfare to stay out of town on Thursday. It was a freelance operation, right, with no help from us, right, and in my book they deserve the good hiding they got from the old bill. And I'm no friend of the old bill, unlike yourself, Ashok, so keep your libellous remarks to yourself, right?'

Mavis moved in to cool the dispute with the expertise of a nanny used to calming the high emotions of the nursery. She reminded them they were all on the same side and should be attacking the political enemy rather than falling out among themselves. Patel was pale and tight-lipped, but managed a more conciliatory mien than Ditchley, who stared defiantly back at Mavis. And when it looked as if they were both going back to their corners, he delivered a parting jab below the belt.

'And so, Ashok,' he said, the drink at last beginning to slur his voice. 'What's your own alibi for Thursday, then?'

'Excuse me,' Patel said indignantly, blinking hard. 'Some of my fellow councillors are waiting to talk to me.'

Mavis immediately said she'd come with him, and slid off her bar stool, her bulbous rump falling into new shapes inside her slacks. The two of them edged through the press of bodies, watched with hostile grins and ill-suppressed sniggers by Ditchley and his friends.

'He's like a crow, that one,' said Mavis, giving Patel's tubby elbow a reassuring squeeze. 'Strutting in the gutter.'

'A twelve-bore shotgun would do the trick,' muttered Patel, mopping his face with a handkerchief and accepting the offer of a drink from the deputy leader of the group, an emaciated young man with an open-necked white nylon shirt.

The last of the light had drained out of the June evening outside, and Saturday night at the Pig and Whistle was nearing its climax. People pressed and jostled, shouting for more drinks, which they spilled liberally on the bare floorboards or down people's backs as they struggled across the overcrowded room. And from the students arguing and embracing at the front to the councillors speechifying at the back, the common word in the hubbub was *Bullock*. A few days earlier, they'd shouted it in aggressive indignation; but now the tone was of wonderment, as if some mystical event had lifted a yoke from their shoulders, as if everything was now going to change. The only exception was among Ditchley and his friends, who were deep into the final and most satisfying phase of their night out: wholesale denunciation of every political faction but their own, with frequent sneering references to the race of Ashok Patel.

The call of last orders produced a final flurry of pushing and a crescendo of noise before people began to drain their glasses and slowly drift off home. They paused on the warm pavement, finishing conversations and exchanging jokes before walking slowly off under a blue-black sky where a few stars were appearing. Patel invited some of the other councillors back to his house for coffee; Mavis waddled off

75

alone to her thin sister in their council flat; Ditchley was one of the last to leave, turning to shout slurred and exaggerated farewells as he walked unsteadily across the road, hands jammed into his pockets, black jeans tight over his skinny rump. He made his way through the narrow side streets of the town centre, his occasional belches echoing violently off the shopfronts and attracting stares of disgust from passers-by. Then he was on the main road towards central London and the block of 1950s council flats where he lived with his girlfriend, a hairdresser with a history of unsatisfactory relationships with men.

It was a twenty-minute walk, and after ten minutes he reached the headquarters of Bullock and Damson, a handsome, detached Victorian house with two tall gables. It was painted white, with black woodwork, and had only been converted into offices a few years before. At the side of it, a space which was once the garden was now an asphalted parking space, partly occupied by a dark-coloured Jaguar. The ground floor was flooded with light, and Ditchley stopped and peered in at the flashy office furniture, the computer screens and display boards crowded with little colour photographs of flats and houses. Then he glanced furtively around, unzipped his jeans, and peed copiously on the front wall. As the urine darkened the stucco, steaming and bubbling around his grubby black winkle-pickers, he raised his eyes to the greenish glow of Venus.

For half a minute after the flow had finished he continued to stand exposed and gazing, bladder and mind relishing the bliss of emptiness. Then a fart jolted his thin body, and he suddenly noticed the word Bullock, suspended above him in two-foot-high illuminated letters. He leaned his head back, blinking tipsily, trying to focus on it. Then he gave up, tucked himself in, zipped himself up, and jerked a V-sign at the building as he turned to cross the road.

'Good riddance, you Tory bastard,' he shouted.

Ditchley had failed to notice that Nigel Damson, John Bullock's partner, was sitting dark and immobile at one of the desks, watching him.

Chapter Ten

'. . . the borough of Beechley was recently praised by the Prime Minister for what she called efficient housekeeping and good value-for-money services. Police have renewed their appeal for people to come forward if they have any information about Mr Bullock's movements in the hours leading to his death. BBC Radio News.'

Barry Rutter snapped off the portable radio and paced up and down the black and white tiles of the kitchen, shoulders hunched and hands balled up in the pockets of his thin blue track suit. He had just returned from his five-mile Sunday morning run, and the fringes of his sparse dark hair were moist with sweat.

'Poor Bullock,' he murmured, shaking his head and shedding drops of water like a dog emerging from a pond. 'Poor old Bullock. I went past the place this morning, you know – all taped off, coppers everywhere asking people if they saw anything.'

His wife Eunice, tucked behind the kitchen table in her pink towelling dressing-gown, looked up from the depths of *Social Work Today* and stared at him sceptically through her round, blue-rimmed glasses. There were crumbs of toast round the edges of her little round mouth and the gummy remains of sleep in the corner of one eye.

'Did they talk to you?' she asked. Her voice was brisk and impatient.

'Yes – some pipsqueak constable, looked about sixteen. Very polite. Nothing I could tell him, of course. Told them everything I knew on Friday, before they found the body.'

'Well, then, stop worrying about it,' said Eunice. 'Nothing you can do will bring him back. And anyway, I seem to remember your last conversation with the leader of the council left you seriously considering an application for the job of chief executive in Liverpool. The Siberia of local government, I think you called it.'

She took a big slurp from an outsize teacup and brought the magazine up in front of her face like a drawbridge. Rutter stared at her, fingering the livid little scar on his forehead, his green eyes glittering like beryl stones behind his thick glasses. Eunice was a lecturer at the University of Surrey, and all her efforts seemed to be going into her career these days. Their sixteen-year-old daughter Beatrice, away for the summer as an *au pair* in Lyons, was nearing the end of her education, and Eunice was seriously interested in going for a professorship. Rutter contemplated his wife, resentment mounting.

'Er, excuse me, Eunice,' he said, his voice loud and indignant. 'Do you think we could continue this conversation for a minute or two longer? That is, if you could spare the time. I could make it easier for you if you like, by removing that magazine from your hands and stuffing it in the bin. Or somewhere more painful.'

Eunice slowly put the magazine on the table, folded her hands on it, sighed, and put an insincere, long-suffering smile on her face. She had shoulder-length hair which was parted in the middle and fell in two curtains down the sides of her face. Upstairs in the wardrobe, she still had several kaftans from her student days.

'Thank you,' said Rutter, more calmly. 'I just want to say that I find your attitude amazingly callous, especially in someone supposed to be linked to the so-called caring professions. It's perfectly true that Bullock and I didn't always hit it off, but that doesn't mean I should be dancing on his grave. He was the council leader, for God's sake, and I'd developed a reasonable working relationship with him. We were both professionals. We got on all right. And so now I'm bloody upset, not least because chaos is going to descend on the borough without him. Can't you understand that?'

Eunice nodded slowly.

'Has your head been hurting again, Barry?' she asked evenly, her face impassive.

'Look, shut up about my head, will you? It's perfectly all right. This has got nothing to do with my head. But I must say, it would help matters a bit if you could spare just a little more time and attention from your work. For God's sake, you've been away at that bloody conference for most of the week, and we've hardly had a conversation since you got back. I know you're tired and busy, but it is the weekend, after all. And stop nodding at me – it's like you're humouring a madman.'

Eunice continued nodding for several seconds, then glanced at her watch.

'I'm sorry, darling, I didn't mean to sound callous. It's just that I knew there was no love lost between you and Bullock and I'm a bit surprised you're so upset. I must say I don't feel very sad about it – I couldn't stand what the bastard was doing to the social services in the borough. Look, why don't I spend the rest of the morning catching up on this reading, and then we can go out or something this afternoon, talk about it a bit more?'

Rutter smiled, mollified, and went over to kiss her pale forehead and brush the crumbs from the corner of her mouth with his thumb. Eunice smiled perfunctorily and lifted the magazine again.

'You could spend a bit of time this morning tidying up outside,' she murmured. 'Those blokes have left the place in a hell of a mess.'

Rutter sighed heavily and walked over to lean in the doorway which led from the kitchen into the garden. Eunice had inherited ten thousand pounds from an aunt in Lyme Regis, and they were using it to build a conservatory outside the french doors of their dining-room. The builders had started work two weeks previously but failed to turn up for half the time, and so far they had only managed to lay the foundations. Rutter stared unhappily at the clods of earth trodden into the lawn, the pile of hard core half-covering a rosemary bush, and the fag ends and empty milk bottles on the dining-room step. The blade of a shovel and the end of a large roll of polythene were sticking out beneath a moth-eaten tarpaulin like unruly hair from a hat, and Rutter walked over to push them back irritably with his foot.

'Bloody layabouts,' he muttered, losing interest and wandering off up the garden. It was Eunice's problem, not his, and he wasn't in the mood to help her out: he'd wanted to use the money for an expensive holiday trekking in the Himalayas, but his wife had never shared his enthusiasm for travelling on foot. Then she'd insisted on using a firm recommended by a friend, instead of inviting several tenders, council-style, as he had suggested. He sniffed at the claret and yellow flowers on a honeysuckle, scraped forty or fifty greenfly off a rose bush to squash them between finger and thumb, and crinkled his nose in disgust as he used his toe to cover a fresh pile of cat turds with loose earth. He strolled past the wooden shed, peering dejectedly through the cobwebby window at the old bicycles and garden tools inside it, and reached the brick wall which separated the garden from the open ground at the back of the row of houses. A wooden door led out to a lacework of pathways which were the starting point for his running expeditions into the nearby countryside. He leant against it now, deep in thought, picking at its crumbly black-painted crosspiece with his fingernail.

His reverie ended brutally when an electric mower leapt into life in the garden next door, where a bank manager called Charles spent his leisure hours in pursuit of the perfect lawn. The sound was like the arrival of a million maddened insects, and Rutter took off briskly towards the house, hands wrapped round his ears, muttering curses under his breath.

'I'm having a shower and then I'm going into the office for a couple of hours,' he said as he passed briskly through the kitchen. 'There's a few things I want to sort out before tomorrow.'

'All right, dear,' said Eunice, sparing him a glance of mild surprise. 'It'll be a cold lunch, so come back whenever you like.'

Rutter stamped up the stairs, through the pools of scarlet and blue thrown on to the carpet by the stained-glass window on the landing. The house was a large, detached Victorian villa in Blackthorn Avenue, a wide, tree-lined street not far from the downs, and they had chosen it because it still had the old cornices, fireplaces and dado rails. But they'd put a high-powered modern shower in a corner of the bathroom, and he switched it on and began to undress.

'Don't come back at all is what you really mean,' he muttered to himself as he pulled his sticky T-shirt over his head and threw it at the washing basket. 'God knows why I bother any more.'

He paused in front of the mirror for a gloomy look at his body: the tuft of curly hair on his white chest, the knobbly stomach muscles so rare in a man of his age, the hard thighs, spare to the point of scrawniness. He ran a forefinger round his weak chin, wondering if he could get away with not shaving.

'I dunno,' he told his reflection meditatively. 'She used to like to watch me shave, and now she gets angry 'cos I'm using the bathroom.'

He heaved a deep sigh, placed his thick glasses on the window-sill, and felt his way myopically into the steaming cabinet. Small gasps and whimpers followed as he varied the temperature and played with the nozzle, switching it from a stinging jet to a soft spray and back again. Eunice saw his love of showering as part of the mid-life crisis she'd decided he was having.

Fifteen minutes later, hair still wet and dressed in a green polo shirt and grey trousers, Rutter skipped down the stairs, picked up his briefcase in the hall and walked out to his car without further words to his wife. The big Rover came with the job, and the colour he'd chosen – red – had been another mild source of friction between himself and the council leader. The door clunked behind him, sealing him in the gadget-lined plastic womb, and he eased out into the sunlit Sunday-morning torpor of suburbia. Charles from next door was out the front now, and responded to Rutter's perfunctory wave with a baring of his teeth and a threatening flourish of his electric hedge clippers.

He stopped at the first parade of shops, where the entrance to the newsagent was almost blocked by placards about John Bullock: DEATH MYSTERY OF TOP TORY, said one. LAST HOURS OF COUNCIL BOSS, said another. Rutter headed straight for the *Observer*, which had rung him up last night, and skimmed through its front-page story. No sign of his name, but the story turned on to page two. Other sections of the paper fell and splayed open on the floor as he turned the page impatiently. Ah, there it was, final paragraph:

Barry Rutter, Beechley's chief executive, said the murder was a mystery and a tragedy. 'Whatever you think of John Bullock's politics, working with him was always a challenge and never dull. All of us will miss him.'

Rutter couldn't remember saying that, but it would have to do.

'I hope you're going to buy that paper,' came the sharp voice of the Asian newsagent, who was watching him make a hash of re-assembling the exploded sections. Rutter smiled back grimly, scooping up copies of all the other papers and plonking them on the counter with a five-pound note. The wad of newsprint was so thick he could hardly tuck it under his arm as he left the shop.

It took him ten minutes to reach the town hall through the near-deserted streets, which looked dirty and shabby in the brightness of the sun. He wound down his window, and the sound of a ringing church bell only increased the sense of desolation created by the shuttered shops and empty pavements. There seemed to be several piles of discarded burger cartons and paper bags within a few yards of every green litter bin emblazoned with the slogan 'Keep Beechley Brighter'. A bus shelter had been newly plastered with 'Stuff the poll tax' stickers, and when Rutter pulled up at the lights facing the town hall a tramp limped across the road, belted tightly into a filthy brown overcoat and carrying handfuls of bulging plastic bags. His little gleaming eyes, hidden in the tangle of hair and beard like those of a furtive animal in a hedgerow, locked on to Rutter for a moment, across the protective snout of the Rover. The tramp was still only halfway over when the lights went green, and Rutter drummed on the steering-wheel as he waited. Beechley was getting more like an inner city borough all the time: a few metal police barriers, standing in a jumble, had been left at the bottom of the town hall steps since Thursday, as if someone had hesitated to remove all the defences just yet.

Behind the town hall, Rutter swung his car into the car park entrance and leaned over to the glove box for the plastic card which would raise the barrier for him. The little blue box swallowed the card with a greedy click, and he stared balefully at it as it ticked, chuckled and eventually pushed the card back through its slot at him, like a thrust-out tongue. At least the new system wasn't yet installed: it would be there in a couple of weeks, logging every arrival and departure instead of just letting card holders in and out without making a record. He anticipated endless hassle from it, but the security review after the poll tax riot had said it was necessary. The unions had been outraged, and had only been mollified by an agreement – opposed by Bullock – that parking records couldn't be used as evidence to discipline staff. Another measure in hand was security cameras inside and out, and Rutter was glad they weren't there yet either.

He parked near the back door and let himself in with the largest key on the bunch he drew from his pocket. He decided against walking all the way to the front hall to tell the security officer he was in the building, and went past the lift and straight up the bare and echoing stairway to his office. It was on the second floor of the back extension, a stained and dilapidated concrete edifice of the 1960s attached like an ungainly hump to the elegant, white-stone back of the original building. Rutter would have much preferred one of the smaller offices at the front, which had wood-panelled walls and art deco light fittings in amber-coloured glass; but these were reserved for the leaders of the political groups, and he unlocked the door to confront the large but soulless expanse of what was known as the chief executive's suite.

There was the big functional desk carrying his personal computer, the glass-fronted bookcase with copies of the *Municipal Year Book* and a few legal volumes, the wide windows with an excellent view of the blank nine-storey face of the local social security headquarters. His heart always sank when he came in here, and he leant back against the door contemplating the shabby green-covered sofa and the spider plants with brown-tipped leaves which sat on the warped mahogany window sills. He had tried to give the room character by putting up some engravings of Victorian Beechley – a view of the parish church, the first steam train arriving at the station – but they were too small to make an impression on the great pale acres of wall. He now took a deep, bracing breath, walked over to the desk, and bent to unlock one of the bottom drawers.

The file he drew out was a thin one, containing several typewritten letters, a slim plastic folder of sheets of printed figures, and a few sheets of paper covered in notes in his own handwriting. He went through the documents slowly, rubbing his forehead and occasionally touching his scar, and then plumped them together and put them back in the plain beige wallet. He drummed his fingers on the desk for a while, staring out at the blue sky above the glass and concrete, and then pulled out his top right-hand drawer and started leafing through a book of phone numbers. He reached for the grey phone, his private direct line, and dialled.

'Simon? It's Barry Rutter here. Sorry to disturb you on a Sunday morning – have you got a few moments?'

His voice sounded unnaturally loud without the usual noise of typing and talking from the adjoining secretary's room and the comings and goings in the corridor outside. Pilkington, at the other end, was his usual smooth self.

'Certainly, Barry. Not too long though – got some people over for lunch and we're just trying to organize a game of croquet.'

'Croquet? On the lawn of your vast estates, eh?' Rutter knew that Pilkington's garden was about fifty foot long, and he pictured the scene sourly: the host in a bow tie, possibly a boater as well, the women in long flowery dresses, a cacophony of squealing and cut-glass vowels.

'Ha, ha, that's right. No, we've got this old croquet set in the attic which my old granny left me, and we thought we'd have a quick bash before lunch. Among all the molehills and dandelions. Anyway, what can I do for you, Barry? Terrible thing about John, isn't it – that why you're calling?'

'I'm afraid it is, actually, Simon,' said Rutter, lowering his voice as if worried he might be overheard. 'There's something on my mind and I think I ought to bring you in on it.'

'Really? Sounds exciting. You don't know who did it, do you? Popular theory seems to be some random nutter, although I'm not so sure myself.'

'No idea who did it, I'm afraid. It's just that some information's come my way recently which might – just might – help the inquiry. The more I think about it, the more I feel I ought to pass it on to the police. But I didn't want to do that without political backup, and you're the leader of the council now, in effect.'

Pilkington suddenly sounded more serious and self-conscious, clearing his throat and pausing as if to collect his thoughts.

'Yes, well, subject to an election in the group of course, I sort of suppose I am. Not that I would have wished it to happen this way, of course.'

'No, no, of course not,' said Rutter in his best smoothing-it-over manner. 'I know there were differences of emphasis between you two, but you were going in the same basic direction.'

Rutter half-listened, nervously turning the pages of his phone book, while Pilkington spent a few careful sentences protesting too much about how loyal he had always been to his arch-rival John Bullock.

' . . . but anyway, Barry, what is this mysterious information which has dropped into your hands?'

'Well, it's about the town centre redevelopment.'

'Aha!' The reaction was undisguised triumph, followed by an embarrassed pause and a studied return to more restrained tones. 'There have been a few whispers about that for some time, you know.'

'Yes, I know, but whispers are one thing and evidence is another. And I'm afraid this looks as though it may be real evidence.'

'What is it? How long have you had it? Where'd it come from?' Pilkington's questions came pumping eagerly down the line, like coins from the jackpot of a slot machine, and Rutter found himself putting up his hand in the empty room, as if to prevent himself being swept away.

'Hang on, hang on, Simon. I don't think it's the sort of thing that's best discussed on the phone. How are you fixed after the croquet? Can you get away at all later on?'

'Hmm. Bit difficult – visit to in-laws this afternoon. Dog house for days if I cried off. Might have to leave it till tomorrow.'

'Town hall, first thing?'

'Fine by me. So, eh, someone playing naughty boys, were they? The brothers'll have a field day with that.'

'We'll talk about it in the morning. Oh, and Simon . . .'

'Yes?'

'If the police call and see you before tomorrow, don't mention this to them just yet, all right?'

Chapter Eleven

Sunday, 12.30 p.m.

When Colin and Judy arrived at Jumpers on Sunday morning, they found Dorothy Bullock loading a suitcase into a maroon Volvo estate car standing tyre-deep in the gravel driveway. The house and garden were gleaming in the warm sunshine, and the widow was wearing a cream-coloured cotton dress and sunglasses. Two teenagers were sitting in the shadows of the back seat, heads bowed, and Judy's stomach lurched as she saw the boy's jawline, a perfect reproduction of the one on the dead body she'd seen splayed in the butterfly bush and dissected on the mortuary slab the previous day.

'Find out what they're up to, will you, Jude?' said Colin dourly. 'I can't face posh women this early in the day.'

'They're doing a bleedin' bunk, that's what,' said one of the two detective constables in the back of the car, who'd come along to help with the search. This one was wearing a self-satisfied expression and too much musky after-shave, and Judy gave him a withering look as she twisted her body to get out of the car.

Dorothy closed the tailgate of the Volvo and turned to meet Judy. She looked pale and exhausted, and her brown hair was dull and tangled. The eyes were unreadable behind the near-black lenses. No, she hadn't slept much, she felt terrible, and Annabel was about to drive them over to her mother's place in Banstead for a few days.

'We'd just like to have a proper look through your husband's things,' said Judy. 'Just in case there's something which might help us.'

'What sort of things?' asked Dorothy, her voice sharp and suspicious. Judy shrugged, screwing up her eyes against the reflections from the highly polished car.

'Clothes, papers, address books, that sort of thing. Just in case. Have you been having a look through them yourself at all?'

'I've been rather too busy with the children and all the phone calls from sympathetic Tories,' said Dorothy, waspishly. 'Is there something in particular? Has anything come up?'

'We've got one or two ideas, but nothing concrete at this stage, I'm afraid.'

Dorothy lowered her head and started kneading the back of her neck with her free hand. The gesture tightened the shoulders of the cream dress, its flowing cut giving a flattering outline to her thickening waist and hips. Judy wondered why bereaved people never chose black any more.

'You know,' said Dorothy, her tone suddenly weak and mild, 'I think it must just be some maniac. John quite often went for walks up on the Downs, if he was feeling upset or was trying to think things out. Something made him miss the meeting, then he must have driven up there in the evening and been attacked by someone after his wallet. The world seems to be crawling with nutcases these days. And there've been two other murders up there quite recently, haven't there?'

'Yes, there have. They were rather different, though.'

'Well, it's up to you,' said Dorothy, sighing and shaking her head. 'You must know what you're doing. I suppose you want to get on with this search?'

'If you don't mind.'

'OK – I'll get Annabel to take the kids and I'll follow later in my car.'

Dorothy crunched her way wearily to the porch to make the arrangements with Annabel Silver, who was standing with her arms folded, staring at the three policemen sitting in the car. Eventually Annabel, glossy and bouncing in contrast to Dorothy, strode out to the Volvo, flashing an ambiguous smile at Colin as he sat behind the steering wheel of the Cavalier. She spoke to the children for a few moments before driving off, revving the engine unnecessarily and churning deep ruts in the gravel. Judy and the three men trooped into the house, where Dorothy showed them Bullock's study and the chest of drawers and wardrobe where he kept his clothes.

'I'll be in the kitchen,' said Dorothy. 'You won't be too long, will you?'

The two constables, muttering sarcastically about not being offered any coffee, stayed upstairs while Judy and Colin started on the study. It was a small red-carpeted room behind the staircase, with a window looking out at the tall beech hedge which separated Jumpers from the next garden. There was a wooden bookcase with a few hardback volumes of popular fiction propping up untidy piles of yellowing council papers, a couple of tarnished golfing trophies on top of a small TV in the corner, and a black and white picture of the boys of Beechley Grammar School in 1964, their ears sticking out from short back and sides haircuts. They began sifting through the drawers of the desk, a Georgian reproduction with a red leather top tooled in gold.

'Bank statements,' said Colin, dropping a black folder into a plastic bag.

'All I've got here is gas bills,' muttered Judy. 'Aha, this looks more interesting – diaries from previous years. Nineteen eighty-nine, opened at random, month of May – hello, it's DK at the Black Swan again. Look, on the 12th – obviously a stable, long-term relationship.'

They stood, elbows touching, in the silent room, peering for longer than necessary at the neat jottings of the dead man. Then Colin gently took the diary from Judy's hand and turned to the notes pages at the back.

'More phone numbers,' he said. 'Just like in the one we found on his body. I'm sure they'll lead us to the tom on the tape recording.'

'Tom? Mind your language, Colin. This is a sex-industry operative we're talking about. You can have a cosy session with the reverse numbers book this afternoon.'

'A treat in store, eh?'

There was a tap on the door and the constable with the aftershave came in, holding a large plastic bag containing a few scraps of paper. He seemed to fill the tiny room with his bulky body, his cloying aroma and his big-jowled, self-satisfied look.

'This is all we could find, sir,' he said jauntily to Colin. 'Been through all his pockets, piles of undies, smelly socks, the lot. Just a few bits and pieces like old train tickets up to London and the odd restaurant bill. Mike's just having a rummage through the tubes of KY in the bedside cabinet.'

'OK,' said Colin, taking the bag without looking at him. 'We'll meet you out at the car in a few minutes.'

'That guy's head's so big it ought to be circumcised,' muttered Judy as the door closed behind the constable.

'Fancy him, do you?' said Colin smoothly, bending over the drawers again. 'What I want to know is, where are the fat insurance policies?'

'And what I want to know,' said Judy, prodding the dark stain left on the armchair by John Bullock's head, 'is whether the wife knew that he was seeing a tart?'

'Gives her a motive, you mean? We'd better find the tart before we ask the wife.'

They took the bag of documents into the hall and called for Dorothy. The house was still and peaceful, and in the sitting-room particles of dust were swimming in the sunlight which poured through the windows on to the blue carpet. In the kitchen was a lingering smell of toast and a few breakfast things on the steel draining board. Through the open back door came the breathless song of a nightingale, bursting its heart high above the downs. They found Dorothy in the paddock, leaning against the wooden railings and staring at the beech copse on the far side of the steep little valley. The bright light showed up the streaks and blotches of badly applied make-up on her cheeks.

'Very peaceful, isn't it?' said Judy. Dorothy, locked in a gloomy trance, nodded dumbly.

'I see there's a little stable as well, over there – were you going to get a pony?'

Dorothy nodded again, pushed her sunglasses back into her hair, and turned her troubled hazel eyes on Judy for a moment.

'For my daughter.'

'I expect you'll still be able to, with the insurance and everything.'

Dorothy's eyes, screwed up against the sunlight, narrowed further.

'What do you know about the insurance?' she asked sharply.

'Nothing. Except what you tell us.'

Dorothy studied Judy and Colin for a moment, then turned away, folding her arms and brushing at the shin-high grass with her foot. She was wearing brightly coloured espadrilles, and Judy noticed the stubbly hairs on her ankle, missed by the razor.

'John's left everything to me, as far as I know,' she said. 'And there's some sort of lump sum on the insurance. But the documents are all in the bank, and I don't know the detail.'

'So you won't be going short?'

Dorothy gave Judy a venomous look.

'Honestly,' she said. 'You talk as if there was something wrong with that.'

'Not at all,' said Judy. 'But it just helps to build up the picture. Did you go anywhere for lunch on Thursday, Mrs Bullock?'

Dorothy heaved a long-suffering sigh, and raised her gaze to the blue sky. The nightingale was still trilling and warbling high above them.

'No, I did not go anywhere for lunch on Thursday. I was here all day. I had two friends round for tea, Annabel and Betty Damson. Is this the Spanish Inquisition, or what?'

'That's all for now, Mrs Bullock.'

Colin and Judy left Dorothy locking up the house and walked back to the car. One constable was telling the other how his wife had attacked him with a rolled-up glossy magazine when he'd arrived home drunk at two in the morning and woken her up by throwing his shoes across the bedroom.

'Fit pair of women, those two,' said the one with the aftershave, jauntily, as Colin eased the car away across the crunching gravel. 'For their age, that is.'

'See the rear on the one who drove off in the Volvo?' said the second constable, who was lanky, with blond hair sticking up in patches like an ill-trimmed hedge. 'Woo-er!'

Judy turned round and looked at them contemptuously, winding down her window and screwing up her nose.

'Does the aftershave help much, pulling the birds?' she asked. 'Or d'you find they just throw up?'

'Whoops, sorry,' said the first constable sarcastically. 'Foot in it again. Sexism. Black mark. Forgetting ourselves again, Arty.'

They drove back to the police station, the sense of space and colour of the leafy outskirts of the borough yielding slowly to the denser, duller fabric of the centre of Beechley. The only break in the silence came when they stopped at traffic lights and Colin sarcastically read out a felt-tipped inscription on a bus shelter: 'I woz 'ere but now I'm gone, so here's my name to turn you on.' There were several suggestions from the back seat about the physical tortures which should be applied to the authors, who signed themselves Rocky and Banjo.

In the incident room, Manningbird was yawning and scratching himself through a thin grey cardigan which matched the colour of his face. He watched Colin and Judy sceptically as they reported the morning's work and dumped the documents among the overflowing ashtrays.

'Give us the other diaries,' he grunted. 'I'll find the tart, while you two get out there again and talk to this Simon Pilkington.'

'What about his business partner?' said Colin. 'Nigel Damson?'

Manningbird looked up at him and sighed irritably, pushing over a leaf from a spiral notebook with Pilkington's address on it.

'Plenty of time for that, don't worry. Anyway, Damson might be in on the blackmail, as you pointed out yourself, Colin. So let's get to the tom first, see what we can get out of her. And mind your Ps and Qs with Pilkington – he's a clever dick, apparently.'

In the corridor Colin nudged Judy with his elbow. 'I'm sure the Fat Man wouldn't want us to disturb Mr Pilkington's Sunday lunch, would he?' he said conspiratorially. 'So what about a team meeting in the Harrow?'

'So you're being nice to me today?' said Judy, deciding against a barbed remark about going home for lunch with the wife and kids.

'Sorry about last night,' said Colin, giving her his creased grin.

As they walked through the scuffed passageways of the station into the brightness of the backyard, Judy felt a sudden lightening of mood, as if she were a child again, being taken out for the kind of summer treat she'd never got from her father. She reclined the passenger seat, closed her eyes and rested her arm on the open window ledge, feeling the warm pinch of the sunshine on her bare skin. Colin's hand brushed against her knee as he moved the gear stick, and it crossed her mind that she should move her legs and start a brisk conversation about professional matters. But she left her knee where it was, eased off her shoes, and let her thoughts drift pleasantly. The headrest felt soft as a pillow.

'Could you stop snoring, please?' said Colin. 'And get your mind back on the case?'

Judy rolled her head sideways and half-opened her eyes. He had pulled the sun visor down, leaving his eyes in shadow and the rest of his face in bright sunlight. For the first time she noticed a sourness in the underlying set of his lips, as if he always had something unpleasant in his mouth.

'Sorry,' she said. 'What d'you want to know?'

'Whether you've still got it in for Mrs Bullock.'

Judy frowned, and brought her seat upright again, resentful at being forced back to reality.

'I haven't got it in for her,' she said. 'I feel very sorry for her, in fact. But I also think she's like what they say about icebergs – there's only about a tenth of the story on show. You can tell by the way she behaves that there was something wrong between her and her husband.'

'But that's true of any marriage, isn't it?' said Colin quietly.

'Yes, but I'm talking about something fundamental. And I'm not convinced that she really doesn't know how much she stands to inherit. You know, I think we ought to get the Telecom to start recording her phone calls. Find out who she's talking to.'

Colin shrugged.

'Can't do any harm, I suppose,' he said. 'Get them to do it first thing tomorrow.'

He turned into the car park of the Harrow, a mock-Tudor 1930s pub crowded with open-topped cars and young people in skimpy clothes drinking and laughing too much. The place was built on a spine of land which led the eye back to Beechley, where the town hall gleamed like a bleached bone among the dross of concrete and glass around it. In the distance was the City, where the towers of the NatWest bank and Canary Wharf – one black periscope and one silver – poked above the sun-soaked haze.

90

Colin had bought rolls and found a table on the terrace before Judy came back from the bar with the orange juice. She sensed him assessing her as she walked towards him, and fought down the impulse to adjust her walk, to defer to the male eye by swinging her hair and her hips and placing her feet more delicately. Her blue skirt was well below the knee, but she wondered if her short-sleeved white blouse was too revealing. She sat down feeling irritated that such things seemed to matter.

'You know, Colin,' she said through a mouthful of stale bread and cheese. 'I'm rather surprised you invited me to a pub today.'

He stopped in mid-chew, his eyes guilty.

'What do you mean?' he said sharply, a crumb shooting across at her from his half-full mouth.

'Well,' she said innocently, brushing the wet crumb from her cheek. 'I thought a church would be more likely. We could have banged a tambourine together to while away the time.'

His face was slowly turning a deep red as he searched for a reply among the beer puddles and fag ends beneath their feet. Judy noticed how long and delicate his eyelashes were before turning away to study the sunlit countryside, determined not to apologize. Eventually he chose candour rather than retaliation.

'It's not that born-again kind of stuff, Judy,' he said gently, sipping his drink. 'Just the half-hearted Church of England. But it does help a bit, when you think all the filth is going to drown you.'

'Filth?' Judy's eyes widened, and she glimpsed the sourness in the line of his mouth again. 'Is that really how you see the world? Christ, Colin, I always took you for a cheerful bloke.'

'Come on, Jude, you read the papers. What about that pensioner who was chopped into dog food in Lewisham a couple of weeks ago? They tied her up, burnt her with cigarettes, raped her and stabbed her fifty-odd times. Not all that unusual these days, either. Sure, you try to stay on an even keel, you crack a few jokes, but filth isn't a bad word for it.'

Judy watched him over her orange juice, remembering how she'd rejected Christianity at sixteen because of all the war and death it had caused.

'You spend all your time as a copper thinking the worst of people, thinking there's no such thing as a good motive. I suppose I just need something to remind me there can be good bits too. You can get to the point of thinking everyone's a villain or a pervert.'

'I suppose I just haven't been in the job long enough to feel like that,' said Judy. 'Maybe it's why so many coppers top themselves.'

91

'Thanks a lot, Judy.' His look was half amusement, half venom.

'Sorry, Colin, I didn't mean . . .'

'No Judy, course you didn't. A few more years of this job and you'll realize a lot of people are just plain evil, and it's not just because they grew up in a single-parent family in a tower block. Original sin, it's called. And the worst thing is when you see yourself beginning to behave like the low life you deal with all the time – following their standards, going down to their level.'

'What you been doing, Colin, chopping up your granny?' Judy hammed it up, trying to lighten the tone. He looked at her reflectively, the grimness slowly fading from his eyes.

'Nah,' he smiled, shoving away his empty glass. 'Drinking with fast women instead of going to church. Come on, we'd better get over and see this Simon Pilkington.'

Judy led the way to the car, wishing she'd controlled the impulse to taunt him. No doubt he felt better for voicing his inner conflicts, but she felt worse: things had been shifted to a new level, where she knew him better but liked him less.

They drove back down the hill, round the roundabout on the main road and into an enclave of middle-market, semi-detached houses with small front gardens and lots of ruched curtains at the windows. Pilkington's small BMW was parked in a tidy driveway.

The tinkle of affected female laughter from inside stopped suddenly when they rang the doorbell, and Pilkington opened the door wearing a festive-looking red and orange bow tie and carrying a glass of white wine. The smile flew from his face like a bird off a wall when he saw Colin's warrant card.

'Oh, no,' he muttered. 'It bloody well would be you, wouldn't it?'

'I'm sorry, sir,' said Colin expressionlessly, his nose twitching at the fish-dominated aromas emerging through the door. 'Were you in the middle of celebrating something?'

Chapter Twelve

Sunday, 2.30 p.m.

'Why, Derek Kingswood, of course,' said Pilkington, raising his elegant blond eyebrows. 'I'd have thought you'd guess that. You must know Derek Kingswood.'

Colin and Judy exchanged cautious glances. They vaguely knew of Kingswood as a local property developer who had expanded fast in the middle eighties and was trying to prop up an empire of vacant space and collapsing values. In Beechley he was known as the man behind Market Walk, which was the name given to the redevelopment of the town centre.

'Know what about Derek Kingswood, exactly?' asked Colin. Pilkington was leaning back, swinging himself gently in a deeply padded lounger, while Judy and Colin perched on white plastic chairs by a table with empty glasses and a half-full jug of Pimms. He had recovered his aplomb, his smooth, lightly tanned face was set in a placatory smile, and his nervousness only showed when he reached up to pat his neatly cut blond hair or tweak his jazzy tie.

'Well, John Bullock and Derek Kingswood have been working together for years over this town centre thing. There was no secret about that. So it was hardly surprising they were having lunch together.'

'No, I suppose not,' said Colin. 'Fairly obvious, as you say. Only trouble is, the time of the appointment was the time he disappeared. You'd better just run through the history of the thing – just to refresh our memories.'

Pilkington sighed and looked out over the garden, allowing one polished brown loafer to fall off his heel and swinging it from his toe. Some of the mallets and brightly painted balls from a battered croquet box were scattered near them on the flagged terrace, and the white-painted hoops were set out on the small lawn, much too close to each other. Judy guessed that Pilkington's recent forebears and occupied a rather larger space in the world than he did at present.

The scheme had first been conceived in the mid-eighties when the property business, as Pilkington put it, was 'all systems go'. Everyone knew that the unremarkable Victorian covered market in the High Street was a wasted asset, with just a few barrows selling fruit and vegetables and the odd hippy with a stall full of silver earrings, joss sticks and scuffed Jefferson Airplane LPs. The late Horace Cardwell had been leader of the council then, with Bullock as chairman of the planning committee, and they and Kingswood had put together the plan to demolish the old market and make the whole area into what they called a modern retail environment.

'I've looked at it,' said Colin gloomily. 'It's going to be one of those places with piped music, security guards, and escalators. Lots of little shops to buy expensive clothes and American ice-cream, but nowhere for a tube of toothpaste or a tin of paint.'

'Must admit I'm not too keen on these shopping malls myself,' said Pilkington ruefully. 'But there you are.'

The idea was that the council would sell to Kingswood's company the market, a dilapidated next-door block of 1950s offices which it owned, and several buildings it would purchase compulsorily: a row of Victorian shops beside the market, and a large working garage behind it. Kingswood would get planning permission for his new development of offices and shops, and lurking in the background was an understanding that the council would lease the new offices and sell off the 1960s extension at the back of the town hall so that could also be demolished and redeveloped, probably into a supermarket.

Then, however, the Greater London Council and the local electorate threw a spanner in the works. On the eve of its abolition by the Government, the GLC used its planning powers to declare the market and High Street a conservation area, making planning permission much trickier; and the Tories lost their overall majority in Beechley at the 1986 borough elections. Horace Cardwell lost his seat and died shortly afterwards, and the whole scheme went on ice until the Conservatives came back to power when two by-elections were held the following year.

'That was when I was elected and Bullock took over as leader,' said Pilkington, his blue eyes suddenly harder and colder. 'And the first thing to be resurrected was the Kingswood scheme.'

'How did they get round the problem of the conservation area?' asked Judy.

'Well, the first set of plans were called in and rejected by the Department of the Environment. So Kingswood had to draw up a new set which preserved the façade and the ornamental ironwork of the market, and the front of some of the Victorian shops. He was exceedingly put out because it was much more expensive to build, of course. But at least it got permission, and in early '88 the property boom was still firing on all cylinders, so the scheme still looked pretty attractive. But then there were all the legal challenges.'

'What were those?'

'Shopkeepers opposing compulsory purchase orders, that sort of thing. The biggest was the Cyril Austin case – now if you're looking for a motive to bump, er, do John Bullock to death, I'd have thought that's a man you'd be taking a close look at. He's saddled with two hundred grand's worth of legal costs which he can't pay, thanks to my late colleague.'

Pilkington explained it was all to do with whether the council had a conflict of interest in giving planning permission to a scheme which the council itself had promoted. Austin was furious at losing his garage to compulsory purchase, and went to the High Court for a judicial review of the decision to give the scheme planning permission. But the law only said, according to the judge, that planning decisions could not be subject to political direction; and while there was plenty of surmise and supposition about political interference, there was actually no hard evidence.

'Ridiculous, really,' said Pilkington, half-laughing, half-indignant. 'Because everyone knows the decision was highly political. Labour and the Lib Dems were against it. It's just that there was nothing on paper from the leadership instructing the planning committee to give permission to the scheme. Costs were given against Austin, and John Bullock stood on the steps of the High Court afterwards and said it served him right for being so stupid. Very compassionate. You must have seen it on TV.'

Pilkington's face had coloured, and he suddenly stopped rocking, leaned forward and picked up the croquet mallet lying nearest to him. He held the handle halfway down and let the heavy wooden head, scarred and splintered like a chopping block, swing gently between his ankles.

'I did see that, now you mention it,' said Colin, hands clasped, watching Pilkington closely. 'He stood there sticking out his chin, like a boxer, talking tough. That was his style, really, wasn't it?'

'I'm afraid it was, officer. A bit of a bruiser, in my view. That sort of approach was all right for the early years of the Prime Minister, knocking heads together and taking on the miners and that sort of thing. But I suspect we're going to need a bit more consensus if we're going to get through the next election in one piece. Someone with a bit less, well, personality, shall we say.'

'Is that why you put yourself up against him for Beechley South-East?' said Judy innocently, yielding at last to the temptation to lean over and pluck a dead head off a potted petunia. She rolled it in her fingers, watching its remnant of purple juice colour her skin.

'Partly, yes,' said Pilkington, blinking. 'I'm not afraid to admit it.'

'And now he's gone, there'll be a new contest? Leaving you free to stand again?'

'I suppose so, now you mention it. Thought hadn't crossed my mind, to be honest. It's so soon after the event. Good Heavens, you chaps – and, er, women – you do have suspicious minds, don't you?'

His nervous laugh stopped suddenly as he looked down at the mallet in his hands. He stopped swinging it, placed it carefully on the grey flagstones a yard away and folded his hands in his lap. Judy thought his smile was becoming less affable.

'It's just that we've had reports Mr Bullock was very angry with you about something,' she said. 'He was talking about knocking heads together, that sort of thing. What was all that about, then?'

A smug look crossed Pilkington's face, and he got up and walked the two steps to the end of the terrace, turning to face them with his hands in his pockets. He had long, elegant legs which seemed cramped by this small, neat garden and would have looked better pacing up and down in grander surroundings. Above and below his polished brown belt were the comfortable swellings of an infant paunch.

'That,' he said, 'would probably be about the new document on spending cuts. You know, the one that was leaked to the local paper. He wasn't too pleased about it.'

'About what, exactly?' asked Colin. 'The leak, or what was in the document? I thought he was all for spending cuts.'

'Oh, he was, he was,' said Pilkington, grinning cleverly. 'The new cuts were all his idea, entirely without consultation with the rest of us in the group. Just to keep the poll tax down to £300. No, what he didn't like was the bit about cancelling the lease.'

'On these offices Kingswood's put up in the High Street re-development?'

'Precisely. If we were going to cut social services and libraries to keep the poll tax down, I could see no reason why we should be taking on a new office lease costing us half a million when there's no longer any guarantee anyone's interested in redeveloping the town hall extension. Bullock didn't agree with me – nor did Elspeth Gorringe, of course – but a majority of the group did. And he was not a happy man.'

Pilkington stepped back to the lounger, sat down, crossed his legs and arms, and smiled at them. He looked like a lawyer who had delivered his bull point, and was resting his case.

'So did this come up at your Conservative group meeting on Thursday morning?' Judy asked. 'Before the full council?'

'We might have touched on it. But we were more concerned with the day of action – you know, the strike. And I think John was going to play a waiting game over Market Walk, try to get round it another way.'

'Presumably Kingswood wouldn't be too pleased about the option on the lease going down the tubes,' said Colin. 'In the present economic climate, and all that.'

'Presumably. But I don't see why the chargepayers should act as a cushion for a property developer. John agreed with the argument politically, he couldn't do otherwise, but at the same time he was, well, what shall we say – beholden?'

Colin and Judy looked at each other, and then back at Pilkington, whose smile was now tight and enigmatic, like a mischievous child withholding a secret. Two grey squirrels chased each other perilously along the top of the fence, and Judy caught sight of a pale face with a blond fringe among the reflections on the sitting-room window, peering out at them anxiously for a second. Pilkington hadn't introduced them to his wife and guests and had led them straight through to the garden.

'Are you implying there was something improper going on?' asked Colin, his voice neutral.

'I'm implying nothing,' said Pilkington, arms still crossed. 'Merely answering your questions.'

'All right then, here's another,' said Colin. 'Where were you for the rest of Thursday?'

Pilkington's eyebrows arched and his voice became rhetorical and sarcastic, as if the lawyer was now pointing out to a jury the full ridiculousness of the statements from the witness in the box. He counted his three points on his fingers, as if he had rehearsed them.

'Where was I? Well, I had lunch with most of the other members of the group, went to the council meeting – rather ill-fated, as you know – and came home to spend the evening with my wife. Really, Inspector, you don't suspect me, do you?'

Colin said nothing, but looked at Judy for a moment. They exchanged little nods and stood up to go. Pilkington looked from one to the other, confused, and began talking again, hurriedly.

'Because if it's motives you're looking for, I would have thought the people with a track record were all over the town centre that afternoon. All those yobbos from Class Warfare, who did all the damage back in May and split poor old Rutter's head open. And our old friend Steve Ditchley, who's crossed swords with Bullock many a time. Have a look at your own videos from the riot, officer: I think you'll find him there, issuing death threats in the clearest possible manner.'

'Thank you, Mr Pilkington,' said Colin. 'We'll be in touch.'

Judy sat in the car at the side of the road while Colin phoned the Fat Man. The conversation was dragging on, and Colin glanced towards her and made placatory gestures from time to time: perhaps there'd been a new lead and they were going to be catapulted off somewhere to make an arrest. She leaned her head towards the open window, catching the scent of hay from the recently mown fields beside the road and trying to imagine the suave features of Simon Pilkington contorting into violence and hatred as he smashed at the skull of his rival; the two faces of the Tory party, patrician and brute, in a murderous confrontation in the hot summer dusk. It all seemed so unlikely on this warm and sleepy afternoon; she smiled to herself, and watched a blue and grey train pass over the little viaduct at the bottom of the hill and disappear into a cutting for the tunnel under the downs. Even the rattling of the wheels seemed gentler, more languorous, than it would in the morning, when the line would be busy carrying perspiring, impatient commuters in and out of the baking city.

'He's too vain to turn violent, I reckon,' said Judy as Colin climbed back into the car. 'He'd be too worried about getting blood on his Daks or his hair falling out of place.'

'What?' Colin was distracted, unfocused. 'Oh, you mean Pilkington? Don't be so sure. These toffs have all kinds of nasty impulses lurking beneath the surface, just like everyone else.'

'What's up?'

'What? Oh, nothing much. Bryan wants you to talk to someone who's come in the front office. Says he knows something about the murder. And he's got an address up in Marylebone, checked it out with the vice squad up there. Mr Bullock's lady friend.'

'Oh. Length of time you took, I thought there was something big.'

'She'll probably be quite big enough.' Colin grinned at her as the crack fell flat. Judy sensed some kind of male conspiracy, but decided to let it go by: she'd had enough heavy conversation for one day, and Colin seemed as happy as she was to drive back to the station in silence.

Sunday, 4 p.m.

The sergeant on the front desk blew a sigh of relief as they came through the door. Sunday afternoons, so peaceful on the middle-class hillsides, only increased the stresses among Beechley's unemployed and unfortunate, and the waiting room was full of people with tearful faces or minor wounds.

'That's the one,' said the sergeant, indicating a blond, blue-eyed young man sitting upright in the corner, watching them alertly. 'Take him in our little interview room here, if you like.'

Colin went off upstairs while the young man was brought round to the interview room. As Judy followed him in, the sergeant mouthed the word 'nutter' to her and told her to leave the door open. He was smiling familiarly, blocking the corridor so she was forced to brush against him as she passed, catching a whiff of sourness from the armpits of his short-sleeved shirt.

'Right, sir,' she said to the youth, pulling up the plastic chair on the other side of the table. 'I understand you've got something for us on the murder inquiry.'

The young man cleared his throat and nodded. He was clean-shaven, his hair was short and neat, and his black jeans and blue T-shirt were in good condition; but there was a greasy black line around his collar, and the warm room was already tainted with the sweetish smell of the long-term unwashed.

'Er, yes, I have,' he said, in a drab middle-class voice drained of intonation. 'It was me, you see. I did it.'

It was the pale blue eyes which gave it away. They were so wide open that the irises were visible all the time, and their expression veered between pain and childlike innocence. The skin around his fingertips was red and peeling where he picked at them constantly with long, dirty nails.

'I see,' Judy said quietly. 'When and where?'

'Thursday night. Up by the quarry.' He nodded solemnly, as if to confirm the truth of what he was saying and satisfaction at the way he was saying it.

'Why did you do it?'

'Because he was a fat bastard politician.' Again, the quiet nodding;

Judy noticed now that some of his teeth were beginning to rot, and he had suspicious-looking marks around the veins in the crook of his elbow.

'Not the voices, then?'

The youth was startled, and the distracted eyes suddenly focused on Judy's face.

'So you know about the voices?' he said eagerly.

'A bit. And how did you do the murder?'

'Hit him with a piece of wood.'

'Where exactly did you hit him?'

The young man's index-finger, its lines and whorls engrained with black grease, shot up and pointed at the centre of his forehead, just below the line of his neat but unwashed hair. He pressed so hard the flesh went white, as if he wanted to pierce his own brain.

Judy sighed, picturing John Bullock's head lying on the mortuary slab, the face and forehead pale and unmarked except for the yellowish graze on one cheek. She drummed her fingers on the table for a moment, wondering whether to bother with even the briefest statement. Then she remembered a phrase from her first Chief Superintendent about the police being the only real twenty-four-hour social service. She brought him a cup of scalding, reddish tea from the canteen and chatted to him gently as he drank it.

The bits of his story she believed were that his first name was Godfrey and he came from a well-off family in Sevenoaks. He'd dropped out of university and spent time in and out of several mental hospitals, but none of them would keep him any more. For the last two years he had been living rough, going back to his parents occasionally until he had a row with them and got thrown out. But now he wanted to live somewhere safe where he'd be looked after: he couldn't face another winter outside.

The bits she found less convincing were that he had forgotten his surname, was very interested in local politics, and had decided that Bullock was to blame for the plight of the homeless. He'd found out where he lived, and had seen him walking on the downs one evening the previous week – he couldn't remember which one, though. They'd had a furious argument, he'd picked up a piece of wood, beaten Bullock over the head with it, and then tipped the body into the quarry.

He finished his tea and put one dirty hand up, pressing his temples with finger and thumb. Judy watched him for a moment, then got up and opened the door.

'Thank you for coming in, Godfrey,' she said quietly. 'You'd better be off now. Everything you've told me has been in the papers, you know.'

He looked up sharply, his eyes growing panicky.

'Aren't you going to take me in?' he asked plaintively. 'Arrest me?'

'Not now,' said Judy. 'But don't worry, we'll find you if we need you.'

'But I've got nowhere to go.'

'Would you like me to ring one of the hospitals? Or your parents?'

He suddenly rose to his feet, knocking over his chair with a clatter, and swung a bony white fist towards Judy's face. Half expecting it, she jumped backwards and lifted the plastic chair in defence. Godfrey's wild lunge threw him off balance, and as he fell forwards across the table she caught a glimpse of his face, puckered and desperate like a child on the verge of tears.

Judy dropped the chair in the corner behind her, grasped the rim of the table and jerked it hard, tipping him on the floor before he could get back to his feet. While he struggled like an overturned beetle, she stepped rapidly round the table, hopped over him, and dropped one knee into the small of his back. As she put a wrist lock on him, grimacing at the drain-like odours wafting out of his clothes, he reached out his other hand and gripped the metal leg of the table.

'You all right, Judy?' The desk sergeant and a square young PC with a crew cut appeared in the doorway above her, excited and ready to have a go. She looked up at them and nodded, her pale blond hair falling into her eyes.

'Think so. Tried to thump me so we'd take him in.'

'We'll charge the bugger with assault, then, stick him in a cell.' The sergeant's voice was thick with distaste as he eyed the back of the young man's neck: the tendons were standing out like thin ropes as he tried to lift his face off the lino.

'Not worth it,' said Judy, letting go the bony wrist and getting to her feet, brushing dust off her skirt. 'He ought to be in hospital, but things being what they are he'll be sleeping in the park again tonight.'

'OK, come on, you – out,' said the sergeant, nudging Godfrey in the ribs with his gleaming toecap. 'We've had enough of you.'

'Easy, Sergeant,' said Judy.

The sergeant's face tightened nastily as she brushed past him and went out through the front door of the station. She watched as Godfrey, hunched over his hands, walked slowly away, the sole of one of his trainers flapping loosely. For a moment she was going to follow him, say something, but she sat down instead on a pavement bench and stared at the street. A rented van stopped at the traffic lights and a couple of yobs inside bent forward to leer at her.

'You a plod? Beating people up again, eh?'

101

Someone sat down beside her and she looked up to see Colin, twirling his car keys and smiling the boyish smile which went so badly with his pessimistic views. She told him about Godfrey.

'Cry for help,' she said ironically. 'The sort we can't give.'

'One of life's mysteries,' he said. 'We can never find the buggers we want, and the ones we don't want are climbing in the windows.'

Chapter Thirteen

Monday, 11 a.m.

Judy slid the car out of the fuming traffic jam of Gloucester Place and pulled into the edge of the road in a small, run-down square near Marylebone Station. On one side, like a wall of sludge-coloured brick and peeling stucco, was a terrace of tall Victorian houses with pillared front porches panelled with a dozen or more bell-pushes. On the other, the blotched and scabby trunks of the square's grey-green plane trees half-hid some straggling rose bushes and a bench where a group of down-and-outs were arguing and swigging from brown bottles. A white-faced woman in a stained grey tracksuit passed by slowly, leaning on a pushchair where a curly-headed child slept, a bottle hanging loosely from its mouth by the teat. The door of one of the houses slammed and a young woman with a red mouth and a tight black skirt clicked down the pavement on high heels, fiddling anxiously inside a small handbag. A man in a suit with a briefcase crossed the road briskly in front of the car, face set and eyes furtive.

'Just look at him,' muttered Colin disgustedly. 'It's not yet eleven in the morning and the buggers are at it.'

'Lust springs eternal,' said Judy. 'Don't you ever feel horny in the morning? On second thoughts, don't answer that.'

'No, but half these blokes must be married. They can have sex at home. There's something perverted about it. Abnormal.'

'Abnormal? You've got a funny view of sex, Colin. Remind me to talk to you about it sometime.'

Judy was half-laughing until she realized from the hard gleam in his eye that she'd strayed into deep waters again. There was a harsh hostility in the way he looked her up and down, as if she was guilty of all the transgressions around them.

'What the hell do you know about it, Judy?' he snapped. 'You're not bloody well married.'

'Marriage and sex don't always go together, Colin,' she said. 'Why d'you think these blokes are sniffing around here?'

103

She turned away and wound down the window, letting in a sudden stream of incoherent curses from one of the men on the bench; they were all bobble-hatted and overcoated despite the warmth of the overcast summer morning, and one of them caught her eye and jerked his middle finger up at her. She looked at her watch and sighed impatiently: she and Colin had arranged to meet a detective sergeant from the central vice squad, and he was already ten minutes late.

'Why don't you tell me what's really on your mind, Colin?' she said eventually. 'You've been a pig all morning.'

Colin sighed and drummed his fingers on the dashboard.

'I can't talk about it, Judy,' he muttered. 'A lot of people have suddenly started twitching about this case. It's all getting a bit too political for my liking.'

'Is that why you were on the phone to Bryan so long after we'd been to see Pilkington?'

He nodded, not looking at her.

'And put me on to interviewing that nutter to keep me out of the way?'

'Not exactly. Well, sort of.'

'I thought there was something going on,' said Judy, trying to control her anger. 'Honestly, you're like a lot of silly kids in the playground – boys' games.'

He looked at her reproachfully, eyes doggy.

'I'd like to tell you more, Jude, but I can't just now. Look, here's our bloke – we'll talk more later on.'

A body blocked the light at the driver's window and Judy looked round to see a large man with receding sandy hair standing in the road chewing gum and smiling, hands stuck in the pockets of a shiny green bomber jacket.

'Hi,' he said, between grindings of his sturdy white teeth. 'Peter Tomkins from West End Central. Shall I jump in the back for a bit?'

He climbed in, shook hands, and settled himself with his beefy jeans-clad knees jammed against the front seats. They chatted for a few minutes, trying to find common experiences or acquaintances; Colin fell back on relating how he'd been in a local vice squad as a probationer and had spent hours lying in the roof space of a men's lavatory, watching homosexuals through a tiny spyhole.

'Really?' said Tomkins, one eyebrow raised. 'Rots the mind, that sort of thing. 'S more protecting juveniles and drug-related round here. Anyway' – the car rocked as he twisted forwards to bring a notebook out of his hip pocket – 'we know all about your young lady. Trades under the name of Elkie – fuck knows what her real name is, to coin a phrase. Pardon my French, Judy.'

'Has she got form?' asked Colin. Tomkins turned down the corners of his mouth and shook his head as he flipped the leaves of the little notebook, which were sprinkled with clumsy handwriting.

'Nah. She's one of the smarter ones. Stays off the streets, doesn't let anyone ponce off her, not using hard drugs as far as we know. Advertises in the back of the girlie mags, which is probably where your dead body got her from. As to whether she was in on the blackmail, haven't the faintest, to be honest. But she answered the phone five minutes ago.'

'Right, then, let's go and knock her up,' said Judy, opening the car door. 'She'll think she's got an early customer when you ring the bell, Colin.'

He flashed her a bad-tempered look over the roof of the car and they crossed to the corner of the square, past a phone box half-filled with advertisements for prostitutes: hand-written invitations to 'executive massage' were stuck flat to the glass, and little orange or pink printed cards with drawings of girls bending over in suspenders were tucked into the frame. 'New,' they announced. 'Eighteen-year-old blonde. Two-way spanking. Rubber and leather. Treat yourself. All fantasies.'

'Growth industry,' grinned Tomkins, as Judy half-turned to stare. 'Telecom and the council strip 'em out one minute, next minute, wham, they're back. Like a fungus.'

Judy wrinkled her nose and stuffed her hands tightly into the pockets of her jeans, as if to protect herself from contamination. Everything around them seemed stained and seedy, everyone who passed them seemed to eye them speculatively, as if they were potential customers for the traffic in flesh and drugs which went on, night and day, in this run-down pocket of central London. But the narrow eyes quickly slid away and went dead: the dealers and hookers round here had learnt long ago to smell police at twenty paces.

They turned a corner and passed a terrace of small hotels with vacant signs on the door and nattily dressed men hanging around on the steps, smoking. The street they wanted was narrower, with lower houses, but it had the same discoloured stucco and loose railings, the same infestation of estate agents' boards leaning at conflicting angles, like the rifles of a badly drilled platoon.

Elkie's basement was in one of the better-looking houses, with a window box full of geraniums and a gate at the top of the steps with a proper catch on it. Nigel said he'd hang around at the end of the street and keep an eye on things while they went in.

105

There were two doors to the basement flat – an outer one consisting of a metal grille, and an inner one with a top panel of frosted glass. The bell rang with an exuberant ding-dong, as it might in some respectable suburban bungalow, and Colin and Judy exchanged amused glances while they waited for the inner door to be unlocked and opened. They were confronted by a slim blonde woman of about thirty wearing a pink towelling dressing-gown and fluffy slippers. She looked at them with cold and unsurprised eyes.

'Yes?' she said in an impatient, slightly hoarse voice. 'What do you want?'

Colin showed her his warrant card and said they wanted a word. She tutted and raised her grey eyes heavenwards. Her hair was cut into a fringe with two blonde wings round her face which almost met under her chin as she shook her head.

'I don't know what's wrong with you people,' she said briskly. 'You ought to know by now that I'm not doing anything illegal. One of your blokes came sniffing around only a couple of weeks ago. You're like a load of randy dogs.'

'This is different,' said Colin. 'It's about a murder.'

'Ooh, that's exciting,' she said sarcastically, widening her unmade-up eyes and fluttering the lashes. 'Makes a change. Come on in, then, but you'd better be quick 'cos I've got to go to the bank.'

It was the same voice as the one on the tape, striving to produce upper-class vowels, asking Bullock in a matter-of-fact way if he wanted beating or babying. She bent to unlock the metal grille, and the dressing-gown fell forward to show the slightly mottled skin of her chest and the top of a black brassière.

As Judy edged through the door, Elkie gave her a tiny smile, her eyes softening for the briefest moment. Judy sensed she was being tested as a potential ally in a world where men were always either punters or predators and help and solace came only from other women. The mushroomy smell of damp rose into her nostrils as she followed Colin through to a brown-carpeted living-room dominated by a large TV with a stack of videotapes on it. There was an oxblood-coloured leather sofa with a pile of folded washing balanced on one arm. As Judy turned she caught a glimpse of a shadowy bedroom with a large, rumpled bed.

'You probably know why we're here,' said Colin, shaking his head at the waved invitation to sit down. Judy sat on the sofa and found her ear being tickled by the frills on a pair of lacy red knickers escaping from the pile of washing.

106

'It's about poor old Mr Bullock, I expect,' said Elkie cheerfully, settling with crossed legs on an armless chair and taking a cigarette out of a silver packet.

'Very good,' said Colin, adopting the same flippant tone. 'Straight to the point. One of your clients.'

'Yes.' Elkie let out a cloud of smoke which hid her face for a moment. 'But I didn't realize it was him, if you see what I mean. Not until I saw his picture on the telly. He called himself Bill when he came round here. If I'd known he was in politics I'd have charged him more.'

She was looking straight back at Colin, evenly and ironically. Colin was less cool, standing in front of the big TV with a vindictive gleam in his eyes, fists clenched inside the pockets of his jacket. The sourness had taken full control of his mouth, and Judy suddenly thought: he hates himself for fancying us.

'Are you sure you didn't know who he was?' he said. 'Are you sure you weren't blackmailing him?'

'Blackmailing him?' Elkie showed emotion for the first time, her eyebrows lifting and her pale mouth falling open slightly. 'You must be joking. I want to keep the punters coming back. They don't do that if you try to blackmail them.'

'So if it wasn't you, then, making tape recordings and threatening to send them to the papers and his wife, who was it?'

'Tape recordings? What of?'

'Of you getting up to your tricks with Mr Bullock, what do you think?'

Elkie fell silent, and her face grew slowly darker as she looked back at him through the blue wisps from her cigarette, pulling her dressing-gown up round her neck and folding her arms defensively.

'I don't know nothing about any tape recordings,' she growled, the posh vowels evaporating. 'Someone must be winding you up.'

'This is no wind-up, Elkie,' said Colin, raising a threatening fore-finger at her. 'Just stay here with her, Judy, while I have a quick look around the flat.'

When Colin was out of the room Elkie gave Judy another ghostly smile through her cigarette smoke. Judy shifted uncomfortably in her seat and had to dart out a hand to prevent the pile of lingerie falling to the carpet. She patted the pile back into place, studied the herd of wild horses on a poster above the chipped fireplace, and noticed the teddy bear propped on a bookshelf. Then she decided she might as well expand her general knowledge.

'How's trade, then?' she asked awkwardly.

'Can't complain,' said Elkie.

'What sort of blokes d'you get these days?'

Elkie produced a little shrug.

'All sorts. A lot of men who don't dare ask their wives for a beating or a blow job. Like your colleague out there.'

Elkie jerked with her chin towards the tiny kitchen, where Colin was banging doors open and closed. Judy was beginning to admire Elkie's repertoire of mannerisms denoting indifference, and decided not to rise to the bait.

'Maybe they do ask, and the wives say no.'

'Maybe.' There was another tiny twitch, this time from the corner of Elkie's mouth. 'Prefer them to the gangsters, anyway.'

'Gangsters?'

'Small-time criminals from the East End. Lots of noise, lots of bragging, but they can't get it up – drink too much. That's why they smoke those big cigars.'

Judy was leaning forward with another question when a muffled shout from Colin summoned them both. Judy glanced into a little green bathroom, where the smell of damp was in combat with the whiff of disinfectant, and stepped into the bedroom, the biggest room of all. It was tightly curtained, with a wall of fitted cupboards and a dressing-table with a mirror next to the bed. The smell changed to stale sweat, and a set of handcuffs dangled from the metal bars of the bedhead.

Colin was rummaging in the wardrobe, pushing aside high-heeled shoes and a selection of whips. Carefully he picked up something large, stood up, and backed over to the bed: it was an outsize baby's changing mat, on which rested a large white folded towel, some safety pins and a brown rubber dummy nearly as big as a tennis ball. Colin's mouth was open in astonishment, but Elkie glanced at the things indifferently, as a cook might look at her saucepans.

'That was a favourite of poor old Bullock's,' she said, almost sadly. 'He did look a bit like a baby with that nappy on, all round and rosy.'

The need to laugh had been mounting in Judy ever since she'd noticed the combination of Elkie's sheer black nylons and pink fluffy slippers, and now she sat on the bed, put her head back and let go. She shook with laughter at the thought of all these respectable men, who were no doubt strict with their children and wanted the world to take them seriously, coming here to be suckled and swaddled like babies or beaten and tortured like prep-school boys: and among them had been

John Bullock, hard and secretive at home and in politics, releasing his tensions by sucking a dummy and having a mummy in suspenders play with his willy. The spasm was passing and she was about to apologize when she opened her eyes and saw it: there was something odd about the light fitting in the centre of the ceiling.

'Hang on,' she said, amusement vanishing as she stood up and climbed on the bed, grabbing one of its brass knobs to steady herself. 'What's this?'

There was a thin brass-coloured ceiling rose from which hung a white flex and a flower-shaped glass shade, and at one side of the rose was a dark half-moon hole in the ceiling, just big enough to insert a finger. Judy looked down and asked Colin and Elkie, staring up at her side by side like kids at a kite, to turn up the light on the dimmer switch.

'Who lives upstairs?' she asked, squinting at the hole but failing to see anything inside it. 'Another prostitute?'

'There's a tart in every house round here,' said Elkie sourly. 'But Mandy up there is on the social.'

'She live by herself?'

'There's a bloke there sometimes. Big ginger-haired sod. Why?'

'Haven't caught on yet, have you?' said Colin nastily. 'Looks like they've been bugging you. Only I'll take a lot of convincing you're not in on it.'

Elkie flopped into the small basket chair by the bed and stared at them, fiddling in her dressing-gown pocket for another cigarette.

'That bastard pig,' she muttered, her face pale as card. 'One of the other girls told me there was someone following punters home. Didn't know it was that scumbag.'

'What d'you mean, following them home?' asked Judy, rocking perilously on the springs as she stepped off the bed.

'Watching people coming out of girls' flats and following them home. Then, you know, if they've got a nice house and that, asking for money.'

'You seem to know plenty about it,' said Colin, his voice vindictive. 'And how come you didn't notice that hole up there, amount of time you spend on your back?'

'Shut up, you,' spat Elkie suddenly, jabbing towards him with the lighted end of her cigarette. 'I've told you, I know fuck all about it, and that hole's been there ever since I moved in. So give it a rest.'

Colin stared back at her, and Judy noticed that he was breathing heavily and his face was glowing. She tensed, thinking he was going to call Elkie names or hit her, but he turned abruptly away.

'Get your clothes on, you,' he said tersely, walking out of the room. 'You're coming with us.'

Monday, 12.30 p.m.

There was no reply to the bell for the ground-floor flat, but as Judy and Colin came back down the half-dozen steps they saw a big ginger-haired man strolling down the street towards them. He was engrossed in a copy of the *Sun*, held up in front of his face, and carried a pint carton of milk in his free hand. His shirt was black, his trousers sand-coloured, and his patent slip-on shoes a gleaming white.

'Reckon we can take him ourselves?' muttered Judy. 'Looks a rough sod to me.'

Colin looked at her. He'd insisted that the reinforcements, called up by Peter Tomkins when they'd taken Elkie round to the car, should stay in the next street while they knocked on the door, and he seemed determined not to change his mind now. There was a hot, sulky look on his face, as if forces he normally kept under control had risen up and taken control of him.

'We'll be OK,' he muttered, tapping the radio in his pocket, lent to them by Tomkins. 'We can call them up on this.'

The man was a few yards from them now, and as he lowered his paper to turn and mount the steps he glanced at them suspiciously. His face was almost liver-coloured, as if he'd spent too long under a sun lamp, and his eyes were a sharp green, the colour of glaciers. Colin began to follow him up the steps, with Judy close behind.

Just as Colin began to speak, the man turned on the top step, lifted the pint of milk in his freckled, tattooed fist and smashed it full into his face. There was an explosion of white liquid and a strangely soft moan, and Colin tumbled back down the steps into Judy's arms, the back of his head hitting the points of the black iron railings and bouncing down them with a series of soft thuds. The man threw his copy of the *Sun* at them, and as Judy staggered back, half laying and half dropping Colin on the pavement, a page-sized colour picture of a girl spraying her glistening breasts with a hosepipe fluttered down on his milk-soaked chest.

Judy dropped to her knees, her hand entangled in the newspaper as she pushed it aside. A trickle of blood was flowing from the corner of Colin's eye and mingling with the milk which covered his hair and face. His eyes were closed, but he was conscious, and his features clenched slowly into a grimace of pain, his hand flapping weakly on a dusty paving stone.

'Christ, Colin, are you all right?' gasped Judy, using the sleeve of her sweatshirt to wipe the milk out of his eyes and putting a hand under the back of his head. His hair felt surprisingly soft and springy, but there was a moistness in it, and when she pulled the hand away it was smeared bright red, a shocking palmful of colour among the drab pavements and houses.

'I'm OK, I'm OK, just nick him,' muttered Colin, irritably, as if the injury had only made his mood worse. The adrenalin was bubbling angrily in Judy, and she took off down the pavement like a sprinter.

'Sod you, sodding Colin,' she panted as she pumped her arms harder. 'That was your own bloody silly fault.'

Ginger was heading away from the street where the van with reinforcements was parked, and Judy had no idea what lay beyond the next corner. He had a slow, flailing gait, and his white shoes seemed to be slipping at every stride. A young man in jeans appeared round the corner and Judy hoped he would come to her help – trip her suspect, or slow him down somehow. But the man skipped rapidly out of the way, grinning at her as if there was some sort of game going on.

She reached the corner, grabbing the railing to slow her down and swing her round, and nearly collided with Ginger, who had stopped and turned and was lunging towards her, teeth set in a grimace of effort. His arms were spread wide, nearly blocking the space between the railings and an old red Cortina parked at the side of the road. For a moment Judy clenched herself, drawing her forearms across her chest to take the impact, then followed her instinct and veered off sideways instead, jumping on to the Cortina's bonnet with a loud booming of flexing metal, and landing in the roadway beyond it. As she turned and reached into her pocket for the warrant card, she heard the click of his flick-knife springing open.

'You are nicked, mate,' she gasped, holding up her card, glad of the bulk of rusting metal which separated them.

'Back off, you tart, or I'll fucking spit you,' said Ginger, his voice rasping and breathless. It was the voice from the tape, a hard, clipped Cockney. He was half-crouching, holding out the gleaming four-inch blade as if he was offering it to her as a present, and his green eyes were panicky.

'Just drop the knife and come quietly,' said Judy, recovering her breath and trying to steady her voice. 'There's a vanload of coppers round the corner, so you've got no chance.'

'Oh, yeah?' His eyes strayed left and right. 'I can't see any fucking coppers. Lying cow.'

He suddenly sprang towards her, landing on his knees on the bonnet of the car and making a series of swipes towards her with the blade. He gave a gasp of effort with each swipe, and Judy leaned backwards as the bright metal swished past, inches from her nose. Then Ginger rolled his bulky body off the bonnet and was running again, his fancy smooth-soled shoes skating awkwardly on the paving stones. Judy ran her left hand down her face, checked that it wasn't bloodied like the right one, and walked round to the pavement, her stomach feeling suddenly drained and empty. She felt too weak to sprint again, and wondered if Peter and his famous reinforcements realized what was going on.

'Sitting in the van picking their noses,' she muttered, breaking into a half-hearted jog after Ginger's retreating black shirt. A pensioner with a toothless mouth opened a door and peered out, and Judy yelled at her to dial 999 and say police needed urgent assistance in whatever the street was.

But as she looked back at the pavement again, she realized with a jolt of fear that Ginger had turned and was running back towards her, holding the knife out in front of him like a lance, his face a desperate, open-mouthed grimace. Beyond him, she saw two uniformed officers had turned the corner and were bearing down behind him. Judy knew she should move off the pavement, dodge behind another car, let him go for the moment. But her muscles felt frozen, and she stood there staring at the huge man lumbering towards her with a deadly weapon.

'Stop, you idiot,' she heard herself yell at him. 'Before you kill someone.'

To her astonishment, he stopped. When he was only ten yards away, he juddered to a halt like a javelin thrower at the line, and leaned against the railings, panting and staring at her, the knife held loosely in his hand. The green eyes locked murderously on to hers for a few seconds, and then he sucked in a huge breath, looked away, and dropped the knife on the pavement. It clattered tinnily and lay there next to his shiny white patent leather shoe.

'Fuck it,' he muttered, as a red-faced PC lumbered up behind him and snapped handcuffs round his wrists. 'I've got nothing to hide. I didn't fucking do it.'

Chapter Fourteen

Monday, 9.30 a.m.

'You've hit the big time, sir,' said Jim Duncan, looking up from his desk as Manningbird waddled through the door. 'The editor of the *Sun*'s been on the blower.'

'Yeah, tell me,' muttered Manningbird, pulling off the jacket of his blue suit and slinging it carelessly round the back of his chair. 'He wants to buy my memoirs, make me a rich man.'

Half a dozen detectives were sitting round the incident room yawning, drinking coffee, scratching themselves and complaining proudly about their hangovers. The metallic, sunless sky was already pushing heat through the grime-streaked windows, and the atmosphere was thickening with cigarette smoke. But Jim Duncan looked alert and fresh, with the sleeves of his carefully ironed white shirt folded back over his muscular forearms.

'Not this time, I'm afraid, sir,' he said cheerily in his mild Scots accent. 'It was about the tape of Bullock with the tart. They were sent a copy of it last Friday. With pictures of Bullock coming out of her flat.'

'So how come we didn't hear from them on Friday?' growled Manningbird, rummaging through his pockets for change for the coffee machine.

'He said he didn't know blackmail was involved and they were planning to check the story out. They were closed on Saturday when the news of the murder broke, had a little think about it on Sunday, and decided to get in touch first thing. Which is now.'

'Yeah? You got any tens? Thanks. And was he saying who gave them the tape? And how much they wanted?'

'Bit coy about that. Said it was complicated. Wanted to talk to us face to face.'

'Well he'll have to wait a bit, won't he? Any luck Colin and Judy will get their hands on the blackmailer this morning, without any help from those hyaenas.'

'Talking of which, are those two having it off?'

Manningbird gave Duncan a pebble-eyed stare.

'You're a crude bastard, Jim, in spite of your fancy clobber. So just excuse me while I get a cup of sludge from that so-called coffee machine of yours.'

Manningbird's lumpy form disappeared into the corridor and Duncan leant back in his chair, rolling his white sleeves further up his arms and looking round his colleagues with an offended expression.

'What's the Fat Man got the hump about?' he asked, pretending innocence.

'Monday morning, what d'you think?' muttered the DC with the aftershave, who was sitting at a computer poking at the keyboard with one finger, as if it was something unpleasantly dead. 'Plus the Yard and the Tories and Uncle Tom Cobbley breathing down his neck. You'd have the hump, an' all.'

Manningbird came back in, spilt the plastic cup of coffee as he put it down on the table, and tucked his scalded fingers between his rubbery lips.

'Ow, bugger it,' he said. 'Anything else so far, Jim?'

'Yeah, the chief executive, Rutter. Wants to talk to you urgently.'

'Oh, yes?' said Manningbird carefully, lowering his yard-wide bulk on to a padded swivel chair. 'We've already got a sergeant and two DCs over there interviewing everyone. And the head of security's an ex-copper. Why can't he talk to any of them?'

Duncan shrugged and leaned back in his chair.

'Wants the top man. Said it was about corruption. Relating to this case.'

'Oh, yes?' Manningbird glanced at Duncan, his little eyes suddenly watchful and calculating. 'And is he over there now?'

'At the town hall? Think so.'

'Right,' said Manningbird, standing up and pulling on his jacket again, moving more rapidly than before. 'I'll get on over there. No point in hanging about.'

'What about that nice cup of coffee?'

'Sod the coffee – you can have it. I might get something decent at the town hall. Certainly deserve it, all the bloody poll tax I've just paid.'

Manningbird swung out through the front door of the station and headed towards the centre of Beechley. There was grim determination on his grey features, and his breath rasped slightly through the dark crevice between his lips. His short legs worked like eager pistons, carrying his tubby body along so rapidly that he brushed against several office-goers as he overtook them. His jacket and his burgundy-coloured

114

tie flapped loosely, revealing the mounds of flesh lurching fluidly under his white shirt.

'Blimey,' said a building worker in a dusty T-shirt to his mate, making a detour to avoid a collision. 'You don't get many of them to the pound.'

Manningbird reached the white stone steps of the town hall and tried to skip up them two at a time, in the manner of a TV host coming on the set. He gave up half-way and pushed slowly through the swing doors, breathing heavily.

'You'd better sit down for a few minutes, sir,' said the reception woman with the neat grey perm. 'We don't want you to have a mischief on council premises, now do we?'

Manningbird collapsed on a nearby chair, which creaked and scraped backwards under the impact. His breathing was a little less laboured by the time Rutter appeared, studying Manningbird through his thick glasses and holding out a lean and wiry hand. The receptionist stared and smiled secretly as the fat man and the thin man made their way side by side up the broad main staircase, underneath the green beeches of the borough's coat of arms.

Manningbird paused at the top of the stairs, gathering breath and taking his first look at the grand vestibule where the councillors of Beechley would gossip and drink tea from a trolley before trooping through the tall wooden doors to the adjoining council chamber. Gold-framed oil paintings of former leaders, including Edwardians with floppy moustaches and Victorians posing with dogs and guns, seemed at odds with the elegant art deco fittings – the amber glass wall lights, the low sofas with foot-wide arms, the mirrors with crenellated tops, the brown carpet with its modernist motif of cream-coloured chevrons.

'Like one of those old Odeons with a few old pictures thrown in,' said Manningbird. Rutter studied him curiously.

'Mmm, could say that. Wait till you see the rear extension, where my office is – more like a multi-storey car park, but without the charm.'

He led the way, past the entrance to the council chamber and along a panelled corridor of committee rooms. Then they went round a corner, through an archway and into a different world: to their left was a bare concrete staircase, and ahead of them stretched a strip-lit linoleum-covered corridor, lined with pale green doors with name cards on them. Rutter turned into the staircase, and their footsteps echoed round the bare walls as they climbed to the second floor and went into his office. Rutter put his head through the door to the adjoining office to ask the secretary for coffee, and Manningbird arranged himself gratefully on a well-padded chair. Outside, the multiple glassy eyes of the Social Security building seemed to peer in at them.

'I'll get straight to the point,' said Rutter, closing the door and bending to get the file out of the bottom drawer of his desk. 'I've received some information which may be relevant to your inquiry.'

Manningbird blinked and smiled patiently. Rutter looked at him anxiously for a moment, as if weighing whether he could trust this grey-faced, overweight police officer with the sharp little eyes. He fingered the little scar on his high forehead for a few moments, then cleared his throat, looked down at the file, and continued in his pernickety lawyer's voice.

'Yes, well, it's been alleged to me, in my capacity as chief executive of the borough council, that the, er, late John Bullock may have been involved in improper dealings. Involving, er, financial matters.'

'Go on, please,' said Manningbird, like a parent cajoling a reluctant child to read aloud.

'Yes, well, you probably know about the town centre redevelopment scheme. Market Walk, as it's called.'

Manningbird put up his hand to an artificial-sounding cough.

'I've, er . . . well, as it happens, someone was talking to me about it only yesterday.'

'Well, the allegation is that Mr Bullock was taking money from the developers.'

'From Mr Kingswood?'

'Quite possibly,' said Rutter with a little smile. 'Although my information doesn't detail the exact source of the money. You see, it's certainly true that Mr Bullock was active in pushing the scheme forwards, but one always attributed his enthusiasm to motives that were entirely political. Partnership between public and private sectors. A matter of belief and ideology, not personal gain.'

They paused while the secretary, smiling and sycophantic, brought in the coffee on a round tin tray with a picture of foaming beer glasses almost erased by years of friction with municipal cups and mugs. Manningbird gratefully lowered his nose into the sweetish steam and sipped noisily.

'Ah, that's better,' he gasped. 'Lovely. Right, then – let's not beat about the bush: who's making these allegations, how much money are we talking about, and how was it done?'

'I was told in confidence, but I've advised my informant to try to obtain the documentary proof with a view to making a formal complaint to the police. At this stage I can't reveal the name.'

Manningbird grunted, his smile less patient.

'As for the money, I'm told a total of two or three hundred thousand pounds. Paid in several instalments to a numbered Swiss bank account held by Mr Bullock.'

Manningbird raised his eyebrows and nodded, holding his coffee mug on his knees with both hands, as if trying to warm them.

'Do you believe the allegations to be true? I mean, knowing what you know of the people involved and the business of the council?'

Rutter clamped his lips together and gave a little snort, looking contemplatively out at the nearby buildings and the bright, overcast sky.

'It must be said that there have always been rumours that the relationship with the developers might have been a little too close. I know my chief planning officer always had his reservations. But no one ever produced any proof.'

'And there still isn't any actual proof, from what you say.'

'No, but there might be soon.'

Manningbird swigged off the last of his coffee and leaned forward with a grunt to put the mug on the desk.

'All right,' he said. 'Supposing it is true, what bearing would it have on Mr Bullock's murder?'

'Ah, you say murder, Mr Manningbird. But I've been thinking hard about this, and the possibility has crossed my mind that Mr Bullock knew that these irregular payments were about to be made public by my informant. He may also have been under pressure from the developers because of the way the recession has hit the Market Walk scheme.'

'So you're suggesting suicide. A man who knew the shit was about to hit the fan.'

'Your phrase, not mine, Superintendent. But yes, I would have thought suicide must be at least a possibility. After all, his business is property and it's no secret that the market has hit a disastrous patch. You see, there was extra pressure on him because of the draft policy document his group had just approved. He wanted to cut services to keep the poll tax down for political reasons, and the price exacted by the rest of the group was cutting out the planned rental of the Market Walk offices as well.'

'Yes – my colleagues have been hearing about that from Mr Pilkington as well. In effect, Mr Bullock was going back on his undertaking to Mr Kingswood? And Kingswood wouldn't be very pleased?'

'Exactly. And if the leader knew anyway that a financial connection was about to be revealed . . . '

Rutter let his voice tail off as Manningbird heaved himself to his feet, shoved his fat hands in his trouser pockets and walked to the window for a brief study of the car park below. In the nearby side streets, several shopkeepers were leaning in doorways waiting for customers.

'It's a nice idea, Mr Rutter,' he said, not turning round. 'It would certainly get everyone off the hook. But I'm afraid it doesn't fit with the medical evidence. The fatal blow was a thump on the side of the head with a blunt instrument – not very easy to inflict that kind of thing on yourself, unless you're some kind of contortionist. All the injuries sustained by the fall into the quarry were sustained after death. Quite a long time after, in fact.'

'Ah,' said Rutter, nodding, suddenly confused. 'Of course, yes, the post-mortem. I wasn't aware of the findings – on Saturday, was it?'

'Yes.' Manningbird turned round and looked at Rutter, who was leaning protectively over the unopened file on his desk. Manningbird's look was long and speculative.

'In fact,' he said, 'there are a couple of paragraphs in some of the papers today about Professor Rutter confirming that Mr Bullock was killed before he was dropped in the quarry. But even if he'd gone over the edge alive we'd have to ask whether he jumped or was pushed.'

'Yes, yes, of course. I just know that Mr Bullock was quite a private man, in spite of being a vocal public figure. Might have been bottling up his tension . . . anyway, Superintendent, I thought it my duty to pass on this information to you. It only came to me last week.'

Manningbird rested his buttocks against the window sill, gripping it with his podgy fists, and put his head on one side, like a quizzical dog.

'Disappointed, are you, Mr Rutter?' he asked lightly.

'What do you mean?' asked Rutter, sharply.

'That it's not suicide, that's what I mean.'

Rutter leant back in his chair and shook his head, smiling ruefully.

'I don't know which is worse for the reputation of the borough, Superintendent – suicide or murder. You probably remember that one of our Liberal Democrat members did away with himself not so long ago. That caused a fair amount of scandal – not to mention one of the by-elections which brought the Conservatives back to power under Mr Bullock. But either way, we can't bring poor Mr Bullock back. I suppose what concerns me more is this allegation of corruption.'

'Which could be highly defamatory of Mr Kingswood.'

'Indeed – that is, if Mr Kingswood is the source of the finance.'

'On the other hand, it gives him something of a motive, eh?'

'How do you mean?'

'Bullock let him down rather badly. The development's up shit creek, not to put too fine a point on it, and now the council's not even going to rent the offices. You know they were due to have lunch together on Thursday?'

'Really?' Rutter suddenly seemed more animated, and his green eyes glittered behind the thick lenses. 'No, I certainly didn't know that.'

'Not hard to guess what would be on the agenda, eh? A bollocking for Mr Bullock. Give me my money back, that sort of thing.'

'Yes, yes, I suppose so,' said Rutter breathlessly, his first and second fingers doing a trill on the little purple line of his scar. 'That is, if it really is Kingswood. But you don't think, surely . . . '

'I don't necessarily think anything at this stage, chief executive,' said Manningbird mildly, returning to his chair and sitting down. 'But we've got to look up all the avenues. Turn over all the stones. Look at all the slimy things underneath.'

They sat looking at each other for a few seconds, thoughts flitting through their eyes, both unsure whether to push the conversation further. Then Rutter bent to return the file to his drawer, and Manningbird banged his palms on his knees and stood up.

'Well, we'll be seeing Mr Kingswood, naturally,' he said. 'So let us know if your, er, informant comes up with the goods. And we'll check it out with Mr Bullock's business colleagues – they might know what was going on.'

Rutter pushed his glasses back up his nose, and an artificial smile twisted his little bird-like mouth.

'Best of luck, Superintendent. By the way, your people were here first thing to start interviewing everyone about what they saw on Thursday – d'you want to have a word with them before you go?'

'Have they interviewed you yet?'

'Er, no, I've arranged to go down at eleven. I wanted to get this little confidential conversation out of the way first. The only other person who knows what I've told you is Mr Pilkington, who's taken over as council leader *pro tem*. Anyway, there we are – let me show you out.'

Manningbird shook Rutter's hand at the head of the main staircase and walked slowly down, running his hand along the smooth oak banister and noticing a new-looking security camera perched high in one corner of the entrance hall, like a vulture on a wall. He nodded at the permed woman and stepped out into the growing warmth, screwing up his eyes to tiny points against the brightness of the sky. All the urgency of his walk to the town hall had drained away, and he thrust his hands into his baggy pockets and shambled off towards the High Street, looking thoughtfully at the pavement. His route took him away from the police station, past the plate glass and cash machines of the building societies and the 'to let' signs of the shops closing under the weight of the recession. As he waited for the traffic lights to change, he looked up and saw the renovated façade of the old covered market, surrounded by the new town centre development like some lumpy old ornament in a crush of flashy knick-knacks.

The block to the right was fronted by hoardings advertising 'modern office and retail environments' at special low rents, and the one to the left which the council had intended to occupy was sealed off at street level with a wall of boards covered with peeling notices of rock concerts and 'Stuff the Poll Tax' posters. Stretched between two vacant first floor windows was a banner reading: 'Working for Beechley – a new partnership between the borough council and Kingswood Properties.'

Manningbird turned away from the scene with a little snort which seemed to bring him out of his torpor. Turning suddenly up a side street, he ignored a woman in a beret who was shaking a tin for the blind, looked craftily around him, and stepped into a phone box. He pulled a coin from one pocket and a diary from the other, dialled, and hunched forward over the receiver.

'Derek? Bryan here.'

Manningbird put his hand over the mouthpiece for a moment and stole a quick look round the handful of shoppers in the narrow street. A stooping pensioner trailing a tattered brown trolley stared back at him mournfully, and Manningbird turned brusquely away and continued talking, fast and quietly.

'Listen, Derek, the chief executive's on to some idea that you've been bunging Bullock over this town centre job. What? No, no proof, but he reckons he might get it. Something about a Swiss bank account he had. Thought I'd better let you know, give you a bit of time. What? No, look, if he was on the level he wouldn't be passing it on like this, would he? And if I'd tried him he might have clammed up. Anyway, I thought I'd tell you in case we can't talk tonight. What? No, like I told you yesterday, there's someone been blackmailing Bullock. We're hoping to pull the bastard in today and pin it on him. Chief exec. knows nothing about that yet. And by the way, it might not be me coming to see you tomorrow – might look bad. OK? OK, better go. See you later.'

Manningbird eased his bulky body out of the phone box and walked off down the street, clearing his throat self-consciously and reaching under the tail of his jacket to hitch up his drooping trousers. At the first junction he passed a pub, glanced up at the sign and did a brief double-take when he saw it was called the Square and Compasses. He checked his watch, found it was just gone eleven, and strolled happily through the glass-panelled door into the dim interior, like a refugee suddenly discovering a club of compatriots.

Chapter Fifteen

Monday, 12.30 p.m.

When Manningbird got back to the incident room, fortified by a couple of large Scotches, he informed Jim Duncan it was time they got round to see Bullock's business partner. Duncan scribbled the phone number on a piece of paper for him, and Manningbird sat down and lifted the phone. He dialled with the blunt end of a pencil, and then leaned back and used the sharp end to probe gently into one ear, an expression of agonized pleasure on his lumpy features.

He was put through immediately to Nigel Damson, who'd been expecting to hear from the police and would be only too delighted to see them in his office at 4 o'clock. He'd look forward to it, would be only too happy to give them all the assistance he could; but in the mean time, since they were talking, he had a complaint to make. It might not sound very important, but it just might have some bearing on the case of his partner's most distressing and unfortunate murder. At the very least, it concerned unacceptable behaviour in a public place.

'OK, Mr Damson, what is it?' growled Manningbird, examining the yellow-black stodge on the point of the pencil with a mixture of triumph and disgust.

'I'm afraid it's about a Mr Steve Ditchley, who received a certain amount of publicity at the time of the poll tax riot,' said the voice at the other end. Nigel Damson's vowels were artificially acute and modulated, and he pronounced Ditchley's name as if its owner was an unmentionable object one would pick up by the corner with finger and thumb and hold at arm's length.

'Ditchley?' said Manningbird. 'Mm. He's already been mentioned to us – the shop steward or whatever they call it, nearly got done for offensive weapon?'

When Manningbird spoke Ditchley's name, Duncan looked up and gestured eagerly, lifting the black cartridge of a videotape off his desk and waving it at him. Manningbird gave him an irritated glare and turned away to listen to Damson.

'I happened to be in my office late on Saturday night, catching up with a few things, when Mr Ditchley turned up outside the windows, somewhat the worse for wear. Rat-arsed, I believe would be the popular term for it. Recognized the great yobbo by his pony-tail and earrings – I ask you, whatever next? Anyway, I was sitting quietly at one of the desks, and for a moment I thought he'd just stopped to have a look at the properties on display, you know, window-shopping, that sort of thing. Then I realized the bugger was peeing. Can you believe it? Peeing on our bloody wall! There was a great cloud of steam rising up!'

'Disgraceful behaviour, I agree,' said Manningbird, his voice serious but his thin lips sliding into a grin. 'Far too much public urination these days.'

'I'm glad to hear you agree. Anyway, that was bad enough in itself – quite possibly amounts to criminal damage, given the corrosive nature of the stuff. He'd probably had about ten pints of lager. But that's only the beginning of it. The bugger then seems to go into a sort of trance for a while, standing there with his organ on display, and finally he looks up at the sign and points at it and shouts something.'

'What did he shout, Mr Damson?' asked Manningbird, through a small yawn. ' "Up the workers, property is theft", something like that?'

'What? No, no, nothing like that. It was more like "Good riddance, you Tory bastard." What d'you think of that, eh?'

Manningbird grunted, leaned forward, and scrawled the phrase on his notepad with the besmirched pencil, which left sticky yellowish traces around the writing.

'Very interesting, Mr Damson. Anything else?'

'Anything else? That's enough, isn't it?'

'Far too much, by the sound of it. What I mean is, did he heave a brick through the window? Did he leave his organ on display? Or did he just move on?'

'Well, he, er, moved on. Staggered might be a better word for it. Deserved to get run down crossing the road, but unfortunately there wasn't very much traffic around at the time. Disappeared towards those God-awful council estates off the London Road.'

'All right, Mr Damson. We'll have a word with Mr Ditchley when we see him. And we'll see you this afternoon.'

Manningbird put the receiver down and asked Jim Duncan vengefully why he wasn't able to make a simple phone call without other police officers waving and grinning at him like lunatics. The mellowing effects of the Scotch were wearing off rapidly.

123

'Sorry, sir. It's just that the name of Ditchley was a bit of a coincidence – I've just dug out that tape of the poll tax riot three months ago.'

'This must be the one Mr Pilkington was going on about to Judy and Colin yesterday – how the hell would he come to know about it?'

Duncan shrugged. 'Got a wide airing at the time of the riot, I suppose. Anyway, if you'd like to watch a dirty video, just step this way.'

Manningbird grunted, got to his feet, and followed Duncan's lean form to a dusty little room along the corridor. Duncan closed the blinds, put the tape in a video machine, and pressed the start button.

'Kill the poll tax! Kill the pigs! Kill the bloody Tories!'

The chant was fizzy and poorly recorded, but its words were clear enough, repeated time after time by the front line of placard-waving demonstrators pushing up against the metal barriers and the line of police in front of the town hall. The picture, taken in the twilight of orange street lamps, jazzed around the TV screen with unexpected lurches of focus and fuzzy surges of red and green. Suddenly a yelling crew-cut youth in a dark jacket could be seen lifting the wooden shaft of a placard and hurling it like a spear towards the police lines. It sailed in a slow arc, gleaming suddenly as it passed under a lamp, and fell in the police lines, hitting an officer on the shoulder and sending him lurching backwards into the arms of colleagues. There was a sudden joyful crescendo in the shouting.

'That fucking scumbag's in court next month, thanks to this little home movie,' said Jim Duncan softly. 'Any luck he'll get six months. Now, look out for our friend Ditchley.'

The chant on the tape was faltering as the focus of the crowd began to change. Several protestors began yelling and pointing, and there was a sudden rush away from the town hall steps. The camera swivelled downwards and caught the flashing light on top of a police car turning into the street alongside the town hall. As it did so, the people at the front could be seen more clearly, and among them was Steve Ditchley, face contorted and shouting, pony-tail swinging round the shoulders of a padded jacket buttoned protectively up to the neck. The old chant died away and a new one took over as a big estate car – John Bullock's Mercedes – glided in front of the camera towards the rear entrance of the town hall. As it turned, there was a glimpse through the windscreen of Dorothy Bullock holding tight to the steering-wheel and John Bullock, impassive and immobile, in the passenger seat.

'Just watch Ditchley's lips,' muttered Duncan. The legs of Manningbird's plastic chair grated on the lino as he leant closer, his wart-surrounded eyes glittering in the half-light filtering through the blinds.

'Bull-ock!' It was a slow sing-song, a high note followed by a low note.

'We want you!' The phrase was threatening and mocking, a low note, a drawn-out high one, and a low one again, with some of the demonstrators jabbing their fingers to emphasize each syllable.

'Dead!' The word came hard, tight and louder, and Ditchley's mouth could be seen barking it out with a greater bare-toothed vehemence than all the youths around him with their high-laced boots, their nose rings and their tufted hair. The chant was repeated several times, then faded rapidly as the crowd's attentions switched to a surging, bucking battle on the right of the picture between a knot of furious demonstrators and a small group of police trying to drag away a black-clad girl.

Duncan reached out to switch the tape off, then went to the window and fiddled with the cords of the blind, letting in more light.

'That's the bit that counts,' he said, leaning against the wall and folding his arms. 'The rest is pretty much more of the same, with a bit of a finale where they all go rushing off down the High Street smashing up the shops, with not a uniform in sight – another triumph for the Metropolitan Police.'

'Ditchley should have been done on the evidence of that tape,' said Manningbird. 'I'd have done it, if I'd been on this division.'

'That's right.'

'So why wasn't he?'

Duncan shrugged.

'Unless we'd done all the others, it would have looked like victimization. The photo of him in the paper was more serious because it was published and complaints came of it, but that was ditched in the end. Political, really.'

'Ditchley got any form?'

'Two convictions from demos in the early eighties – obstruction and behaviour likely to cause a breach of the peace.'

'Mm. Nothing to impress a magistrate with. Well, you interviewed him over the demo, and this Pilkington seems to reckon he's a candidate – what d'you reckon?'

'Nasty piece of work. No doubt he hated Bullock. Just possible he came across Bullock somewhere later on Thursday and lost his rag . . .'

'And then pissed on his office on the way home two nights later? Just to round it off nicely?'

Duncan grinned complicitly at Manningbird's sceptical tone, and shrugged his muscular shoulders again.

'All right, I know. But he's worth a call, if only because if anyone so much as breaks wind in Beechley borough council, Ditchley tends to get to hear about it. He's only round at Churchill Park – I checked.'

'Right,' said Manningbird, his voice wheezing as he pushed himself up off the little chair. 'We'll stop in after lunch, on the way to see Mr Nigel lah-di-dah Damson.'

The news from the West End about Judy and Colin making an arrest dominated the lunchtime talk in the Cat and Mouse, round the corner from the police station. The consensus among half a dozen young detective constables from the inquiry team was that Colin had been a prat to get himself hospitalized but would recover quickly enough with Judy at his bedside, holding part of his anatomy. As for the arrest, they were torn between euphoria at the prospect of a result and disappointment that they hadn't been in on the action. Jim Duncan was sitting at a table at the back with Manningbird, drinking orange juice and trying to consolidate the relationship.

'Just look at them all,' he said wonderingly, like a zoo visitor surveying the ape house. 'Jumping to fucking conclusions left, right and centre. Why don't they wait for some solid evidence?'

'My view entirely, Jim,' said Manningbird, finishing his Scotch and smacking his lips. 'Just getting a cough from this blackmailer wouldn't be enough if he changed his mind and pleaded not guilty in court – not these days, anyway. We need a witness, some decent forensic – bit of a breakthrough somewhere. C'mon, let's go and see this Ditchley character.'

It was Manningbird's second big walk of the day, and he set an ambling pace along to the town hall, which he gave a malevolent stare, down the High Street again, and past Market Walk towards Churchill Park. The streets were busier than they had been mid-morning, but there were queues at the sandwich shops and empty seats in the wine bars and restaurants. People looked stressed and weary under the pewter-coloured sky; there had been hot weather for a week now, and the air was thick and humid. Duncan chatted on, describing his role in recent cases and disparaging women detectives, but Manningbird gave briefer answers as his breath grew shorter, and the conversation petered out. After ten minutes they passed under a wrought-iron arch into the park, half a square mile of green space and begonia beds covering one of the gentle early foothills of the Downs. They strolled past the tennis courts, where Duncan took an intense interest in two girls in shorts hitting slow, looping shots to each other; Manningbird took a greater interest in the bowling green, where pensioners in long white trousers sent their spheres of dark wood curving gently across the perfect grass.

Behind the white-painted wooden pavilion was the park supervisor's office, where they found Ditchley sitting with his boots up on a desk, finishing a mug of tea and a newspaper full of vinegary chips. He looked at them standing in the doorway, froze for a second, and then continued his meal with exaggerated normality.

'Ah, the constabulary,' he said sarcastically, putting his head back and lowering a long, pale chip into his mouth. 'I knew it was only a matter of time.'

Duncan took a slow look round the office, taking in the kettle, the tin tray of mugs and sugar packets, the toaster, the two old armchairs, the tattered 'coal not dole' posters from five years before. There was even a little radio tuned at low volume to a pop station.

'Busy, are you, Mr Ditchley?' he asked neutrally, leaning on the lower half of the split door. 'Urgent trade union business?'

'Nah,' said Ditchley, screwing up the soggy chip paper and tossing it with casual accuracy into a bin in the corner. 'Lunch break. Have yours in the pub, did you?'

'This is Superintendent Manningbird, Mr Ditchley,' said Duncan, his Glaswegian accent hardening. 'He's in charge of the investigation into the murder of Mr Bullock, and we'd like to have a word with you. If you can spare the time.'

'Can't help you, guv,' said Ditchley, picking up his mug with one hand and opening the *Daily Mirror* with the other. 'Don't know nuffin about it.'

Duncan and Manningbird looked at each other impassively for a moment, then Duncan reached inside the door and slid the bolt back. He strolled into the office and gently pulled the newspaper off Ditchley's knees while Manningbird followed him in and lowered himself gratefully into one of the armchairs.

'All the same,' said Duncan, folding the newspaper carefully and hitching one buttock on to the desk next to Ditchley's unpolished boots. 'Perhaps you could spare us a few minutes. Unless, of course, you'd prefer to come down to the station.'

The two stared hard at each other for a few seconds, a streetwise mongrel facing up to a lean and eager terrier. It was the mongrel's eyes which slipped away first.

'All right,' said Ditchley, indifferently. 'What you want to know?'

'We've heard from a couple of people at the town hall that you had a shouting match with Mr Bullock a short while before he disappeared last Thursday.'

Ditchley gave his shoulders a quick up-and-down twitch, and reached up to give his pony-tail a casual flick.

'We had an exchange of views on the steps, if that's what you mean,' he said. 'Par for the course when you've got scabs crossing picket lines. Feelings running high over the cuts.'

'So where'd you spend Thursday afternoon and evening?'

'Easy: demo, Labour Party office, Pig and Whistle, home. Witnesses all the way.'

Duncan slid off the desk, stuck his hands in his pockets and paced slowly up and down. There was a sudden rattling of machinery, and a tractor dragging a mowing machine sped past twenty yards from the door, throwing up a shower of chopped grass.

'Even on the way home?' asked Duncan, stopping behind Ditchley and studying the dull, ill-washed pony-tail, secured with a thick rubber band. Ditchley coughed and took his feet off the desk.

'Ten-minute walk. Can't do a murder and dump a body in ten minutes.'

'Who said anything about doing a murder, Mr Ditchley? That's your idea. I was just wondering if you stopped for a piss.'

Ditchley swivelled his head to look up at Duncan, his eyes suddenly confused. Duncan gave him a sadistic little grin, like a schoolmaster baiting a dim pupil.

'Because,' Duncan continued, 'that's what you did on Saturday, wasn't it? We have a complaint about it.'

'Complaint? Who from?'

'From Mr Bullock's partner, if you must know. Doesn't like you pissing on his windows.'

'I didn't piss on his windows,' muttered Ditchley, picking his fingers and looking down at the scruffy offcuts of red carpet on the floor. 'I pissed on the wall. Anyway, what the fuck's he doing there at bleeding midnight?'

Manningbird suddenly interrupted from the depths of the old armchair, his voice thick and gravelly.

'What we really want you to tell us, Mr Ditchley, is whether you saw anything when you stopped off for a piss there on Thursday at midnight. Cast your mind back – Thursday, not Saturday.'

Ditchley grabbed the arms of his chair and turned it round to face

Manningbird, who looked calmly back at him, squat and grey.

'What you mean?' he said hesitantly.

'Did you see Mr Bullock, perhaps?'

'Nah, course I didn't.' Ditchley's voice was higher now, his pasty complexion pinking up.

'Or his car? Big Merc? In that parking space at the side?'

Ditchley threw his head back and gave a sudden little yap of a laugh, which reverberated off the wooden roof above them.

'Come on, Mr Ditchley,' said Manningbird softly. 'We're not trying to trap you. We're just trying to work out Mr Bullock's movements.'

'Like fuck you're not trying to trap me,' his voice low and suspicious. 'Just like you weren't trying to fit me up after the poll tax demo. I can't remember if there was any car there or not, right? I'd had a few drinks.'

Duncan gave an impatient tut and turned away. The rattling mower passed in front of the doorway again, its teenage driver hanging on desperately to the steering-wheel of the tractor, like a rider on a runaway horse.

'Same sort of time, though, was it?' asked Manningbird. 'Coming up to midnight?'

'Yeah, must have been.'

Ditchley was regaining his bounce and defiance, and seemed disappointed when Manningbird thanked him, rose from his chair and headed for the door. Duncan was already outside on the asphalt path, peering round the back of the building to the tennis courts where the girls had been playing. Manningbird paused in the doorway, his bulk shutting out most of the daylight, and gave Ditchley a final look.

'Stop pissing on other people's property,' he said wearily. 'Or we'll do you for it, see?'

Ditchley grinned silently as Manningbird waddled off down the path. The air was laden with the fresh scent of the new-mown grass, but the girls had gone, and Duncan had his hands in his pockets, pushing bits of loose gravel and dust into a little pile with his foot.

'Lying bastard,' he said, looking up at Manningbird. 'I wouldn't be surprised if he was pissing on the Merc when Bullock comes out and finds him. Argument, fight, Ditchley drives the body up to the quarry.'

Manningbird's face went into a sudden gasping contortion, and he pulled out a grey handkerchief just in time to capture an explosive sneeze. Duncan jumped back a pace.

'Sorry, Jim,' gasped Manningbird. 'All this bloody pollen about the place. That's why I never mow the lawn. Nice idea, I grant you, but who's jumping to conclusions now? And where's it leave Bullock all afternoon?'

'Long lunch with the property man?'

'Nah – I had a word with him on the phone. Bullock didn't show for the lunch. And he wouldn't have missed the council meeting.'

'Didn't show for the lunch?' said Duncan, raising his eyebrows in surprise. 'You never let on.'

'Yeah, well, we'll get the full story in the morning when we go and see this Kingswood bloke.'

There was a call from behind them, and they turned to see Ditchley's grinning head protruding from the doorway of the little office, his pony-tail swinging slowly behind his head.

''Ere,' he called. 'You sorted out that other body yet? The one in a barrow?'

'What d'you know about that?' asked Duncan, walking slowly back towards him. Ditchley's grin spread triumphally.

'Enough. What's it worth?'

Duncan lifted a threatening white forefinger and was about to thrust it under Ditchley's nose when he stepped back into the office and raised both palms in surrender.

'All right, all right,' he said mockingly. 'I'll give you this one for free. You see that geezer on the tractor, tearing about like Nigel Mansell?'

The officers turned to watch the tractor do a rapid U-turn at the far end of the park and head back towards them in a green halo of flying grass.

'Him and his mate,' said Ditchley. 'Fart-arsing around.'

'What d'you mean?' asked Duncan, narrow-eyed.

'Straight up. The two of them got so pissed they couldn't make it to the demo. One of 'em falls down in the street, and the other comes over here, gets his barrow, and carts him home in it. That Paki can't tell the difference between a stiff and a pisshead.'

The two officers looked at each other uncertainly, then back at Ditchley. Duncan cocked his neatly trimmed head.

'You winding us up, Ditchley? Because if you are . . .'

'Would I wind you up? Stop the little bugger and ask him.'

Duncan glanced uncertainly at Manningbird, and the two of them began crossing the freshly mown grass towards the tractor as it raced towards them. Ditchley watched them go with a smile of delighted malice, then suddenly jabbed a finger towards their retreating backs.

'I'm way ahead of you blokes,' he shouted. 'Always will be.'

But his words were drowned by a series of seismic sneezes from Manningbird and the roaring clatter of the mower, which only subsided when Duncan stepped forward like a traffic warden at a busy junction and held up his hand.

Chapter Sixteen

Monday, 2 p.m.

'They're all bloody Freemasons,' said Colin weakly. 'On the square, on the level, taught to be cautious, however you want to put it. That's what I'm not supposed to tell you. That's why I was in a filthy mood.'

He was lying on a trolley in a cubicle of the casualty department of University College Hospital, propped on a pile of crisp pillows with a square white dressing on his left cheek. The green curtain pulled across the entrance made the cubicle cosy and intimate, despite the oxygen respirator hanging on the wall and the kidney bowls and packets of sterile supplies on the locker. Judy was half-sitting on a tall stool next to the trolley, one foot on the ground, with her hands tucked into the pockets of her jeans. She was smiling at him and he was looking back at her sentimentally, like a loyal dog repenting after chasing a cat.

'What d'you mean, all of them?'

'Well, the Fat Man for a start – Bryan. I always knew he was one. But when I told him that Bullock's lunch date was Derek Kingswood, he started acting all careful, so I knew something was up. In fact, I'm pretty sure he and Kingswood are in the same lodge.'

'So that would be why Bryan's in no hurry to get round and interview Derek Kingswood?'

'That's right. Between you and me, I think he's been giving him advance warning. Which is well out of order.'

'And what about Bullock?'

'Well, I'm just assuming. He was doing business with Kingswood – rather more than just business, in fact, if we're to believe fancy-pants Pilkington. So it's odd-on they're rolling up their trouser legs together as well.'

'Well, if Bullock was one too, it confirms my theory about his wife not telling us everything. But why didn't we find any of the gear at his house? I mean, they prance around in gloves and pinnies and chant things out of little books, don't they? All about tongues being cut out and buried below low-water mark?'

The vision gave her a spasm of amusement, and she put her head back and laughed. Colin's eyes travelled attentively over her pale blonde hair, her grey eyes and boyish features, the hints of dimples as she smiled.

'Dunno,' he said. 'Maybe those two DCs who did the upstairs didn't search very well. Or maybe he keeps his stuff at work instead. Some people do – want to keep it away from their family.'

Judy controlled her laughing, pushed herself off the stool and walked slowly down to the curtain. Somewhere on the other side, a man with a Geordie accent was complaining loudly that he'd been there two hours, hadn't seen a doctor yet, and could bloody well die, for all they cared. Judy turned back to the trolley and stood over Colin, looking at him teasingly, lips pursed and eyes narrowed.

'You know,' she said. 'You seem to know an awful lot about this Freemasonry business. Who's in, who's out. I thought it was all supposed to be under wraps.'

He gave her a sheepish grin and held out his hand, like a child needing help crossing the road. Judy looked at it wide-eyed, putting her fingers to her throat and grimacing in mock horror.

'Oh no! Not the secret handshake! Spare me!'

He had already turned his eyes away and started to withdraw the hand when she reached out suddenly and took hold of it. She began kneading it gently, relishing the dry warmth of the skin and the mobility of the bones underneath. His hair was curly and dishevelled against the white pillow, and his shirt had the top two buttons undone, exposing the white bump of one collarbone. The man outside had stopped warning of his imminent death, leaving just a faint bustle from the main casualty area outside. The cubicle felt separate, safely screened off, and the subject of Freemasons suddenly evaporated.

'Like a bedroom in here, isn't it?' she said softly. He nodded, and she watched his Adam's apple move as he swallowed heavily.

'How's your head?' she asked.

He leaned forward and turned round to show her the small shaved area where another dressing covered the two stitches put in to close the wound in his scalp.

'Aches a bit,' he said, subsiding on the pillows again.

'You'll have to wear a hairpiece,' she said, still kneading his hand.

'No,' he whispered, like a man in a confessional. 'I'll have it all cut, like a skinhead.'

She was leaning closer to him, a slight flush climbing her neck from under her pale sweatshirt, when the curtain suddenly swished back and a young Asian doctor breezed in, brandishing a sheaf of X-rays at them. Judy snatched her hand back and stepped away from the cot.

'Well, everything seems to be intact,' the doctor said cheerfully. 'Bones all in one piece. Good thing really, we don't have any spare beds at the moment.'

'So I can go?' asked Colin, who was blushing.

'If you like,' said the doctor, fiddling with a long row of pens in his breast pocket and looking at the pair of them with amused interest. 'Don't get up to anything too strenuous for a day or two, though, eh? And go to your doctor or the nearest casualty if you feel dizzy or faint, anything like that.'

Colin swung his legs over the side of the trolley, and Judy noticed that the nail of his big toe was protruding through one of his blue socks. She muttered something about giving him some privacy to get dressed, and followed the doctor out into the casualty room, where a bedraggled woman with a face as white as flour was being wheeled past in a chair. The man who had been threatening to die had fallen asleep with his head on a table, his open mouth revealing a set of orange incisor teeth.

Judy sat on a plastic chair, feeling confused and foolish and remembering all the reasons why she shouldn't be having anything to do with Colin Borden. He was married, he was a colleague, and behind the boyish ways and crinkly smile there were things she didn't like. There was his cynicism and self-dislike, which squared poorly with the Christianity; there was his lack of judgement over the arrest, and now there was the Masonic connection. She told herself to put him down, that he wouldn't be good for her. If she wasn't careful, he'd be telling her what a lovely mother she'd make.

The drive back to Beechley started in silence, Judy concentrating on her driving and Colin staring out of the window at the whey-faced office workers on the hot pavements. But when they were crossing Waterloo Bridge, with its sudden open vistas of grand buildings and the busy waterway, Judy turned to him.

'Were you one of them, then?' she asked.

'You guessed it,' he said grimly, not looking at her.

'But you left?'

'Yes.' He gave her a wry grin. 'Why d'you think I haven't been promoted for so long?'

'Why d'you leave, then?'

He studied the dashboard and began tracing hieroglyphics on it with the little finger of his free hand, like a child being pressed to describe something humiliating that had happened in the playground.

'It was getting too much,' he said. 'Too much time, too much money, too much mumbo-jumbo. Never saw my family. But the worst thing was, I began to think it was actually evil. You know, they have this ritual which mimics resurrection, where they lay you down on a shroud and the master of the lodge raises you up with a third-degree handshake.'

'Sounds weird. Repulsive.'

'It's blasphemous,' he said vehemently, turning to face her, the colour pumping back into his pallid face, his eyes screwed up and anxious. 'It's only a short step away from devil worship. It was after I went through that ceremony that I began to feel I was possessed. I was actually having nightmares about the devil, waking up in cold sweats . . .'

'So it isn't just the mugging and raping of old women that keeps you in the clutches of the Church?' said Judy. 'There are all these Satanists in aprons after you, waving their spirit levels, or whatever?'

'Well, I left out the Masons when I was talking to you in the pub yesterday. I suppose the old habit of keeping it quiet dies hard.'

'Well, you're out of it now, that's the main thing,' said Judy.

'That's right. The thing that gets me, looking back, is that they're all weak characters, all looking for something to prop them up. Makes them feel big, being part of this little in-crowd with the silly handshakes and the nasty oaths. And there they all are, giving each other jobs and contracts and pretending it's all just harmless fun.'

'Isn't joining the Christians just another version of the same sort of thing?' said Judy. 'We're in the know, you're out in the cold?'

'It couldn't be more different, Judy,' he said, starting to shake his head but stopping immediately with a grimace of pain. 'Christianity's open to everyone – you've actually got to be pretty tough to proclaim it these days.'

'Well, your mates certainly take the piss out of you,' said Judy. 'But just wait till you proclaim that Ginger knocked you over with a carton of milk. Life among the hard men won't be worth living.'

Silence set in again as they toiled through Walworth and Camberwell, past the great soiled blocks of flats and the parades of cheap shops. Outside the magistrates' courts a lanky black youth sat on a wall and watched them pass with dead eyes, as if he knew who they were and would be seeing them later.

'Shall I take you home, then?' asked Judy, as they eventually climbed up Denmark Hill, out of the fume-filled claustrophobia of the Thames flatlands. 'Let the little wife tuck you up in bed?'

'No way,' said Colin vehemently. 'We're going to see Bullock's business partner on the way back. See what he knows about the worshipful brothers. And anything else, for that matter. Remember all that stuff from the widow about him being pissed off with Bullock, jealous of his house, all the rest of it?'

'Hang on a minute – what about Ginger? The van from West End Central will have him down at our nick pretty soon.'

'He can wait a couple of hours before we interview him. Give him time to get nicely in the mood.'

'Hadn't we better square it with the Fat Man?'

'Sod that,' said Colin smoothly, reaching out of the window and drumming on the roof with his fingers. 'There's enough squaring going on already. The Fat Man'll find out soon enough.'

He flashed Judy a reckless little grin, but she didn't smile back. It wasn't the first time she'd found feuds forming within an investigation, and she didn't want to get involved. It was like two gangs of boys wasting the whole playtime arguing about what game to play.

Monday, 3.30 p.m.

Judy turned the car on to the little square of asphalt next to the whitepainted offices of Bullock and Damson and squeezed into a space between a dark green Jaguar and a rusty Mini. Colin pulled the rearview mirror towards him to comb his hair and tie his tie. It was in mock-regimental blue and white stripes rather than the vivid splashes of colour favoured by the younger CID men. Judy took the comb from him and rearranged the hair at the back of his head to cover most of the dressing. She resisted the temptation to touch and pat his hair, and looked instead at the loosening flesh under his chin.

Colin had just started introducing himself when the young secretary with long blonde hair interrupted to say that Mr Damson was expecting them and they should go straight up to his office. He and Judy followed her through a door at the back and up a wide staircase. Damson was waiting for them at the top, wearing a dark blue suit and holding out his hand. He was a little man, about five foot six tall, with neat, almost fragile features. Judy noticed the vivid contrast between the darkness of his cheeks and the moist redness of his lips.

'Superintendent Manningbird?' asked Damson. He pronounced the *a* as an *e* and his tone was ingratiating, as if he hoped to earn a chunky commission by selling them a high-priced piece of property.

'Er, no,' said Colin, taking the hand and shaking it. 'I'm Inspector Borden, this is Detective Sergeant Best.'

Damson's smile faded as he eyed Colin's injured face and turned to Judy, shaking her hand hesitantly, as if he wasn't quite convinced a woman could be a detective.

'I see,' said Damson. 'It's just that Mr Manningbird gave me to understand he'd be along himself. Oh, well, you'd better come in.'

Damson's office was large and light, with a grey carpet and a big desk in dark wood. There was a conference table with a heavy glass top, and two reproduction Georgian bookcases with rows of red-backed books which looked as if they had been bought by the yard. Damson settled himself behind the desk and started fiddling with a silver paper knife, while Judy and Colin sat on padded chairs opposite him and asked him about Thursday. Bullock had been in the office briefly in the morning before walking to the town hall; the chief executive's secretary had rung mid-afternoon to say that Bullock was missing, and he'd rung Dorothy at six to say her husband's car was still outside the office.

'Tell me, Mr Damson,' said Colin. 'Is it true that Mr Bullock was spending an increasing amount of time on council business?'

Damson smiled sourly, holding the paper knife between thumb and finger and pushing the sharp tip gently into the palm of his other hand. It was a Turkish or Middle Eastern artefact, with elaborate Islamic designs engraved on the blade and handle.

'He was indeed,' said Damson.

'And that put a bigger burden on you? In the business?'

'You could say that.'

'Was that the cause of friction between you?'

The sour smile turned into a frown, and Damson hesitated. 'Friction's a bit of a strong word, perhaps.'

'And were there any other claims on Mr Bullock's time? Other than politics?'

'Not sure what you mean.'

'Was he a Freemason?'

Damson tossed the knife on to the blotter in front of him and laughed. The sound was a series of little explosions of contempt and cynicism. Judy and Colin glanced at each other and waited for his amusement to subside.

'You mean to say you didn't know? I would have thought his wife would have told you.'

'She didn't volunteer it,' said Colin. 'And we didn't suspect it at the time we saw her.'

'Mmm,' said Damson, nodding, as if savouring some private significance. 'Interesting.'

'Oh, yes? Why?'

Damson got up and walked towards the door, indicating with a jerk of his sleekly brushed head that they should follow him. Out on the landing he took a bunch of keys from his pocket and opened a door to a room which was the mirror image of the one they'd just left.

'John's office,' he said over his shoulder. 'I've kept it locked all along, in case you wanted to search it.'

'We do,' said Colin, following him in. 'Very thoughtful of you.'

While Damson's office had grey walls, pretentious prints of stately homes, and a green leather desk top, Bullock's office had magnolia walls, pretentious prints of racecourse scenes, and a red leather desk top. Otherwise the rooms seemed identical, and Judy remembered Dorothy Bullock describing her husband's efforts to make the partnership equal after the takeover of Damson's firm. The next thing she noticed was the small tape recorder lying on the blotter, with a line connected to the telephone receiver. Colin reached it first and picked it up, raising his eyebrows at her.

Damson, meanwhile, had bent over a cupboard under one of the bookcases and when he turned round he was holding up a small leather suitcase, like a chancellor about to present his budget to the nation.

'The box of tricks,' he announced sarcastically. 'Come back into my office and we'll investigate further.'

Damson laid the battered case on the thick glass of the conference table and snapped open the twin catches. The first thing they saw was a pair of immaculate white cloth gloves, which Damson took out and laid on the table. There followed an assortment of regalia: a small leather apron with rose-like designs on it, several medals and pendants inscribed with pictures of compasses, squares, levels and gavels. Last of all came some dark, heavily bound books, among them *The Masonic Year Book* and *A Treasury of Masonic Thought*.

'You ever been tempted by this stuff?' Colin asked Damson, pushing the objects around with a forefinger, like a man poking ashes with a stick.

'I'm a Catholic,' said Damson grimly. 'I'd be excommunicated.'

Judy picked up the apron, held it across her hips and minced down the room, as if on a catwalk.

'What d'you think, chaps?' she asked. 'Reckon they'd let me in to the lodge?'

At that moment the door opened and Manningbird appeared. He looked tense and agitated, and when he saw Judy with the apron stretched across her pelvis his face turned rapidly from grey to a dirty puce and horror appeared in his eyes. He began swaying and breathing heavily, like a man witnessing a dreadful sacrilege, and only his tight grip on the door handle seemed to prevent him falling.

'Ah, you must be Mr Manningbird,' said Damson jovially. 'Your colleagues and I were just talking about poor John's little hobby.'

'Hobby?' gasped Manningbird, outraged.

'Well, er, whatever you call it,' said Damson. 'I see you found your way up here all right.'

'They told me to come straight up,' said Manningbird, sticking a fat finger between collar and neck to ease his breathing.

Judy folded the apron, put it back on the table, and sat down demurely. Damson shook Manningbird's hand, then led him solicitously to a chair and left the room to get him a glass of water.

'What the fuck are you two doing here?' gasped Manningbird vehemently as Damson left the room.

'It was on our way back, Bryan,' said Colin calmly. 'We needed to know if Bullock was a Mason, and I'd say it was fairly clear that he was, wouldn't you?'

Colin gestured at the objects laid out on the table next to him, like the offerings at a jumble sale. Manningbird stared at him, then glanced nervously at Judy, his tongue darting out and moistening his thin grey lips.

'Yes, well, we'd better talk about that later,' he muttered. 'Profane ears.'

'Look, Judy's working on the inquiry, Bryan, and she knows, one, that Bullock and Derek Kingswood were Freemasons, and two, that allegations are being made about corruption.'

'That's as may be,' snapped Manningbird. 'But what we're investigating here is murder, not some wild allegations about backhanders in the borough council.'

'Who's to say the two aren't connected?' Colin's face was colouring, his fists balling. Judy was turning from one to the other, like a spectator at a tennis match.

'This blackmailer you've arrested, for one,' said Manningbird. 'He's the prime bloody candidate, and here you are wasting time on side issues like who's a Mason and who isn't.'

'Side issues?' Colin was shouting. 'Why are *you* here, then?'

There was a diplomatic cough from the doorway as Damson returned with the glass of water. Manningbird took a sip, his hands trembling so much he spilt some of it down his chin and tie. Damson walked back behind his desk and picked up the paperknife, staring at it with his lips pursed judiciously.

'I, er, couldn't help hearing you mention the relationship between

John and Derek Kingswood just now,' he said, looking hesitantly at them all across the yard-wide desk top.

'Well, it's just as well you did hear it,' said Manningbird feverishly, waving his tie like a tassel to dry it. 'Because it's been alleged to me – and I know it's far-fetched – that your partner may have been using a numbered Swiss bank account for certain dirty dealings. Perhaps you could help us scotch that one.'

Judy and Colin exchanged puzzled looks. Damson sat down, coughed, and looked out the window for a moment. Then he looked defiantly at the police officers, one after the other.

'Well, I couldn't prove it one way or the other,' he said. 'But I'm pretty sure he did have one. And since you mention Kingswood, it's my belief Kingswood was using the Swiss account to pay him off.'

Manningbird opened and closed his mouth silently, like a fish out of water. Colin put a question into the silence.

'How would he do that?' he asked. 'I mean, without the tax authorities knowing and so on?'

Damson's cherry lips took on a bitter smile.

'Hah!' he said. 'Easy. Kingswood's got a little outfit in France, calls it Deekay Europe. Flogs ruined farmhouses in Normandy to gullible yuppies. Shouldn't say that about property buyers, of course, but I'm afraid it's true. The money goes from the French company to the Swiss account, and no one in the UK is any the wiser.'

Manningbird, blotting beads of sweat from the warty skin around his eyes, had recovered enough for a quick comeback.

'Yes, well, Mr Damson,' he snapped. 'We do happen to know that you've got every motive to blacken Mr Bullock's reputation. You were none too pleased with him leaving you to run the business while he spent his time on politics. And then he bought the house you and your wife had your eye on.'

Damson's features turned from swarthy to a muddy scarlet. He jabbed the point of the paperknife into the blotter in front of it and twisted it, as if boring a hole in the desk.

'All right, I won't deny it,' he said, his voice unsteady. 'It's true that my wife was keen on the house. And if you ask me, John's Swiss account was used in buying that place.'

'What d'you mean?'

'I reckon he did a deal with the previous owner to drop the sale price by a ridiculous amount and pay at least a hundred and fifty thou. to him overseas. The vendor's company was going down and he needed to keep some capital out of reach of the creditors. He dropped the price paid in this country from £600,000 to £400,000. The difference was meant to be explained by the collapse in the property market, but you can't blame it for a drop as big as that. Fifty thousand, yes, but not two hundred.'

'I see what you mean,' said Colin. 'Listen, you sure these bank statements aren't in the safe here?'

Damson tossed the paperknife on the blotter, exasperated, and walked over to the window, where his body was silhouetted against the gunmetal sky, his face in shadow.

'Look,' he said. 'I know exactly what's in that bloody safe, and if those records were there I'd be the first to shove them in your hot little hands. I didn't like what was going on, one bit. But John was a clever operator.'

'Maybe he was. But someone was blackmailing him,' said Manningbird nastily. 'Now, you knew that too, didn't you, Mr Damson?'

Damson shrugged his narrow shoulders. His back was to the light, his face unreadable.

'Wouldn't surprise me,' he said. 'John had a lot of secrets.'

'Well, we've arrested the blackmailer,' said Manningbird decisively, standing up and pushing the knot of his tie up tightly again, 'And it's time we went and had a little chat with him. Come on, you two. There'll be some officers round later to search the office, Mr Damson – maybe your partner's tucked that file under the carpet.'

The other two followed him to the door. But Colin paused with his hand on the knob and turned back to Damson, head on one side, eyes half-closed.

'One last thing,' he said. 'You're the one who reported Mr Bullock's Mercedes still here at six o'clock. Think anyone else saw it at all?'

'I've no idea,' said Damson, his agitation all gone and his smooth manner restored. 'Maybe you should ask around.'

'We might just do that, Mr Damson. 'Bye for now.'

Colin grinned at him, and followed Manningbird and Judy down the blue-carpeted stairway, holding on to the mahogany banisters and moving more carefully than usual. Damson stood on the landing and watched them go, his eyes glittering and his hand jiggling the bunch of keys in his jacket pocket.

Chapter Seventeen

Monday, 7.30 p.m.

Martin Donovan was around forty years old, six foot two, and ginger-haired. His limbs were big and bony, and his movements were slow and laborious, as if joints were seizing up or his muscles couldn't manage the weight of his skeleton. His great rounded knees sprawled awkwardly off the little plastic chair, and he seemed to fill up most of the space in the interview room. Judy and Colin were sitting opposite him, and his glacier-green eyes stared at them, modulating between defiance and anxiety. A large uniformed constable was standing in the corner, his eyes fixed uneasily on Donovan's big pale hands, clasped together on the table. Judy watched them too, thinking they were what a strangler's hands would be like – clumsy, strong and unrelenting.

'So tell me how you made that recording,' asked Colin.

'You know how I made the bloody recording,' said Donovan, his Cockney voice sullen and tight. 'You had the floorboard up, didn't you?'

'I didn't get to see it myself,' said Colin, keeping his tone light and conversational. 'I was at the casualty department, having a carton of milk pulled out of my face.'

'Yeah, well, she saw it,' said Donovan, jerking his doorstep of a chin towards Judy and eyeing her unpleasantly. 'She can tell you all about it.'

'But I want it from you. The full story.'

Donovan fell silent, looking at his own fingers as they wrestled together, the big knuckles showing white and bloodless. After a few seconds he looked up at Colin and Judy with a pleading, abased expression; the gingery freckles on his face sat strangely on a background of skin the colour of raw liver.

'Look,' he said. 'I'll do you a deal. I'll give you the full story on the blackmail, you can do me for that, for assault, resisting arrest, anything you like. Only leave off the murder bit, OK? The geezer didn't show up. So I went home and sent the stuff to the papers. Simple. End of story.'

'Can't give you any guarantees, Martin.'

'Right, then.' Donovan leaned back, smacking the plastic table top with a palm the size of a plate and producing a little jump from the PC in the corner. 'I'm saying nothing. Not until I see a solicitor.'

'Duty solicitor's on his way, Martin, I told you that. He'll only tell you to co-operate and give us the truth.'

Donovan folded his arms defensively, his eyes sulky and his voice bitter.

'You aren't interested in the truth,' he said. 'You're just interested in stitching someone up for a quick result. Fucking coppers – I been through all this crap before.'

'Had a lot to do with coppers, have you, in your time?' Colin's tone was needling, designed to provoke. Judy looked at him warily, while Donovan looked at the floor, shaking his head as if all his lamentable expectations of police behaviour were being fulfilled. The ginger hair was dry and unruly, peppered with dandruff.

'Martin,' said Judy, leaning towards him and opening her hands. 'Just tell us the story, start to finish. We won't interrupt you, and you can go through it all again when the lawyer's here. We can't do fairer than that.'

Donovan eyed her cautiously while he thought about it. Judy looked steadily back at him, maintaining a guileless expression and trying not to remember how, that very morning, the same face had clenched and grimaced as the knife flashed back and forth beneath her nose. Donovan cleared his throat.

'OK if I smoke?' he asked.

Judy nodded. Colin passed him a crumpled red packet and a box of matches, and he lit up with heavy, fumbling fingers. Blue wisps floated upwards from the cigarette and grey clouds began escaping through Donovan's stained front teeth, as if an overstressed boiler was gently letting off steam. Judy quickly broke out two cassettes, put them in the recording machine, and explained the taping system to Donovan. He nodded, and after a few more hungry drags on the cigarette he began to talk.

'I moved in with Mandy last year, all right? I wasn't working that much, a bit here and a bit there, and it soon seems to me there's a lot of men calling at the flat downstairs. Anyway, wasn't long before I twigged – the bird's on the game, like a lot of the others round that area. You can hear her down there with the punters sometimes, moaning and groaning and cracking whips and what have you, talking filth. Bloody sickening, it is. I hit on the idea of following a couple of the punters, seeing who they were, like, whether there was any mileage in it. So Bullock turns up one afternoon, looking all furtive like the rest of them, and when he comes out I jump in the car and follow him, right? He looks a well-off sort of bloke, and sure enough he gets this big Merc out of the multi-storey. Drives down this way, out of town. Stops at his office, right? So I make one or two enquiries in the pub down the road, find out who he is . . .'

'You don't know Mr Bullock's partner, by any chance?' cut in Colin.

'What? Nah, course not. What's that got to do with it? Anyway, I follow Bullock home – turns out he lives in a bleeding mansion, up towards the downs. Same time next week, sure enough, there he is, collar turned up, creeping along next to the wall like a fucking cockroach. Only by now I've got the floorboard up and stuck the mike by the little hole in her bedroom ceiling. Christ, that bloke was a real pervert, you know that? You know what he got her to do to him?'

'We've heard the recording,' said Judy gently. 'We've got a tape he made of one of your phone calls.'

'What?' Donovan stared at them, not understanding for a moment. 'Recorded it? Did he do that? Cunning sod.'

He ground out his cigarette in the little tinfoil ash tray, shaking his head and grinning faintly, as if Bullock had risen slightly in his estimation.

'So you've heard all the stuff about who's a naughty baby with a big John Willy, then? What the fuck's the matter with some of these toffs? It's all torture chambers and spanking and dressing up in women's knickers and wearing nappies – you'd think they'd never heard of straight sex. What's the matter with them, eh?'

He looked from one to the other appealingly, as if he needed an answer for his peace of mind, to restore his faith in the human race. Judy and Colin glanced at each other, then both looked down at the floor. The PC in the corner was wrestling to keep a grin off his face.

'Can't help you with that one, Martin,' said Judy impassively. 'Unless it's something to do with their upbringing.'

'Fucking perverts,' declared Donovan, after a few more moments of perplexed silence. 'He was one of the worst, and when I rang the bugger up he tried to deny it. Got all threatening, said he'd have the old bill on me and fuck knows what. But I'd got the pictures of him coming out of the basement, and second time I rang I played him a bit of the tape. That seemed to shut him up all right. Didn't know the bugger was recording it, though.'

'So what happened next?' asked Judy. 'After the phone call?'

'I told him to meet me at the car park next day, one o'clock, up on the downs. Halliloo Hill. I left a note for him on the tree, like I said, and drove off to the spot I wanted him to make the drop.'

'Where was that?'

'Little bridge over a road by the M25. Down a little lane where I can see all around, make sure no one's following him, no clever tricks and that. Idea is he puts the cash in a little case I leave at one end of the bridge. When the coast is clear I pull the case down the bank with the bit of rope, and two minutes later I'm on the motorway.'

'Pleased with that, were you?' asked Colin, sarcastically.

'Yeah,' said Donovan, his chin jerking up defiantly. 'I reckon it would've worked. Only Bullock didn't show up.'

'Are you sure?' asked Colin. 'You sure you didn't meet him in the car park that lunchtime and bash him on the head when he didn't have the money?'

Donovan turned to Judy, spreading his hands and appealing silently for fair play and protection. She nodded at him reassuringly and motioned him to continue.

'When he didn't show up after a couple of hours I nipped back to the car park, took the note off the tree. Then I went back to town and got in contact with a bloke at the *Sun*. I met him on the Friday and handed over the stuff – the tape, the pictures, the lot. Not the negs, though. He was wetting himself, said it would make a great story. Then on Saturday I heard it all on the news – found in a quarry with his head bashed in. Nasty business.'

'The quarry's only a few yards from where you arranged to meet him,' said Colin, his tone implacable.

'Look!' Donovan's big body stiffened, his fists clenching and his green eyes glittering. 'I've already told you – don't you understand bleeding English? I didn't arrange to meet him at the car park, that would've been too easy for him to set up a trap with you lot. What I told him was, get more instructions at the car park. And that's all on the tape you've got, so you can't accuse me of making it up at the last minute. And he never showed at the bridge. If he had done, why would I send all the stuff to the papers, eh? You talked to the *Sun* about it?'

He stared angrily from one to the other. Colin nodded at Judy, who spoke a few concluding phrases into the recorder, clicked it off, and began re-sealing the tapes. Colin told Donovan he'd be charged with assault causing grievous bodily harm and resisting arrest and kept in custody for more interviews about the blackmail and murder.

'Where's the bloody lawyer?' said Donovan resentfully, holding out his clumsy paws so the PC could handcuff him for the return to the cells.

'I'm sure he'll be here any moment,' murmured Colin vaguely, walking out into the corridor.

'You've gone back on your word!' shouted Donovan. 'Typical fucking copper!'

Back in the incident room half a dozen officers were checking through lists and statements or slumping on chairs with ties awry, smoking cigarettes. Jim Duncan, crisp and sharp by comparison, breezily told Colin and Judy that there were several reporters and a couple of TV crews outside; they'd heard someone was about to be charged with the murder.

'I don't know who the hell gave them that idea,' he added; his voice was light and melodious, as if the case was suddenly a source of irony and humour to him.

'Someone who wants it to be true, perhaps,' muttered Colin, leading Judy over to his desk in the corner. He sat down, put his elbows on the desk, and held his head in his hands for a few moments. Then he took a deep breath and exhaled noisily.

'What d'you think of Donovan, then?' he asked, emerging from behind his hands. His eyes were tired and bloodshot.

'The spyhole he used for the microphone reminded me of your story this morning about the vice squad,' she said wryly. 'You know – lying in the roof space of the public lavatories, peeping at the gays.'

'Yes – but we were applying the law while he was breaking it,' said Colin sharply.

'Yes, well. It's a fair point about why did he go to the papers,' said Judy. 'And the *Sun* did ring Jim this morning to say they'd got the stuff.'

'That's right. On the other hand' – Colin picked up and let fall some printouts on his desk – 'he's got plenty of form, including some quite nasty woundings. Two stabbings – nearly three, if you count this morning.'

'True. The other thing, though, is he told Bullock on the tape to park down at the right of the car park, by the big tree? That wasn't where we found the car. It was down the other end.'

'Uh-huh. That's right.' His face went vague and he looked at his watch.

'Listen,' he said. 'I'd better go down and throw some raw meat to the animals.'

'What you going to tell them?'

'That we'll be continuing to interview a number of people to eliminate them from our inquiries and we don't anticipate substantive charges at this stage. Or some such bullshit.'

'Shouldn't it be the Fat Man talking to the press?'

Colin grinned ironically.

'Ideally, I suppose. But he's a bit busy tonight – that's why he wasn't in the interview with Donovan.'

'Busy doing what? It's the height of the bloody inquiry.'

Colin ran his hand over his face and rubbed the back of his neck, looking at her speculatively.

'I'll show you what, if you like, on the way home. When I've got the press off my back we could grab a bite in the canteen and go for a little drive.'

Judy hesitated, looking at the window. It was after nine and a few slanting rays of the sunset were breaking through the gunmetal clouds. She wasn't sure about late-night wanderings with Colin after what had happened in the hospital cubicle that morning; on the other hand, it was better than baked beans on toast by herself.

'You ought to be in bed,' she said, 'with a head like yours.'

'Nonsense – it's tuned up the brain. See you downstairs in fifteen minutes.'

Monday, 10.15 p.m.

Colin turned off the main road, squeezed into a parking spot down a side-street, and cut the engine and lights.

'There we are,' he said, nodding towards the big stone building, silhouetted against the still-glowing sky fifty yards away. 'The Penge and Catford Masonic Temple.'

'So they'll all be in there now, baring their breasts and blindfolding each other and rabbiting on about Egypt and Solomon?'

'That sort of thing. Only they usually get the ceremonies out of the way first and then get stuck into a big meal and a few drinks. Or a lot of drinks, in many cases.'

'And you reckon Kingswood's in this lodge as well as Bryan?'

'I'm sure he is. They'll probably be out soon.'

They got out of the car and strolled along the warm pavement, breathing in the few stirrings of breeze which rustled the leaves of a lime tree above them, bringing the day's first touch of coolness. The great metal lattice of the Crystal Palace TV mast loomed high over the end of the street like a watchtower, elegant but menacing, its white warning light blinking implacably every few seconds. A weary evening hum, punctuated by the occasional shout or roaring engine from the nearby pubs, had replaced the frenetic noise of daytime London, and

Judy felt herself at last relaxing, allowing the fatigue of the day to flow unchecked into her limbs. They drew level with the Masonic Hall and she stopped to look at it, yawning luxuriously.

Like Beechley Town Hall, it was a two-storey building of the 1930s, with spare modernist lines and friezes of carved and patterned stone. But the walls were of dark granite, and above the heavy wood and brass doors of the main entrance rose a stubby, obelisk-shaped tower. The light behind the metal-framed windows was dim and sepulchral, and Judy had a vision of gloomy corridors, graven images and muttered rituals.

'Psst . . . look at this.'

Colin had walked on a few paces and was motioning at her to join him. A bronze-coloured Rolls-Royce was sitting at the kerb, foursquare and complacent on its fat tyres, like some great roosting bird.

'Clock the index number,' said Colin, nodding at the car's bulging rear end.

'DK 1989,' read Judy. 'As in lunch, Black Swan. Which is Fat Man's car, then?

'Haven't seen it, but it'll be around somewhere. Unless he's left early, which I doubt.'

Judy yawned again, folding her arms across her chest, and they strolled up to the top of the road. At the corner they paused and leaned against the wall, watching the few passers-by, who stared back at them incuriously. Judy could feel her shoulder touching Colin's elbow as they watched the entrance of the hall fifty yards away. There was a slight smell of warm sweat emanating from him, but she found herself leaning closer rather than recoiling.

'Come on, Bryan,' she murmured. 'Finish your bloody drink and get on home.'

'Right on cue,' said Colin. 'Here they come now.'

A rectangle of warm light had appeared at the hall doorway, and a gaggle of middle-aged men in suits began to emerge. A few walked off down the street or got into cars, while others stayed in little knots near the doorway, talking and laughing. All of them carried little cases and projected an air of good humour and self-importance.

'Look at them,' muttered Colin contemptuously. 'Southern Cross Lodge number 4921 – all puffed up and full of themselves after spouting all that gibberish. It'd be pathetic if it wasn't so sinister.'

'Was this your lodge, then?'

'No, mine was a different one. Just as bad, though. Look, here we are – I'd recognize that silhouette anywhere. Like a cupboard with feet.'

148

Manningbird had emerged from the lighted doorway and was walking slowly up the street towards them beside a small man in his mid-forties with dark hair and a short-stepped, strutting gait. Both men were looking down at their feet, nodding and talking with none of the *bonhomie* of their colleagues. Colin suddenly took Judy by the elbow and propelled her a few yards along the wall into the doorway of an unlighted shop, where they leaned back together into the shadows, away from the light of the street lamps.

The two men looked up before crossing the street, and Judy saw Kingswood's face for the first time – round and pale, with a puffy, debauched look around the eyes. He had his hands in his pockets, pulling the lapels of his suit back to reveal an aggressive little paunch pushing against his white shirt.

'I bet he's got gold taps in his bathroom, all right,' muttered Judy.

'He lives in some big place on the edge of the downs with an electric fence,' said Colin. 'They reckon he's into porn as well as property.'

The two men, one strutting, the other waddling, reached the bronze Rolls-Royce and stood leaning against it, still deep in serious conversation. Manningbird looked up, his face scrunched into a frown, and for a moment he seemed to be staring directly at the shop doorway. Judy shrank backwards and found herself leaning full length against Colin, who put his hands on her shoulders to steady her, and then kept them there, kneading gently through her sweatshirt.

They watched in silence as Manningbird and Kingswood shook hands. Then Manningbird crossed to the other side of the road again, giving a wave to a couple of other men leaving the hall. Kingswood, dwarfed like a ventriloquist's dummy in the huge leather driving seat of the Rolls, started the motor and glided away with a smooth whooshing sound. Judy half-turned to look at Colin, and found herself being kissed awkwardly on the mouth.

His lips were dry and warm, and she turned round fully to put her arms around his neck. Her hand slid up to the dressing on the back of his head, then moved round to the other one on his cheek. As she pulled away from him to speak she had to detach a few strands of her hair which stayed stuck to the dressing.

'You were a right clown this morning, you know that?' she said softly.

'I know,' he whispered, his eyes intense and troubled in the orange half-light from the street lamps. 'A lot on my mind, including you – not thinking straight.'

'And showing off,' said Judy, kissing him maternally on his uninjured cheek. 'Come on, let me take you home.'

He took her arm and pulled her back towards him. Judy wanted to

149

fall back into the darkness, to push aside all the sensible reservations in her mind. Instead she grabbed Colin playfully with both hands and pulled him out into the street like a naughty child. He came without much resistance, and began walking along with her arm in arm, looking half-relieved.

'Did I ever tell you what happened to the last bloke who got fresh with me in a shop doorway?' she asked, jovially.

Chapter Eighteen

Tuesday, 9 a.m.

Judy sat silently in the passenger seat, wondering what she was going to do about Colin, as Jim Duncan drove out through the suburbs of Beechley. On the way back from the Masonic hall the previous night, she'd told Colin all about her brief flirtation with a City yuppie two years earlier, and how she and her boyfriend had both been suspected of killing him. It had been intended as a cautionary tale, but Colin hadn't been put off at all: he'd kissed her again when he dropped her off at her flat, and was clearly expecting greater things. She liked him, for his worn good looks, his humour, and even the moody contradictions and pessimism which were tied up with his Christianity; but she was wondering if his attraction was as a better father figure than the one she had, and there were also the streaks of vindictiveness and misogyny she'd recently divined in him. On top of that was the plain fact that he had a wife and family, and something else had already started in the last couple of days – the little smirks from their colleagues when they entered or left the room together. It was a relief being sent out with Jim Duncan this morning to see Dorothy Bullock again, while Colin went off with Manningbird to interview Derek Kingswood in his mansion up on the edge of the downs.

Duncan, however, was not happy at being asked to work alongside his main rival like this. They'd already argued about whether or not Martin Donovan was the murderer as well as the blackmailer, and now Duncan was venting his usually well-concealed spleen on middle-class women drivers. His Scots voice was a low, tense monotone of dislike.

'Just look at them all, bloody ice-maidens in their bloody armoured personnel carriers – Volvo estate, Mercedes estate, Range Rover. Who needs a Range Rover in a London suburb, for Christ's sake? Only time they go off the road is when they park on the pavement and smash up the slabs. Place is crawling with them, bloody toffs – look at that one in front, silly bloody hair band, shirt collar turned up, string of bloody pearls, rather die than look at you. Look at her bloody expression!

Thinks she owns the road, nobody else exists, she's the only bloody member of the human race. Now she thinks she's going to park. Oh no, you bloody don't, madam! Selfish cow. You can park down a side-street and walk, like everybody else. Who do they think they are, these people?'

He drove the Cavalier hard up behind the Volvo, blocking the tiny space the driver wanted to back into, and tooted menacingly on the horn. She was turned in her seat, giving them a long, disdainful stare, but after half a minute of confrontation she gave up and drove off again, the big estate car lurching clumsily. Jim Duncan was delighted.

'Another small victory for the common people,' he chuckled. 'Stuck-up cow, looking down her nose at everyone.'

'They might actually be more frightened than stuck-up, you know,' said Judy crossly. Duncan looked at her with an expression of inno-cent astonishment.

'Frightened? Frightened of what?'

'Of people like you, for a start. And of all the people who might come along and take their big cars and strings of pearls away from them.'

'In that case they should buy smaller cars. And leave the bloody pearls in the safe.'

'Jim, I'm amazed. Ten years of Thatcherism and you're still a social-ist. Congratulations.'

Duncan snorted.

'There's a great career for you in social work, Jude,' he said.

They drove on in silence, overtaking a three-wheeled invalid car with an unnecessary swerve and roar of the engine. Soon they were snaking up the narrow lane of Hunter's Combe, past the high garden walls and the big metal gates. Just as Jumpers came into view a woman in a blue track suit stepped off a stile in the fence and walked stiffly into the road without looking at them. Duncan braked hard, cursing, and the car skidded and came to a stop a yard from Dorothy. Judy snapped off her belt, jumped out of the car and took her by the elbow, asking her if she was all right. At first Dorothy didn't realize who she was, but after a moment recognition entered her wide hazel eyes.

'Oh, it's you again,' she said, her voice low and distracted. 'No, I'm not all right, actually.'

'What's the matter? You nearly got yourself run over just then.'

'Did I? I'm terribly sorry. My mind's on other things. I've been up to the quarry, you see. I thought I needed to look at the . . . well, you know, the place.'

The arm under Judy's hand felt slight and insubstantial, and she pictured Dorothy walking alone under the bright grey sky and looking down into the rubbishy bottom of Slump Quarry.

'And that's not all,' said Dorothy, swallowing hard, her eyes seeming to roll slightly as she turned to look at Judy. 'There's someone prowling around up there – among the trees.'

Duncan had parked the car on the verge and joined them in time to hear the last sentence. They both looked down at Dorothy's wet boots and legs, and Duncan raised his eyebrows and placed a forefinger against his temple. Judy shook her head at him, leading Dorothy towards the house and asking her gently for more details.

'I told you the place was full of weird people these days,' said Dorothy, treading heavily through the deep gravel. 'We're too close to London, that's what it is. It's probably the same one who killed John, the one we've seen hanging around among the trees. He's probably looking for someone else to attack, don't you think?'

They went into the kitchen and sat around the big pine table while Dorothy, calm and numb, described her morning. She'd come home from her mother's the previous night, had woken early, and decided to go out. It was only when she'd been halfway up the Downs, walking between the wide stretches of ripening corn, that she'd realized she was going to the quarry. It was like a visit to John's grave, she said, painful but necessary. Duncan was getting fidgety.

'This prowler of yours,' he said brusquely. 'You sure you're not imagining things? You've been under a lot of stress, probably been taking drugs and what have you. It might just have been, well, the shadows in the trees up there.'

Dorothy looked up at him wearily.

'No. That's what I thought at first. But I definitely saw him. A young man, sort of shambling around. I'm sure of it.'

'And you say you've seen him before?' asked Judy, thinking for a moment of Godfrey, of his horrible smell and his thin shoulders.

'Well, I can't be certain it was the same man. But we've seen someone up there before – both of us. It isn't just me. Why don't you have a look for yourself?'

Duncan immediately looked more cheerful and flashed Judy an eager glance. She nodded and he got to his feet, asked Dorothy for more exact directions, and walked through the back door. He gave them a cheery little wave as he passed in front of the kitchen window. For a while the two women sat motionless, immersed in the silence of the bright morning. Judy watched Dorothy's pale face and bloodshot eyes, reluctant to add to her burdens with the news about the prostitute and the blackmailer – if indeed it was news to her. She was about to speak when the phone rang out in the hall.

'Shall I answer that for you?' said Judy, half-rising to her feet. A look of consternation shot on to Dorothy's face, and she stretched out and took hold of Judy's forearm. Judy looked down at the slender white fingers, the expensive diamond and the narrow gold band.

'No, no, it's all right, I'll go,' she said quickly. 'It'll only be my mother, I expect. Won't be a moment. She keeps on ringing, I'm afraid.'

'I expect she's very worried about you,' said Judy, subsiding on to the chair again. Dorothy went into the hall, shutting the door behind her, and Judy immediately got up and stood close to the door. All she could hear was Dorothy telling someone in a low voice that she couldn't talk now and would the other person please stop ringing. Then the phone went down and Judy had to scuttle back to her chair to avoid being caught eavesdropping.

'Yes, mothers,' said Dorothy, filling the kettle and taking two mugs and a biscuit tin from a cupboard. 'Over-anxious. You know. You're always a child to them, aren't you? Would you like some coffee?'

Judy said yes; Dorothy was suddenly brighter and more chatty, but it seemed forced, as if she was still struggling with the feeling aroused by the visit to the quarry.

'We've arrested someone, Mrs Bullock,' said Judy, her voice sounding harsher than she meant it to. 'But not necessarily for the murder.'

A series of expressions seemed to flow across Dorothy's features: surprise, disbelief, anxiety. The one which remained was confusion.

'What do you mean, not for the murder?'

'We've found someone who was blackmailing your husband, Mrs Bullock.'

'Blackmailing him? What about?' Dorothy opened her palms on the table in front of her, as if they were the book of John Bullock's blameless life. Her incomprehension seemed genuine.

'I'm afraid it was to do with his sex life, Mrs Bullock. He appears to have been visiting a prostitute, and someone took photos and made recordings and was blackmailing him. We traced the blackmailer and arrested him.'

Dorothy closed her eyes quietly, interlaced her fingers and clamped her hands hard together. Judy steeled herself, wondering if she could cope with any more tragic emotion so early in the day. But when Dorothy opened her eyes again they were dry, and seemed only to plead for her to say that she hadn't meant it, that it was just a joke. When

154

Judy looked steadily back, saying nothing, Dorothy's features dropped slowly into resignation.

'I'm not surprised, I suppose,' she said quietly. 'Our sex life was lousy, and he was out all the time, so I suppose something like that had to happen. I was naive enough to think it was just the Freemasons. Where was this, then? Up in town, I suppose?'

'Yes – near Marylebone Station.'

'He was up in town every week or two, various political meetings, the boroughs association. But you said the blackmailer wasn't the murderer?'

'We don't know. He wanted your husband to go up to the car park on Halliloo Hill last Thursday, just by the quarry, and follow some instructions to hand over the money.'

'So did this man meet him there?'

'The man says not. And of course we don't know when your husband drove up there. After all, Mr Damson says his car was still in town at six o'clock.'

Dorothy nodded, her face screwed into a frown. Then she suddenly noticed the boiled kettle, emitting wisps of steam and clouding the big window overlooking the garden. The chair legs squealed on the floor as she stood up and went over to make the coffee.

'Will this all have to come out?' she asked cautiously, her face turned away from Judy as the teaspoon clinked against the mugs. 'I mean about the prostitute and everything?'

'Eventually, yes. In court. But not in too much detail if he pleads guilty. Which he probably will.'

Dorothy asked about milk and sugar, brought the mugs back to the table, and rested her head on one hand. Her face seemed more haggard by the minute.

'Hard on everyone,' she whispered. 'The kids.'

'Mrs Bullock,' Judy said. 'You didn't tell us about the Freemasons the other times we came to see you.'

'But you must have known,' said Dorothy, a sudden spark of defiance in her look and tone. 'Half your lot are in it too.'

'Well, we did find out before long. It turns out he kept all his stuff at the office, the regalia and everything, and Mr Damson showed it to us.'

'Did he indeed?' Dorothy was suddenly angry. 'I bet he did. I'm surprised bloody Nigel wasn't doing the blackmailing.'

'We haven't ruled anything out,' said Judy softly, hoping she was going to hear more. But Dorothy lowered her eyes and sipped her coffee.

155

'Are you married?' she asked abruptly.

'No.'

'Well, make sure you don't marry a Mason. And make the man you marry sign in blood that he'll never join the Masons. Or else you'll be a Masonic widow, like I've been, and I can tell you it's no life at all.'

'So I've heard,' said Judy.

'That's why I didn't tell you. I was ashamed of it. D'you know, he once wanted me to rehearse one of the rituals with him? With blindfolds and God knows what. I made him keep all his stuff outside the house after that, I was so disgusted with it all. But none of the rows we had ever stopped him, and in the end I gave up trying. It was a huge wedge between us, and it ruined our marriage. All that secrecy and sinister gobbledegook. There's the ladies' night once a year when they're all over you, giving you presents and singing your praises. And the rest of the year they're out at the lodge once, twice, three times a week, and nothing – nothing – is allowed to get in the way of that.'

Dorothy's voice and body were vibrating with indignation and tears were flowing from her eyes, each drop following the other over her cheeks and dropping from her chin like a dripping tap.

'Sounds like you might almost be glad to be rid of him,' said Judy quietly.

'Yes, no, I don't know.' Dorothy shook her head sharply, and one of the fat tears was hurled through the air and landed on the back of Judy's hand. 'But why did he have to go and have it off with some tart? Why didn't he have it off with me?'

Judy got up and paced up and down the kitchen a couple of times, smoothing her blue skirt round her hips and tweaking the cuffs of her blouse while Dorothy's feelings subsided a little. Judy controlled the impulse to grasp the other woman's shoulders, pat her back and murmur soothing words to her: it wasn't her job, especially while Dorothy's role in the case was far from clear. She looked out the window and wondered where Duncan was, what was happening up beyond the copse. For a moment she thought she could see a dark-clad figure moving rapidly along the edge of the trees, and then it disappeared. She turned back to Dorothy, who was drying her eyes on a piece of kitchen towel ripped from a wooden roller.

'Mrs Bullock,' she said. 'Do you know if your husband had a Swiss bank account?'

Dorothy showed no reaction and continued dabbing at her eyes.

'And was someone called Derek Kingswood paying a lot of money into it?'

Dorothy continued dabbing at her eyes, and frowned a little as she tried to place the name.

'Derek Kingswood? Isn't that the property man – doing up the town centre?'

'Yes, and another Freemason, as it happens. And the man your husband was meant to meet for lunch last Thursday.'

'Oh, so that was the DK you asked me about? I should have thought of him, I suppose, only I've never actually met him. Why d'you think John would have been getting money from him?'

'For smoothing the path of the redevelopment, perhaps. Only the scheme's hit the sand and the council's pulling out of the deal to rent the offices.'

Dorothy shook her head and leaned back in her chair. The tears were gone now, but her eyes were redder, and an expression of firm refusal was taking hold of her face.

'I'm sorry,' she said. 'You're suggesting John was corrupt, and I just don't know. I've no idea about all the financial side of things, and to be honest I didn't want anything to do with it. I just left it all to John, and he wouldn't have told me much even if I'd asked.'

'Were you surprised you were able to afford this house?'

Dorothy turned down the corners of her mouth and waggled her head cluelessly.

'Not really. John did say it might mean shelving our long-term plan of buying something in the south of France or somewhere in the Mediterranean. But I never knew the ins and outs of it. Why don't you ask Mr Kingswood?'

'I hope,' said Judy, unable to keep the sarcasm out of her voice, 'that my senior colleagues are doing that right now. So, Mrs Bullock, you haven't found a file anywhere in the house which . . .'

Dorothy let out a sudden little scream, one hand jumping splay-fingered up to her mouth. Judy whipped round in her chair and saw Jim Duncan standing outside the window, his face flushed, and his lips twisted in a maniacal grin. He was holding up a crooked forefinger, gesturing for Judy to come outside. She threw back her chair and walked angrily out of the back door.

'D'you have to, Jim?' she snapped. 'You look like something out of a horror film. Scared Mrs Bullock to death.'

'Sorry, Jude,' said Duncan, panting slightly. He was not his normal controlled and tidy self: the trousers of his blue suit were wet from pushing through the long, dewy grass, and his blond hair was dishevelled, falling on his forehead.

'Find the psycho, then?' asked Judy. 'Lurking in the undergrowth, grinning at you?'

'Yes and no,' said Duncan, still grinning and savouring the enigma. Judy looked impatiently at the sky and sighed.

'What I mean is, I didn't find him. But when I radioed in just now, turns out that the others have found him, bit further up the hill. Turns out he's just the man we're looking for.'

Chapter Nineteen

Tuesday, 9.15 a.m.

'You seen my bloody gateposts?' said Derek Kingswood indignantly, hurrying across the black and white marble hallway of his mock-Regency mansion. 'Have you? You seen what those little buggers have done to them?'

Colin Borden and Bryan Manningbird, standing on the wide slab of coconut matting just inside the double-doored entrance, glanced uncertainly at each other. It would have been hard to miss the bloody gateposts, which stood twelve feet tall on either side of two ornate wrought-iron gates with the initials DK worked into the middle of them.

'Yes, we, er, did see the gateposts, on the way in,' said Manningbird. 'Nasty mess, I agree.'

'Well, what you planning to do about it?' asked Kingswood, his portly little body coming to a halt, hands on hips, a couple of yards from the two policemen. He was wearing red braces which pulled his white shirt tightly on to his aggressive-looking pot belly.

'We'll, er, look into it,' said Manningbird lamely, running the back of his hand across his grey brow and staring at Kingswood's round, pale face; this muggy weather didn't suit him a bit.

'Look into it, will you? Right then, you'd better come outside and see what else they've been up to. Follow me, please, gents.'

Kingswood pushed past them and led the way down the steps between the Doric columns which supported the porch. He swung left, past his gleaming bronze Rolls-Royce and the officers' down-at-heel maroon Cavalier, and disappeared round the side of the house. A splendid view opened up of the hazy mauve and green patchwork of the weald of Kent, with its knolls of woodland and tidy valleys where an occasional white-painted building gleamed back at them. The garden had been recently landscaped, and the thin yellowing grass and straggling shrubs were redeemed only by a stand of tall Scots pines down one side, looking down haughtily on all the newness.

'There you are,' said Kingswood, gesturing with his chubby hand at his white-stuccoed front wall. 'That's even worse, if anything. Bloody vandals – God knows how they got over the frigging walls.'

Beneath the tall windows which reflected the high, grey sky, there was a twenty-foot long message written in red spray paint in easy, looping letters: 'Stuff the poll tax, not the poor. Class warfare now!' It was a variation on the theme which Manningbird and Colin had seen all along the winding lane which gave access to the dozen large and well-protected mansions which perched, like this one, on this eastward-facing edge of the downs. 'Bash the rich!' and 'Greedy pig house' were the slogans on the gateposts which seemed to have touched Kingswood's sorest nerves.

'Good thing they didn't have a go at your motor,' said Colin, squinting up at the windows of the upper floor. 'They didn't get inside as well, did they?'

'No they bleeding didn't,' muttered Kingswood grimly. 'The Dobermann would've had their bollocks off.'

'They've done a bit of a sweep all along the road,' said Colin. 'Some of your neighbours got it even worse than you. Funny, I've never seen them operate so far out of town before.'

'Should make 'em easier to catch,' said Kingswood, running his hand over his swept-back black hair and sticking out his pale jaw. 'Good thrashing's what they need. Birch – like the Isle of Man.'

'They could be in Wales by now,' said Colin, scraping at the spray paint with a fingernail. 'But we'll do our best, sir. There's a car on its way to cruise round the area, see what they can find, and someone else will be up later to take statements.'

'Statements?' said Kingswood, his little eyes bulging. 'I want a full bloody investigation – fingerprints, forensics, the lot. It's a bloody outrage.'

Colin sighed and stared out over the hazy, distant landscape, rolling up his sleeves in the growing heat of the morning. There was a thundery quality in the sky now, with occasional patches of dirty yellow and darker grey lurking around the horizon.

'Of course it's a bloody outrage, sir,' he said. 'But we're here because of an even bigger outrage, which is the murder of your business associate John Bullock in the quarry not six miles away. So d'you think we could move on and talk about that?'

Kingswood looked angrily at Manningbird, who looked at the ground. He'd admitted to Colin in a heated phone call at 7 a.m. that he ought not to take part in any interviews with Kingswood, but a compromise had been struck that Colin would do the talking while he kept to the sidelines. They walked down the garden to a circular pond surrounded by a paved area where there was a large sun umbrella poking through a round table and a few padded sun-loungers. A small goldfish floated immobile in the cloudy water, belly-up. Kingswood looked steadily back at Colin, his eyes hard and beady above the loosening flesh of his white cheeks.

Yes, he said, he'd arranged to meet Bullock for lunch the previous Thursday. The plan was to pick him up from the town hall at quarter to one and drive out to the Black Swan, where they had a business meal together in the upstairs restaurant from time to time. But when he'd called at the town hall to pick him up, his driver was told he wasn't there and they assumed he'd made his own way to the pub. When Bullock didn't show up there, either, Kingswood had assumed that more urgent business or politics had intervened. He'd tried phoning the following day, was told Bullock was missing, and was deeply shocked when the bad news came through on Saturday – very deeply shocked.

'What was the meeting meant to be about?' asked Colin.

Kingswood glanced uneasily at Manningbird, as if hoping that the other man would take over the story, or at least prompt him. Manningbird cleared his throat, licked his grey lips, and narrowed his eyes for a better appreciation of the delightful vistas of the garden of England spread out before him.

'This and that,' said Kingswood. 'But there was a bit of a problem over Market Walk.'

'Oh yes, what was that?'

Kingswood lifted one foot from the imitation stone flags and crossed his legs. His feet were as small as a girl's, and he was wearing a pair of shiny patent-leather moccasins with a little gold buckle on the instep.

'The council was changing its mind about taking a lease on the offices,' he said grumpily.

'And you wanted it to change its mind back again?'

'Naturally,' shrugged Kingswood. 'I'm a businessman. But I'm a reasonable man too, and I appreciated that John had a political problem on his hands.'

'What would that be?'

'Taking on a big lease on nice new offices when they're trying to keep the poll tax down. Especially difficult for him without a guarantee they'd find a developer for their present premises. You know, that heap of crap behind the town hall.'

161

He flashed an aggressive, mirthless smile at Colin, who suddenly became aware of something moving at the corner of his eye. He looked round to see a bulky man with a crew cut walking towards them across the lawn: this would be the driver. The man leaned over Kingswood's shoulder and whispered in his ear, eyeing the two officers suspiciously at the same time. Kingswood nodded, and the man stepped back; a complex red and green tattoo was half-visible under the sleeve of his dark polo shirt, and there was a military stiffness in his movements.

'There's a telephone call for you, Bry ... er, Superintendent Manningbird,' said Kingswood. 'If you follow young Mark here, you can take it in the house.'

Manningbird heaved himself to his feet with a grunt and lumbered off after the beefy ex-soldier. Colin had a vague memory of seeing the man's face in a file of known offenders. Kingswood treated him to a repeat of the mirthless smile, which revealed a set of teeth which looked healthier than the rest of his face.

'Did John Bullock owe you any favours, Mr Kingswood?'

Kingswood's face was suddenly blank and shuttered, his eyes harder and smaller. He folded his hands together on his thigh, leaned a few inches forward, and cocked his head to one side.

'I'm not sure I like your implication, Inspector,' he said quietly. 'What exactly are you driving at?'

'You worked closely together over the market redevelopment.' Colin had unconsciously adopted the same attitude of crossed legs and clasped hands, and was looking calmly back at Kingswood.

'We did indeed. A very fruitful partnership between public and private sector, though I say it myself. Until the frigging Chancellor threw a spanner in the works, that is.'

'Were you rewarding Mr Bullock for his co-operation, in any way? I understand he had a foreign bank account.'

Colin put the suggestion in a pleasant and relaxed tone, as if the idea were no more reprehensible than a holiday in Majorca. Kingswood leaned back in his chair, shaking his head and sucking his breath gently through his teeth, as if Colin had just suggested paedophilia or desecrating the Union Jack. One white forefinger rose from his clasped hands, like a worm from a hole, and wiggled warningly.

'That's a very naughty suggestion, Inspector,' he said. 'And very disrespectful of the dead, if I may say so. John was a fine man, a pillar of the community, and it's out of order to go round suggesting he was on the take. Unless, of course, you've got some proof?'

Colin smiled back, keeping his voice conversational, as if they were having a friendly chat in a pub.

162

'Because if you'd been forking out for a certain result, and things were turning out quite differently, you'd have every reason to feel aggrieved, wouldn't you, Mr Kingswood? Most natural thing in the world.'

Kingswood threw back his head and laughed up at the sky, revealing the gold caps on some of his rear teeth and the little bushes of black hair inside his nostrils. The laugh was dry and mirthless and ended in a minor coughing fit which flushed his pale face with blood.

'You're a card, Inspector, you know that?' he spluttered eventually, the shutters sliding down over his face again. 'Let's say I kidnap John Bullock, take him up the quarry and knock him on the head. Now, apart from the sheer improbability of it, what good's that going to do me? He was my best hope of getting over this temporary problem with the town centre. He was a business partner. And he was a personal friend.'

'I see. You wouldn't kill the goose which laid the golden egg.'

'You've been watching too many Hollywood movies, Inspector. Warped the old mind a bit, if you don't mind me saying so. And if you continue like this I'll have to ask for my lawyer to be present.'

'No need,' said Colin lightly. 'Here's Bryan.'

Manningbird was bowling briskly towards them across the thin grass, his face like a lighted window on a dark night. The thick cushion on the chair gave a winded wheeze as he flopped on to it, exuding good humour and grinning at them with lips the colour of a boiled ox-tongue.

'The lads have picked him up,' he announced between heavy breaths. 'In a bus shelter, a mile or so down the road.'

Colin and Kingswood looked at each other, suddenly united in wanting a clearer explanation of the Fat Man's excitement.

'Picked up who, exactly?' said Kingswood roughly. 'The sodding Pope?'

'No, no,' said Manningbird, gesturing impatiently with one over-stuffed hand. 'The murderer. Or at least, he says he's the murderer, which is good enough for me.'

Colin's eyes wrinkled up as he stared out over the landscape, an expression of foreboding taking shape on his face. Manningbird was too excited to notice.

'Come on then, Superintendent, let's hear the gory details,' said Kingswood, recrossing his legs. 'Your man here's been busy trying to stitch me up.'

'Has he indeed?' said Manningbird jovially, his little eyes fixing on Colin for a moment. 'Well, that may not be necessary any more – just a joke, Mr Kingswood, just a joke. No, that phone call was from the incident room. That patrol car we told you about, the one cruising around looking for these Class Warfare lunatics. They found this young bloke hiding in a bus shelter down the lane, and he introduces himself as the man who killed John Bullock. In fact' – Manningbird's face suddenly clouded as he turned to Colin – 'he says he's already been to the station and confessed, but got kicked out. You know anything about that, do you, Colin?'

Colin looked at Kingswood with grim regret, like a dog just deprived of a bone, and stood up slowly.

'I'll tell you on the way back, sir,' he said. 'Keep in touch, Mr Kingswood,' he said. 'Let us know if you remember anything about owing favours.'

'I certainly will,' said Kingswood, rubbing his little white hands together as he stood up lightly from his chair and winked at Manningbird. 'I'd be only too glad to offer you gents a little drink, but I can see how busy you are.'

Tuesday, 2.30 p.m.

Godfrey's clothes had been taken away to the forensic lab, and he sat in a set of white paper overalls, moving his wrists ceaselessly inside his handcuffs, testing them with a gentle, obsessional movement, as regular as a metronome. He had a fresh cut above one eye, and the knuckles of his left hand were swollen purple and yellow. Judy, sitting in the corner behind Manningbird, found it impossible to imagine these small, weak-looking hands, with the skin picked raw round the fingernails, picking up a weapon and striking murderous blows, or tipping a great heavy body over the edge of a quarry. They were at the other extreme from the big, meaty strangler's hands of Martin Donovan which she'd been looking at in the same room the previous day. The Fat Man was taking Godfrey through his story.

'Just what are these voices like then, Godfrey?' asked Manningbird, in the slow, patronizing tones of a Christmas Santa addressing a half-witted child. Even his great rounded shoulders and the folds of grey skin on the back of his neck seemed to exude the optimism of a man who thought his worries might soon be over. Judy shifted uneasily in her chair and glanced over at Colin, who was leaning forward staring at the floor, hands clasped, as if in prayer.

'Inside my head,' muttered Godfrey, glancing up at Manningbird with pale, tormented eyes. 'Loud. Tell me what to do. I don't get them all the time, though.'

164

'But you got them last week, did you, Godfrey? Last Thursday?'

Godfrey looked up at his interrogator, his eyes submissive but uncomprehending.

'Last Thursday? Dunno – should have taken my medicine. I sort of go on long walks, up there, 'cos of my voices.'

'Up where, Godfrey?' The eagerness of Manningbird's voice made Judy feel hot with frustration and anger, and she took several deep, slow breaths to calm herself. She remembered Dorothy's repeated sightings of a figure moving in the shadows of the trees.

'Up round there,' said Godfrey, making a vague gesture with his thin, pinioned arms. 'On the downs. Sleep up there sometimes.'

'Round the quarry, eh, that sort of place? Were you up there last Thursday?'

Godfrey shook his head, then grimaced and nodded.

'You were, eh? And what did you do up there? Who did you see?'

Godfrey looked up suddenly and pointed at Judy, the handcuffs obliging him to use both hands. She saw that there were traces of tears among the grime and dried blood on his face. His voice rose and wavered.

'I told her. I told her the other day. He's behind it all. I've been watching him.'

Manningbird twisted his lumpy body to look at Judy, his expression impassive and hostile. His mouth was like two slugs pressed together, she thought. She gave a tiny shrug and looked back at him expressionlessly.

'All right, now, Godfrey,' resumed Manningbird. 'Let's not get too excited. You were up there last Thursday, you've been there before. Now, did you see the man, the man who's behind it all? Getting out of his car, perhaps? A big Mercedes?'

Judy got up as quietly as she could and left the interview room. Manningbird had already torn many strips off her in front of the entire team for failing to tell him about Godfrey's attempted confession two days previously, and she didn't see why she had to suffer the further humiliation of watching this pitiful young vagrant being cynically stitched up. Manningbird had brushed aside her protestations that Godfrey couldn't describe Bullock's injuries accurately, and made it clear he had high hopes of persuading him to admit to the two other unsolved killings on the downs as well. Colin had stayed silent and failed to defend her.

She stood listlessly in the corridor for a moment, trying to control her feelings of bitterness and injustice, then sighed and headed towards the lift and the universal police remedy of a cup of stewed tea. Perhaps she'd also get home early for a good night's sleep, to wipe some of the aggravation from her mind. She had just pressed the call button when the door to the incident room opened and Jim Duncan put his head round it.

'Jude,' he shouted. 'Call for you.'

His attitude towards her had become sublime and sunny ever since her public bollocking by Manningbird. He was beaming at her sarcastically as she walked slowly back to the incident room, but she kept her head averted, refusing to meet his eyes. She picked up the receiver lying on the desk.

'Hullo, this is Annabel Silver.'

'Oh, yes. Mrs Bullock's friend.'

'That's right. Listen, there's a couple of things I should have told you. About what happened on Thursday.'

The voice was confident, middle-class, peremptory, and Judy thought of Duncan's diatribe against ice-maidens in Volvos. But there was an edge of tension and anxiety as well.

'All right,' said Judy. 'Can you drop in at the station sometime?'

'I'd rather not. To be honest, I don't want it to be on the record, if you see what I mean. Can't I speak to you privately? This evening?'

Judy remembered the luxurious dark hair, the knowing manner, the ripeness. Annabel Silver was what male police officers would call a bit of a goer, and she was a close friend of the Bullock family; so it was unlikely that what she had to say was trivial, especially if she wanted to keep it quiet. Judy had a dim but alluring vision of herself pulling a rabbit out of a hat and waving it under Manningbird's nose, and she could feel a gentle new wave of adrenalin pushing aside the despondency of the last few hours.

'OK, Mrs Silver,' she said. 'Why don't you pick me up at about nine? Let's say the town hall steps.'

Chapter Twenty

Elspeth Gorringe approached silently down the shadowy corridor on her rubber-soled shoes, stopped just behind Simon Pilkington and stared balefully for a moment at his impeccable blazer and the neat blond curls on the back of his neck. Then she rose unsteadily on her tiptoes and struck.

'Snake!' she hissed in his ear from point-blank range, spraying him with specks of saliva and tiny blackened particles which had probably spent several weeks stuck between her gold and brown teeth. Pilkington jumped as if he'd been goosed, but by the time he'd turned round Elspeth Gorringe had glided away towards the queue for the tea trolley. She adopted an innocent pose and smiled sweetly at those of her fellow-councillors who had seen what she'd done and were looking at her in amusement or disbelief.

Pilkington, who was talking to the Labour group leader Ashok Patel when Elspeth struck, took a single impulsive stride after her, hand raised, before controlling himself and redirecting the hand into his pocket. In a gesture reminiscent of John Bullock, he brought out a large white handkerchief and used it to rub the side of his reddening face.

'Mad old bat,' he muttered to himself, as Patel, trying to control a smile, moved away and started talking to Barry Rutter, who had just arrived from the rear of the town hall, carrying a heavy stack of papers. He was looking more careworn than usual, and from behind his thick spectacles he seemed to be trying to catch the eye of the distracted Pilkington. It was their first meeting since Rutter had told him the contents of his file the previous morning.

'How are you, then, Barry?' asked Patel, affably. 'Bearing up under the strain?'

'Not too bad, thanks, Ashok,' replied Rutter, flashing him a harassed glance and resting the pile of papers on the corner of a table. 'Everything's in turmoil because of the Bullock affair, of course, and now the committee clerk's gone AWOL. Sometimes I feel I'm running this council single-handed.'

It was the strategy committee tonight, the first formal meeting of councillors since the demise of the leader. In the old days it was called the policy and resources committee, but John Bullock had soon kicked that into touch in favour of something a bit snappier. Normally he would be standing there impatiently, jaw set and eyes roving, alert for signs of dissent or mutiny, silently dominating the committee members as they sipped the tea and bolted the curling egg mayonnaise sandwiches which were meant to sustain them through the meeting but usually gave them indigestion and attacks of wind.

Tonight, on both Tory and Labour sides, there was a strange mixture of shock, mourning and relief: on the one hand, their guiding light had gone out, leaving them alone in the world and frightened; on the other, their tormentor was no longer on their backs, he would never return, and the new sense of freedom secretly thrilled them. It was another oppressive evening, everyone was edgy and perspiring, and nobody was behaving quite normally, as Elspeth Gorringe had already demonstrated. She was now glowering at Pilkington, smiling at anyone else who met her eye, and dropping bits of egg mayonnaise down the front of her blouse. Fortunately the stains blended well with the pattern, which consisted of whorls and splatterings of bright colour.

'Well, it's all bound to be a bit confused for a while,' said Patel, his large, dark eyes flicking over Rutter's scarred and furrowed brow. 'Have you heard of any developments? In the police investigation, I mean?'

Rutter looked down to check his pile of documents, and several seconds went past before he replied.

'Nothing one could exactly call a development,' he said, his brisk and complaining tone of a few moments before replaced by one of slowness and caution. 'They're having a few people in for questioning, but that's all. You're probably in a far better position than me to hear what's going on, Ashok.'

It was a remark subtly directed at Patel's weak spot: he was always worried that people were keeping him in the dark or that some of the nuances were escaping him because he was an Asian, an outsider. The implication that he had his finger on the pulse of the borough of Beechley brought a grin of boyish pride to his face and loosened his tongue.

'Well, there have been a few rumours floating around,' he said, his voice low and confiding. 'I gather they're taking a certain amount of interest in what you might call the Kingswood connection.'

168

'Really?' said Rutter evenly; his voice and demeanour gave away nothing about his conversation with Manningbird the previous morning or the contents of the file in his bottom drawer, but his eyes gleamed a little behind the thick, greenish lenses.

'Uh-huh,' said Patel, taking a contented and knowing sip from his Styrofoam cup of tea. 'I mean, Kingswood must be a very angry man now this leaseback's fallen through – am I right? And rumour has it he and Bullock were due to have lunch together last Thursday.'

'Well,' said Rutter, looking at his watch and glancing round the waiting group, 'as a lawyer, I'm reluctant to speculate, of course, especially while it's all in the hands of the police. But naturally I'm aware that the Labour side had its doubts about the whole town centre redevelopment from the start. You don't seriously think there was any actual financial impropriety, do you?'

Patel's eyebrows rose slowly upwards as the seed fell on fertile ground and started to sprout.

'Well, you know, come to think of it I wouldn't be at all surprised,' he said, nodding so vigorously that his tea slopped on to the polished parquet under their feet.

'Very difficult area, though – I think we'd better go on in, don't you?' said Rutter, picking up his papers and stepping carefully round the puddle. Patel looked guiltily round the lobby and followed him.

As people began to file into the wood-panelled committee room, Ernest Jinks, a white-haired Tory with twenty-five years in local government, came alongside Elspeth and took her shakily by the elbow.

'I say, old girl,' he murmured towards an ear stretched downwards by orange stones which clashed hideously with her henna-dyed hair. 'Bit uncalled-for, don't you think? Not exactly Simon's fault, after all.'

'What on earth are you talking about, Ernest?' said Elspeth, removing his hand from her bony arm and turning towards him. Her smile of defiant innocence contained such an unmistakable gleam of irrationality that the old man quailed and shuffled off to his seat with foreboding on his face: the demise of Elspeth's hero had obviously pushed her closer to the brink.

Pilkington sat at the head of the long table, coughed, adjusted his tie, and called the meeting to order. Rutter sat at his right hand, shuffling his files and papers like some outsize pack of cards.

'I think, ladies and gentlemen,' Pilkington said uncertainly, 'that we ought to start with a minute's silence to remember our leader and colleague John Bullock, who was killed in such a brutal and tragic manner only a few days ago. I'm sure we all hope the police will soon

169

find the culprit and submit him to the full rigour of the law.'

There were embarrassed throat-clearings, murmurs of 'hear, hear', and the scraping of chair legs on the wooden floor. But through the noise there rose the querulous voice of Elspeth Gorringe, loud and determined.

'Point of order, Mr Chairman,' she said, fixing Pilkington with a pale and laser-like eye. 'In my opinion anything less than two minutes would be an insult, and I'd like to propose an amendment to that effect.'

Pilkington stared back for a moment, going red, then looked down at his blotter.

'All right, Mrs Gorringe,' he muttered. 'No need for an amendment – this isn't a formal motion. Two minutes' silence, if you're sure you can manage it.'

'And what's that supposed to mean?' flared Elspeth, leaning forward. The room was hot and airless in spite of the opened windows, and there were hectic red spots on her sallow cheeks now.

'Er, nothing,' said Pilkington, running his finger round his collar as if it had suddenly become too tight. 'I withdraw the remark unconditionally. Two minutes' silence, please, ladies and gentlemen.'

'Hypocrite!' hissed Elspeth, leaning back and fiercely studying the embarrassed faces of the committee one by one as they stared at the ceiling or checked the condition of their fingernails. A few stomachs were heard gurgling as they engaged in combat with the egg sandwiches, and someone on the pavement outside shouted in furious tones that Tony was a wanker. Pilkington looked at his watch several times, and eventually cleared his throat and broke the silence.

'Well, now, ladies and gentlemen, we've a very full agenda, so . . .'

'Ten more seconds, I make it,' interrupted Elspeth, her braceleted arm producing a sound like a tambourine as she waved it imperiously in front of her, tapping the face of her watch with the forefinger of her other hand.

'Oh, really!' snapped Pilkington, slapping his palm on the table and turning to Rutter, like a lawyer to the judge. 'Do we really have to put up with this kind of thing?'

Rutter looked up and was about to say something, but Elspeth beat him to it.

'I'd like to remind you, young man,' she said, waving the scrawny forefinger at Pilkington now, 'that what you call "this kind of thing" is nothing less than democracy in action. You can't stifle the voice of the elected representative, you know, even if you have appointed yourself leader.'

'Oh, come on, Elspeth,' muttered Ernest Jinks, running a liver-spotted hand over his face, and glancing nervously at Patel and two Labour colleagues who had begun to snigger openly. 'Do give it a rest.'

'Give it a rest?' screeched Elspeth, throwing restraint aside and waving both hands. 'What do you mean, give it a rest? Have you seen this agenda? It's a travesty, a whitewash, and I'm proposing to put forward several emergency items for debate.'

'Such as?' drawled Pilkington. 'Because we'd need the agreement of the whole committee to add them to the agenda.'

Pilkington had clearly realized that his momentary loss of cool had played into her hands, and had recovered some of his smooth professional aplomb. But there were beads of sweat on his smooth forehead, and his fingers were playing nervously with his pen.

'Such as? Such as why is this man in the chair, for a start,' said Elspeth savagely. 'We haven't had a leadership election, you know, and he just assumes that he can take over and start dictating terms. Such as why he's planning to sell out to old-style municipal socialism by having secret meetings with Steve Ditchley. Such as why he's giving interviews to the press about the Conservative group changing direction – oh, yes! I know it's true, you can't deny it. And there are several other things I could mention.'

Rutter had half-risen to his feet and raised both arms like a conductor trying to gain the attention of the orchestra.

'If I could possibly assist in this matter, Mr Chairman,' he said obsequiously, nodding at Pilkington. 'It seems to me, with respect, Mrs Gorringe, that some of the matters you've mentioned, if not most – all, in fact – could be more suitably dealt with in the forum of your political group. You do have a full agenda of exclusively council business before you right now.'

'Hah!' exploded Elspeth, looking round in triumphant challenge at her fellow Conservative councillors, some of whom looked back at her doubtfully, wondering now if she was on to something. Ernest Jinks cleared his throat and spoke.

'Well, Mr Chairman, I entirely agree with the Chief Executive in as far as leadership questions are concerned, but since we're all here I can't see any harm in hearing a brief account of these other matters raised by Mrs Gorringe . . .'

Pilkington looked round, trying to gauge whether he'd have to give some sort of reply. He knew that many of his colleagues would take some time to transfer any loyalty to him, and there was enough dawning suspicion in their eyes to make him realize that he couldn't just give a blank refusal, as John Bullock would almost certainly have been able to do.

'Well, naturally I'm quite happy to take a few moments to put the record straight before we get started,' he said. 'Of course I can't go into much detail, given the presence of members of other parties. Suffice it to say that I have had a brief meeting with the leader of the joint shop stewards' committee, a meeting which was entirely at his request and at which I gave no undertakings whatsoever. And I have given a brief interview to the town hall correspondent of the *Examiner,* entirely at the paper's request once again, at which I said it was business as usual, no more, no less. Now, I would very much like to move on to today's agenda, starting with the new customer contracts on refuse disposal.'

'Hah!' ejaculated Elspeth again. 'Refuse disposal! I suppose that's how you regarded it, eh?'

Pilkington looked at her blankly for a moment, then went pale.

'What on earth do you mean?' he said quietly.

'What do I mean? Perhaps you'd like to explain to the committee why you've had a visit from the police. If not more than one. Eh? Eh?'

Elspeth's blood was fully up now: her bird-like ribcage was rising and falling rapidly, her eyes held a hectic, unnatural gleam, and each shouted word was delivered in a thin shower of spittle. Her two neighbours were leaning away from her, their faces torn between distaste and a fascinated admiration. At the far end of the table, Pilkington's tongue emerged lizard-like from his mouth and flicked over his dry lips. Everybody was looking at him now, and the room fell silent. Rutter had resumed fiddling with papers, but his hand had crept up to play with his scar.

'This is outrageous,' muttered Pilkington. 'The police are interviewing practically everybody who was in the town hall last week, and for Mrs Gorringe to single me out like this and try to draw some sort of damaging inference verges on the slanderous. It really is time for this meeting to come to order and—'

'Yes!' yelled Elspeth. 'They've interviewed Mr Patel here – not that he could tell them anything, poor sap – and they've interviewed Steve Ditchley, who was one of John's worst enemies from the word go. A nasty piece of work, I think even the Labour members agree on that. I'm sure there's more than one of us in this room who'd like him to be the leading suspect. But who's really got most to gain from John's assassination, that's what we've got to ask. No, Ernest, you can stop flapping your hand around like that, you're a wet willy and you always will be, so shut up. What we've got to ask is, who's got most to gain? Who thinks he's going to be the new leader of London's most go-ahead borough, and who thinks he's going to be the next Member of Parliament for Beechley South-East? We all know the answer to that one, don't we, and if I have my way he's got another think coming. When did you do it, eh? Right after the meeting? Or was it . . .'

It was Elspeth's finest hour, a *tour de force* of trembling, obsessive rhetoric, but it was too much for her. In the space of half a sentence, the blood drained out of her face, her voice dried into a hoarse gargle, her pale eyes revolved like dying Catherine wheels and she flopped back into her chair. For a moment people continued to stare at her in fascination, as if the collapse was part of the act. Then they realized that she was unconscious, that her torso was twitching unpleasantly, and that no actress could reproduce the terrifying noises she was producing in her struggle for breath.

'Call an ambulance!' said Pilkington loudly, unable to disguise the relief in his voice. Rutter jumped up and went to a phone on a table in the corner of the room. Una Granby, a former nurse in a grey twin-set, bustled round the table and supervised the laying of Elspeth on the ground and the administration of first aid. All but a couple of councillors backed off as if from the plague, and formed into little knots to gasp and gossip sotto voce. Rutter put the phone down and joined Pilkington by one of the windows, which he had pushed as far open as possible to get more air.

'Ambulance should be here in five minutes,' he said.

'Does she know something we don't?' muttered Pilkington, dabbing his face with his handkerchief. 'Or has she finally flipped?'

Rutter glanced over at the recumbent body and its kneeling attendants.

'Well, she was his greatest fan,' he sighed. 'She'd have died for him, and now he's died on her. Big shock to the system. She's obviously casting around for someone to blame – guided by her feelings rather than any evidence, to judge by that little performance. So I shouldn't worry too much.'

'She's taken against me in a big way, for some reason. I think she reckons I'm some sort of throwback who wants to betray the new Tory party and take us back to Butskellism, or some such nonsense. Total fantasy. Couldn't be further from the truth. But how come she knows all this stuff about who's been interviewed and who hasn't?'

'Beechley's quite a small place, Simon,' said Rutter. 'People talk. Ah look, here's the ambulance.'

Elspeth was rolled on to a stretcher, covered in a red blanket in spite of the heat, and loaded into the back of the ambulance. Shortly after it had pulled away from the kerb Pilkington, still watching at the window, saw a woman who looked familiar walk up and stop at the bottom of the town hall steps. She leaned against one of the pillars and scanned the passing traffic as if she was waiting for someone. She was a blonde, fit-looking woman in jeans, and for a moment, in his need for relief from the current drama, he slipped into a fantasy about picking her up himself and driving off for a little encounter somewhere. Then he realized she was the policewoman who'd sat in his garden at the weekend asking him questions, and immediately stopped fancying her. Instead he watched her more closely, and just as Rutter called him back to the committee table a maroon Volvo pulled up at the side of the road and Judy Best walked over to get into the passenger seat. Pilkington made a mental note of the index number and jotted it down as soon as he returned to his seat.

' . . . it may have been just a fainting fit, but there's always the possibility it was a mild stroke,' Una Granby was telling the others. 'I'll call at the hospital on my way home and see how she is – poor old duck.'

Pilkington found himself unable to share the general sympathy for Elspeth which was flowing around the table. Game old bird, they were saying, bit barmy, but we need her sort. He let them gossip on for a few minutes, his face set in grim silence as he wondered what that policewoman was up to and whether he would really have to go through a full-blown leadership election at the next group meeting. Then he sighed and called the meeting to order to tackle the item on waste collection: a nearby Labour council had recently offered people a pound for every occasion the dustmen failed to empty their bins on time, and John Bullock had angrily ordered the officers to draw up a superior scheme without delay. It looked like his last bequest to the people of Beechley was going to be a bin-owners' charter which offered let-down customers a choice of free tickets for an ailing local theme park or dinner at an Italian restaurant with the Lord Mayor and Lady Mayoress.

Chapter Twenty-One

Tuesday, 9.30 p.m.

Annabel Silver switched on the headlights of her maroon Volvo as she turned off the main road into Tupwood Lane. There was still plenty of light in the evening sky, but here it was filtered by the overhanging trees to a pond-like, grey-green gloom. The car's engine sounded suddenly louder in the enclosed space, and the bright lights swept briefly over bushes, great trunks of beech trees, tangled clusters of exposed roots on the banks of the semi-sunken road. A rabbit jinked in front of them for a few moments before veering into a patch of undergrowth. They were suddenly in the wild wood, a place of mystery and excitement, where hidden eyes might be watching and the skin began to prickle. It was the place where hundreds of citizens of Beechley came for their secret conversations and clandestine back-seat couplings; and three-quarters of a mile up this winding lane lay Halliloo Hill and Slump Quarry, where John Bullock had been unceremoniously discarded.

Judy sat quietly in the passenger seat, waiting for Annabel to start explaining. She'd picked Judy up at the town hall wearing sunglasses and heavy make-up, and said tersely that they'd go and park somewhere before they talked. For fifteen minutes they'd driven in silence, with Annabel, dressed in expensive-looking jeans and pink cotton sweater, exuding elegant perfume and high tension. She drove the big car rapidly and with confidence, and Judy considered how different their two lives must be: Annabel was moneyed, bored, and probably adulterous, while she was hard up, too busy for boredom, and celibate – for the moment, at least.

The canopy of trees opened out on one side of the lane, and they could see across to the Summerhill Estate a mile away, a decaying forest of system-built maisonettes familiar to Judy as the home of some of the borough's petty villains. The street lamps were on now, mapping Beechley's straggling suburbs, and to the north the great orange glow of the London night was taking over from the fading sun. On the other side were the beechwoods, with little rutted tracks leading off the road to secluded parking spots among the trees. Every few seconds Judy caught a glimpse of a car tucked away in the gloom, and as they took a bend the headlights swept across a windscreen, picking up two white, open-mouthed faces, like ghouls in a ghost train ride.

'Here we are,' muttered Annabel, slowing the car as they approached the set of steep climbing curves which took the lane up the final slope to the car park. The gearbox went into reverse with a grind and a clunk, and the engine whined as she turned in her seat to steer deftly backwards into the trees. Judy watched Annabel out of the corner of her eye, taking in the bounce of her dark hair, the ripeness in the curves of her face, the beautiful rings on the well-fleshed fingers. Then Annabel jerked on the handbrake, unclipped her safety belt and leaned back into the corner between her seat and the door. She looked nervous and defensive.

'Right,' she said, like a businesswoman starting a meeting. 'First of all, I want this to be confidential. It could land me in deep trouble. Personally, I mean.'

'I'll do my best, Mrs Silver,' said Judy. 'But it depends on the nature of what you've got to tell me.'

'What d'you mean?'

'Well, for example, it's very difficult to get round the requirement that a witness to a serious crime would have to appear in court.'

Annabel gave a little laugh, and glanced out of the driver's window, tapping the steering wheel with one finger. The car was almost enclosed by holly bushes on three sides; in front of them was the lane, and beyond that, in the twilight, was a field sweeping and undulating into the thickening twilight.

'Witness to a crime? It's not exactly that. It's just something that might help you.'

'What is it?'

'I saw John Bullock driving up here late on Thursday night. Half twelve, quarter to one in the morning, something like that.'

Judy tensed in her seat as a note of triumph sounded inside her, but she restrained herself from moving.

'How d'you know it was him?' she asked calmly.

'Well, I can't be absolutely certain it *was* him. But it was his car all right. Number plate and everything – I've seen it a hundred times.'

'And presumably you were sitting right here when you saw it?'

'That's right.'

'Did anyone else see it? Were you by yourself?'

176

Annabel waited a few seconds, tapping again on the steering-wheel before answering carefully, her voice thick with embarrassment.

'Yes, and no, respectively. That's the part that's confidential.'

'OK, I can see your difficulty. So it was about half twelve, and definitely his car, the silver Mercedes estate, right? Just him in it?'

'Just him, far as I could see.'

'The darkness must have made it a bit difficult.'

'Yes. So I couldn't swear it was him. But the thing which made me feel sure was the glasses. He wears glasses when he drives – drove, I should say – and there was enough light for me to see them glinting. He was sort of leaning forward over the wheel.'

'And was he driving fast?'

'Pretty fast, yes. Fast enough not to see us, anyway.'

'You must have thought it was pretty strange for him to be coming up here at that time of night.'

'Certainly did,' said Annabel ironically. 'People don't come up here late at night just to sniff the air or recite poetry.'

Judy glanced into the gloomy rear part of the car, wondering just how Annabel and her lover went about their business. Front seat? Back seat? Or did they lower the rear seats, creating a bed-like space for greater pyrotechnics and spreading of limbs? She imagined the rocking and the groaning, and found herself surreptitiously nosing the air for any lingering hint of sex among the plastic odours of the car interior. There was a sudden raucous cry out in the darkness somewhere, and Judy couldn't decide if it came from a bird or a human.

'So why didn't you tell us earlier? As soon as he disappeared? And more particularly, when he was murdered?'

Annabel shrugged and turned away, sighing. The darkness around them was near-complete now; Judy wound down her window to let in some air, and something rustled suddenly in the bushes nearby.

'I'd hoped it would be sorted out without too much trouble,' said Annabel eventually. 'I assumed that there'd be a simple explanation. After all, someone like John Bullock doesn't usually get mixed up in, well, crime. And the other thing was I wanted to protect Dorothy.'

'Not to mention yourself?'

'There was my situation, I grant you. I know it looks entirely selfish, but in fact it wasn't.'

'Go on, convince me.'

'Well, Dorothy had a bad enough time with John, with all the politics and Freemasonry, and I didn't want to be the one breaking the news that he was up to no good in some other way as well. I didn't want to upset her further. But in the end, with no sign of a breakthrough, I thought I'd better get in touch. I don't know if it helps, but there you are.'

Judy's mind was scurrying around trying to work out the implications of Annabel's information. It didn't fit too well with the pathologist's views about time of death, but he'd admitted himself that time of death was only a rough and ready business. It chimed well enough with Damson saying the car was still in town at six. It tended, if anything, to lend weight to Martin Donovan's protestations that Bullock hadn't responded to the blackmail note – not at lunchtime, at any rate, and Donovan had an alibi for the evening. It threw no new light on where Bullock would have spent the afternoon and evening. But the most frustrating thing for Judy just now was that it wouldn't prevent Manningbird from pinning the murder on poor Godfrey. She needed more.

'Mrs Silver,' she said cautiously, gently, 'I gather you've known Mrs Bullock and her husband a long time.'

'That's right. She and I went to school together. Shared the same cubicle in the dorm, had our first boyfriends at the same time, all that sort of thing. Less close since we got married and had children, of course. Life pulls you apart somewhat, doesn't it?'

She said it wearily and cynically, searching out Judy's eyes in the gloom for some sympathetic response to the shortcomings of her existence. Judy met her eyes and smiled noncommittally, struck by the thought that she could be like Annabel in ten years' time: children growing up, husband away a lot, career slipped out of reach, years flashing past.

'Certainly does,' she said neutrally. 'The Bullocks, though – what was their marriage like?'

Annabel shrugged and shook her head.

'Like so many other middle-class marriages round here – pretty conventional. He worked, she stayed at home. He earned it, she spent it. He did what he liked, she was tied to the house and kids. On the surface everything was normal. Underneath it was pretty rocky. Did you know he was a Mason?'

'Yes, she told me about the damage that did. But in what other way was it rocky?'

'Same way as most marriages. Lots of obligations, plenty of resentment, not much sex.'

'So did you know that Mr Bullock had been visiting a prostitute?'

'What?' Annabel's eyes lit up in the gloom, and she gave an excited little laugh. 'Really? The dirty bugger. How d'you find that out?'

'Someone was trying to blackmail him over it.'

'Does Dorothy know?' asked Annabel, suddenly concerned and protective again.

'Yes – I told her earlier today. She might have known already, I suppose, but she didn't let on.'

Annabel shook her head.

'I doubt it – she had a great capacity to stick her head in the sand. She didn't want anyone or anything to upset her safe little nest. Not like me, I'm afraid, taking silly risks all the time.'

'But every worm turns in the end, doesn't it, Mrs Silver?'

'What?' Annabel peered at Judy in the gloom. 'Oh, you mean Dorothy gets wind, decides she's had enough, and hits him on the head with a candlestick? Doesn't sound much like my Dorothy, I'm afraid. John was a secretive, manipulative bastard, but I don't think she'd ever turn on him.'

'Well, what about something a bit less dramatic? She's put up with the Freemasonry for years, she realizes he's playing away, for want of a better phrase, and decides it's time to do something similar herself.'

'An affair, you mean?'

Annabel was smiling enigmatically, the fading light glinting on her full, shiny lips, her moist white teeth. Affairs were her province, it seemed, and the suggestion of her tame and repressed little friend having one as well didn't seem to appeal to her. It would be a crossing of long-agreed boundaries, an invasion of territory, like the fat ugly schoolgirl stealing the admirer of her pretty best friend. But Annabel's smile faded as she thought, and her tone became more reflective.

'Well,' she said, sighing, 'it's possible, I suppose. The thought has crossed my mind recently, there's been something about her. But even if she was up to something, she probably wouldn't tell me. Look, the way it works is this: I tell her everything, lots of jokes, she listens, I say, "What about you," and she says, "Oh, there's nothing to tell." It's always been like that, that's the nature of the relationship. I know there's probably plenty for her to tell, but I suspect it would all be too miserable and messy and I'm not sure I want to hear it. No laughs. So I don't press.'

They heard the sound of an engine climbing up the lane, slowing, changing gear, speeding up, slowing again. Headlamps suddenly lanced through the foliage in front of them, creating a patchwork of bleached brilliance which made them blink and put their hands up to their eyes. Then the lights swung onwards, and as the car passed they caught a glimpse of two faces turning to see if the spot the Volvo occupied was free. For a few seconds afterwards, the outward curve of the lane allowed them to see the car's rear index number, lit by the little lamp beneath it.

'A bit of a one-way street, then?' asked Judy. 'The relationship with Dorothy, I mean?'

'Yes,' said Annabel, nodding sadly and sighing. 'But it was changing a bit over the last few days, at her mother's place. She was opening up a bit more.'

'In what way?'

'Well, there was a definite sense of relief, which rather surprised me. I thought it would be all grief and doom, but it wasn't.'

'D'you think she has any idea who'd done it?'

'I almost got the feeling she'd rather not know. You know – it had happened, nothing could bring him back, let's forget it and move on. No desire for revenge or anything like that, not that I could see.'

'Know anything about his financial affairs? Swiss bank accounts, things like that?'

Annabel held up a hand, palm outwards, and turned her face away. Her voice became indifferent, distant, and firm.

'Don't ask me anything about that sort of stuff, because I just don't know. And I don't think Dorothy did either. Everyone was a bit surprised when they bought their new house just as the property business was taking a dive, but I suppose the price of houses was dropping as well. You know what men are like with money, they keep it close to their chest, that's how they control things. And John was worse than most in that way. I dare say he had fingers in all sorts of pies.'

Annabel stopped and bent over her forearm, holding her watch between finger and thumb and twisting it round to the dwindling light. There was more rustling from the bushes outside, and Judy looked round nervously, half-expecting a face to loom up at the window and leer at her.

'Listen,' said Annabel, the brisk businesswoman again. 'I really must be getting back. My excuse is running out. Now, you will keep this confidential, won't you?'

'I'll do my best.'

Annabel started the car, eased it forward off the rutted leaf-mould beneath the trees, and drove slowly down the lane. There seemed to be more cars parked among the trees now, and as the lights of the Volvo passed close to one of them Judy was sure she saw a naked back, white as a slug, hunched over the front passenger seat.

'What the hell if it does come out,' Annabel muttered with a sudden vehemence. 'If Adrian doesn't like it, he can bloody well lump it.'

Judy was about to slide her key in the lock when she heard a footstep on the path behind her and wheeled round rapidly, lifting the key as a weapon. A tall man was walking towards her, faster than she would like, and she didn't recognize him until she saw the pale plaster on his cheek.

'Colin!' she said. 'You had me worried. What d'you want?'

'Charming,' he said, coming to a halt a few feet away and sounding aggrieved. 'I wanted to see you. Didn't know where you'd gone.'

'Sorry,' said Judy, turning and opening the door. 'I didn't mean to sound so hostile. But you shouldn't come at people in the dark like that.'

He followed her into the hallway, and as she reached out for the light switch he grabbed her round the waist from behind and buried his face in her hair, kissing her ear and cheek like a clumsy child. She smelt the beer on his breath and gently pushed him backwards with her elbows as the unshaded bulb snapped on above them, showing up the shabbiness of the hallway and the tortured look on Colin's face.

'You'd better come up for a coffee,' she said coolly. 'And I mean coffee.'

Judy pushed Colin into the sitting-room, and when she returned from the kitchen with steaming mugs and a packet of biscuits he was half-lying on the sofa staring moodily at the Japanese print of the big wave.

'That's how I feel sometimes,' he said, gesturing at it loosely. 'Just like those guys in the boat.'

'We all do,' said Judy, flopping into the armchair. 'That's the whole idea. So please don't tell me about it.'

Colin pulled himself into a more upright position, picked up the packet of ginger nuts and began wrestling ineffectually with the cellophane. He was breathing heavily, his emotions on the surface.

'You're in a crabby mood tonight,' he said, eyeing her with a mixture of desire and resentment. 'Where've you been, out with your women's group? Feminist collective?'

'You could call it that,' said Judy, taking the packet of biscuits from him and slicing it open with a knife, as if she were cutting a salami. 'Was there anything on the case, after I left the station? Has the Fat Man fitted up poor little Godfrey yet?'

'Now then, Judy, where's your respect?' said Colin, biting into a biscuit and crunching it aggressively, as if it was the cause of his confusion. 'There were a couple of things, as a matter of fact. I reckon it's the widow who did it.'

'Why d'you say that?

'We had the forensic lab on earlier.' Colin was dragging it out, enjoying the power of holding back information.

'And?'

'Blue fibres sticking to his blazer and trousers, and caught in the heels of his shoes. Carpet fibres, probably. You remember their front room? Or lounge, or drawing-room, or whatever they'd call it?'

Judy nodded slowly, munching her biscuit.

'Blue carpet. Very interesting.'

'Interesting?' There was a sudden liveliness in Colin as the job took over from introspection. 'Isn't that enough for you? She gets him to come home at lunchtime – picks him up in her car, maybe. Then she bashes him on the head, and stuffs him in a cupboard while her friends come to tea. He wasn't bleeding, remember. Then she goes down at night to collect his motor, takes him up and dumps him, walks back.'

'You really believe that?'

'Well, it's a theory, isn't it? Fits better than any of the others I've heard.'

'Well, the lab can test it out pretty easily, see if the fibres match. The only trouble is, if the Fat Man wants to pin it on Godfrey, he'll just say it's not surprising that a few fibres from a man's front room are on his clothes. And your theory doesn't fit with what I've been hearing at the feminist collective.'

'Go on then,' sighed Colin, staring at her with doggy eyes. 'Tell me about it.'

She related her evening with Annabel among the courting couples of Tupwood Lane. Colin listened carefully, sipping at his coffee. When she'd finished he put the mug on the table and gave a deprecatory little sniff.

'How sure was she that it was him driving?'

'Pretty sure. A car came past while we were there, and you could see enough of the faces inside as it went past.'

Judy yawned and pulled her hair back from her face with both hands. She was short of sleep, she wanted to forget about everything and make a fresh start in the morning. But she'd allowed things to start happening with Colin, and now here he was, tired and emotional, looking like a Labrador expecting its biscuits and indicating with the occasional growl that it might turn nasty if it didn't get them. This wasn't the best time or place, but she had no choice but to sort things out.

'Why'd you come here tonight, Colin?' she asked harshly. 'Why didn't you go home like a good Christian?'

He looked up at her with a sudden expression of surprise and shame, like a boy accused of stealing sweets. He looked at her silently, waiting for clemency. Judy ploughed on.

'Because I think we ought to get a grip on this thing, to use a slightly unfortunate expression. I like you a lot, Colin, and I fancy you a bit too, but it would be a disaster for us to have an affair.'

'Why?' His tone was hurt and pleading, the wrinkles on his face drawn tight.

'Well, I don't know what it would do to you, but in my case it would ruin my career. I've seen it happen to other women who get mixed up with married officers. D'you think word wouldn't get around if I went to bed with you? Course it would. I'd be a slag, a pushover, a home-breaker, an offender against the whole two-faced bloody code. I'd rather be a flat-chested dyke or a nigger-lover or a hard-faced bitch, or whatever it is I'm meant to be at the moment. My prospects are rather better that way. And besides, I don't want to get into the sort of hole and corner stuff that woman Annabel goes in for, touring around the countryside at night and fucking in the back seat. That's what adultery's all about, Colin. It doesn't make her happy, and I had enough of that kind of thing when I was about nineteen. They're already grinning behind our backs and making stupid jokes, you know that, don't you?'

There was a mixture of delight and pain on his face, as if he agreed with her but couldn't bear to hear it. Judy thought she saw a tinge of vanity there as well, which made her suddenly angry.

'Come on, you,' she said. 'You're a bloody hypocrite. You've got God, which means family values and fidelity – presumably. And here you are sneaking round the place trying to get your leg over. And afterwards you'll be sniggering about it with your mates. Done this sort of thing before, have you? It's time to go home, Colin.'

But instead of getting up and going to the door, Colin slid forward off the sofa on to his knees, planted his elbows among the curling newspapers on the low table, and took his face in his hands with a tormented grunt. Judy watched in horror: he was going to pray, to confess, to spill his soul. His shoulders and heels had the awkward boniness of a body no longer buoyant and supple, and she felt an internal twist of revulsion at the decay of middle age.

'You're right, Judy, you're right,' he moaned. 'I'm a hypocrite, I'm as rotten as the rest of them. It's because I'm weak, and you're so lovely, and I can't resist you, and I know it's wrong, but I can't help it.'

He took one hand away from his face and held it out to her. She sat well back in her chair, her arms folded and her face cold: it was hard to believe someone fancied you, she thought, if he despised himself for it. A bit more animal conviction, and she might have given in by now, wife or no wife, career or not. She found herself speaking to him as she would to a drunk lurching around outside a pub, haranguing passers-by.

'OK, Colin, you've had a lot to drink, it's all got a bit out of hand, I know, but now's not the time for all this. You've had your say, I know how you feel, but it's time to forget it and get on home to bed. OK?'

It had the wrong effect on Colin. His face suddenly appeared, red and twisted, from behind his hand, and he began to jab at her with an accusing forefinger.

'No, it's not OK!' he shouted, a fleck of white appearing at the corner of his mouth. 'It's your fault too, you're as much to blame as me. You're a, you're a . . .'

'Tart? Jezebel? Or would "prick-teaser" be the word you're looking for?'

The taunt, spoken lightly and coolly, was too much for him. He suddenly sprang for her, knocking over a coffee mug on the table, and grabbed her by the wrists. At first Judy thought he was trying to force her hands together in prayer, but then he seemed to abandon that in favour of pulling her out of the chair, pushing her on to the floor and falling on top of her.

'Colin!' she gasped. 'What the hell are you doing?'

'I'm, I'm,' he muttered desperately, wrestling her arms back onto the carpet. 'I'm trying to, I'm going to . . . oh, fuck, I don't know.'

He suddenly went limp, his mouth panting and moist against her neck. The weight of his body, suddenly inert and motionless, gave Judy a strange sense of peace and mild amusement. She lay still for a while and looked up at the ceiling, watching a dirty strand of cobweb twisting in the currents of warm air from the light. Her hand came round and gently stroked the back of Colin's head, her fingers delicately feeling round the dressing on the little shaved patch.

'Colin?' she asked quietly. He grunted into her hair.

'Colin, why aren't there any suitable men around?'

'All men are unsuitable,' he slurred, not lifting his face.

'Pigs and rapists?' At least it wasn't just himself he despised.

'That sort of thing.'

'Ah,' she said, yawning. 'So that's it. I'd always wondered.'

184

Chapter Twenty-Two

Wednesday, 11.30 a.m.

'Officer, why does this prisoner look as if he's been dragged through a bush backwards?'

The custody sergeant, pale and sunken-cheeked, looked round the court, as if hoping that the chairman of the bench was addressing someone else. But the blue marbles of her eyes were fixed on him, and he licked his lips uneasily.

'Er, my apologies, ma'am,' he muttered, looking sideways at the scruffy youth in the dock, who smirked back at him gleefully.

'Kindly see to it that prisoners are a little more presentable when they appear in my court. This individual hasn't shaved or brushed his hair in weeks. Now then, what was the charge?'

Mrs Camilla Todhunter was at her most imperious this morning, slapping down solicitors, being rude to the clerk, and treating defendants like mentally defective children. Judy, who had witnessed the perform-ance many times, lounged on the benches at the back of the court, yawning and worrying about what was going on back at the station. It was taking so long for Martin Donovan's case to come up she was beginning to suspect that Manningbird had arranged it like that: the longer she was out of the way, the easier it would be for him and Jim Duncan to pursue their attempts to get a confession out of Godfrey.

The scruffy youth was remanded in custody and Donovan, hulking and impassive, was finally ushered through the door from the cells. Mrs Todhunter looked sceptically at his creased black shirt and dishevel-led ginger hair, while Donovan's icy green eyes roved round until they found Judy. He raised a great forefinger and was halfway through mouthing a threat at her when the piercing contralto of the magistrate rang out.

'Any more of these childish gestures, Donovan, and you'll go straight back to the cells. I don't mind hearing your case in your absence – in fact, I might prefer it.'

The charges were read out – blackmail, actual bodily harm, resisting arrest – and Mrs Todhunter decided after brief evidence from Judy that Donovan should be remanded in custody to have his case dealt with by the Crown Court. Donovan raised a middle finger at Judy as he was bundled out of the court, but she ignored him and walked out into the lobby, where the usual crowd of anxious and confused people were huddled round the noticeboard or sitting on the tattered chairs, smoking.

She was heading for the stairs when she was waylaid by two local reporters, a man and a woman. They were both in their early twenties, with lank hair and battered clothes, and while one asked a question or scribbled down a note, the other would chew on a finger and look around anxiously.

'This Godfrey bloke, then,' said the man. 'He going to be charged with the Bullock thing, or what?'

'No idea,' said Judy impassively. 'Inquiries are continuing. That's all I can say.'

'But Donovan's off the hook?'

'Looks like it, doesn't it? You two investigators got anything to tell me, then?'

The two suddenly lost interest and drifted off, conferring and gesturing intensely, like vagrants arguing over cans of lager. As she walked out into the bright noonday heat, Judy felt suddenly weak and exhausted: she'd hardly slept for three nights, she hadn't been eating properly, and her senior officer was barking up the wrong tree. She stopped a few yards along the pavement and glanced back at the magistrates' court, a stained, slab-sided creation of the 1960s with a dirty concrete lion and unicorn clutching the royal shield: someone else could worry about the case for an hour or so.

She bought a sandwich and coffee and made her way to the garden round the war memorial, a white stone obelisk flanked by four First World War soldiers leaning on rifles and staring gloomily at their feet. She sat next to a bony old woman feeding the squabbling pigeons and stared at the public symbol of ancient Egypt, adopted first by the Freemasons and then by the state, and now bearing spray-painted swastikas, erased by council workmen but still visible. Her mind returned to the Masonic widow, to the discussion with Annabel about an affair, to Colin's latest suspicions over the blue fibres. She'd been trying not to think of Colin, but now she remembered: he'd promised to go over to the Telecom building this morning and get the printout of Dorothy's telephone contacts. She finished her sandwich, and threw the screwed-up papers in a bin, sending the pigeons flapping and earning a reproachful stare from the old woman.

'Sorry,' said Judy cheerfully, setting off for the station. The sky was turning yellow at the edges with the threat of an approaching storm, and she suddenly felt confident there would soon be a breakthrough.

Wednesday, 1.30 p.m.

Judy was passing through the swing doors when she spotted someone half-familiar among the people in the waiting-room. She paused and peered through the glass at the nut-brown face, out of place among the maggot-white complexions around it, and recognized the farmer from Slump Quarry. His sleeves were rolled up over broad forearms, his hands were planted on his knees, and he was grinning back at her, his little eyes gleaming cleverly. Judy opened the door and put her head round it.

'Hello, Miss Detective,' said the farmer sarcastically, before she could open her mouth. 'I've got something for you, I have.'

Judy glanced round at the other faces, all of them watching with the heightened tension of visitors to enemy territory, alert for detail which might help or harm them. There was a heavily pregnant woman with red eyes, smoking a cigarette, and a sharp-faced man in a suit, playing impatiently with a bunch of keys.

'You'd better come with me, then,' said Judy, holding the door open for him.

He picked up a white plastic bag from between his dusty black boots and followed her, leaning against the wall in the corridor and hitching up his loose trousers while Judy spoke to the desk sergeant. It was the same officer who'd been there when she'd been attacked by Godfrey, and he looked at her as if she was diseased.

The interview room quickly filled with farming smells of milk, dust and cow hide. Before Judy could say anything the stout little man sat down heavily, lifted the plastic bag and up-ended it above the table. Out tumbled a large piece of thick white polythene, folded to the size of a bulky magazine and bound up with shiny, honey-coloured tape.

'Don't think much of your search,' he said mockingly. 'All those coppers poking round the place for days. Me and my dog found this in half an hour.'

Judy met his eyes for a moment; his manner was humorous, but there was an underlying remorselessness which made her wonder if he was the sort who liked badger-baiting and illegal dog fights: he would sit there, smiling beadily at the blood and screams.

'Let's have a look, then,' she said. 'Where exactly did you find it?'

'Foot of the face, fifty, sixty yards from where you found that

187

Conservative chappie. Place where people chuck their rubbish over.'

Judy picked up the package of polythene and held it up to the strip light, squinting to see if there was anything inside it.

'What made you think this had anything to do with the case?' she asked.

'That's a new piece of stuff, that is,' said the farmer. 'Not the usual sort of shite gets tipped over the edge. And I thought you lot had all these forensics and that these days. I'll take it home if you don't want it – nice bit of plastic, that, use it on the farm.'

'No, don't worry, we'll have a look,' said Judy, keeping her hand on the shiny bundle. 'What were you doing searching the quarry, then – looking for another body?'

The hard grin didn't flicker, the round brown face gave nothing away, and the voice remained mocking and sarcastic.

'I have a look round in there time to time – never know what people leave behind or chuck over the edge. Found a very nice old radio once – worked a treat. Anyway, they reckon you've got a nutcase lined up for this one.'

'How d'you know that?' asked Judy sharply, pushing her hair out of her perspiring face.

'Plenty of 'em around, all right,' said the farmer cannily, ignoring her question. 'Probably did those other two, and all, eh? The old bloke and the old bag? Strangled, weren't they?'

Judy looked at him carefully and tried to dredge up what she remembered about psychopaths from the lectures at training school: lacking conventional notions of right and wrong, without appreciation of the sufferings of others. He'd certainly be used to hitting animals on the head and the other routine cruelties of farming work.

'We're still working on the case,' said Judy evenly. 'You seem very interested, though – any other theories, while you're at it?'

'Me? Why me?' He opened his palms and shrugged his shoulders, still grinning. 'I'm just a farmer. I'm not a clever detective like you. Usually sex or money, though, ain't it?'

Judy picked up the polythene, went to bag and label it, and came back to take a statement from him. His name was Archie Harrison, he lived at White Rocks Farm, he'd found the object yesterday; he signed his name as if he was stirring paint, and clumped out of the station again, still grinning and giving off a whiff of silage.

Up in the incident room, Manningbird stared at Judy, hard-faced, as she told him first about Annabel's story and then about the polythene.

188

For a while he seemed edgy, then relaxed when he realized that it was nothing conclusive.

'We'll forensicate the sheet if you like,' he said. 'But I can't see where it'll take us. Bit like the fibres from the sitting-room.'

'The polythene might have been used to wrap the body,' said Judy. 'Or transport it from one place to another.'

Manningbird eyed her impatiently for a moment, irritated at having to think about yet another theory.

'I thought the body drove itself up there, according to your Mrs Silver,' he said tersely. 'So what are you talking about – moving it from where to where?'

'Not sure, really,' said Judy, hesitating. 'I'm still thinking about it.'

Manningbird raised his eyes to heaven. Judy could sense Jim Duncan watching them and grinning, and she steeled herself against turning to look at him.

'Listen, Judy,' said Manningbird. 'I know you're concerned about young Godfrey, so we've held off interviewing him again this morning while his parents lay on a solicitor. The police surgeon says he's all right today, and we'll only question him again with the lawyer there – now, how's that?'

'Better, sir,' said Judy, her face impassive. 'But I can't see the point. Apart from anything else, it doesn't square with the post-mortem evidence, like I said before – there's no way that kid killed Bullock.'

'Well, you're bound to feel that, aren't you, Judy? Otherwise you'd have to admit you made a mistake when he first came in. And your woman's evidence doesn't fit the forensic either – time of death would be wrong.'

His eyes were hard and unforgiving for a moment, and Judy looked back, controlled her anger. Then he reached out and tapped her matily on the elbow, his voice suddenly low and confiding.

'Come on, Judy,' he cajoled. 'You've got to take the breaks when you get them – why make it hard for yourself? After all, it won't make much difference to the kid. Broadmoor's the best place for him, get the right treatment at last.'

Judy flicked the corners of her mouth up and down in a mock-smile, and glanced round the room. Duncan was sidling up, hands in pockets, a knowing grin on his face.

'Whatever you say, sir,' she said tonelessly. 'Colin around, is he?'

'Out on a burglary, back any minute,' said Manningbird, standing up and buttoning his jacket over his vast paunch. 'He'll explain – Jim and I are just going to grab some lunch.'

189

'He said he had something to show you,' said Duncan insinuatingly from behind her.

'Something big,' smirked Manningbird.

'Yes, sir,' said Judy, restraining the urge to smack his rubbery grey face. 'Isn't that what all the boys say?'

Chapter Twenty-Three

Wednesday, 2.30 p.m.

Judy found the printout in Colin's top drawer, among the paper clips and expenses forms. There were about two dozen phone calls in the forty-eight hours since Dorothy's return from her mother's house, and Judy already knew some of the names and addresses scrawled next to the numbers by the Telecom manager – Dorothy's mother, Annabel Silver, Nigel and Betty Damson. Then there was a local funeral director, the schools of the son and daughter, neighbours who had probably phoned to commiserate. But most interesting of all were four calls made to Jumpers from a number in Beechley town hall.

Judy sat down in Colin's chair and ran her fingernail carefully along the figures. The first call, lasting two minutes twenty seconds, was made just before six o'clock in the evening on Monday – soon after Dorothy would have got home. The second was made at 10.14 in the morning on Tuesday and lasted twelve seconds; the third was at 3.41 on Tuesday afternoon and lasted five seconds; and the last one, also five seconds, was just after ten on Wednesday – this morning – which must have been immediately before Colin collected the list. She scrabbled about in the dusty drawer until she found a highlighter pen, and slowly put a thick orange mark over the call made midmorning on Tuesday: she'd been sitting in Dorothy's kitchen at the time, hearing how intolerable it had been living with John Bullock. Dorothy had tried to say the call was from her mother, but what had Judy heard through the door? Something like 'No, no, I can't talk to you – and please, don't phone back.'

'Interesting, eh?'

It was Colin, who'd come up quietly behind her and was now leaning over the desk at her side. His face looked blotchy and hung-over, and the wrinkles round his eyes were deeper and darker than usual. The dressing on his cheek was dirty, and she wondered if he had delayed shock from his injuries two days before.

191

'Very interesting,' she said, putting a large orange cross next to the 10.14 call and telling him what she'd overheard.

'Her mother? No way it could be her mother,' he said. Judy could smell the sourness of his breath and remembered his mouth against her neck on the floor of her living room.

'Definitely not the mother. Don't the Telecom know who this town hall number belongs to?'

'No – it's one of dozens. Only the internal switchboard could tell us who's got which number.'

'Why don't we get over there now?' said Judy, standing up and pulling back a swath of hair from her face, glad of a reason to move away from him.

'Hang about,' said Colin, taking her place in his chair with a little gasp of tiredness. 'I've got to get shot of the paperwork on this Damson burglary.'

'This what?'

'They didn't tell you? The Damsons got burgled last night.'

Judy blinked at him in surprise.

'No, really? I can't keep up with this case any longer. What happened?'

'Well, it looked like a very professional job to me. They forced a small window at the side and used the service engineer's code to silence the alarm – God knows how they got hold of that. Neighbours heard it ring for about twenty seconds and stop – didn't call the police because they thought it must just be a fault. The Damsons were out to dinner, came back to find the study and all the paperwork ransacked, but some quite valuable jewellery left in an unlocked drawer in the bedroom.'

'Looks like someone thinks Damson's got the Swiss bank statements.'

'Yeah. And I didn't tell Damson which large person might have told someone where to look.'

'Damson still swears he never had them?'

'That's right. I tend to believe his line that if he had them he'd hand them straight to us.'

'Unless he's planning to blackmail Kingswood with them, of course.'

'Give it a rest,' said Colin wearily, blotting little beads of sweat from his forehead with a grubby-looking handkerchief. 'Bullock might have a safe deposit box, or he might have destroyed all the records. Someone might be making the whole thing up.'

'I'm just trying to think,' said Judy, staring out of the window. 'Was there a blue carpet in Damson's office?'

Colin gave her a bilious look.

'For God's sake, Judy, leave off. This case plus a hangover is giving me a headache, I don't mind telling you. Why don't you go and get the coffees while I sort this lot out?'

'*Me* get the coffees? That's a woman's job, is it?'

'Don't be boring, Judy,' he said, not looking up. 'I got it about four times yesterday.'

Judy fetched him some coffee and went off to the locker room to change out of her suit into jeans and a T-shirt. As she took her skirt off she noticed a large bruise near her hip and remembered how heavily Colin had landed on top of her. After he'd abased himself and men in general for ten minutes, he'd climbed off her and gone home, crestfallen but evidently feeling better. Judy had gone to bed feeling worse, determined never to accept his promised invitation to go round for dinner with him and his family. Neither of them mentioned the episode until they were in the lift, on the way out to the town hall.

'Sorry about last night, Judy,' he muttered as the little cubicle lurched and banged. She had just embarked on a luxurious yawn, eyes tightly closed, and he stared haggardly into her open, quivering mouth.

'Don't worry about it,' she said eventually, wiping an involuntary tear from the corner of her eyes. 'Put it down to that nasty bang on the head.'

'That's a good excuse.'

Outside the yellow tinge round the rim of sky was creeping higher. People toiling along the hot pavements were lifting their faces to feel occasional breaths of wind in the air. Faint grumblings of far-away thunder produced little smiles of expectation, as if they had already tired of the longed-for warmth of summer and were relishing the prospect of rain to chill the air and sluice away the dust. BULLOCK MURDER: MAN HELD proclaimed a *Standard* poster outside a newsagent; Judy glowered at it. A few minutes later they trotted slowly up the shallow steps of the town hall, under the gaze of the cheerful, useful citizens on the stone-carved frieze above them.

Wednesday, 4 p.m.

It was cooler in the entrance hall, and Judy strolled slowly up and down while they waited for the head of security. She took in the wide staircase with its oak-topped banisters, the polished wooden floor, the pale brown marble walls with the new security camera high in a corner. At the far end a couple of workmen were reglazing the last of the windows smashed during Steve Ditchley's day of action the previous week. A wiry, harassed-looking man in thick spectacles clipped busily down the stairs and went out, nodding to the tightly permed receptionist.

'That was the chief executive,' said Colin, slumped on a bench, as Judy patrolled past.

'Really? Looks as if he needs a holiday.'

The head of security was a paunchy ex-policeman with brilliantined hair and a nicotine-stained smile. He shook their hands unnecessarily long and hard, as if to convince them he hadn't gone to seed, and let his veiny eyes trail up and down Judy's body. As they followed him through a door under the staircase, Judy asked him about the security review: the new cameras were going to be switched on next week, and before long there would be swipe cards, plastic name badges, and a turnstile by the front desk.

'You used to get winos off the street wandering round these corridors,' he said, grinning at them as he stopped to open a door. 'But soon you won't even be able to fart in this place without me knowing about it. Here we are – switchboard.'

Three women in headsets were sitting in a dim, cupboard-like room confronting banks of little levers and blinking lights. They were all sing-songing the same phrases to distant callers, as if taking part in some endless, demented canon. 'Hello, London Borough of Beechley, can I help you? Engaged, will you hold? Putting you through now, caller. No reply on that extension. Hello, London Borough of Beechley, can I help you?'

The head of security touched one of them on the shoulder. She started, pulled off her headset, and swivelled on her chair to face them. She had a pallid, underground face, spiky black hair, and one of her hands began groping urgently for her packet of cigarettes, like a suspect facing the third degree. She lit up with a practised flick of the lighter and disappeared behind a film of smoke with the piece of paper Judy passed to her. Then she reached behind her, flicked through a sheaf of papers stapled together, and ran her finger down one of the dog-eared pages.

'Small conference room,' she declared eventually, pulling her cigarette off her peeling lower lip. 'Second floor, rear extension.'

'So it's not in someone's office?' asked Judy, fanning the trails of smoke away from her face with one hand.

'Nah,' said the woman, blowing out more smoke.

'So who uses it?'

'All sorts. Senior officers go in there if their own offices aren't big

194

enough. Like if they have big meetings with people from outside, contractors and that. Most of the time it's empty.'

'So why's it got a direct line?'

The woman crossed her short but shapely legs and dangled a pink fluffy slipper off one toe, giving Judy a look which said that she didn't take kindly to being interrogated by another woman, especially a younger one.

'Search me,' she said indifferently.

Judy looked round at the head of security, who put his hand on her waist to steer her towards the door.

'The line might be there so people from outside can make confidential calls,' he said, so close to her ear she heard the constant wheeze in his breath. 'Let's just go along to my office for a moment.'

Judy stepped fast through the door and the hand fell away. At the far end of the parquet-floored corridor, his office had a large desk and several shelves of brochures for security equipment.

'More I think about it,' the security man said, sitting down on his leather chair and swivelling self-importantly, 'it's probably just staff who knew Mrs Bullock – you know, ringing up to express their regrets.'

'What's wrong with their own phones?' asked Colin.

'No personal calls on office phones, so they nip in there instead of using the payphone.'

'But these were five-second calls,' cut in Judy.

The security man shrugged his shoulders irritably, tiring of the inquisition and picking up a computer printout from his desk.

'Just a theory,' he said. 'Anyway, I'm glad you've come in, because I was going to get in touch with you. There's something else I think you ought to know.'

'What is it?' asked Colin, rubbing his face wearily.

The security man felt in his pocket for his cigarettes, drawing out his moment of importance with the ritual of selecting, tapping, lighting, exhaling.

'I don't know how much help it's going to be,' he said slowly, judiciously studying the far corner of the room. 'Might just confuse things for you further.'

'Do spit it out,' muttered Colin in a sickly voice from behind his hands.

'Well, there's this greengrocer over the road there, out the side of the town hall, lives in the flat above the shop. Got this little Yorkshire terrier, nasty bit of dogflesh, if you ask me, all flaking and mangy, know the kind of thing? Leaves a trail behind it. Anyway, he takes it out for a dump late at night, and he swears he saw a big Merc, station wagon, coming into the car park last Thursday. After midnight. He was telling me in the pub this lunchtime.'

Colin had emerged from behind his hands and was paying more attention.

'Bullock's, you reckon?'

'Who else's? No one else with a Merc has got a card to let them through the barrier. In fact, no one else has got a Merc, full stop.'

'So what do the car park records say?'

The security man took a deep drag and shook his head, his grin halfway between triumph and regret.

'No use, I'm afraid. Two weeks' time we're getting a new machine, log all the movements, little printout often as you like. But the one we've got now just lets people in and out. No records. Bit of a bugger, eh?'

Colin looked at Judy with an exasperated sigh. She was staring at the security man, her face tense and glowing.

'Did this greengrocer see who was in the car?' she asked.

'Said he didn't notice.'

'Why the hell didn't he come to us about it?'

The security man shrugged.

'He didn't know whose car it was – didn't know you'd be interested. You know how it is. He only mentioned it when I was chatting to him about this new system. Said he'd noticed it because cars hardly ever go in there so late.'

'OK, we'll go and see him,' said Judy briskly. 'Now, any security staff here at that time?'

'After midnight? No.'

'And would Bullock have had keys?'

'Not normally, no.'

'So who has keys all the time?'

'Myself, the member of my staff due to open up the next day. Chief executive and a couple of the chief officers have got a key to the back. That's all.'

Judy paused and looked over at Colin.

'I think maybe the next stop is the chief executive, don't you?' she said.

'Yes,' said Colin, looking more blotchy and haggard than before. 'There's more than one man who wears glasses to drive.'

'Is Mr Rutter still out?' asked Judy. The security man, looking sulky and baffled, dialled a number and spoke briefly to someone called Stella.

'Gone until the morning,' he said, putting the phone down. 'Last few days have knackered him, I reckon.'

Colin struggled to his feet with a little gasp and followed Judy to the door.

'There's just one more thing,' Judy said, standing well clear of the security man's hands. 'Got any blue carpets in the town hall?'

The security man pursed his lips, shook his head.

'Can't think of any, offhand. Apart from the council chamber, that is. Why?'

'Never mind,' said Colin. 'We'll tell you later.'

Chapter Twenty-Four

Wednesday, 6 p.m.

The first drops of rain began to splatter on the dusty windscreen as they turned into Blackthorn Avenue and cruised along close to the kerb, checking the house numbers. It was a wide, wealthy-looking road with a grass verge planted with ornamental fruit trees, and the houses, neatly tiled and painted and with clean windows, were set back behind little walls or neatly sculpted hedges. Judy peered through the passenger window at names like Tantallon and Robin's Rest, carved on oval varnished boards cut to look like slices from logs. By the time they located number 99, among a row of detached Victorian houses, the rain was drumming on the roof and the windscreen wipers were squeaking their way through a thinning soup of water and grime. Each long grumble of thunder seemed to be closer, and now and then the gloom was lit by brilliant silver sheets of lightning.

'Got your mac?' murmured Colin, slowing to a halt and watching in the mirror for the second unmarked car with three detective constables in it. Judy grimaced and shivered as she opened the door and stepped out. Colin ran behind her up the drive, past Rutter's red Rover and a battered yellow Mini, and into the shelter of the little brick porch. Rutter's wife Eunice, wearing a flowery dress and sandals, opened the door and looked at them from behind her round, blue-rimmed glasses.

'Yes?' she said impatiently, her round red mouth half-covered by a curtain of blonde hair. 'What is it?'

Colin told her who they were and asked if they could speak to her husband. Eunice returned to pulling a thick academic journal out of a brown envelope, her face almost disappearing behind the hair.

'I'm afraid you can't,' she said. 'He's out. Running.'

She looked up at them with a perfunctory smile and placed a hand on the edge of the door, ready to close it again. Colin put his hand gently against one of the white-painted panels.

'He won't be long, will he? Do you mind if we wait?'

Eunice seemed suddenly to realize that it must be serious if two police officers were on her doorstep refusing to go away. She looked speculatively from one to the other, then pulled the door wide and waved the journal to invite them inside.

'Not at all. Go straight through to the kitchen.'

Colin and Judy walked through the tiled hallway with its scattering of shoes and briefcases, past the massive dark-brown stair posts and into a kitchen which stretched across the back of the house. Rain was driving onto the windows now, and Judy peered through them at the garden, which rose towards a wall thirty yards away.

'Nice location here,' she said, as Eunice walked to the table to continue opening her mail. 'Gives straight on to open country at the back, does it?'

Eunice, running a sharp kitchen knife through an envelope, flashed her a glance which said she wasn't interested in small talk.

'What's all this about, then?' she asked briskly. 'Presumably it's the Bullock murder, is it?'

'That's right,' said Colin. 'A couple of things have come up which we need to check out with your husband.'

'Well, he's bloody upset about it, I can tell you that much,' said Eunice, reaching for another large envelope, hair swinging, knife at the ready.

'Did he ever say much about Mr Bullock? Before the murder, I mean?'

'Nothing very complimentary, I'm afraid. That's why I was a bit surprised at him taking it so badly. You see, Bullock wanted to get rid of him because he didn't fall in with the new privatizing, service-cutting ideology. You know how it is in local government these days.'

'So you didn't know the Bullocks socially, at all?'

'I never get mixed up with things to do with Barry's work,' said Eunice firmly, screwing up the dismembered envelopes and dropping them into a swing-top bin. 'He had to go to various functions with them, of course. And it was Mrs Bullock who patched him up when he got his head split open at the riot.'

Judy looked at Colin, raising her eyebrows and nodding. Eunice noticed it and glared at her, putting one hand on her thick, flowery hip.

'And what's that supposed to mean?' she asked sharply. 'Little signs and signals?'

'Not at all, Mrs Rutter,' said Judy smoothly. 'Listen, do you mind if I have a quick look outside? I see you've been having a bit of work done on the house.'

'Please yourself,' said Eunice, gesturing at the back door. 'Get as wet as you like.'

Judy twisted the brass knob and stepped out onto a strip of paving along the rear wall of the house. The rain was coming down hard now, driven by a swelling south-west wind. She screwed up her face and crossed her arms across her chest as she trotted over to the foundations of the new conservatory.

On the newly laid concrete floor stood a small cement mixer and a mound covered with a dark tarpaulin. Judy pulled up the corner, revealing a rusty wheelbarrow, a battered spirit level and a couple of shovels. Lying among them was a thick cardboard tube about six feet long, which she lifted and looked at for a moment, feeling the cold rain striking through her T-shirt on to her back. Then she bent and studied the edge of the new floor until she found what she was looking for: a crinkled edge of thick polythene, laid as a damp-proof course four inches beneath the surface.

There was a loose bang from the wooden door at the end of the garden, and she straightened up to see Barry Rutter walking slowly into the garden in dark shorts and singlet, hands on hips and shoulders heaving. His sparse hair was plastered close to his head, his hairy shinbones were splashed with spots of wet dust, and he was watching her warily through his thick, rain-streaked glasses.

'What are you doing?' he called nervously. 'Who are you?'

Judy smiled at him placatingly and stood still, hoping he would come right down to the house. But he stopped halfway down the garden, and one of his hands moved up to finger the thin, two-inch scar on his forehead.

'Didn't I see you in the town hall today?' he asked, his voice wavering. 'You're not police, are you?'

At that moment Colin opened the kitchen door, and the sound seemed to act as a starting gun for Barry Rutter. He turned and ran back up the garden, flailing his arms to build up speed. Judy jumped over a flower-bed and raced after him to try to stop him escaping through the door in the wall. But her feet skidded on the wet lawn and she found herself struggling up from her knees as Rutter pulled the door open and disappeared through it, slamming it behind him with a bang and a rattle.

'We should have had the others out the back,' said Colin, exasperated, helping her up. 'There are no roads for miles across the back here.'

'Never mind that now,' said Judy angrily, shaking his hand off her arm and brushing the wet hair off her face. 'Give me the radio, and

200

I'll follow him. Come on, quick, before he disappears.'

Colin pulled the radio from his jacket pocket and handed it to her. Judy sprinted towards the door in the wall and pulled it open.

'Don't go near him,' Colin yelled after her. 'Keep your distance till you've got help.'

Beyond the door was a stretch of bumpy, open grassland leading away from the houses up towards the downs. Rutter was a couple of hundred yards away, and as she started to follow him through the gusting rain the sky was suddenly lit by a curtain of lightning which seemed to linger and pulsate, fading and brightening again. For a full five seconds the tiny, dark figure of the man ahead of her was silhouetted against the great sheet of light, and then the gloom returned and a crackling peal of thunder rolled overhead.

After a few hundred yards, Judy's eyes were full of water, her breath was beginning to judder in her throat, and her sodden jeans were shrinking on to her thighs like elastic bandages. The pain in her legs and lungs made her want simply to stop, to let the stupid bastard go. Scores of officers and vehicles would be surrounding this patch of the downs by now, closing every road and path: even if she lost him, even if they had to wait overnight, he'd soon be found. And if by some fluke he even got through the police lines, how far was he going to get? He was a drenched, middle-aged, middle-class man in shorts and a singlet, at large in an overpopulated countryside that would soon be echoing with public announcements that he was wanted by police; he wouldn't stay out of custody more than a few hours.

But stronger than the voice of reason was the stubborn desire within her to stick with her suspect, make the arrest and take the credit. If it hadn't been for her, she told herself, they'd probably still be pinning it on poor, crazy Godfrey, laying themselves open to an acquittal, a humiliating appeal, another scandal about police oppression of vulnerable suspects. She wasn't going to lose Rutter, leaving the cavalry to thunder in, snatch him from under her nose and make snide remarks to each other afterwards about how she couldn't stand the pace. And besides, Rutter had already run several miles, and she would get her second wind soon. She hawked up the phlegm that was closing her throat and spat into a puddle, leaving a thin liana of spittle trailing over her face. She brushed it off with her hand, feeling the heat of her cheek under the film of water.

They had run over a mile now, and through the stinging rain Judy could see ahead of her the broken line of trees which marked the escarpment of the downs. Even in the early dusk of the thunderstorm

201

there was a feeling of approaching openness, of escape and relief from the inward-looking entanglement of suburbia. She imagined, beyond the ridge, the blue-green spread of the Weald, and beyond it more downs, the English Channel, the freedom of the ocean. Her breath was coming more easily now, and Rutter was still only two or three hundred yards ahead of her. Where was he aiming for? Up to the right was Flinty Hill with its pair of radio masts, and not far beyond that would be the broken edges of Slump Quarry, where John Bullock had lain and decayed for a day and a half. Was Rutter following the instinct of the penitent killer, returning to the scene of the crime? She looked down for a moment as she brushed back the swinging wet rat-tails of her hair, and when she looked up again Barry Rutter had disappeared.

Judy slowed to a walk, one hand on the stitch in her right side, the other still grasping the dripping black radio. Apart from a little copse at the side of the path, she was surrounded by waist-high ripening grain, stretching away for hundreds of yards, its surface waving and rolling in the wind and rain. Judy came alongside the copse, no more than a hundred yards square, and stopped beside a gap in the wall of tall grass and foliage. Cautiously, like someone inspecting a cellar or manhole, she bent and stuck her head inside. The canopy of the trees made it almost dark, and she blinked rapidly to adjust her eyes. Brambles and undergrowth seemed to seal all the gaps between the burgeoning little sycamores and birches, and there was no sign of Rutter. It was time to use the radio, she decided, stepping back on to the path.

But two minutes later, after much shaking and pressing of buttons, she realized it wasn't working. Either the batteries were dead, or water had got in, or she'd managed to damage it, but whatever had happened she was on her own. She resisted the urge to fling the thing down among the grey and orange shards of flint which littered the path, and stuck her head inside the copse again.

'Mr Rutter!' she shouted, trying to control the gasping in her breath. 'Come out and give yourself up. You're surrounded by police. You'll be treated properly.'

She listened, head cocked, for the sound of swishing undergrowth or crackling branches, but all she could hear was rain dripping from branches. Then there was another flash of lightning, and in the brilliance she saw a thin path through wet grass and nettles to a dark opening in the ground, with a mound of chalky rocks around it. The gloom returned with the thunder, and when her eyes had adjusted again she collected her nerves and stepped into the copse.

There was an ancient damp smell in spite of the recent dry weather, and the shrivelled flowers of a few of last month's bluebells hung dead on their stalks beneath the trees. She stopped after each step, holding her breath and looking round in the twilight. But she saw and heard nothing, and soon she was looking at the mouth of a cave, some six feet tall and four feet wide, leading into the chalky earth beneath ivy-covered sycamores. She knelt and peered into it: there'd been an article in the local paper about ancient chalk workings on the Downs, one of which was said to have an underground passage to a nearby village. They were also used by bats in the winter, she remembered, shuddering at the thought of tiny bits of flying fur brushing against her face in the darkness. She studied the chalky scree of the entrance for footmarks, but there was nothing. Five yards in, the white walls, soiled with green slime and studded with fragments of flint, gave way to silent blackness.

As she straightened up to look around her, the back of her neck prickling with the fear of attack, Judy heard a rustling sound beyond the mound, the sound of grass and undergrowth being pushed aside. She clambered quickly up the side of the cave entrance, hands and feet slipping on the chalky stones, and caught sight of a dark figure, forty or fifty yards away, pushing through the undergrowth, back towards the path. He must have stopped by the cave, thought better of it, and hidden when she'd entered the copse. Judy slithered back down the piles of chalk and dashed for the gap in the trees.

This time Rutter seemed further ahead, and she felt suddenly weak, her stomach like water, as she tried to get into the rhythm of running again. She struggled on, head down and arms pumping, for half a minute, and when she next looked up she gave a little yelp of delight: up ahead, in the gloom of the sweeping rain, she could see a flashing blue light.

Rutter must have seen it too, because he had plunged off the path towards the right and was fighting his way forward through the waist-high corn. Four hundred yards ahead of him was a ragged hedge which hid a bridleway: there'd be police there by now, ready to capture him as he emerged from the field. But at the top of the cornfield, to the left, rearing into the stormy sky from a hillock which stood higher than the crest of the downs itself, were the two radio masts of Flinty Hill. One of the great latticeworks of steel carried two fiery red lights at its tip, like the mesmerizing eyes of some monster of the clouds. Rutter had changed direction and was heading towards it.

Judy veered into the passage he had cut through the corn, her feet crunching on the toppled stalks and her nostrils filling with the fermenting, floury smell of ripening barley. She was suddenly moving far faster than him as he flailed and kicked his way along, but he was already on the final steep slope to the fence surrounding the towers. Surely, she thought, he'd stop there and give himself up. But Rutter didn't even pause at the fence; instead he began to climb it, hooking his fingers into the wire mesh like a monkey in a zoo. It was only eight feet high, and the three outward-sloping strands of barbed wire at the top were hanging in loose loops, leaving space for him to squeeze through and slide down the other side. By the time Judy had clawed her way up the loose earth to the fence, panting and gasping, Rutter was walking around underneath the tower, hands on hips, kicking out his scrawny legs to loosen the muscles, like a middle-distance runner about to start his heat. His face was sheet-white, his dark hair lying in wet streaks on his skull, and beneath his rainy spectacles his beak-like mouth was opening and closing in time with the heaving of his chest. He looked like a man whose mind was turned inward, and seemed not to notice Judy as she called to him through the fence.

'Come on, Mr Rutter,' she gasped. 'Time to call it off. You're surrounded. Nowhere to go.'

He was silent for a few seconds, pacing and circling, and behind him Judy caught a glimpse of a revolving blue light, appearing and disappearing behind a hedgerow. Then Rutter suddenly stopped, looked up, and pointed at Judy.

'I didn't mean to do it,' he shouted. 'He provoked me, started a fight. It was self-defence.'

Judy raised her arms in a gesture of acquiescence, then hooked them on to the fence and leaned against it like a scarecrow.

'All right,' she gasped. 'Give yourself up and tell us about it. You'll be properly dealt with, I promise you.'

Again the circling with downcast eyes before he pointed and shouted again.

'She put you on to me, didn't she? It happened because of her, and she's ratted on me.'

'No, she didn't,' called Judy. 'She didn't say a thing.'

'She wouldn't even talk to me,' shouted Rutter. 'She . . .'

The whirring of a powerful engine stopped him in mid-sentence, and he turned abruptly to see a police Range Rover surge from between the hedges behind the compound, headlights ablaze and blue light flashing. As the vehicle slithered to a halt and two black-jacketed officers jumped from the front doors, Rutter threw a desperate look at Judy and then ran for the ladder which led up the tower.

'Don't go up there,' yelled Judy, trying to climb the fence, her wet toes sliding off the mesh. 'You'll kill yourself.'

Rutter had already reached a locked grille which blocked the ladder ten feet from the ground, and was beginning to climb carefully out and around it. Judy fought harder with the fence, tearing her upper arm against a strand of barbed wire as she swung herself over the top, rushing to get her hands on Rutter before he got round the obstacle. She jarred her ankle as she hit the ground, and as she ran to the tower she saw the two officers standing helplessly beyond the gate of the compound, like spectators at a fairground.

She knew as soon as she grabbed the rungs and started climbing that she was too late. Rutter was lifting his legs above the locked grille and was now climbing steadily beyond it. He paused at the first platform, looked grimly down at her, and started steadily up the second ladder, towards the two blazing red lights and the grey-black clouds rushing past behind them.

Chapter Twenty-Five

Wednesday, 7.30 p.m.

'What's this, then, Sarge – a wet T-shirt competition?'

The PC from the traffic division Range Rover leered at Judy as she walked over to the gate of the compound, pushing back her sodden hair and trying to get her breath back. As she lowered her arms and folded them across her chest, the blood from the long scratch on her arm, diluted to pink by the rain, began to soak into the white cotton.

'Have you got a loud hailer with you, by any chance?' said Judy, staring coldly into a fleshy face which was pink and warm from the cosy interior of the vehicle. 'Because I'd like you to pass it over instead of making sexist remarks.'

The rain was flowing into her mouth and the words came out less crisply than she'd wanted, but the leer faded from his face and he switched his attention to the tower, where the shrinking figure of Barry Rutter was still climbing into the darkening sky. The other officer, smaller and darker, went to the back of the Range Rover and started digging among the traffic cones.

'Where's he think he's going?' said the fleshy one, squinting upwards into the rain and hunching his shoulders inside his coat. 'He a fucking jumper, or what?'

'He's the main suspect in this case,' said Judy. 'And our job is to get him down in one piece. So would you mind spreading the good news on the radio – and get them to contact the site owners. Looks like it's an aircraft beacon.'

She pointed at the notice attached to the fence which gave a telephone number for the Civil Aviation Authority. The officer gave her a dirty look and turned away while his colleague approached with a white loud hailer in one hand and a spare police sweater in the other.

'Looks like you might need this too,' he said, slinging the sweater over the gate and grinning at her from beneath his flat hat. Judy thanked him and pulled it on, huddling into its heavy, sweat-impregnated depths and rolling up the sleeves.

'How near's everyone else?' she asked.

'There'll be a screaming motorcade arriving in about five minutes.'

'That's what I was worried about,' muttered Judy, putting up a hand to protect her eyes from the stinging rain as she looked up the tower, searching vainly for Rutter. 'Might just freak him out.'

'Procedure's to back off and sweat it out, isn't it?' said the young officer. 'Get the trick cyclists in.'

Judy gave him a sour look; he was right, but it wasn't what she wanted to hear. A little voice was still nagging at the back of her mind: This is my arrest, and I want it. The fleshy officer was talking into the mobile radio now, saying what had happened and giving the location.

'Female DS in hot pursuit,' he was saying sarcastically. 'Looks like a drowned rat.'

Judy closed her mind to him and walked back towards the mast, the loud hailer hanging from her hand. Even under the low sky and the sheeting rain, this place felt as if it was the top of the world. To the north, the landscape rolled and swept away into the thirty-mile sprawl of London, half-obscured by the storm but still punctuated by the blinking pinnacles of Crystal Palace and the Canary Wharf tower. For a few seconds she stared at the huge panorama, thinking of nothing, but then a great bolt of lightning fizzed and jerked among the black clouds above, and her thoughts suddenly returned to Barry Rutter, perched on the steel tower a hundred and thirty feet above her, exhausted and desperate. She waited for the crash and roll of the thunder to subside, then raised the loud hailer to her mouth.

'Come on down, Mr Rutter,' she yelled shakily, still breathless. 'It's not safe up there.'

Despite the amplification, her voice was swallowed by the sounds of the storm. She stood still for a few seconds, feeling foolish at her efforts and straining to hear an answering call from the tower. But she could hear nothing except the trees thrashing and swishing in the wind, the rain rattling on the little plastic building in the compound. She couldn't even see Rutter, let alone hear him.

She glanced round at the gate and saw the two officers from the traffic vehicle watching her, water streaming from caps and coats. The dark one who had given her the sweater looked worried and uncertain, but his fleshy colleague was standing there with hands on hips and a mocking grin on his face.

'You'd better wait for someone who knows what he's doing, hadn't you, love?' he called sarcastically.

Judy stared back at him for a moment, failing to find the crushing

207

repartee. She forced herself to turn her back on him silently and concentrate on what she was going to do.

He was right – the proper thing was to back off and wait. There'd be others here soon who had talked potential suicides off high buildings and persuaded homicidal maniacs to hand over loaded guns. They'd maybe get Rutter's wife here to talk to him, or his mother or a close friend, and there'd be a psychologist to advise on his state of mind. There'd be little bribes and deals and undertakings, and the whole affair was unlikely to last more than a few hours. He would be down soon enough.

But as Judy strained to see the top of the tower through the stinging rain, the other possibility preoccupied her: that he'd come down by the fast route, unassisted by ladders, bouncing and snagging on the iron-work and ending up with a wet smack on the hard ground, like a bag of jelly. This man had killed someone, probably in the heat of the moment, and spent a week feeling shocked and friendless, trying to cover his tracks; now that he had failed and was facing ruin, jumping off might seem the best option. The longer he was left alone up there, cold and exhausted with no one to talk to, the more likely he was to do it. Judy moved forward to the ladder and started to climb, the loud hailer dangling from her wrist and banging against the rungs.

Ten feet up, she met the overhanging grille designed to deter passing vandals. But she managed, like Rutter, to climb out and round it and back on to the ladder. As she pulled herself on to the lowest platform, the edge of the loud hailer swung hard against her shin, and as she swore and bent down to rub it she realized she was already twenty-five feet off the ground. The little building with the cables running out of it, the two officers shouting and gesticulating at her to come down, the Range Rover with its revolving light, all seemed small and far away, and her stomach lurched with sudden vertigo. She glanced upwards instead, and the sight of the grey sky rushing past above the two glaring red eyes at the top of the mast only made it worse. As she grasped a rung of the second ladder to steady herself, her hand slipped along a smear of chalky mud left behind by one of Rutter's shoes. She wiped it off on her jeans, taking a deep breath and allowing the rain to run off her top lip into her mouth, moistening the sudden dryness of her tongue and throat, the dryness of deep fear. Don't look up, she told herself, and don't look down. Just look at the bit of iron you're holding, and climb.

She paused at the second platform, sixty feet off the ground, rubbing her hands together to relieve the numbness left by the cold, thin rungs.

208

Then she took hold of a safety railing and steeled herself to look up towards the top of the tower and the low sky skidding past it. For a moment she was sickeningly aware that the world was a moving thing, that she was on a planet hurtling and spinning through space, with only the fragile push of gravity preventing her from reeling off into the darkness like an astronaut severed from the ship. She closed her eyes to stop her stomach turning over, and when she opened them again she focused sharply on the expanded metal floor of the next platform, another thirty feet above her: Rutter could be sitting there, waiting for her, ready to kick her off the ladder as she reached him. But there was no sign of him: he must have gone right to the top, to the final platform just beneath the monstrous red eyes. She'd have to climb again.

Judy was halfway up the next ladder when another sheet of lightning shimmered and danced across the sky. It faded after the first blinding burst, then flashed up brightly again, as if some child of the gods was fiddling with a dimmer switch. When the glare finally ebbed and the earthquaking crack of the thunder began, she found herself clinging to the ladder, trembling and whimpering, her cheek pressed hard against the cold metal. If she moved at all, up or down, she was going to fall, and all she could do was cling on, fighting off panic and cursing herself for having left the ground: how stupid she was, climbing up here, putting her life at risk for the sake of a suspect. She'd been driven by pride and vanity – the need to defy the fat-faced constable from the Range Rover, the hope for some kind of spectacular arrest. What if lightning were to strike the tower? What about the current in the arm-thick cables, yellow and black, running to the top of the tower? She had a hellish vision of herself twitching and jerking, falling and spinning off the tower, her hair on fire and her flesh turning to carbon.

But after a minute or two the crisis subsided and a strange new calm took over. The paralysis drained from her limbs, and the pride and stubbornness were returning: it was just as dangerous to go back as to go on, she told herself, and she still had the job to do – make contact with Rutter, talk him down, arrest him. One hand to the next rung, then a foot, then another hand: she closed her mind to the weather and the terrifying height, fixing her eyes on her own white knuckles and the bar of galvanized metal beneath them. Ten seconds, twenty, half a minute, and then she was on her hands and knees on the third platform, nearly a hundred feet up. Slowly she crawled across its metal floor, dragging the loud hailer, fighting a primal voice at the base of her brain which nagged at her to ball up like a foetus, cover her eyes, and wait for rescue. She jammed herself carefully in the corner of the safety railings, and this time when she looked up, almost closing her eyes against the rain, she finally saw the dark-vested figure of Barry Rutter. He was standing against the railings of the highest platform, his thick spectacles catching and reflecting the blood-red glare from the huge warning lights a few feet above him. Judy waited a few moments for her breathing to steady, then raised the loud hailer to her mouth.

'Mr Rutter,' she called. 'Are you all right?'

The figure above her leaned out over the waist-high railings to peer down at her. His movements were swaying and unbalanced, as if he were drunk, and Judy saw how easy it would be for him to topple over and fall, even if he didn't mean to.

'No, I'm not all right,' came the answering shout from above. His voice, just audible above the sounds of the storm, was cracked and unsteady.

Judy decided that the distortions of the loud hailer were the last thing to reassure a frightened man; she set it down on the metal grille and cupped her hands round her mouth instead.

'I know how you feel,' she shouted. 'But you must come down and talk – it's too dangerous up here.'

Again Rutter swayed forward over the railing, and Judy braced herself to see him topple over and plummet past in a cartwheel of white limbs.

'You bloody well don't know,' shouted Rutter, his voice shriller this time. 'You won't be going to prison.'

Judy could feel the mast swaying slightly in the rainy gusts. Every fibre of her jeans and T-shirt was sodden, and there were rivulets of cold water flowing down the neck of the sweater, beneath her underclothes and into her trainers. A fit of shivering was hitting her every few seconds, making her teeth chatter, and she knew that unless the weather eased up she would soon be suffering from exposure as well as vertigo. She had to get them both down fast, even if it meant misleading Rutter about his prospects. She remembered what he'd yelled to her just before he started up the ladder.

'You might not go to prison if it was self-defence,' she shouted. 'Come on down – let's talk about it.'

'What's the point?' Rutter shouted back, swaying dangerously, haloed by the red glow behind him. 'My job's gone, marriage gone. Nothing left. Might as well jump.'

'No, no, don't do that,' called Judy, her voice fraying. 'What about Dorothy?'

'Ha!' It was a shout of bitterness and pain, as if Judy had twisted

210

the knife in the wound. 'She doesn't care! She won't even talk to me.'

'She was trying to protect you – both of you.'

'Where is she, then, eh? Where is she?'

His voice was wild, and he was leaning out again, dangerously off balance, as if searching for the brown hair and wide mouth of Dorothy Bullock somewhere out in the storm. Judy braced herself for the giddiness and craned her head through the platform's safety railings. A hundred feet below was a chaotic scene, lit like some mad discotheque by blue lights revolving and flashing out of phase with each other. In the gloom and rain, each tiny upturned face looked much like the next, and unless Colin had thought of sending for Dorothy, she would have no idea what was going on. As Judy watched, a group of yellow-helmeted firemen pushed open the gates to the compound, the first wedge of the assault. They must have used bolt cutters, she thought: dark-jacketed policemen were pouring through the gates behind them and milling around the base of the tower.

'What are they doing?' called Rutter hysterically. 'If they come up, I'll jump! I'm not joking! I'll jump.'

Judy didn't doubt him. She reached for the loud hailer, her hands clumsy with cold, and managed to jam it halfway through the railings so it was pointing down at the mêlée in the compound.

'Please back off!' she shouted. 'He might jump. Let me talk to him!'

For half a minute, men continued to crowd round the bottom of the ladder, gesticulating and pointing upwards. Judy lay watching on the metal grille, wondering if they were going to start arguing with her through another loud hailer, ordering her to come down. Then they suddenly began retreating through the gates and climbing back into their vehicles, like spectators after a football match. The blue lights were switched off one by one, and a strange calm descended, as if the crowd of vehicles were just part of the sodden landscape. Judy blew a sigh of relief and rolled over to talk to Rutter again.

'There you are!' she shouted. 'They're not coming up – there's just you and me.'

There was no answer, but he was no longer leaning over and swaying. The wind seemed to be softening now, and the rain changing from a stinging fusillade to larger, softer drops. The sky was still low and dark overhead, but far away on the western horizon Judy could see a thin strip of brightness. In half an hour it would have passed, leaving the countryside fresh and steaming in the evening twilight.

'Tell me what happened.' She no longer had to shout to make herself

211

heard, and her voice was weary and almost conversational. Again there was no reply, and she settled back against the railings to wait, hugging herself for warmth.

She could hardly hear him when he began to talk, and rather than interrupt him she got to her feet, suddenly unworried by the emptiness around her, holding the railing and craning upwards. She couldn't hear every word, but bit by bit, with gaps and pauses, it came together – the story of an unplanned encounter where a few ill-tempered remarks had pushed a bad relationship into sudden but fatal violence. On another day, with different moods and pressures, they might have laughed off such a trivial conflict and the tragedy would not have happened. But on this particular day, Bullock had blackmail and political rebellion on his mind, Rutter was worried about his marriage, and both men were anxious about the day of action and the afternoon's council meeting. A gibe from Bullock about wasting money on nameplates for the council chamber, a riposte from Rutter about Bullock's wife, a push from one, a moment of blind fury from the other, and suddenly it was over – the blows were struck and a man was dead. Rutter had never realized until too late how delicately life was suspended, how easy it could be to kill a large man without meaning to do anything but shut him up, stop his goading. He'd never hit anyone before, not even at school, and now he was a killer, full of fear and remorse. It was as good a place as any to hear a man's confession, thought Judy, this platform high above the earth, detached from the ordinary world, lit by the fiery glow from the two red beacons, the wind blending with his breaking voice and whisking half his words away.

Rutter was half-collapsed on the railings, his body shivering violently every few seconds, his elbows on the ironwork and his head in his hands. He was leaning a long way out, but he no longer looked like a man about to jump. Judy watched him from below, confident that he would come down now, providing she chose the right moment. Another little flurry of wind and rain had blown in, but the sky to the west was brightening rapidly. When the bolt of lightning struck she'd already opened her mouth to reassure Rutter that the charge he'd face would be manslaughter, not murder.

It was as if all her senses were, in a fraction of a second, overloaded to the point of bursting: an explosion of brilliant light blinded her, a great thudding and fizzing forced itself into her ears, and her body seemed to be snatched out of contact with the real world by a wave of impersonal, irresistible energy. She was suddenly back in a terrifying moment of her adolescence, when she'd been caught by a great Atlantic breaker off a Cornish beach and rolled along helplessly underwater, the bright, foaming surf filling her eyes and ears and the terror of death bursting open in her mind like the door to a furnace. But just as the breaker had suddenly tired of her and tossed her casually on to the sand, this wave also disappeared as quickly as it had come, abandoning her to a strange stillness. She could see nothing but dazzling whiteness, as if she was lying on a stage with all the spotlights focused on her face. Some reflex made her try to sit up, but as she did so a sudden explosion of noise seemed to push her down on her back again.

She lay there, slowly realizing what had happened, as the thunder came and went around her. At first it was like a great bellow of triumph, and then it dwindled to a distant drum roll, funereal and almost benevolent. Judy lay still, dazed and blinking, as the normal colours of the world returned and her surroundings took shape again: there in front of her were the metal railings of the platform with the heavy grey clouds behind them. She swivelled her eyes upwards, and at first she didn't realize what the object was which hung like a giant dishcloth on the railings of the uppermost platform. It was blackened and smoking and did not move, and it was only when the aroma of burnt flesh bit her nostrils that she understood what had happened to Barry Rutter.

Judy brought her hands up from her sides to cover her eyes, but a sudden shock of agony made her stop, her palms a foot from her face. Across each hand was a broad red weal, its pain suddenly brought to life by the movement of her arms. With every beat of her blood the pain grew worse, she heard her own moans growing louder. She had just filled her lungs and was about to scream with all her strength when the light disappeared completely and the pain stopped.

Chapter Twenty-Six

Thursday, 1 p.m.

'Well,' said Steve Ditchley, putting his first pint of the day down on the bar after a long, grim swig. 'Shows you can't get away with bumping off a Tory, spite of all the crimes they've perpetrated on millions of British workers.'

'Even bleedin' God's on their side,' muttered Todger, nodding unhappily and pulling the brim of his baseball cap to the side of his head.

'And I hope you wouldn't want it different,' said Mavis Tench, massively ensconced on a nearby stool and eyeing them with distaste. 'Can't murder people 'cos of their politics. Not even Tories.'

'Don't start an argument, Mavis,' said Ditchley, who would be ready to argue with all comers in three or four pints' time. 'Anyway, it was sex, not politics, wonnit? Crime of passion.'

'Oh, yeah? Know all the details already, do you?' Mavis took a pull at her Guinness, leaving a dirty white moustache on her upper lip.

'Course I do,' said Ditchley, pretending outrage that anyone might think otherwise. 'It was Barry Rutter, in the council chamber, with the gavel. Just like a game of bleeding Cluedo.'

The other drinkers in the Pig and Whistle only knew what they'd heard on the morning radio or read in the early edition of the *Evening Standard*: that Rutter was a suspect in the Bullock case, that Judy had pursued him up the tower, and that the bolt of lightning had hit him as he stood on the top platform. The police were giving no more details.

'Easy to say, isn't it?' said Mavis suspiciously. 'Now both the poor buggers are dead you can make up any old cock and bull.'

Ditchley looked slowly round his little coterie of gardeners and doorkeepers, smiling and giving his pony-tail a reassuring twitch.

'What d'you think, lads – give her chapter and verse?'

'Yeah, go on,' said Todger grimly, as if it was a punishment she thoroughly deserved.

'Right then,' said Ditchley, pausing to relight his roll-up and blow the first jet of smoke at Mavis. 'Plods have been all over the council chamber this morning, haven't they? Snipping off bits of carpet, taking the gavel away in a plastic bag.'

'What's that prove?' said Mavis sulkily. Ditchley sighed and raised his eyes to heaven.

'C'mon, Mave. Everyone knows Rutter and Bullock didn't hit it off. Only got to look at them, haven't you? Fat ugly Tory, on the make, bending the rules, and this beanpole chief exec., big on procedure, getting up his nose all the time. So when the bonking begins, something's got to give, right?'

'Who said anything about bonking?' Mavis sounded suddenly edgy, her eyes roving the bar.

'Not your subject, I know, Mavis,' said Ditchley, winking at Todger. 'But putting it simply, Rutter was knocking off Bullock's wife, see? Common or garden leg over situation. Carrying on ever since she patched him up at the poll tax demo. You know how patients feel about nurses.'

'Yeah,' came a fervent grunt from Todger, who'd spent a week in hospital after putting a garden fork through his foot the previous year. 'You're lying there with a hard-on and they're rushing up and down in those tight little aprons.'

'Couldn't have put it better, Todge,' said Ditchley mockingly. 'Nice turn of phrase, this boy. Anyway, there they are last Thursday, both got out of bed the wrong side. So they end up having words, Rutter bops him on the nut and off he goes to that big marble council chamber in the sky – which I sincerely hope is Labour controlled.'

'Don't you believe it, mate,' said a small man in a cloth cap, hunched over his pint. 'Don't you bleedin' believe it.'

'Yeah, anyway,' said Ditchley, eyeing the man as if he was a beetle. 'That leaves Rutter with a stiff on his hands, so he sticks it in the cupboard at the back of the chamber, and . . .'

'In the cupboard?' Mavis interrupted, her little eyes wide with horror. 'While the meeting was going on?'

'That's right,' grinned Ditchley. 'So he didn't miss it after all.'

Mavis stared at him in stony disgust as he finished his pint in a single slow draught, the laughter of his acolytes echoing around him. Todger picked up Ditchley's glass and beckoned at the barman with an earth-encrusted forefinger topped by a blackened nail.

'So how'd he end up in the quarry?' Mavis asked weakly as Ditchley wiped his mouth with the back of his hand.

'Rutter takes his keys, comes back with his car after midnight, wraps him up and takes him for a drive. And I should know.'

'Why's that, Sherlock?'

'Saw Rutter's red Rover outside Bullock's office on my way back from the boozer – must have parked it there while he brought the Merc round to the town hall.'

'You tell the police?' asked Mavis sharply.

'No way did I tell the bleeding police,' said Ditchley, suddenly red and vehement, banging down his glass. 'They got the wrong bleeding attitude, coming round asking questions like I was some kind of criminal. Fuck them, they can sort it out themselves.'

He turned his back on her as the news flashed up on the TV screen in the corner of the bar. A picture appeared of Flinty Hill with a few police officers standing around the mast, hands on hips, staring up into a serene blue sky. A reporter with a big chin spun out the brief police statement, said the full story would be told at the inquest, and started interviewing a man in a suit about why DS Judy Best hadn't been killed along with Barry Rutter.

'Well,' said the man, swallowing and grimacing nervously. 'Our installations do in fact get hit by lightning all the time, and in the normal way of things they just conduct the electricity down to the ground without any damage. And if someone was on the tower, they'd get a nasty surprise and a few burns, but that's all – providing they didn't fall off.'

'That seems to have happened with the police officer,' said the big chin. 'So why did Mr Rutter suffer this horrific death?'

'Well, he does appear to have been right at the top of the mast, and possibly leaning out some distance. And by some appalling mischance the lightning appears to have hit him before it hit the tower. It's a bit like the situation where a golfer shelters under a tree in a thunderstorm, but still gets hit.'

'So what would have been the effect on Mr Rutter?'

'Er, well, a bit like swinging on high voltage power lines and letting your feet touch the ground.'

'Carbonized?'

'Er, you could say that, basically.'

The barman hit the mute button as an item came on about world trade talks, and the drinkers turned back to the bar, shaking their heads and tutting under their breath.

'Well,' declared Ditchley, 'the atmosphere must have been electric, *boo-boom*. Who says local government is boring, eh? Come on, Mavis, I'll buy you a drink.'

216

Manningbird was a man transformed. There was a new briskness in his heavy gait, a new pinkness in his complexion, and a playful sparkle in his eyes. With him was a beaming Chief Superintendent Blackman, in full uniform, with his hat under his arm. They handed a bouquet of flowers to the nurse, who muttered something about finding a vase that was big enough. Manningbird sat down matily on the end of Judy's bed, nearly capsizing it.

'How you feeling, Judy?' he said, like a solicitous uncle, gesturing at bandages the size of boxing gloves round both her hands.

'Fine,' mumbled Judy, face as pale as the hospital nightgown which hung below her collarbones. She wiggled her fingertips, which stuck out like pink lozenges from the gauze and tape.

'Glad to hear it,' said Manningbird. 'You did a great job, Judy, very nice result.'

'Result was a dead body,' mumbled Judy, semi-stunned by painkillers. 'Not very nice at all.'

'Not your fault the lightning struck,' said Blackman heartily. 'Even the Met Police can't control acts of God.'

There'd been jokes all day about how the Almighty had saved the police a lot of trouble and the Home Office should take out a contract with Him for similar disposal of all killers: so much per hundred, no paperwork, no trial, no putting the buggers up in prison for the rest of their lives.

'What's happening about Kingswood?' muttered Judy. Manningbird suddenly conceived an interest in the other patients round the ward. The Chief Superintendent ran a hand over his brilliantined head and cleared his throat as if to address a committee.

'Well, we found the Swiss banking records in a file in Rutter's desk – he must have removed them from the dead man's briefcase. Very clever of him, pretending someone else was feeding him the information contained in them. Suggesting suicide, revenge by the developers.'

'Good thing for us he didn't take the blackmail tape as well,' said Judy slowly, screwing up her face with the effort of thinking and talking. 'But since the statements were good for his cover-up, you'd think he'd just have handed them over to Superintendent Manningbird the other morning.'

'He'd have had a lot of trouble explaining where he'd found them,' said Blackman. 'Maybe he was going to arrange for them to come to light in some other way, later on.'

217

'Well, now we've got them, do they confirm all the stuff about the bribes and how he bought his house?'

'Well,' said Blackman, coughing awkwardly into his hand. 'Hard to be entirely sure, at this stage. We've, er, referred the matter to the fraud squad at Scotland Yard.'

Judy sighed and closed her eyes.

'And what about Godfrey?'

Manningbird suddenly concluded his survey of conditions in the ward, and turned towards her, folding and unfolding his slabby hands like a nervous shopwalker.

'Yes, well, obviously, Godfrey's well and truly exonerated on this one,' he said rapidly. 'Parents have taken him home, for the present at least.'

'Good,' whispered Judy vehemently. Manningbird wriggled uncomfortably, and a hint of truculence came into his voice.

'Course, we had to check out if there was any involvement in those other two stranglings of course, very remiss of us not to have done. But in the event there doesn't seem to be. Poor bastard, eh? Poor bastard. Ah, look, here comes Jim.'

Jim Duncan was approaching now, heels clicking on the polished lino as if he was on parade. He turned in by Judy's bed and held a small box of chocolates out to her. She raised her swathed hands like a beggar's stumps, and he put the box on her locker.

'Sorry,' he said coolly. 'Have to get Colin to feed them to you – he'll be along in a wee while.'

A silence enveloped them. A woman in the next bed was explaining to a visitor the difficulties of using a bedpan. Duncan winced and went to perch on the edge of the armchair beside Judy, like a reluctant member of a family gathering.

'Well, you'll never believe it,' he said eventually, rubbing his muscular hands together. 'But it was one of the kids who found him who lifted the wallet. Little bastard. The parents handed it in today.'

'I'm surprised by less and less,' said Judy, shifting her arms and grimacing with pain. 'What about the widows?'

'Mrs Rutter seems pretty unmoved. Says she didn't know about any affair, but her husband had been behaving a little strangely since the riot. She just put it down to stress and the bump on the head.'

'And Dorothy Rutter?'

'She was trying to tell us it wasn't really an affair, that they'd only got together two or three times.'

'That's what they all say,' broke in Manningbird, wriggling on the

218

bed and making it rock. 'But while Bullock was up in town getting a good spanking, Rutter would be trotting over the downs for a tryst with the neglected wife. Bloody hell, the way people behave – you'd think there was no such thing as Aids.'

'Amazing no one knew about the affair after, what, nearly three months,' said Duncan. 'I mean, someone must have seen them meeting and so on.'

'Knowing it's one thing,' said Judy, craning round to look at him. 'Saying it's another, especially to the police. I felt pretty sure there was something going on after I saw her friend Annabel – it was just a question of working out who with. And Rutter obviously didn't realize what these new digital exchanges can do.'

Blackman had been shifting and glancing at his watch, and now he cleared his throat and interrupted.

'Er, Judy, I don't want to rush you or anything, but there's about fifty press and TV downstairs. The sister says it's OK just to let a few in, and if we don't they'll be dressing up in white coats and popping out from under your bed in the middle of the night.'

Judy moaned and raised her bandages like a boxer who'd had enough.

'Good PR, Judy,' said Manningbird cajolingly. 'For you and the force.'

'Doesn't sound like I've got much choice,' said Judy eventually, peering at them from between her arms like a victim of a lynch mob.

'Don't worry, love, the nurse'll comb your hair for you,' said Manningbird. Judy gave him a little snarl.

'They always ask such bloody silly questions,' she complained. 'How do you feel, and are you married, and would you do it again? It's complete crap.'

'That last one's quite good, in fact,' said Jim Duncan craftily. '*Would* you do it again?'

Judy heaved a slow sigh and gazed down the ward for a few seconds, thinking. A toothless old man who'd set his chip pan on fire grinned at her in fellow-feeling and waved his bandaged hands.

'The stupid thing is,' said Judy eventually, 'that I probably would.'